THE PROPHECY OF
AN ELF MAID...

"So, you have had your will, King. Know, we got a child together. When you took me in, I wished you well; and I do not yet wish you ill. Do as I say, and it may be we can still halt the bad luck you have sown in my womb.

"Our child," she continued, "must be born undersea; for mine is the blood of Ran. Be down by your boathouses this time next winter, and look for her." Pain crossed her mouth. "If you fail, the Skjoldungs will suffer."

But as the seasons went by, the king forgot what his elf-love had asked of him. Indeed, she seemed so strange to everything else he knew, he sometimes wondered if she had been a dream.

But she had not been a dream—and what she had augured would most tragically come to pass.

HROLF KRAKI'S SAGA

Poul Anderson

A Del Rey Book

BALLANTINE BOOKS • NEW YORK

To my favorite Finnish spellbinders—
Chelsea Quinn Yarbro and Emil Petaja

A Del Rey Book
Published by Ballantine Books

ISBN 0-345-25846-0

Manufactured in the United States of America

First Edition: October 1973
Second Printing: July 1977

Cover art by Darrell Sweet

CONTENTS

THE HISTORY OF HROLF KRAKI:
A Foreword by Poul Anderson

A book should speak for itself. But since this is not a modern fantasy, you the reader may like to know its background.

In contrast to the *Volsungasaga*, whose core is a story from the Rhineland, the cycle of Hrolf Kraki and his heroes is purely Northern. Once it was widely known and many-branched, deep in the souls and the songs of the folk. But it did not have the same good luck as the tale of Sigmund, Sigurdh Fafnir's-Bane, Brynhild, and Gudhrun: to get a sinewy prose narrative and to inspire poems which have survived in their entirety. Hence, today it is nearly forgotten. It deserves to be remembered anew.

The germ of it is close in age to that of the *Nibelungenlied* and contemporary with *Beowulf*. In fact, it and the latter throw a great deal of light on each other and include a number of the same people. The most conspicuous example is King Hrothgar, whose hall Beowulf rid of the monsters. In the homeland version he is Hrolf's uncle Hroar. Enough additional identifications have been made to leave no doubt.

Now this can be dated rather closely. Gregory of Tours, in his *History of the Franks*, mentions a Danish king—whom a slightly later chronicle calls Geatish—Chochilaicus, who fell in the course of a massive raid on Holland. He has to be that lord whom *Beowulf* calls Hygelac and *Hrolf* (and certain other Northern remnants) Hugleik. On that basis, we can say with reasonable confidence that he was indeed a Geat. We are not sure whether this people lived in Jutland or the Göta-land part of Sweden, then an independent kingdom. I think the second is more likely. In any case, since that leader was real, no doubt others were whose names loom far larger in tradition: such as Beowulf and Hrolf themselves.

Hugleik died between 512 and 520 A.D. Thus Hrolf flourished two or three decades later. This was during the *Völkerwanderung* period, when Rome had gone under and the Germanic tribes were on the move, as wild a time as the world has ever seen. We can understand why Hrolf Kraki was gloriously remembered, why the saga tellers generation by generation brought every hero they could to his court, even if this meant giving less and less of the cycle to the king himself. His reign was—by comparison, anyhow; in story, at least —a moment of sunshine during a storm which raged for centuries. He became to the North what Arthur did to Britain and Charlemagne, afterward, to France. On the morning of Stiklestad, five hundred years later and away off in Norway, the men of King Olaf the Saint were wakened by a skald who chanted aloud a *Bjarkamaal:* one of those lays wherein the warriors of the pagan Dane-King Hrolf were called to their last battle.

Fragments of it have come down to us. We know also the *Bjarkarímur,* a different and late set of verses. In his chronicle of Danish legend and history, the monk Saxo Grammaticus (c. 1150–1206) gives still another poem, in a long Latin paraphrase from which we can only attempt to reconstruct the original. (A sample is in Chapter I of "The Tale of Skuld," and some other parts have been worked into a form more in period for Chapters II and III.) This book—which likewise includes the oldest extant account of Hamlet—tells the story of Hrolf. In addition we find mention of it in Snorri Sturlason's *Younger Edda* and *Heimskringla,* the synopsized *Skjoldunga-saga,* and scattered references elsewhere. The principal sources are a few Icelandic manuscripts devoted wholly to the legend. Unfortunately, no copy of these is from before c. 1650, and both the style and the logic leave something to be desired.

All the sources contradict each other, and occasionally themselves, on various points. Moreover, they are too sparse, leave too much unexplained, for the modern reader who is not a specialist in the early North.

I have long wanted to make *a* reconstruction, if not *the* reconstruction: put together the best parts, fill in the gaps, use the old words where they seem right and otherwise find new ones. My gratitude is great to Ian and Betty Ballantine and to Lin Carter for this chance to try.

Many such choices and suppositions must be controversial, or sheerly arbitrary. However, we can leave to scholars the pleasant pastime of arguing over details. To me, the most important questions turned on how the narrative might be made enjoyable to read while staying faithful to its originals.

For instance, from my viewpoint and doubtless yours, too many names begin with *H-* and even *Hr-*. I did not feel free to change this, unless one of the sources gave an alternative; but I have tried to write so as to minimize the chance of confusion. For similar reasons I have used modern place names throughout, generally the English versions, except for territories like Svithjodh which no longer exist.

A greater hazard lies in the very spirit of the saga. Here is no *Lord of the Rings,* work of a civilized, Christian author—though probably it was one of Tolkien's many wellsprings. Hrolf Kraki lived in the midnight of the Dark Ages. Slaughter, slavery, robbery, rape, torture, heathen rites bloody or obscene, were parts of daily life. Finns in particular will note the brutality and superstition to which the Scandinavians subjected their harmless people.* Love, loyalty, honesty beyond the most niggling technicalities, were only for one's kindred, chieftain, and closest friends. The rest of mankind were foemen or prey. And often anger or treachery broke what bonds there had been.

Adam Oehlenschläger, writing in the Romantic era, could sentimentalize Helgi, Hroar, and Hrolf. I would not. If nothing else, we today need a reminder that we must never take civilization for granted.

I hope you will bear with that, as well as the necessarily sprawling character of the tale and what we today feel as a lack of psychological depth. The latter merely reflects how those folk thought of themselves. To us, their behavior seems insanely egoistic; but to them, each was first a member of his family and only second—however greedy for wealth or fame—himself. The hero is no one of them, but rather the blood of Skjold the Sheaf-Child, which coursed through many different hearts.

I felt obliged to give you some idea of how those lives and that society worked. Yet my aim was not at a hypothetical historical reality, but a myth. Therefore I have put the narrative in the mouth of a person in tenth-century England, when the cycle would have reached its full development—a woman, who would be less likely than a man to use the spare saga style. Of course, she brings in not just the supernatural, but numerous anachronisms. The Scandinavia she describes is, in most respects, the one she herself knows.

As for personal names, those of the gods are in their

---

*At least, the sagas call them Finns, though many of them were doubtless actually Lapps.

modern forms. Since those of humans are exotic anyway, they have been left in the Old Norse. Spellings have occasionally been modified, though, to make both printing and reading easier. For those readers who care, pronunciations go about as follows, accents always being on the first syllable:

a: Generally broad as in *ah*.

aa: Midway between *aw* and *oh*.

dh: The edh, like *th* in *this*.

ei, ey: As in *rein, they*.

g: Always hard, as in *get*.

gn: Both letters pronounced.

j: like *y* in *yet*.

kn: Both letters pronounced.

ng: Always as in *ring*.

ö: As in German or, roughly, English *oo* in *good*.

oa: Two vowels, *oh-ah*.

th: The thorn, like *th* in *thunder*.

u: Long except when followed by a doubled consonant (*Skuld* vs. *Gunnar*.)

y: Like German *ü* or, roughly, English *ee*.

æ: Like German *ä* or, roughly, English *eh*.

But never mind any of this unless you are especially interested. All that really matters is the story.

—Poul Anderson

HROLF KRAKI'S SAGA

Though life is lost, one thing will outlive us:
memory sinks not beneath the mould.
Till the Weird of the World stands, unforgotten,
high under heaven, the hero's name.
                                    —The Bjarkamaal

THE SKJOLDUNGS

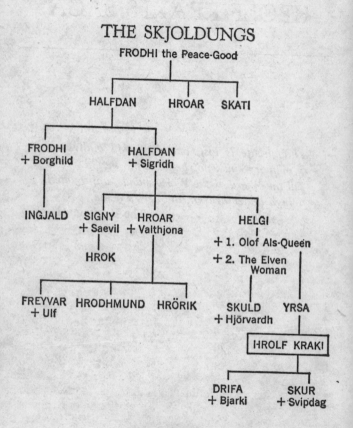

I

OF THE TELLING

There was a man called Eyvind the Red, who dwelt in the Danelaw of England while Æthelstan was king. His father was Svein Kolbeinsson, who had come there from Denmark and often made trading voyages back. When old enough, Eyvind went along. Yet he was more restless and eager for a name than Svein, and at last took service under the king. In a few years he rose high, until at Brunanburh he fought so mightily and led his followers so well that Æthelstan gave him full friendship and wished him to stay always in the royal household. Eyvind was not sure if he wanted that for the rest of his life, and asked leave to go visit his old homestead.

He found Svein readying for another journey, and decided to embark. In Denmark they got hospitality from the chieftain Sigurdh Haraldsson. This man had a daughter, Gunnvor, a fair maiden whom Eyvind soon began to woo. The fathers thought it would be a match good for both their houses; and when Eyvind returned to England, he brought Gunnvor as his bride.

Then he must attend the king, who spent that winter in travel. Gunnvor came too. She won the heart of ladies in the court, for she could speak much about foreign lands and ways. Though Æthelstan was unwed, news of this came to him: especially of a long saga from olden days that she was relating. He called her to the building where he sat among his men. "These are gloomy nights," he chided her, laughing. "Why do you give the women a pleasure you refuse me?"

"I was only telling stories, lord," she said.

"Good ones, though, from what I hear," answered the king.

Still she looked unhappy. Eyvind took the word on her behalf: "Lord, I know something of this, and it may not be fit for your company." His eye dwelt on the bishop who sat near. "It is a heathen tale." He had not given out that he still offered to the elves.

"Well, what of that?" asked Æthelstan. "If I have among my friends a man like Egil Skallagrimsson—"

"There is no harm in hearing about the forefathers, if we do not forget they were in error," said the bishop. "Rather, it helps us to understand today's heathen, and thus learn how best to bring them to the Faith." After a little, he added thoughtfully: "I must confess, I spent my youth studying abroad and know less about you Danes than do most Englishmen. I would be grateful if you could explain things as you go along, Lady Gunnvor."

The end of it was that she spent many evenings that winter telling them about Hrolf Kraki.

II

THE TALE OF FRODHI

I

In those days, Denmark was less than it is now. There were Zealand and the smaller islands about this great one. Save for the chalk cliffs of Mön in the south, it is a low country, hills rolling as easily as the rivers flow. Then eastward across the Sound lay Scania. At the narrowest part of that strait, swimmable by any boy, it looks much like its sister; and they say that in an olden year the goddess Gefion plowed Zealand free of the peninsula that she might have it for herself and her man Skjold, Odin's son. But northward, where it juts into the Kattegat, Scania lifts in red heights, the southern end of the Keel.

This is a land whose soil bears well, whose waters swarm with fish and seal and whale, whose marshes are darkened and made thunderous by the wings of wildfowl, whose timber fares afar in the strakes of goodly ships. But that same timber grows in woods well-nigh impassable, the haunt of deer and elk, aurochs and wisent, wolf and bear. In former times the wildernesses reached further and darker than they do now, cut the settlements of men off from each other in loneliness, sheltered not only outlaws but elves and trolls and other uncanny beings.

North of Scania is the land of the Götar, whom the English call Geats. It was then a realm in its own right. North of it in turn lay Svithjodh, where dwelt the Swedes; theirs was the biggest and strongest of the Northern countries. West across mountains was Norway, but it was a lot of little quarreling kingdoms and tribes. Beyond it and Svithjodh live the Finns. They are mostly wandering hunters and reindeer herders, who speak no tongue akin to any of ours. But they are so rich in furs that, in spite of numbering many among them who are skilled in witchcraft, they are always being raided or laid under scot by Dane, Swede, and Norseman.

Turning south again, to the west of Zealand we find the Great Belt, and beyond that water the island of Fyn. Then comes the Little Belt and then the Jutland peninsula. Jutland is an earth more steep and stern than the rest of what is today the Danish realm. From the wide wind-whistling strands of the Skaw, south to the bogs where men stride on stilts as if they would be storks, and so to the mouth of the mighty Elbe, here is the mother of whole folk who have wandered widely across the world—Cimbri, Teutons, Vandals, Heruli, Angles who gave their name to England, Jutes, Saxons, and more and more.

Not only to gain strength, wealth, and fame, but to halt endless wars and reavings, the Danish kings who held Zealand and Scania strove to bring these others beneath them. And sometimes they would win a battle and be acknowledged overlords here or there. But erelong blades were again unsheathed, and on the roofs of the jarls they had set to steer yonder lands, the red cock crowed. As often as not, this happened because royal brothers fell out with each other.

Theirs was the house of Skjold and Gefion. In England it is told that he—they call him Scyld—drifted to shore in an oarless boat. It was filled with weapons but bore also a sheaf of grain whereon rested the head of the child. The Danes took him for their king, and a great one he grew to be, who gave law and peace and the groundwork of a country. When at last he died, his grieving folk set him adrift in a ship richly laden, that he might go home to that unknownness whence he had come. They believed his father had been Odin. And truth to tell, the blood of the One-Eyed showed itself afterward in many ways, so that some of the Skjoldungs were wise and forbearing landfathers, others wild and greedy, still others given to peering into things best left alone.

This last was more often true of the Svithjodh kings.

They were the Ynglings, stemming from Frey, and he is no god of the sky but of the earth, its fruitfulness to be called forth by strange rites, likewise its shadows and all-devouring mould. In their seat of Uppsala, no few of these lords worshipped beasts and wrought wizardries. Withal, they bred their share of doughty warriors, and when at last Ivar Widespan drove them out—long after the tale I will tell you—a man of them became the ancestor of that Harald Fairhair who made Norway into one kingdom.

Between Skjoldungs and Ynglings was scant love and much bloodshed. Between them was also the land of the Götar. Being fewer in numbers than either set of neighbors, these sought the friendship of both, or at least to play a double game. Yet the Götar were no weaklings either. Among them was to arise that man the English call Beowulf.

Thus matters stood in the days when Frodhi the Peace-Good became king of Denmark. Of him are many things told, how he won overlordship through battle and craftiness, then went on to give such laws and keep such a calm that a maiden might carry a sackful of gold from end to end of his realm and be safe. Yet in him was likewise that ravenousness which could show in the Skjoldungs and which had, earlier, caused his own forebear Hermodh to be driven from the royal seat in Leidhra town, into the wilderness. We hear different tales about King Frodhi's ending; but this is the one the skalds like best.

A ship from Norway brought for sale some captured uplanders. Out of these, Frodhi chose two huge young women, long-haired, tangle-haired, dark-haired, high of cheekbone, broad of mouth and nose, slant of eye, clad in stinking skins. They called themselves, in thunder-deep voices, Fenja and Menja. It was told how men's lives were lost in binding them and how they were not really human but of the Jötun race. A wiseman warned Frodhi that they could never have been made captive were there not the will of a Norn in this. But the king did not listen.

He owned a quern named Grotti. Whence it came, no one knows—maybe from one of those dolmens which

stand stark around the Danish lands, the very names of
their builders long ago forgotten. A witch had said that it
could grind forth whatever he wanted; but none had
strength to wield the oaken shaft which turned the upper
stone. He thought that these women might.

And they did. He set them in a gloomy shed where
stood the quern. An old lay tells the story of what followed.

Now are they come   to the house of the king,
the twain foresighted,   Fenja and Menja.
Sold to Frodhi,   the son of Fridhleif,
were these two maidens,   mighty in thralldom.

There were the women   set to working,
there must they heave   the heavy millstone,
and never did Frodhi   give aught of freedom.
He bade them sing   without cease at the quern.

Then gave the maidens   a voice to the mill;
the stones were groaning;   it growled in the earth.
Yet told he the maidens   they must mill and must
      mill.

They swung and swung   the swift-flying millstone.
To sleep went most   of the slaves of Frodhi.
Then sang Menja,   beside the millshaft:

"We grind you welfare,   Frodhi, and wealth,
manyfold kine,   on the mill of luck.
You shall sit in riches   and sleep on down
and wake when you wish.   Well is it milled!

"Here shall nobody   harm any other,
sunder the peace,   or slay his fellow,
nor kill the bane   of his own dear brother,
though he have the murderer   bound and helpless."

But Frodhi for them   had no words save these:
"As long may you sleep   as the cuckoo keeps still,
or while one may voice   a single verse."

"Unwise you were, Frodhi,   you darling of folk,
when you did buy us   to be your thralls
and saw that we looked   to be likely workers,
yet left off asking   what land we hail from.

"Hard was the giant   known as Hrungnir,
but even more   of might had Thjazi.
Idhi and Aarnir   are of our blood:
berg-trolls' brethren;   of them are we born.

"Never was Grotti   made out of granite,
nor out of cliffs   were cloven its stones.
Nor do they mill—   the maids from the mountains—
knowing not what   they are whirling forth.

"Through nine whole winters   our strength was
      waxing
while still we played games   beneath the ground.
Then were the maidens   ripe in their mightiness.
Hills we upheaved   and had on our backs.

"We tumbled boulders   on Jötun buildings
and down to the dales,   with a noise of doom.
So did we fling   the flinders of cliffs
that afterward men   made houses out of them.

"Then did we fare,   we foresighted sisters,
off to Svithjodh,   seeking for war.
Bears we slaughtered   and shields we split,
breaking a road   through byrnie-clad men.
One king did we raise,   and cast down another,
giving the goodly   Guthorm our help,
with killing and fire,   till Knui had fallen.

"Through all those years   we were yare for battle
and widely were known   as warrior maidens.
We shore our way   with the sharpened spears,
and blood made dim   the blinking blade.

"Now are we come   to the house of the king.
Bad luck has made us   thralls at the millstone.

Gravel gnaws our feet,   we freeze above,
but have room to work—   and woe with Frodhi.

"Let the stone now stand   and the hands rest still.
I have ground what I must;   I will grind no more."
But never the hands   may know any rest
until Frodhi says   that his greed is sated.

"Now hands shall grasp   the hardened spears
and the reddened weapons.   Waken, Frodhi!
Waken, Frodhi,   if you are willing
to hear our songs   and sagas of old.

"Fire I see burning,   eastward beacons,
signs which warn   of war oncoming.
A host is abroad   and hither it hastens
to burn the stronghold   that Frodhi built.

"You shall be cast   from Leidhra's kingship,
from ruddy rings   and the quern of riches.
Grip harder, maiden,   the millstone-handle,
for now we are grinding   blood on the ground.

"Mightily grinding   the grist of doom,
we see how many   are marked for death.
Now we are shaking   the iron shafts
upholding the quern.   Hard will we swing it.

"Hard will we swing it.   The son of Yrsa
alone may redeem   what is lost to you:
he who is both   the brother of Yrsa
and the child she has nursed,   as well we do know."

The maidens were grinding,   and great was their
    might;
young they stood there   in Jötun wrath.
The quern fell down   and lay in the dust,
the millstones shivered   and shattered to bits.

Then sang the maidens   who came from the moun-
    tains:

"Now have we toiled   as you told us, Frodhi,
and ground out your weird.   We have worked long
  enough!"

And so in their anger Fenja and Menja brought forth
a viking host which fell upon the king's burg and slew
him. As to what became of those giantesses, there are
different stories; but all agree that here a fate was laid
upon the Skjoldungs.

Frodhi left three sons, Halfdan, Hroar, and Skati. They
fell into strife over who should be foremost. It has ever
been the curse of the lands across the North Sea, that
their kings beget many sons and one's claim is as good
as another's, whether he be born of a queen, a leman,
a thrall-woman, or a chance meeting—can he but raise
men who hope to gain if he wins.

This time luck chose Halfdan. He even died in bed,
albeit rather young. He left two sons of his own. The
older was called Frodhi from the grandfather. The younger, being born after Halfdan's death, got the name of the
latter.

I have spoken of jarls. They are not the same as
English earls, though the words sound much alike. A jarl
is a headman second only to the king. Sometimes a king
will set him over a part of the country; or sometimes
a jarl will himself become king in all but name. So it was
while these boys Frodhi and Halfdan were small. Einar,
jarl of the lands around the royal seat Leidhra, took
charge.

He was a sensible man who did not want to see Denmark again ripped apart. To this end, he got each of the
brothers taken as king by the yeomen, when these gathered
at the meetings known as Things. But they were hailed
separately. Halfdan was to rule in Zealand, Frodhi in
Scania.

Einar Jarl likewise arranged marriages after the lads
were grown. Halfdan wed Sigridh, daughter of a small
king on the island of Fyn. By her he got three children
who lived. Oldest was the daughter Signy, who in due
course married Einar's son and heir Sævil. Five years

younger than her was the boy Hroar, and two years younger than him was his brother Helgi.

The custom was that high-born children should be reared in the homes of folk of somewhat lower rank. Thus they learned those skills which become a youth or a maiden; and bonds of friendship were forged. Hroar and Helgi Halfdansson were taken by Regin Erlingsson, the reeve of the shire which held Leidhra. He grew as fond of them as if they had been his own.

King Halfdan was mild and easygoing. The folk loved him for his openhandedness and for the just judgments he gave.

But meanwhile King Frodhi in Scania had turned into a man harsh and hungry. He married Borghild, a king's daughter from among those Saxons who dwell just south of Jutland. By this means he got allies who, able to cross the Baltic Sea, awed Svithjodh enough that the Swedes kept off his back. She died in giving birth to their son Ingjald. Frodhi sent the babe to its grandfather to raise. Nevertheless, on behalf of it, he dreamed greatly.

And now, full of years, Einar died. Then matters stood like this:

In Leidhra on Zealand dwelt King Halfdan and his queen Sigridh. He was well-liked; but, with scant hankering for war, he kept no very strong guard, nor did he offer restless men much chance to win fame and booty abroad. His daughter Signy was wife to the jarl Sævil Einarsson. His sons Hroar and Helgi were mere boys, living with Regin the sheriff about twenty miles from the royal town.

And in Scania brooded King Frodhi.

He plotted with discontented men in Denmark, as well as with headmen among Swedes, Götar, and Jutes. Erelong he could call on a great host.

So he took ship across the Sound, lifted his banner and let blow the lur horns. Warriors flocked to him. Too late did the arrow pass from garth to garth, summoning those who would fight for King Halfdan. Looting and burning, Frodhi carried victory wherever he went. In a clash at darkest midnight, he fell upon Halfdan's army, overthrew it, and himself put his brother to death.

Thereafter he called the Danish chieftains to a Thing and made them plight faith. Among those who, to save their lives, laid hands on the golden rings and swore by Njörd and Frey and almighty Thor that they would never forsake him—among them was Sævil Jarl, husband of Halfdan's daughter Signy.

Thereupon Frodhi clinched his standing by marriage to his brother's widow, Sigridh. She had no choice about this, but it was with a bleak face that she went to his bed. And now Frodhi sent after her sons. He gave out that he wanted to see they were well taken care of. Most men supposed the care would be a quick throat-cutting, lest they grow up to avenge their father.

II

Regin the sheriff had not been at that Thing. When Halfdan's host broke, he sought back to his own home as fast as might be, together with what followers of his were left alive. He knew he would have a few days to batten down against Frodhi—few days indeed. "We can't withstand him," he said. "And I gave my oath to look after those youngsters."

"What can you do?" asked a warrior.

Regin uttered a dour chuckle. "You're a trustworthy enough fellow. However, you have no need to know."

He was a big man, face reddened and eyes bleached by a lifetime of weathers, hair and beard iron-gray, rather paunchy but still a strong and shrewd leader of his shire. The children his wife Aasta had borne to him were long since wedded. Because of this as well as the honor, they two had been glad to give Hroar and Helgi a home.

This was on the Isefjord. It is a broad, well-sheltered bay; the land reaches green to the very edge of the waters, which are ever aclamor with ducks, brant, swans, curlews, gulls, all kinds of fowl. Most trees had been cleared away. But wilderness still brooded on the southern rim of sight; and closer at hand, woodlots remained for squirrels and boys to scramble in. The homes of yeomen were strewn widely amidst the fields, built of planks, with sod roofs from whose smokeholes curled blacknesses that the salt winds quickly scattered. This is a good land, smiling with rye, barley, wheat, and flax beneath the sun and the dizzyingly tall clouds of summer.

Though Regin's dwelling was no royal hall, its black-painted side made one whole edge of a flagged courtyard. The other three were taken up by shed, byre, stable, workshop, and lesser outbuildings. The gable beams of the house were carved into dragon heads to frighten off trolls. On the eastern end, these looked into a shaw where Regin led the neighborhood in offering to the gods.

A path sloped down to a boatshed. Out upon the bay lay several islands. The nearest, while small, was thickly wooded. There dwelt an aged yeoman named Vifil, alone save for two great hounds. Most folk shunned him, for he was a strange and curt-spoken one and it was said that now and then he wrought wizardry. But Regin and he were old friends. "If he can tie a breeze in a bag, why should I not take his help?" the sheriff would laugh. "Or do you *want* to row through a foul wind?" Moreover, Vifil had always been a staunch upholder of Halfdan, whenever younger men grumbled that the king was a sluggard. Sometimes Hroar and Helgi took a boat and called upon him.

No mirth uprose now when Regin rode into his garth. The boys burst forth at the hoof-clatter. Shouts, questions, boasts torrented from their lips. Then they looked upon their fosterfather, and it was as if a sword chopped off their voices. Aasta came out behind them, followed by the household workers, and saw, and spoke naught. For a time stillness filled the long evening light.

At last the sheriff dismounted, with a creak of leather and jingle of iron. He stood hunched, his hands dangling empty. Wordless, a carl of his led the horse away. Hroar clenched fists at sides and all but screamed: "Our father is fallen! He's fallen, is he not?"

"Aye," sighed from Regin. "I saw his banner go down, where we tried to rally by firelight after Frodhi surprised us in our camp. Later I hid myself—"

"I would not have skulked from my father's need," said Helgi, half strangled by tears he failed to hold back.

"We could do naught," Regin told him, "and I had you, his sons, to think about. Toward dawn we began to find each other, we Isefjord men. One had been wounded and lay with no one paying much heed to him till at last he got strength to crawl away. He told how Frodhi slew the bound Halfdan." After a wait, he added: "They spoke together first. Frodhi said he must do this because only thus could he bring back a single kingdom, as it was in the days of his namesake the Peace-Good. Halfdan answered him steadfastly. May you two meet your own endings as well."

Aasta's fingers twisted a towel she held. "So young!" she wept.

Regin nodded heavily. A breeze ruffled his sweat-dank mane; a gull mewed. "I don't suppose Frodhi, having slain the lynx, will leave the cubs in their den," he said.

His gaze dwelt on them. Hroar had twelve winters and Helgi ten; but already the younger brother was more tall and broad-shouldered, for the older was of short and slender build. Both had great shocks of sun-whitened hair falling around their necks, around brown faces which had begun to show the Skjoldung cragginess; amidst that, their big eyes gleamed lightning-blue. They were clad alike, in leather doublets over plain gray wadmal shirts and trews. But Hroar clutched a wooden staff whereon he had been carving runes, to help himself learn those signs, while Helgi bore at his belt a sling, a pouchful of stones, and a hunting knife.

"I . . . wish . . . I might have known my father better," Hroar whispered.

"I'll be content to get revenge for him," Helgi gulped. He did not sound altogether like a child.

"For that, you must stay alive," Regin warned. "I cannot keep you. Did I try, we'd burn in this house after Frodhi's men ringed us in. Better for you that we, your friends, live to help another day."

"They can't flee into the woods as if they—as if they were outlaws!" Aasta cried.

Helgi tossed his head. "We can live quite well among the wolves, Fostermother," said he.

"Maybe; but wolves command no swords," Regin said. "I have a plan. We'll talk of it later." He shuffled toward his wife. "Now give me food and a draught of beer, and let me sleep. O gods, let me sleep!"

It was a silent welcoming feast.

Before dawn, Regin rose. He went to the shut-bed which the brothers shared, drew back its panel, and shook them awake, a finger laid on his mouth. Mutely they donned their clothes and followed him down to the water. The season was midsummer and the night was light, a paleness overhead where only a few stars glimmered, the bay like a burnished shield. Most softly and slowly, so as to make the least lap-lap of wavelets, he rowed them to Vifil's island.

The yeoman dwelt in a sod hut on the north side. Grounding the boat, man and boys stepped ashore into thick shadows. Frightfully baying came two black shapes, the hounds called Hopp and Ho. When they knew who the guests were, they wagged their tails and licked hands.

Vifil, aroused, stoked up the hearthfire in the single room, half underground, which was his. Smoke and stench roiled in its air. Through the gloom one had glimpses of his few poor tools—knife, ax, fishnet, bone hooks, soapstone dish, and such-like—also of the kettle and runestaves and oddly knotted ropes wherewith he was said to make magic. He was a tall, gaunt white-beard, dirty and ill-smelling in his motheaten woolens and badgerskin cloak. Yet from beneath their overhanging brows, his eyes sought not unkindly toward the athelings.

Regin told what had happened. Vifil nodded; did he have the news beforehand? "Well, I hope you can hide these lads," the sheriff finished, "for if you can't, then I know of no other way to save them."

Vifil tugged his whiskers. "That's a bad 'un to strive against, him Frodhi," he muttered. But in the end he agreed he had a duty to help as far as he was able.

Regin hugged them farewell. "May luck abide with you," he said roughly.

"I think the Norns who stood at their cradles sang them no common weird," said Vifil.

Regin hastened to the strand ere dawn should break. He spent the rest of that day faring widely about the Isefjord, making sure he was seen. Thus, when Hroar and Helgi were no longer at his home, folk would guess he had taken them away but would not know whither.

Vifil gave them bread, cheese, and stockfish before he led them into the woods. Yonder he had a place for cool storage of the meat and milk he got from his few beasts. It was hardly more than a pit with a roof of branches and turf. One climbed in or out on a kraki, a fir trunk whose stubbed-off limbs made a kind of ladder. The three toiled together, replanting brush till it decked every trace of man-work.

"Belike the king's men will come search this island," Vifil said. "That Frodhi's no fool, him, and he'll learn how your fosterfather and me has long been friends. Maybe they'll not find you if you crouch in here. Meanwhile, don't let nobody spy you from the shore. And . . . I'll do whatever else I can."

He would not let them watch what next he wrought, either in the hut or in a dolmen which stood among gnarled trees.

For a while thereafter, Helgi and Hroar were fairly well off. No boy can grieve long; and they had never really known their father anyway. The fare here was coarse, but their stomachs were young. If they slept on bare dirt, why, this they had done often before when hunting. That Vifil uttered few words was all to the good: it gave them time to swap daydreams. When the sun was high they must keep to the woods, where they ranged with Hopp and Ho after small game or birds' nests. In the light nights before seeking rest, they could swim or even fish. Sometimes, peering across the water to the home of Regin, they felt it as a fading dream, no longer quite real.

But their peace was short-lived. When a thorough

rooting about over the sheriff's holdings failed to turn
them out, Frodhi bade men scour the whole kingdom. Far
and near, north, south, east, west, he kept watches out;
he promised rich reward for news of his nephews, and
threatened to torture to death whoever dared shelter them.
Yet never a worthwhile word did anyone bring him; and
in the look of Queen Sigridh there began to wax a chilly
joy.

At length Frodhi decided a magic must lie in this, and
sent for those who had knowledge of darknesses.

III

For a time the great hall at Leidhra guested one spaewife
and wiseman after another. Frodhi told them to use their
farsight and scan Denmark up and down, islands and
skerries as well as mainland. But they saw nothing.

Thereafter he had wizards sought out, not merely those
with a little spellcraft or forecasting dreams, but men
who seethed witchy brews in cauldrons and were said
to ride on the night wind or raise the dead or call upon
beings more fearsome than that. These were most often
wanderers, shunned by all goodfolk. The household hirelings and thralls shrank from them and drew signs to
ward off a curse; the burliest guardsman could not wholly
hide a shudder.

Three came at last whom Frodhi received well, seating
them straight across the longfire from him and bidding
the queen bring them meat and drink with her own
hands. "The days are changed from when I served kings
and warriors," said the tall ruddy-braided woman sadly.
"Never did I look to play hostess to those who would
ferret out the sons of my body."

Her new husband gave her a cool regard. "Serve them
you shall, my Sigridh," he answered; and she yielded. It
was whispered among the workers, who sometimes overheard what went on in the royal bower, that Frodhi was
fast taming her, not by beatings which would have
aroused rage, but by skilled lust and unbending will. He
was one of the short Skjoldungs, yet quick on his feet,

quicker with a blade, swiftest and deadliest in his cunning.
Sleek brown hair and close-trimmed beard lay around a
face lean, hook-nosed, and wintry-eyed. He dressed well:
on this evening, a gold headband and arm-ring, a green
kirtle trimmed with marten, red trews cross-gaitered in
white kid.

With Sigridh he had made a lawful settlement, paying
her weregild for Halfdan's killing and a costly morning
gift after he wed her. She spoke little and laughed never,
but doubtless she hoped to work on him enough to save
something from the wreck. As for the rest of the Danes,
mostly they disliked him because of his laying heavy scot
on them and making judgments which went harshly to
his own advantage. But no other Skjoldung was in sight,
and surely Odin would lay wrath on this land, did it not
go beneath a man of his own house.

The wizards were an unkempt gang in musty black
robes; Finnish blood showed in them. After the tables
had been cleared away, they trod forth, set up their kettles
above the fire, cast their runes and cried their jagged
chants before the pillars of the high seat. The right-hand
post was carved to show Odin, father of magic; the left
showed Thor, but it was as if that night a murk lay
across the Hammerswinger. Somewhere a wolf howled and
a wildcat squalled, sounds which had not been heard near
Leidhra for many years. Men huddled back on the
benches. Frodhi sat moveless, waiting.

At last the gray and wrinkled spokesman of the three
said: "Lord, we can only learn that the boys are not on
land-earth; yet they are not far away from you."

The king stroked his beard and spoke slowly: "We
have sought them far and wide. I hardly think they're
nearby. Still, I remember now that islands do lie close
offshore from the house of their fosterfather."

"Then seek the nearest of those first, lord," said the
wizard. "Nobody lives there save a poor smallholder.
However, such a fog was around the island, we could
not peer into his home. We think he must be very wise
and not all that he seems."

"Well, we'll try," said the king. "Strange would it be if

a wretched fisherman could hide those fellows and dare hold them back from me."

Indeed a thick mist had arisen on the Isefjord that night. Early in the morning, Vifil awoke and told his charges: "Much strangeness is in flight, and mighty fetches have come hither to us. I heard them whisper in the dark, I hear them still in the gray. Rise up, Hroar and Helgi Halfdansson, and keep to my woods this day!"

They sprang to do his bidding.

Before noon, a troop of royal guardsmen rode to the water's edge and told Regin he must furnish them boats. By then the fog had lifted, and sunlight flared off their helmets and spears. Vifil greeted them as sullenly as he watched them while they searched. After hours, they had found nothing. At night Regin must needs guest them, though he did so in stingy wise.

Next day they returned to Leidhra and told of their failure. "Ill must you have hunted," snapped the king. "That yeoman is a master of witchcraft. Go back the same way and see if you can't take him by surprise."

Again the king's men landed to ransack the place. Though Vifil opened everything for them that they asked, never did they see trace of their prey. Again they must go home draggle-tailed.

Meanwhile the wizards had told Frodhi more about eeriness lurking on yonder island, blindnesses which neither they nor those which they sent to spy for them could pierce. When he heard the marshal of his guard, Frodhi grew red and white by turns. He slapped the high seat and shouted: "We've taken enough from that yokel! Tomorrow morning, I myself will seek him out."

Vifil awoke at dawn from a heavy sleep. Troubled, he roused Hroar and Helgi and said to them: "Now it goes ill, for your kinsman Frodhi is himself afoot, and he'll seek your lives with every kind of trick and ill-doing. I'm no longer sure I can save you." He tugged his beard and brooded. "If you try to sit the whole while in the storehouse like before, his kind of search may well turn you up. Best you keep flitting amongst brush and trees. Yet they'll beat the woods for you, so you'll need that lair at the right time. . . . Well, stay in earshot. And when you hear me shout for the hounds, Hopp and Ho, remember it'll be you two I mean, and go to earth."

Hroar nodded grimly, sweat on his cheeks. Helgi grinned; to him, this had been a great game.

The king arrived, not on horseback but in a ship which had sailed from what we today call Roskilde Fjord. The hull bore far more men than Regin's boats might readily carry over. They ran her onto a sandbar, dropped anchor, and waded ashore. Vifil stood leaning on a staff, beneath trees which had begun faintly to turn color. A wind blew cold and shrill, fluttering cloaks. Spearheads blinked, ringmail rattled.

"Grab him!" Frodhi cried. Hard hands pushed the yeoman forward to meet the king.

Frodhi glowered at him and said word by word: "You're a foul, sly one, aren't you? Tell me at once where my nephews are—for I know that you know!"

Vifil shrugged. "Hail to you, lord," he answered. "How can I ward myself against that kind of charge? Why, if you keep me here, I can't even hold the wolf off my little flock." The guardsmen were spreading out over the cleared patches, headed for the woods. Vifil filled his lungs and yelled, "Hopp and Ho, help out the beasts!"

"What's that you're calling?" asked Frodhi.

"The names of my hounds," said the yeoman blandly. "Look as hard as you want. I don't think you'll be a-finding of any king's sons hereabouts. And really, I don't understand what makes you think I'd hide aught from you, a poor old fisher like me."

Frodhi growled, told off a warrior to watch the islander, and himself took command of the chase. Today they uncovered the storehouse. However, by then the brothers had slipped from it—after the beaters went past—and were in treetops well back of the onward-moving troop.

At eventide the men returned to the hut. Vifil waited. Dithering with rage, the king told him: "Indeed you're a sly one, and I ought to have you killed."

The yeoman met his eyes and said, "That stands within your might, if not your right. Then you'll at least have gotten somewhat for your trek here. Otherwise you'll go home bootless, eh?"

Frodhi clamped fists together and stared around the crowding ring of his warriors. His slaying of bound Halfdan had not really sat well with them. To order death for a helpless gaffer against whom naught could be shown would truly brand him unmanly. No few would forsake him on that account alone, should a foeman arise.

"I cannot let you be slain," said Frodhi between his teeth; "but I do think it's unwise to let you live."

He turned and stalked to his ship.

The crew rowed him to Regin's garth, where he spent the night. And here he demanded the sheriff swear him troth, as the rest of the Danish headmen had already done.

"You give me a thin choice," said Regin. "Besides my holdings, I have wife, children, and grandchildren. So be it, then. As for your unasked question, I tell you as I earlier told your men, I do *not* know where Hroar and Helgi Halfdansson are."

"No," sneered the king. "Not within a foot or two." Nevertheless he kept from pressing the matter. He could not afford to goad those folk who looked upon Regin as their leader.

Vifil saw where the ship went, and either guessed or foreknew what happened. He called the boys to him and said: "Here you can bide no longer. We'll be under too narrow a watch, the more so when men of the neighborhood will've given up hope of overthrowing Frodhi. Tonight I'll ferry you over. Stay off the highroads while you get out of this shire."

"Where should we go?" wondered Hroar.

"Well," said Vifil, "I've heard as how Sævil Jarl is your brother-in-law. He'll have a big household, where none'll much mark a couple of newcomers. But he too is now the king's handfast man, so don't you go straight off giving yourselves away to him, or to anybody. Lynx cubs got to fare wary."

IV

Sævil and Signy dwelt near Haven. Each year when the herring ran, this hamlet came aswarm with fishermen who had beaten their way south down the Kattegat or north out of Baltic waters; merchants joined them, and it roared among the booths ashore. In other seasons Haven was a base for warcraft which lay out on watch lest vikings slip by to harry the Danish coasts. Thus it was no small charge which Sævil had and he was not a man to whom Frodhi would willingly give grave offense. Maybe one reason the king married Signy's mother was to try to make a bond between himself and the strand-jarl.

When the English first came hither, their great men doubtless built halls like those in the Northlands. They do no more. Let me therefore tell about such a house. It is a long wooden building, with a roof of sod or of shakes, oft-times a clerestory; the beam-ends are apt to be carved in fanciful shapes. If there are two floors, a gallery runs around the walls. Windows are shuttered in bad weather, and belike covered by thin-scraped skins. Inside, one enters through a foreroom, where feet are wiped and outer garments left hanging. Unless the lord is suspicious and commands his guests to leave their weapons here as well, these are brought into the main room and hung up, that the luster of metal and of the painted leather on shields help brighten its gloom.

The ground floor of the hall is hard-packed earth, thickly strewn with rushes, juniper boughs, or other sweet things, often changed. Down the middle run two or three trenches, or sometimes only one, wherein roar the long-fires, that servants feed with wood taken from stacks at the far end. Flanking them goes a double row of great wooden pillars, upbearing the top floor, or the rafters if there is none. They too are graven and colored, to show gods or heroes or beasts and intertwining vines. Against the wainscoted walls, earthern platforms raise the benches a foot or two above the floor. In the middle

of one wall, commonly the north, stands the high seat of
the master and his lady, held by two lesser posts which
are especially holy. Straight across the chamber is a
slightly lower seat for the most honored guest. Between
the weapons ablink behind the benches are other carvings,
skins, horns, torches or rushlights flaring in their sconces.

At mealtimes the women and servants set trestles in
front of the benches and lay boards across them. On
these go meat and drink, prepared usually in a separate
cookhouse for dread of ·wildfire. Later the tables are
removed, and when men have drunk enough, those of
higher standing stretch out on the benches to sleep; their
followers use the floor.

Shut-beds for the master, mistress, and chief guests may
be at either end; or there may be upper rooms; or there
may be a bower standing aside from the hall, a narrow
building of one or two floors where women spin and
weave by day in well-lighted airiness, and at night the
well-born sleep free from snoring and eavesdropping.

Around a courtyard cluster the outbuildings. Beyond
them may lie the homes, byres, and worksteads of hum-
bler families; and a stockade may enclose everything. Thus
many a hall and its attendants make up a whole small
town, always abustle with men and women, children and
beasts, always alive with talk, song, shouts, smithing,
baking, brewing, gaming, jesting, courting, weeping, whatever it is that living beings do.

Besides the dwellers—lord, lady, children, and kin;
warriors; yeomen; artisans; craftsmen; free hirelings;
thralls—there are sure to be visitors. Some are neighborhood men, come for a bit of trade or gossip or talk
about deeper matters. Some are guests invited from further
off, as to a wedding or a Yuletide feast. Some are travelers
passing through. And some are footloose, fallen on ill days
if ever they knew good ones, given food and a strawheap
in a stable for the sake of the lord's honor and for whatever tales they can tell from elsewhere.

To this kind of steading did Hroar and Helgi make
their way. Vifil had given them food to pack along, and

they found no dearth of brooks to drink from. Nonetheless that was a stiff and dangerous trek. He had likewise patched together a pair of hooded cloaks for them, and sent them off with keen redes.

They drew little heed when they limped into Sævil's garth and begged shelter. Many were tramping that year, after Frodhi's host had cast them out and taken their land for its pay. These two sat quietly in dimness, and next day lent a hand with feeding the kine and cleaning the stalls. "Bide your time," Vifil had said, over and over. "Get your growth first, *then* your revenge."

After a week the cowherd foreman felt they had better speak to the jarl if they wished to stay on. They neared him toward evening, when he had had several horns of beer before he ate and was feeling cheery. They kept the cowls on their heads and the mantles drawn around their shoulders. In the dull unrestful light, neither Sævil nor their busy sister Signy knew them. These kin had seldom been together anyway after Regin took in the boys. The jarl shrugged and said, "Small help do I think there is in you; but I shan't refuse you food for a while longer."

Helgi flushed and might have spoken hotly, save that Hroar gave his hand a warning squeeze. They muttered thanks, louted low, and withdrew.

And now through three winters they abode with Sævil.

They hardly saw him or his wife, save as grandness on the high seat or on horseback. For the most part, they were off doing the meanest work of herding, harvesting, and barnyard chores—more apt to sleep in a haymow or a meadow than in any house. Ever they kept the secret of who they were. Hroar called himself Hrani, while Helgi was Ham, and they said in a few words that they were sons of a smallholder killed in battle, themselves driven off his land. To this same end, they always wore their coverings when in sight of anyone else.

A number of carls teased them, saying they must have misformed skulls or breasts like women. They bit their mouths shut and endured. Alone, they could yarn about that which would someday be theirs, or take out their blood-anger on fowl and hare, or spend hour upon bruising hour in weapon-practice, staves for swords and shields made from stolen planks.

But after the three years, Helgi was thirteen and really starting to shoot up. Hroar, fifteen, was smaller, though lean and lightfooted; he was the thoughtful one of them.

King Frodhi had dwelt in peace all this while, and thus his fears had eased a good deal. He sent word, asking Sævil and Signy to a midwinter feast. When Helgi heard, he smote the frozen ground and said, "Hroar, we're going along." Nor could his brother talk him out of that. Instead, it was the other way around, until both were eagerly busking themselves to seek their revenge.

V

Sævil rode off with his lady and twoscore men. The urchins Ham and Hrani plucked at his arm and asked leave to come along. He barked a laugh and told them, "Of course not."

Little snow had fallen thus far. The air lay cold beneath a sky low and heavy as a slab of slate. Fields reached brown, trees stood leafless, farmsteads crouched inward. Here and there a flock of crows jeered "Ha-kra-kra!" Hoofs and wheels rang on the road. Against this, the jarl's troop splashed brightness. All his warriors owned helmets, more than half had byrnies, which gleamed; the blues and greens, yellows and reds of cloaks fluttered back from their shoulders; they were mostly young men, whose merriment stood forth in steam-puffs. Their shaggy ponies trotted briskly ahead.

Signy rode in a wagon carved and painted, trimmed with gold and silver, drawn by four horses of the big Southland stock. With her were a driver, two serving wenches, and supplies of food and gifts. She was a tall woman, the Skjoldung handsomeness in her face and amber-hued braids. Inside a fur coat she wore gaily dyed clothes and lovely ornaments. But no mirth was in her eyes.

Jouncing slowly over the ruts, her cart went at the end of the train. Hence she heard the racket at her back before her husband or his men did. Turning about, she saw two ragged, dirty shapes in hooded cloaks, overhauling.

Because those beasts fit to ride were gone from the hall, Ham and Hrani had caught a pair of unbroken foals in a paddock. With bridles of rope and sticks broken off thornbushes, they somewhat made these mounts carry them. The bucking, plunging, and shying were wild to behold. Ham sat backwards, yelled, flapped his arms, and behaved in every way like a fool. Hrani rode more soberly. Even so, it was his horse which made such a leap as he drew nigh that his cowl fell off.

Signy saw fair locks fly around a face whereon, through grime and gauntness and untrimmed fuzz of beard, she knew her father's looks. She remembered—and had she maybe, during these past three years, begun to suspect? "Hroar!" she gasped as if he had stabbed her. "Then . . . then your mate must be Helgi—"

Hroar fought his steed till he mastered it. He covered himself anew and sought back to his lolloping brother. Signy buried her head in her hands and wept.

Word passed along the line that she was troubled. Sævil trotted rearward. He was a dark man, fork-bearded, given to keeping his own counsel. There in the wagon, beneath the frightened gaze of her servants, sat his wife crying. He drew alongside and asked what her trouble was. How she answered need not be from a later tale-teller. The well-born were expected to be able to make a verse at any time, and a gift of skaldcraft ran in her blood.

"The end has come
of Skjoldung athelings.
The oak has fallen,
leaving only twigs.
My darling brothers
are riding bareback
while Sævil's folk
go off to feast."

The jarl sat quiet in the saddle for a bit until he said, most sternly, as he stared at the driver and girls: "Great tidings, but let them not come out."

He spurred toward the lads. They dismounted, to show him respect and listen more readily. "Go home, you shameless whelps!" he bellowed. "I ought to hang you! It's not fitting for you to be in a troop of good men!" He whirled his horse around and cantered back.

Helgi bristled. "If he thinks——" he began.

Hroar cut him off: "If *you* think, brother mine, you'll recall how his hand moved, hidden from his followers. It signed us a warning, not a threat. And see, our sister weeps. She must have known me and told him. He doesn't want anybody else to learn it from his words."

"Well," said Helgi, "what should we do now?" They had had no fast-set plan. They merely hoped to spy things out while seeming a pair of nitwits, and afterward do whatever looked best. Could they get near enough to King Frodhi to sink their knives in him, then before the guardsmen slew them call out who they were—but Hroar called that a daydream.

"We'd better not keep these nags," the older youth decided. "Too open a defiance of Sævil. If he didn't punish us, the rest would ask why. They're more trouble than they're worth, anyway. Let's leave them off at yonder garth and tag along afoot."

Thus they did. When the early dusk fell, Sævil and Signy took hospitality from a yeoman. Their folk spread warm sleeping bags outside. Hroar and Helgi shivered hungry in a thicket.

They had not far to fare, however. Frodhi was not keeping this Yuletide at Leidhra, but in a lesser hall he owned north of Haven. Most kings traveled about for part of each year, in order to gather news, hear complaints, give judgments, and on the whole strengthen their grips. Besides, truth to tell, their main dwellings must from time to time be cleaned, aired out, and let sweeten.

That tip of Zealand is wind-whipped, a land of moor and sandy hills, thinly peopled. The hall and its out-buildings stood alone, to north a rolling reach of ling gone gray with winter, to south a darkling skeleton woods, one farmstead barely in sight across empty miles. Most months none dwelt here save a few caretakers, who tended, slaughtered, smoked and salted those cattle and swine which guests would eat. The chief building had a single floor, and in front a single door; at the rear it abutted on a wellhouse.

Frodhi the Peace-Good had raised it for two reasons. First, this spot was handily near the middle of what fishermen lived on the north coast and the bay to westward, what farmers plowed the heaths, what hunters or charcoal burners ranged the wilds. Second, here was a clump of oaks taller than elsewhere in these parts, where offerings had always been made. A hall hard by it would gain in holiness, and when its owner was on hand he would be the head butcher and spokesman to the gods.

That was why Frodhi his grandson now chose to keep Yuletide here. Among the heathen, the midwinter rites honor chiefly Thor, who stands between our earth and the giants of endless ice and night. Belief is that on the eve of it, all kinds of trolls and spooks run loose across the world; but next day the sun turns again homeward and hope is reborn.

Moreover, the king meant to talk with different leading men, sound them out, win their friendship by an openhandedness which inwardly griped him. Hence for days, wagons creaked hither, bearing food, beer, mead, and gifts—golden arm-rings and other jewelry, weapons, furs, clothes, silver-mounted harness and drinking horns, glass goblets and stamped coins from the far Southlands. Kine, sheep, and horses, to be slain for the gods and eaten by the folk, milled around in pens. Thralls filled what lowly shelters they could find. Then arrived the king, the queen, and the royal guards.

Since he was asking great men here, each of whom would bring followers, the troop of Frodhi was smaller than was common for him. Besides servants, he brought just his berserkers and a chosen few of those younger sons of yeomen who most often take royal service— chosen for looks, manners, and garb. The rest he gave leave to spend the holy season with their kindred. As I have said, Frodhi had begun to feel at ease in his over-lordship.

Soon guests came, until the stead was a roaring whirl-pool. Most shire-dwellers stayed home. There would be no room indoors for them, and they did not like the thought of camping out on Yule Eve. A number of landloupers risked it, for the sake of meat and beer during those few days of their starveling lives. Among them was a witchwife known as Heidh. When Frodhi heard about her, he said she should enter the hall.

VI

Hroar and Helgi reached the place in mid-afternoon, an hour or two behind Jarl Sævil's band. They mingled easily with the throng in the courtyard. Kegs had been broached, bread and cheese and cold meats stood out for whoever would partake, the smell of roasting oxen welled from the cookhouse to warm the bitter air. Men laughed and bragged, ladies gossiped while eyeing each other's gowns and gauds, children tumbled in play, dogs yammered.

Between their own rawness, and the blow that a stoup or three of beer can give to a hollow belly, the brothers more than carried out their aim of behaving like loons. They sprang around, somersaulted, cracked foolish jokes, stood on their heads, waved legs in air, and all in all made themselves out as silly and loud-mouthed. So folk merely looked down on them, or away from them.

Day drew to a close. At this season, it was hardly more than a glimmer between two gaping darknesses. Guests streamed indoors. Frodhi required that weapons be left in the foreroom. His excuse was that on Yule Eve men always drank heavily; quarrels might well flare, and if edged metal was to hand, a blood feud could much too easily start. The truth was, he did not really trust them. To be sure, he must lay the same command on his own warriors; anything else would have been a deadly insult. But those who were armed only with eating knives would hardly attack household troops who, outnumbered or not, were highly skilled fighters.

The foreroom thus grew crowded and agleam. Despite the longfires and many lesser flames, the chamber beyond seemed murky. Smokeholes were not drawing well and a blue haze thickened, stinging eyes and lungs.

When they had pushed deep into the crowd, the boys suddenly stiffened. They could make out a man who sat near the seat of guest-honor that Sævil and Signy would share. Stout, gray, coarsely clad, he must have stayed within this whole while. "Regin!" Helgi cried in joy. "Old Fosterfather!"

He started toward the sheriff. Hroar grabbed his cloak. "Hold back, you staggerpate," the elder hissed. "Do you want to get us slain?"

Helgi yielded. Still, he could not keep from leaping and dancing down the length of the hall. Hroar must needs pace his sibling. He cast a glance through reek and dimness and elbowing, chattering folk, toward the high seat. There sat his uncle and his mother. The king was leaned forward, in earnest talk with a beggarly-looking crone who bore a crooked staff. He would not mark what anybody else did. Across from him was Signy. Her husband had not yet joined her. The longfires roared high, red, blue, yellow, casting sparks and a surf of heat. Among huge hunchbacked shadows glittered the gold on Signy's arms, at her throat, in the coiled braids beneath her headdress. She was signing to her brothers.

Hroar urged Helgi thither. They stood before her, their faces beclouded by the cowls. Hers was drawn taut. She beckoned them close and whispered wildly, just to be heard by them amidst the din: "Don't stay here in the hall. Don't! Your strength is so little."

Helgi started to answer. Hroar thrust him onward. It would not do for others to see the strand-jarl's lady beseech two witlings. They sought the far end of the chamber and squatted down among the wanderers and dogs that waited for whatever the king would order given to them or the great men deign to throw their way.

The feast came forth. Good and plentiful were both food and drink: trenchers heaped to overflowing with juicy meat, flatbread and loaves stacked beside tubs of butter and cheese, servants scurrying ceaselessly to keep horns full of beer or mead. Yet there was no mirth. Talk buzzed dull and low. Few youths invited maidens to come sit and drink at their sides. A skald chanted forth old lays, and new ones in praise of King Frodhi, but his tones seemed lost in the smoke. Only the row of fires was loud, brawling and spitting above white-hot coals.

That downheartedness stemmed from the mood of the host. He sat withdrawn and curt-spoken, giving off chill like an iceberg. Sigridh his queen was wholly woeful; her fingers twisted and twisted together.

At last the tables were cleared away. The king rose and made the sign of the Hammer above a great silver cup which he then drained. Next should have come the turn of the earth-god Frey. In his honor, a boar made of gold should have been carried in, for those who wished to lay hands upon and make vows.

Instead Frodhi said, flat-voiced and tight-lipped while glooms went hunting around his head: "I want to make known that ill faith is among us tonight, yes, and a will to do murder. If we end it not at once, surely the gods will feel themselves aggrieved, and we may look in the coming year for famine or worse." He was silent for a bit; the eyes upon him glistened white; some guests could not help coughing, an ugly noise. "A witchwife has told me," Frodhi went on, "that she smells danger nigh, stemming from my own blood.

"Well, you know how I've sought after the sons of my brother and my lady. I would heal the breach, I would bring back the peace which ought to dwell among kinsmen. Ever have they hidden from me, though. Why else save in hopes of uprising and murder? And who else might be hereabouts, wishing me harm, save those two?

"I will give rich rewards, and forgive whatever he may formerly have done or plotted against me, to whoever will tell me where Hroar and Helgi Halfdansson are."

Queen Sigridh fought not to weep. King Frodhi peered

about. He could not see well in the gloom. Besides, the faces of men like Sævil Jarl and Regin the sheriff were cold and shut.

"Stand forth, then, Heidh," ordered the king, "and tell me what you need to learn what you must."

The woman hobbled from her seat. Shadows blent with her rags while firelight reddened her unkempt gray locks. She leaned on her staff and spoke in low tones.

Among the stinking paupers, Helgi and Hroar squatted on the floor and gripped their knives. A hound smelled their sweat and growled.

Frodhi spoke to his frightened thralls. They fetched a witching seat. He often had to do with spellcasters and therefore kept such things on all his garths. It was a high beechwood stool whose three legs were of ash, elm, and thorn. Heidh put it before the king and herself like a raven upon it. She closed her eyes, moved her withered hands, and muttered.

No firepit lay between the royal seat and the place of honor opposite. Frodhi squinted across at Signy and Sævil. The jarl sat quiet—the carven pillars seemed to have more movement in this uneasy light—but his wife breathed hard and her gaze roved. Heidh fell silent. "Well, what have you seen?" Frodhi shrilled. "I know much has been opened to you. I see you have luck with you. Answer me, witchwife!"

She parted her jaws and gasped. A cracked croaking came from her mouth:

"Here are two
I do not trust—
they who sit
beside the fire."

The king trembled. A hand clasped his knife-hilt. "Do you mean the boys," he asked, "or those who've hidden them?"

Quoth she:

"They who stayed
there with Vifil
and who had
the names of hounds,
Hopp and Ho."

At this, Signy called, "Well spoken, wise-woman! You've done more than could have been awaited of you." Pulling off her arm-ring, she cast the heavy gold coil across the room, into the lap of Heidh.

The hag snatched it. "What's this about?" Frodhi rasped.

Heidh looked from him to Signy and back. "I'm sorry, lord," she said. "What was that nonsense I spoke? All my spells went astray, this whole day and eventide."

Racked by shuddering and gulping, Signy rose to go. Frodhi stood too, shook his fist at the witch and yelled, "If you won't speak forth freely, I'll torture you into it! For now I know no better than before what you think about those in this hall. And why is Signy out of her seat? I wonder if wolves are not in council with foxes here."

"I, I beg your leave," stammered his niece. "I've grown sick from the smoke."

Frodhi glared. Sævil drew her back down beside him. "I'm sure another horn of mead will make her feel better," said the jarl smoothly. He beckoned to a girl, who hastened—teeth clattering—to pour for his wife. She drank deeply. He leaned close, arm about her waist as if to uphold her, and breathed in her ear: "Keep quiet. Hold your place. Much can happen yet to save the boys, if that be their lot. Whatever you do, show not what you think. As matters stand, we can't do a thing to help them."

Frodhi well-nigh screamed: "Tell the truth, witch, or I'll haul your limb-bones from their sockets and cast you in the fire!"

Heidh cowered from him. She did not let go of the ring, but she gaped widely and struggled with her spell, until she uttered:

"I see sitting
the sons of Halfdan,
Hroar and Helgi,
both of them hale.
Forth their revenge
on Frodhi comes—

"unless somebody hastens to stop it, but that'd doubtless

be unwise," she added low. Jumping from the stool, she cackled:

"Hard are the eyes
in Ham and Hrani.
Grown from kidhood
are kingly children."

A stir and rustle went among those of Sævil's men who recalled the names. "Ham and Hrani?" said Frodhi. "Who? Where?"

But the spaewife had, in her way, given the brothers warning. They had sidled backward through the poor guests to the wellhouse door. As uproar arose, they slipped out and fled toward the woods.

"Somebody ran from here!" yelled a beggar, and: "After them!" the king.

He and his warriors dashed toward that end of the hall. Regin surged from his seat. Blundering along, as if eager to help but very drunk, he knocked a number of faggots from their brackets to the floor. They guttered out. His followers saw what he was about and did likewise. Darkness and tumult filled the space beyond the last fire-trench. There Regin's men got in the way of Frodhi's. By the time the mess had been straightened, no trace of the boys was to see. Outside lay nothing save frost.

Frodhi gnawed his mustache as he led the way back in. Sigridh and Signy were sobbing in each other's arms. Heidh had scuttled out the front door with her golden ring. He paid scant heed to this. When the lights were kindled anew, he stood forth above all stony eyes and told the gathering in bitterness:

"I've lost them again. There seem to be no few here in dealings with them, and this I will punish when the time comes. Meanwhile, you may as well drink—you who are so glad they've gotten away."

"Lord," said Regin, and hiccoughed, "you misunderstand us. Surely tomorrow will be happier. Tonight, let's drink indeed . . . as friends . . . for who knows how long the Norns will let him stay among those he holds dear?"

He kept shouting for brew to be fetched. Shaken by what had happened, the king's men and most others were glad to swill the stuff down as fast as their gullets would take it. Regin—and after Regin had whispered to him, Sævil—passed secret word among their followers: "Pretend to get as drunk as the rest, but keep your wits. Mighty weirds are abroad, and we far from our homes."

Loudness and laughter soon lifted, harsh, not really happy, but at least staving off the stillness of the night. Booze flowed until the household troopers and many more fell asleep, one atop the next. By then Frodhi and Sigridh had gone to bed. Thus Sævil and Regin drew no remark when they led their own bands out, to a barn which had been cleaned and spread with straw and skins for the overflow of guests, even though these quarters were not meant for them. In the hall resounded only hoglike snores and the sputter of the dying longfires.

VII

During those hours, a breeze scattered the overcast. Huddled and ashiver in a brake at the edge of the woods, Hroar and Helgi saw the heaven-signs blink forth—the Great Wain, the Little Wain in whose tongue is the Lodestar, Freyja's Spindle, more and more until the land lay grey and the hall bulked black beneath that icy light.

"Nothing have we done," said Hroar.

"No, much," Helgi told him, "for now men know that the Halfdanssons live—Hold! Yonder!"

A man came riding from the stables, across the open ground between dwelling and wilds. At first he was a blot and a clash of hoofs on rime. As he drew nigh, they knew him. "Regin!" Helgi cried. He bounded forth, Hroar close behind. "Oh, Fosterfather, we've missed you so!"

The sheriff gave no greeting. The shadowy shape of him and his steed turned about and moved back toward the hall. Stricken, the boys gaped after him. The cold gnawed deeper into their bones.

"What?" Hroar whispered. Starlight glistened on tears. "Is he disowning us? Is he off to tell Frodhi?"

"No, never will I believe that of him." Helgi's tone wavered.

Regin brought his beast around. A second time he neared them. He drew his sword and, when he was upon them, they saw how he scowled. He made as if to hew at them. Hroar choked but stood his ground. Helgi snapped numb fingers and breathed: "Hoy, I think I get what he means."

Regin sheathed blade, twitched reins, and again rode toward the hall. He went at a very slow walk. Helgi urged Hroar along, and they trailed. "I don't understand," said the latter weakly.

Said Helgi, and his voice clanged: "My fosterfather behaves like this because he will not break his oath to King Frodhi. So he won't speak to us; but nonetheless he wants to help us."

They closed in on the garth. A few dogs bayed. No man roused, nor did any stand watch. A shadow of looming trees swallowed Regin. The youths heard him speak aloud: "If I had great things to avenge on King Frodhi, I would burn this shaw." Thereupon he spurred his horse to a trot, rounded the main building and was gone from their sight.

The boys halted. "Burn the holy shaw?" wondered Hroar. "What can that mean?"

Helgi seized his brother's arm. "Not the trees themselves. He wishes we'd set the hall afire—as near as may be to its door."

"How can we do that, two mere lads, with such might against us?"

"There's no help for it," Helgi snarled. "*Sometime* we must dare it, if ever we're to get revenge for the harm done us."

Hroar stood a while until, slowly: "Yes. Right. Here we have men gathered who'll know we're the doers. If we make the first move, some of them will rally to us, for our father's sake and in hopes we'll deal better with them than Frodhi has. A chance like this may never come again."

"Let's go, then!" Helgi laughed aloud.

Eager or no, they moved thereafter with every trick of silence and concealment they had learned in hunting.

And surely their hearts hammered thickly when they entered the hall itself.

Stacked weapons gleamed in the foreroom. The chamber beyond was a blindness full of bitter smoke, heat, man-stench, noises of drunken slumber. Fire-trenches glowed dull red, but the pillar-gods upbearing the rafters were lost to sight.

With unsteady fingers, the athelings took war-gear. Outside once more, they helped each other don padded undercoat and coif, noseguarded helmet, byrnie of ringmail whose weight they felt only briefly, sword at waist and shield laid handy. What they chose did not fit them too ill, since Hroar was fifteen and Helgi, thirteen, big for his age.

"Man's arms!" Helgi grew dizzy from gladness. "After three years like thralls—warriors!"

"Hush," warned Hroar, though hope drove the winter out of him too.

Most quietly, they flitted everything from the foreroom and laid it on the ground. Then they slipped into the main room. On hands and knees they went, fumbling a way among sprawled bodies. When someone stirred or mumbled, they froze. Yet a tide of sureness carried them. No boy really believes he can die.

Groping along a trench, they found sticks not quite eaten away and plucked them forth. The light from these made them more sure of not kicking anybody awake. Helgi bore an extra one in his teeth.

Under the stars, they straightened. They whipped the brands to flapping life. They reached high and put torch to low-sweeping eaves.

At first these would not catch. Helgi muttered a stream of oaths. Hroar worked patiently, trying first this spot and then that.

A flame stirred. It was tiny, pale blue, a bird of Surt newly hatched and frail. It trembled in the cold breeze, cowered down between two shakes, peeped a weak little song as if to keep up its own heart. But all the while it fed; and it grew; now strength flowed into it out of the wind; it stood forth boldly, flaunted bright feathers, looked around and crackled a greeting to the sisters it saw.

The timber of the hall was old and weathered. Moss that chinked the cracks had gone dead-leaf dry. Pitch in the roof drank fire as once in its pine trees it drank a summer sun.

Helgi took stance near the foredoor. "If they waken in there before this way is blocked," he said, "we'll have to keep them from boiling out." He scowled. "The wellhouse! Best you go kindle that end right off."

"What of our mother?" Hroar fretted. In his thrill he had hitherto forgotten Queen Sigridh.

"Oh, warriors always let women and children and thralls and such go free," said Helgi. "But—" He broke off and spun around. From the courtyard stole a band of armed men.

At their head was Sævil. He turned to them and said: "Stoke up the fire and help these lads. *You* have no duty toward King Frodhi."

They hastened to obey. Many already bore torches, the rest ranked themselves by the athelings. Helgi cheered. Hroar stuttered, "L-l-lord Jarl—"

Sævil stroked his beard. "I think erelong you will be my lord . . . Hrani," he murmured.

"There's an escape through the wellhouse—"

"Regin is taking care of that."

The sheriff joined them. Firelight waxed till it skipped across metal and lured stern faces out of shadow. As yet, however, the burning was not far along. Neither noise nor heat aroused King Frodhi.

He stirred in his shut-bed. One like that is built short, for its users sleep sitting up. The mattress rustled beneath him. "Ugh, ugh!" he choked. "It's close and black in here as a grave." He slid back the panel. A bloody glow crept over him from the trenches.

Beside him, Sigridh asked, "What's the matter?"

He sighed heavily before he cried: "Awake! Waken, my men! I've had a dream and it bodes no good."

Much though they drank, his warriors had remembered

to lie near him. The call brought them fast out of their rest. "What was it, lord?" asked a man. In murk and reek, he seemed to bear the shape of a troll.

Frodhi snapped after air. "I'll tell you how it went. I dreamed I heard a shouting at us: 'Now are you come home, King, you and your men.' I heard an answer, and grim was the tone: 'What home is that?' Then the shout came so near me that I felt the breath of the one who shouted: 'Home to Hel, home to Hel!' And I awoke."

"O-o-oh," crooned Sigridh.

The dogs indoors had not thus far marked, in their sleep, anything that seemed worth barking at. Now they also stirred, caught the first whiff of death, and set up a hubbub.

Those outside heard. It was needful to lull fears until the trap was sprung tight. Frodhi had two smiths who were both good handworkers and both called Var, which means Wary. Regin boomed:

"Outside it is Regin"—which could mean "raining"—
"and also the king's sons,
fiercest of foemen;
say it to Frodhi.
Wary wrought nails,
Wary set the heads on,
and for Wary did Wary
forge wary nails."

A guardsman grumbled, "What's this to make a verse about? That it's raining, or the king's smiths are at work, whatever they make—"

Frodhi answered starkly: "Don't you see these are tidings? We'll find a different meaning, be sure of that. Regin swore an oath to me, and so he warns me of danger. But sly and and underhanded is that fellow."

Most who thought about it afterward felt that Regin kept his word by thus saying that Hroar—a wary one— was wreaking a crookedness which Helgi—another wary one—put to work, while Regin—a third wary one—gave warning of this to a fourth wary one who was Frodhi himself. The sheriff had never promised not to give news in riddles too twisted for easy reading.

Finding no rest, Frodhi rose a short time later. He threw a cloak over his nakedness and sought the foreroom. There he saw how the roof was ablaze, the weapons were gone, and armed men waited beyond. After an eyeblink he spoke steadily: "Who rules over this fire?"

Helgi and Hroar stepped from the line. In their young faces was no ruth. "We do," said Hroar, "the sons of your brother Halfdan whom you slew."

"What terms of peace do you want?" asked Frodhi. "It's an unseemly doing among us kinsmen, that one should seek the life of the other."

Helgi spat. "None can have faith in you," he said. "Would you be less ready to betray us than you were our father? This night you pay."

An ember fell upon Frodhi and scorched his hair. He walked back into the hall and shouted for everyone to make ready for battle.

The guardsmen had neither mail nor shields nor any arm better than a knife. They fueled the longfires within for light and broke up furnishings for clubs and rams. Some of the guests helped them. The rest were too befuddled, and only stumbled about gibbering and getting in the way.

In a rush together, as nearly as the narrow doorways allowed, the king's men attacked. Most fell, speared or sliced or hewn down as they came. A handful, holding a bench between them, smashed through their foes and gained a clear space. Sævil's folk surrounded these. One was a berserker, a shaggy giant upon whom the madness had fallen. He howled, foamed, gnawed his club which was a high seat pillar, and dashed forth heedless of cuts and thrusts into his bare flesh. His weapon crashed on a helmet. It rang and crumpled; the man beneath dropped dead.

Helgi broke from the line still guarding the door, and sped against the berserker. "*No—!*" yelled Sævil and Regin together, aghast. The atheling heard them not. He took stance, feet apart, legs bent and tautened, shield decking his body from just below the eyes, sword slanted back past his shoulder. After three years of planks and sticks, it was as if these well-made things were alive. The club raged downward. He eased his right knee and thus swiftly moved that way. The blow smote merely the rim of his shield. That was enough to stagger him, and leave his left wrist sore for days afterward. But his blade was already moving. Across the top of the shield it whistled. Deeply it bit, into the berserker's neck. Blood spurted. He toppled. For a small time he flopped, struggling to rise. Then he went empty and lay there in a widening pool.

Sævil hugged Helgi. "Your first man, your first man!" Regin hastened to the back of the hall.

Frodhi had not been in that doomed charge. He took his wife by the arm. "Come," he said. "Maybe a way is still open." They ran to the wellhouse. At its outer doorway stood Regin's men and the sheriff himself.

"We Skjoldungs are not a long-lived breed," said Frodhi, and returned.

The last king's man died. The flames stood ever taller and ate their way ever further back along the roof. Walls caught. Heat hammered. The house thundered and flared. Helgi bawled in his uneven boy-voice: "Let women and servants, men who are friends to the sons of Halfdan, come forth. Quick, before too late!"

They were not many. Most hirelings, thralls, and beggars had slept elsewhere and were gathered terrified at the uneasy edge of firelight. A few crept out, and rather more yeoman guests, those who had not unforgiveably worked on Frodhi's behalf. They babbled of how they had hoped for this wonderful day.

"But where is my mother?" Hroar called.

Sigridh came to the door. Pillars of flame stood on either side and above. "Hurry!" shouted Helgi. She stopped, cloak drawn tightly around the gown she had donned, and looked upon her sons.

At last she said—they could barely hear her through the roaring—"Well have you wrought, Hroar and Helgi, and everything good do I wish for you in all of your life to come. But myself, I forsook one husband after he was dead. Ill would they speak of your mother, my darlings, did she forsake another husband while yet he lived." She raised a hand. "Upon you, my blessing."

She walked back into the hall.

The brothers shrieked and tried to follow. Men held them fast. The doorway crashed asunder. The roof began to fall in. Sparks drowned every star. The noise grew even greater. It smothered the weeping of Hroar and Helgi.

III

THE TALE OF THE BROTHERS

I

Jarl and sheriff took the athelings to Leidhra. There they called a Thing, and when men were gathered, they told what had happened. Standing on the high stone, the youths saw blades flash free, gleam aloft and bang upon shields, while the throng shouted to hail them its kings.

They in their turn promised to abide by olden law, give justice, and restore the lands which Frodhi's gang had grabbed. They thanked their sister's husband Sævil for good help, and likewise Regin their fosterfather, and the men of these; and they handed out gifts to many, taken from the great hall and storehouses which now were theirs.

Thence they traveled about Denmark with their two elders and a well-armed troop. In each shire they got themselves taken as lords.

On the way, Hroar asked Helgi if he wished to split the rule between them, one in Zealand and one in Scania. Regin tugged his beard and said, "I'm not sure that would be wise, remembering what happened before."

Helgi flushed. "Never will I bear a spear against my brother!" he said. "We'll dwell together and share all things."

This would be at Leidhra. Since Scania needed a trusty man in charge, they bade Sævil be theirs. He agreed, moved thither with Signy and their children, and lived long in peace. Often he and his brothers-in-law guested each other; but on the whole, he is now out of the saga.

The new kings were very unlike. Hroar remained

small, albeit quick and deft. He was soft-spoken, not given to more show than he must put on, mild, friendly, and deep-minded. Helgi, though, grew uncommonly tall and strong, until he was reckoned to be about the mightiest warrior in the land. He was gustily merry when not crossed, openhanded, one whose house folk made excuses to seek because they knew how the food and drink and mirth would flow. He either dressed as roughly as the meanest smallholder, or in the costliest furs and stuffs, a dragon's hoard of gold on his arms and about his neck. Against this can be set that he was headlong, short-tempered, unsparing of whoever thwarted his will, and too early restless when seated in council.

Some men felt Hroar was like the father Halfdan and Helgi like the uncle Frodhi, and dreaded a breach. But it never came. The love between the brothers stayed unshakeable while they both lived.

The first year they must keep moving, learning the ins and outs of their realm, binding its headmen to them. Thereafter was no reason to look for trouble from that quarter. Hroar settled down quietly to master the skills of kingship. Helgi trained himself in fighting and in the ways of the sea.

This was to a good end. As soon as weather allowed next year, he led warriors forth. Bands of robbers and nests of vikings had always harassed the land, and gotten worse under Frodhi. Helgi scoured woods and waters, going in with fire and sword, ax and noose; yeomen blessed his name. At first he fared under the guidance of experienced leaders. By fall they admitted that he had no further call on them.

He spent the winter in a cheery round of feasts, also in planning the summer's faring. That was a cruise along as much of Jutland, Fyn, and other islands as he could make, trading, fighting, and scouting out these lands against a later day.

While Helgi was gone that year, Regin, now a jarl, came to Hroar. They went aside and spoke under four eyes, as the saying is. "I am unwell," the king's foster-father told him. "Ever oftener my heart pains me and flutters like a bird trying to escape a cage. It would gladden me if, before I go hence, I can lay one more strong timber to the house of the Skjoldungs."

Hroar gripped his hand. Nothing else was needful between those two.

He went on: "I've asked about, and sent men of mine to look. I think I've found you a wife, who'd not only bring a rich dower and stout friends. She'd be the right lady for you."

"I've always done well to follow your redes," said Hroar low.

She was Valthjona, daughter of Ægthjof, the chief jarl in Götaland and near kin to its king. Thus Hroar would gain spokesmen for himself in that realm between his own and the Yngling-led Swedes.

There went more talk, with faring of messengers and gifts. Ere Yule, Valthjona reached Leidhra. She was a big, good-looking woman, firm at need but otherwise kindly, shrewd and steadfast. She and Hroar dwelt together in happiness.

Soon after the Hammer had hallowed them, Regin died. Folk called that great scathe. The kings gave him burial in a ship laden with costly goods, and raised a howe which reared high above the Isefjord, as if trying to see where old Vifil had laid his bones. Aasta did not long outlive her man. She too got a mound and farewell gifts from her fosterlings.

Hroar said sadly, "Now we must lean on our own wisdom, such as it is."

"If that fails," answered his brother, "we have our strength."

"Our great-grandfather owned more might than we do, yet he went under." Hroar ran fingers through his thin new beard. They sat alone in a loftroom, with only a stone lamp to hold off night. The air was winter-bleak. "We're safer eastward than erstwhile, thanks to Regin. But few are our kinfolk westward across the Great Belt."

"Are you saying I should seek a wife of my own?"

"Well, we'd better begin thinking about it."

"H'm. I'm young for that."

"Not as we Skjoldungs go."

From time to time in the following months, Hroar brought the matter up. Helgi put him off, usually with a jest. This was not because of shyness. Almost the first thing Helgi did when they came to Leidhra, after the slaying of Frodhi, was beckon a thrall girl to his bed. Since then, if he wasn't at sea, he seldom slept alone.

"You're breeding sons who may well bring down the kingdom in grasping after it," Hroar scolded him.

"Oh, I've not had to take one on my knee and give him a name," Helgi laughed. "I never keep a wench long enough. I send her back to work, or home with a gift if she's free-born, and that's that."

"Still, you should have acknowledged children, not to speak of in-laws."

"Let me be, will you?" And Helgi stalked from the house.

He brooded, however, until in the end he decided to astonish the world by showing how he could steer his own affairs—and, at the same time, do a thing which would make him famous far beyond Denmark. Therefore he sent spies out in secret. Openly, he gathered ships and men, promising a cruise come summer which ought to win wealth.

There was no dearth of younger sons glad to join him. After sowing season a big fleet rowed out of Haven.

Hroar had spoken against this—"We've plenty of vikings and foemen close to home, without turning vikings ourselves"—but Helgi said, "Men won't stay willing to go beneath our banners unless we give them a chance at real booty," and would not be swayed.

His ships went down the Sound, their avowed aim to harry the southern Baltic coasts. Then at Mön, camped ashore, he told his skippers that first they would turn west. After he broached his wish, a few said it was too reckless. But they were shouted down and soon gave in. Remember, these were young men. Helgi himself had but sixteen winters.

II

The Saxons began in the neck of the Jutland peninsula. Like all Northland folk other than Finns, they speak a tongue the rest can understand. As their numbers waxed, they spilled forth until they had overrun realms from the Elbe to the Rhine—and Britain as well, along with their Anglic and Jutish kinsmen. A few clung to the old country.

One such kingdom was on the island of Als between Flensborg and Aabenraa Fjords. Its masters stemmed from both Odin and Frey, though they also had blood in them of the Wendish tribes who dwell eastward beyond Ironwood and talk like neither Danes nor Finns. Though doughty, they lacked great numbers of men and must plight faith and pay scot to the kings of Slesvik on the mainland.

The last of these royal underlings hight Sigmund. He married a daughter of his overlord Hunding. She bore him a girl-child they named Olof, but no sons who lived past her own early death. This led Sigmund to raise the girl rather like a boy, take her on hunts, teach her weapon-play, tell her of warlike doings, let her listen while he talked with men. She grew harsh and haughty, scorned womanly skills, sometimes even went about carrying shield and byrnie, sword at belt and helm on head.

Her father reached no high age either. When he died, her grandfather King Hunding of Slesvik feared a struggle for the seat which might lead to a breakaway from him. Therefore he pressed the Alsmen to take Olof for their queen. This was not wholly unheard of among Saxons; besides, the wiser chieftains agreed it was better than uproar. So it was done.

Later Hunding died and *his* realm fell into disorder. Cunningly playing sides off against each other, Queen Olof became able to do what she wanted. Taking a man was not among those things. She was reckoned the best match in the North—if only because this island was well-placed for war and trade—but every suitor she sent away, and not very politely either.

Her own folk did not like her much, finding her over-bearing and niggardly. Still, she was not bad enough to rise up against, bearing in mind that she was the last of their royal house and hence surely under the ward of her forebears the gods.

Matters had stood thus for several years when Helgi's craft turned prows toward her kingdom.

He had learned that she spent her summers on the eastern shore of the island. There she kept a dwelling, less a hall than a lodge and some outbuildings, the Little Belt before it and miles of greenwood behind. It was a stead where she could hunt, which she loved, and seldom have to give outsiders food or gifts, which she cared little to do.

The house stood on a bluff looking widely over strand and water. Thus she reckoned on warning of ships in time to send after help or, at worst, flee down the road inland. Helgi lay to behind Lee Island across the Belt and waited for a fog. At that time of year he soon got it. The fleet crossed in single file, men stealthily rowing. Oft-times in that thick, dripping grayness, a steersman in the stern of one craft could not see the lookout in the bows of her follower. Ropes linked them. In the lead went the king. For pilot he had a fisherman who knew well every tide, current, skerry, and bight of these straits. They made landfall almost at their goal. Helgi sent warriors ashore and then cast anchor below the bluff

The fog lifted quite suddenly toward evening—and there were those lean hulls, ablink with mail and spears, while armored men loafed grinning around the edge of the woods. They made no threat; and the mast of the fore-most ship had been raised to bear at its top the white shield which betokens peace. Yet the queen was boxed in and outnumbered beyond hope.

In stiff-faced calm she received the messengers. "Helgi Halfdansson, Dane-King, greets Olof Sigmundsdottir, Als-Queen, and will accept hospitality" was their word. She could only choose that which was safest, and bid him and his be her guests.

They clattered up the strand-path and into the yard, youths boisterous as a sea-wind, toplofty as eagles. Olof waited in her high seat. Sunset light turned golden the mane and downy beard of him who entered and hailed her. They stared hard across the shadows between them.

Helgi was taller than most of his tall following, wide-shouldered, deep-chested, narrow-hipped, craggy of nose, long of head and chin. Fire-blue eyes danced in a leather-brown face. He was roughly clad, and wetness still dripped off his kirtle and cloak; but golden rings wound their way up his thick forearms, and gold-inlaid was the haft of his sword.

Olof was rather short, though her form showed goodly within her gown and hunting had given her uncommon grace of movement. Her head was round, wide in the cheekbones, nostrils, and mouth; her eyes were big, the same deep brown as her coiled hair; all in all, she was well-favored, and not too many years older than Helgi. The look she gave him smoldered. She bade him welcome in a flat voice.

"I have heard so much of you," laughed he, "I could not but pay this call." Without waiting to be asked, he joined her in the high seat and told a servant to bring them drink.

"Do everything well," said Olof to her folk. "Let our guests lack naught."

To cook for such a big and unawaited company took time. Meanwhile beer and mead ran freely. The Danes jammed the lodge, clamored, grabbed at women, swaggered, boasted, and swilled. Helgi and Olof, side by side in the high seat, must nearly shout to hear each other. She let him do most of the talking—about himself—and he was nothing loth, the more so as he got drunker. She showed no outward unhappiness.

When at last they were eating, he said to her, "You must have guessed I came here for more than a feast. It's thus: I wish us to drink our bridal ale this evening."

She tautened. "You fare too swiftly, my lord."

"No, no." Helgi wagged a beef bone. "We've enough folk gathered here for a wedding. Great will be my honor and gain if I win as high-souled and, um, useful a queen as you for my own. Later we can hallow it, and speak of dowries and morning gifts and whatnot else. But we'll lie in one bed this night, you and me."

"If I must be wed," she answered, knuckles white over the handle of her knife, "then I know of no man who stands above you. I trust you'll not let me get shame out of this."

Helgi leered. "Indeed it's fitting that you, uppish as you behave—that we should live together long's I like."

"I could wish more of my friends were here," said Olof. "But your will be done. I'm sure you'll act in seemly wise toward me."

"Aye, aye, aye!" said Helgi slurrily. He hauled her to him, crushed her mouth against his and pawed across her in sight of everyone. Then he stood and bellowed forth the tidings.

The Danes roared their glee. The Saxons knew not what to do, save for those wenches who giggled in dark corners beside sailors. Queen Olof arose, as if her gown were not soiled and hair tumbled, and called: "Let this bridal be drunk in the best we have. Break out the wine!"

Southland traders bore some to these parts. It was little known elsewhere in the North. Helgi whooped at the taste. Olof smiled—in the flickering shadow-haunted light, it passed for a real smile—and plied him until far into the night.

None marked how she only pretended to match his huge draughts, save her trustiest men to whom she whispered to do likewise.

At last Helgi belched that they'd better put her to bed, else her wedding night would become a forenoon. Shouting, howling, bawling their bawdiest songs and jests, those Danes who could still walk took torches and escorted her across the courtyard to a bower where she slept. This is the Northland custom, that a bride be thus led in ahead of her groom. It is supposed to ward off evil beings, and the earthy words are to bring love and children. But for Olof waited no flowers and green boughs; nor had she been spoken for long beforehand, or had old friends around for this day out of her life, or been hallowed, or laid her maiden's garland down as an offering to Freyja.

The troop went back after Helgi. "In a while, in a while," he grunted. "You scuts won't finish this wine without me." The night was grizzled when he staggered away. Few were left hardy enough to come along.

These closed the door behind him, shouted their last randy good wishes, and lurched off to join the rest in slumber.

One dim lamp lit the room. "Whoof!" cried Helgi, and fumbled at the queen. "Take off your clothes."

"Lie down," she murmured, guiding him, "and I will come to you."

He did. She slipped from sight, as if to make ready. Erelong she heard his snores.

Doubtless she stood a while, then, looking down upon him, turning a knife over and over in her fingers. No matter how drunk, though, his crews were too much for her few guards and carls. Furthermore, his killing would bring on a blood-feud with the mighty Skjoldungs. She had already decided what to do.

Some say she pricked a sleep-thorn into Helgi to keep him from waking. Others say that was not needful.

She slipped forth into chill dimness, under paling stars, and bespoke her men. They dared not bring out a horse; but among them was a fast runner. He started at once down the woodland roadway. Olof fetched what she wanted, and brought back a couple of men for help.

"Is this wise?" she heard asked.

Her head lifted. "I have my honor to think of," she said. "With shame shall shame be avenged."

They hogtied the king; they took scissors and razor, and cut all the hair off him; they smeared him everywhere with pitch; they stuffed him and a lot of rags into a leather sack, and tied it shut; and the men bore him down to the strand.

At dawn, on her orders, Olof's carls roused the Danes —freely using bucketsful of cold water—and told them

Helgi had gone to the ships and wanted to sail off, since there was now an ebb tide and a fair wind.

They sprang up as fast as they could but, numb from drink, hardly knew what they were about. When they reached the shore, they saw their king nowhere. He would soon come, they thought muzzily. Meanwhile, here lay a fat leather sack. They got a wish to find out what it held.

When they undid the ties, there he lay, and in sorry shape. The sleep-thorn fell out of him, if it was ever in, and he awakened, not from any happy dream. He raved with rage.

Now they heard horns bray, feet and hoofs tramp, iron clang, voices call. Athwart the morning sky on the bluff-top stood a host of warriors against whom it was hopeless to go, especially in their wretchedness of headache and bowking. They crawled aboard ship and rowed off. They rowed very badly. The Saxon taunts followed them a long ways; and afterward the seagulls jeered.

III

Huge was the wonder, and wide flew the tale, that Queen Olof should have been able to mock a king like Helgi Halfdansson. The Alsmen looked awed upon her. That made her overbearingness and stubbornness wax beyond measure. Just the same, from then on she always kept a strong guard wherever she went.

As for him, he was in such a mood that none dared speak of the matter in his hearing, nor even let eyes linger on him. He took the fleet to Wendland as promised, where he went forward in a recklessness, slaughter, and burning that shook the toughest of the crew. They carried every battle, and in fall turned home laden with spoils and thralls. Helgi showed no gladness. Landing at Haven, he snapped a few orders as to unloading and care of the ships, took a horse, and galloped off alone.

The tale had reached Leidhra. When Helgi arrived, Hroar sought him in his house. They climbed into a loft-room to speak away from other ears. "I would have readied a welcoming feast for you," said the older brother mildly. "However, I thought this year you'd rather I didn't."

"I would not have come to it, forsooth," Helgi mumbled, glaring at the floor.

"You will outlive this thing," Hroar said.

Helgi flared: "It's a shame on *us!*"

"And who brought it?" Hroar answered, suddenly sharp-tongued. "Who deserved it?"

Helgi lifted a fist as if to strike him, then snarled and flung down the ladder and out of the house.

Through that winter he kept to himself as much as might be, was harsh toward underlings, curt and niggardly toward those of higher rank. Men whispered their fear that the blood of the dark-souled Skjoldungs was rising in him. After he began holding secret talks with those fighters who had ever been closest to him, many thought he must be plotting to do what Frodhi did.

But when gloom waned before daylight, snow melted in rushing streams, the storks and the swallows came home, Helgi grew calmer. His household knew he was busy readying something, though what it was, he told nobody save chosen men. One morning early in summer they were gone, and the king, and the speediest of his ships.

Mast raised, raven sail unfurled, she flew before a following wind. It skirled, cold and salt, kissed cheeks and tousled hair. Waves rumbled and gurgled, spindrift scudded above their wrinkled gray crests and blue-black troughs, sunbeams aslant through clouds struck green fire off them. The hull bounded, strakes sang, walrus-hide tackle thrummed. Helgi took the steering oar. While the land which was his rolled by him to starboard, he smiled, for the first time in almost a year.

When Mön lay aft, he had the dragon head of war set onto the prow.

Yet they fared carefully, that crew, sheering off from whatever other vessels they saw, camping nowhere. At the Little Belt they hove-to until dark, then rowed on north by moonlight.

Ere dawn they reached the cove which their pilot had chosen for them. It lay several miles south of Olof's lodge. Trees crowded a small beach. Helgi ordered the ship grounded. Her boat he put on watch at the mouth, lest a foe take them unawares and block their flight. Thereafter he slept a few hours. Those who stood guard ashore heard him chuckle in his dreams.

At sunrise he bolted some food and busked himself. He went clad in beggarly rags. Slung across his shoulders were a sword and two chests full of gold and silver.

The going is hard through a wildwood. Trees soar, oak, beech, elm, larch; their crowns rustle green-gold in sunlight that speckles the shadowiness beneath; birds sing in their thousands, squirrels streak up the boles like red fire; the air is warm and full of the smells of growth. But underbrush makes a wall, snagging feet, blocking breast, stabbing at eyes, scornfully crackling. It is not strange how often settlements are only reachable by sea.

Helgi was a huntsman. He found game trails and glided along them as readily as a deer. Soon he drew nigh his goal. In a hollow trunk he left his sword, under a bush he half hid his chests, and went onward. At the roadway, out of sight of the lodge, he waited.

A thrall of the queen's came by. He carried a basketful of eggs, bought for the household from a farmstead. At sight of the big man he drew back. Helgi smiled, spread empty hands, and said, "Have no fears. I'm homeless but harmless."

The thrall was not surprised. Gangrels were common, in these days when Slesvik suffered upheaval. As for reaching this island from there, that is the narrowest of channels. "How go things hereabouts?" the stranger asked him.

"Naught save peace," said the thrall, easing a bit. "Whence do you hail?"

"No matter. I'm just a poor stave-carl. See here, though. I've stumbled on a hoard in these woods. Shall I show it to you?"

The thrall saw no reason why the wanderer should attack him. Besides, he bore a stout staff. He came along, and drew a shaken breath when he saw the glitter beneath leaves. "Great things indeed!" he said. "Who might have left that here? King Helgi, maybe, for some reason, before he sought our queen last year and she made a laughingstock of him?"

"I know not," said the gangrel roughly. "Tell me, is she greedy for gold?"

"In that wise, there's none like her."

"I'd heard the same. Well, then, she'll like this, and she's bound to claim it, here being her land. Now I don't want to turn my good luck into bad and try hiding a treasure. How could one like me grow rich overnight, and not be supposed a robber and strung up for crowbait? No, let her take it, and give me what part she sees fit; that's best. D'you think she'll trouble herself to come after the hoard?"

"That I do, if she can go unbeknownst save for a close-mouthed warrior or two."

"I was about to say that's how she'd better fare," nodded the wanderer. "If her find got noised abroad, the headmen of the kingdom would await feasts and gifts; and they tell me as how she's a chary one. But look here, I don't want anybody else about. Only you and her. You can see I'm nothing to be afraid of." He stooped and reached. "Here's a jewel and a ring I'll bury offside and give you afterward, can you get her to come alone. Should she grow angry at you, I'll take care of that."

At first the thrall refused. Smooth swift-flowing talk turned his mind. He guessed the stranger knew of more gold elsewhere, and wanted to bargain about it under four eyes. So glib a tongue could surely turn the queen's wrath. And later he, the thrall, could give her those two costly things in payment for his freedom and a bit of a farm.

Thus he left the stave-carl on guard and himself hastened to the lodge, his heart thumping. He needed a while to get Olof aside, where he panted to her how he had found a mighty hoard, and asked her to follow him and lay hands on it, telling no one else lest envy of him make them spiteful.

Her rust-brown eyes weighed him. A flush crept over her broad-boned face. "If you're telling the truth," she answered, "this news will bring you luck. Otherwise it'll cost you your head. However, I've always found you faithful. I'll trust what you say."

She set a meeting after dark. At that time she arose, dressed, and sneaked from her bower. The watch was against a band or a fleet of foes. A single person, used to stalking game, went easily past. Beneath a moon-silvered oak stood the thrall. He guided her into the murk beyond.

The chests lay close to a small glade. Moonlight drifted between leaves and boughs to pick out the glint of metal —on a drawn sword in the hand of the man who stepped from night.

"Greeting, Queen Olof," laughed his hidden lips. "Do you remember Helgi Halfdansson?"

She shrieked, whirled, and started to run. In a long stride, he caught her. The thrall whimpered and struck at him with his staff. Helgi's blade knocked it aside. "I could slay you, fellow," said the king, as steadily as if the woman were not yelling, writhing, clawing, and kicking in his grasp. "But since we'll be gone before you can fetch help, my rede is that you flee elsewhere." The thrall gibbered. Helgi pointed downward with his sword. "There lies that which I promised you." The thrall was not too stunned to pick it up. Helgi poked swordpoint at him. "Go!" The thrall crashed off through the brush.

Helgi sheathed his blade. "Be still," he told Olof, and gave her a cuff that rattled her teeth. "Did you think I'd leave your treachery unavenged?"

She fell to hands and knees, sobbed a short while, rose and stammered, "Yes, right, I've borne myself ill toward you. In payment, I'll . . . now . . . become your lawful wife."

"No," said he, "you won't get by so easily this time. You're coming along to my ship, and there you'll stay as long as I want. For the sake of my honor I can't do aught but treat you as grossly and shamefully as you did me."

"Tonight must your will be done," she whispered.

He used woodcraft to hide their trail the first part of the way. Later was no need, in that spear-wall of brush. He did not drag her along. Once she tried to break from the deerpath he found. The withes stopped her with claws.

His own wayfaring was none too easy in the gloom. She reached the cove as ragged as he, footsore, bleeding, tripping, and gasping.

Waves clinked on the strand. A nightingale sang. The moon, low, made a gleaming bridge across the waters, against which hull and dragon head of the beached ship reared black. Not many stars showed through its brightness, in the dusky sky. A breeze strolled cool, bearing a smell of kelp.

When he trod forth, Helgi's watchmen ashore leaped from their little fire. He greeted them. Their cheers roused the rest from sleeping bags, to crowd about, pound him on the back and offer their coarsest good wishes. He grinned and urged Olof onward, over the side, into the hull of his ship.

"_Now_ take off your clothes," he said; and this she must do in the moonlight before them all.

He pointed under the foredeck. She crept into the tarry-thick darkness beneath and lay down on a mattress, fists clenched at sides. He sought her.

At dawn he fetched his chests, then stood out across the Belt. On lonely Ærö the Danes made a safer camp. For a week they hunted, fished, wrestled, swam, gambled, yarned, or idled. The king joined them, save when he took the queen.

She gave him no trouble; she only suffered him. She never wept; nor did she speak more than she barely must. "You are a fair woman, Olof," he whispered one night into her hair. "I wish our weird had been otherwise." She lay stiff. He sighed. "I think you cannot care for men. And now it's too late between us two."

"We may not be done yet, you and I," she said.

"What?" he asked. She would speak no further. A curlew shrilled through rising chill mist. Helgi shivered and drew close to her, merely for warmth. She did not flow to meet him.

Next day he crossed the Belt again and set her off near her lodge. Neither said farewell. She waded ashore in the grimy tatters of her gown. His men shoved the ship clear, hauled themselves back aboard, and took oars. Olof did not watch them spider-walk from her. She was already trudging home.

IV

That same summer, to King Hroar in Leidhra came his father-in-law Ægthjof the Göta jarl. Feuds had broken out. Ægthjof slew Heidhleif of the Ulfing family, but the kinsmen proved too strong and he must flee.

Young though he was, Hroar did not order the war-arrow passed from steading to steading. "What boots it to raise a host, kill and burn and sack, making still more death-foes for ourselves?" he asked. "Oh, the Ynglings in Uppsala would like that! What was left of Götaland would stand firm on their side."

He sent word to Jarl Sævil in Scania, who in turn sought the heads of the Ulfings. As go-between, Sævil arranged peace. Ægthjof must pay a high weregild, but Hroar helped him. A pair of marriages were made as well, to bind the houses together for at least a while.

"You have served me most wonderfully," said Ægthjof, wringing Hroar's hand before leaving for home. "I hope I or child of mine may someday do the like for you."

"That's a kindly thought," smiled the king. "However, for me to need help, first I must be in trouble."

"Thence comes fame," said Ægthjof.

"May not a fame better and longer-lived come from building the land? We've work for many lifetimes—nailing down peace within and without this kingdom, clearing fields, raising houses, launching ships for fishery and trade, making good laws and seeing that they're kept, bringing in outland arts. . . . Well, kinsman, I need not talk as if I stood on the Thingstone!"

Helgi returned in the best of humor and was thereafter his old self. At first he lost no chance to make known how he had avenged himself upon Queen Olof. In time he stopped speaking or even thinking about it.

Not so the woman.

She knew folk would guess what had befallen her, and word floating to Saxland from Denmark would soon end any doubts. This would not unseat her if she showed strength. Hence she refused to talk about that week. When she learned that a thrall and a hireling had been gossiping, she had them haled before her; for besmirching her name, she ordered the freeman slain out of hand, the thrall flogged to death. In other ways, too, she fared forward so sternly—withal, skilfully—that men said she was a king, not a queen, in all save body.

They did not know how long she lay awake of nights, how ill she slept, how alone in the woods she raised crooked fingers to heaven and screamed.

Worst for her was when she knew she was fruitful.

After a witchwife failed to bring the child forth early, Olof made plans. Never should the world snicker or Helgi Halfdansson gloat because of this. She gave out that she would fare to Slesvik on the mainland, travel around and see what might be done to end the strife between houses which was wrecking that kingdom.

And indeed she did, and did it well, sometimes bringing two sides together, sometimes throwing the weight of her small but good host on one pan of the scales. None thought it strange that now and then she vanished. She must talk to the headmen in secret.

Heavy clothes for winter weather hid the rounding of her belly. Did some wonder, they knew well to keep their lips sewn.

When her time drew nigh, she went to a lonely hut chosen and readied beforehand. Guards ringed it. The queen did not let them in, on the grounds that it was cramped and she wanted peace to think and (she hinted) work magics. They pitched tents against rain, huddled in the mud over smoky fires, blew on blue fingers and tried to keep the worst rust off their iron. Olof stayed indoors, with none but a midwife and two old women servants.

On a night of storm, dankness and darkness, hail dashed against walls, trees groaning in wind, she brought forth a girl-child. "Cry out," said the midwife, seeing the sweat upon her. "It eases pain."

"No," said the queen between clamped jaws. "Not for this."

No father being on hand, the midwife took the babe, newly washed and swaddled, and laid it on the earthern floor at the mother's bedside. Olof stared dull-eyed through unrestful redness of torches, at the tiny squalling thing. "Will you keep it, my lady?" asked the midwife.

"Never will I lay that at my breast," said Olof. She raised a hand. "Hold, though. Don't do away with it. It may come in useful, somehow, someday . . . I know not. . . ."

"Then what will you name her?"

Olof's gaze wandered listlessly about until it fell on a hound she had, a bitch called Yrsa. Laughter clanked in her throat. She pointed from dog to baby. "Yes, I'll give her a name," she said. "Name her Yrsa." She lay back.

The midwife and the crones shivered.

They could but obey, however. And, this being not unawaited, they had already found a wet-nurse.

When Olof was ready again for travel, they dared ask what she wanted done about Yrsa. "A single word about the brat will be your banes," she snapped. "But bring her along. I'll find the right house for her to adopted in, as highborn children are adopted."

Back on Als, she got hold of a poor crofter and his wife. She handed them the baby and some gifts, and told them this was the offspring of a faithful thrall-woman who died giving birth, and hight Yrsa. They were to raise the girl in every way as if she were their own.

Thereafter Olof never saw or asked about the daughter she hated.

Years went by.

Denmark waxed in might and wealth. The kingly brothers worked well together. Hroar steered the realm and strove to better it, with a wisdom that grew as he himself did. Showing enough manly skills to keep the respect of warriors, he became much loved. He and his queen Valthjona had three children who lived: a girl Freyvar and two boys, Hrodhmund and Hrörik, the latter being born rather late in their lives. They were a happy pair. Hroar only took another woman to his bed when he had long been away from home.

He must travel a lot, building up the land as he wished. Yearly he made a round of the shire-Things, and also heard men out alone at great length. He went to see for himself how matters stood here or there. He sailed abroad, under the white shield, though oftener he guested outlanders in one of his own halls and listened closely to what they told.

Before men could do good work, they must know that what they wrought would not merely become bait for the greedy and ruthless. To this end, Hroar took the field himself every now and then. Mostly, though, he left war to a willing Helgi.

Each summer the younger king sought battle. Sometimes these were plundering cruises, to keep his guardsmen content and make yeomen eager to join him between sowing and harvest. But mainly he stayed around Denmark. In the earlier years he tracked down robbers, he ransacked viking lairs, he overawed whoever might have thought of troubling the peace.

Outlanders stayed all too likely to do this, especially if egged on by Svithjodh or Saxland. When he and Hroar felt themselves firm-seated at home, Helgi began to make them sorry for their mischief. Would they not yield on being asked, take his sword in their hands, plight faith and pay scot to the lords of Leidhra, they were apt to wake one morning and see dragons on the water, or inland a host in the swine-array of battle, a red shield and a raven banner.

These little chieftains could never match Danish strength. Nor did they often league together; the brothers soon learned how to bring their quarrels to a boil.

Armed clashes gladdened the wolves and carrion birds. Helgi gained scars, and a few times lay at the head of hell-road. Always he healed, and always he snatched victory.

In the course of those years, he overran Fyn and every lesser island. He bragged he had brought nearly as many kings under him as he had women.

"And when will you marry?" Hroar would ask.

"When I'm ready," Helgi would shrug. "No haste. The one time I did go wooing, it went not well." He could joke about that fading memory. "I know how you dangle the idea of a tie with me before great men, to get what you want from them. Why not keep the lure useable?"

"When you and I are dead—"

"Then you've already a son. You fear by-blows of mine may challenge him? Unlikely. My bastards come cheap, they're so many. Indeed, Hroar, best for the Skjoldungs may be that I do *not* ever take a queen, whose children may think they have a claim. Now do pull together that long face of yours and let's fill another horn of mead."

The brothers no longer saw each other daily, even in winter, and thus their meetings called for merriment as much as for council. Hroar had gone from Leidhra.

He did not leave in anger. The understanding between those two was such that once, when he came back and Helgi gave a feast for him, Hroar could say:

"You look like the greater of us, in that you keep the olden seat of the Dane-Kings; and this I'll freely give to you, and to any heirs you may have. In return I want the ring you hold—for I have as much right to that as you do."

Men who overheard caught their breath. They knew Hroar could only be speaking of one ring. It was not a plain gold coil, off which pieces might be broken to reward a skald for making a lay or someone else for some other service. No, this was a thick band in the form of a snake which twisted about and about itself until it bit its own tail, there where its garnet eyes glittered baleful. A story says it was first among the riches which Fenja and Menja ground for King Frodhi the Peace-Good. In any case, it had long been the pride of the Skjoldungs.

Helgi merely smiled and answered: "Nothing would be more seemly, kinsman, than that you got that ring."

Nonetheless, Hroar had sound reasons for moving away. Two royal households in the same town, each holding its troop of mettlesome young men, spelled fights that might become deadly. Not always could a feud then be stopped, between families who ought to war on the enemies of Denmark instead of each other.

Furthermore, Leidhra was ill-placed for his uses. The tale went that formerly the fjord had reached this far inland. That was no longer true. Only a sluggish brook wound past. A sheltered harbor, open to the sea but deep within the island, would draw traders and their wealth.

Hroar founded Roskilde on the bay named for it. This became the chief town of the kingdom. An easy ride from Leidhra, it was still far enough away to hold off most trouble. In his day men called it Hroarskildi, Hroar's Spring, from an outpouring of pure water which gave the stead not only drink but holiness.

Of course, the settlement did not leap into being overnight. At first naught was there but a hall which the king had made, with its outbuildings and the houses of freeborn hirelings, sheds and wharfs on the shore for ships. Though fields rolled away southward, heath and marsh lay to the east, wildwood gloomed to the west. Yet men said no goodlier home had been in the North since Odin dwelt on earth.

Huge it was, of the finest timbers, cunningly carved and painted. The beam-ends atop the gables branched out in the shape of mighty antlers, gilded to blaze beneath sunlight: wherefore the hall was called Hart.

Upon this house came grief.

It may have been ill luck. It may have been the wrath of a god. Open-handed toward men, the brothers were rather heedless about offering to Æsir and Vanir. They did what kings were supposed to do at the high holy times. Otherwise, Helgi might slay a cock or the like, once in a while for luck; but mainly he trusted in his own strength. When Hroar's thoughts turned from kingship or kindred, they went more to outland learning than what he might owe any gods or buried forebears.

Be that as it may, the tale goes that Hart became haunted. Long ago a king named Hermodh was driven from home for his greed and cruelty: he was among the worst of the dark Skjoldungs. Skulking in the fens, he got children on a trollwife. Of his blood was that being hight Grendel, who entered the new hall at night and grabbed men for his food.

In England they say this went on for twelve years. The Danes call that unlikely. Would not a warrior like Helgi have rid his brother of woe? Suppose, instead, Hroar built Hart soon after he had done well by Ægthjof and Helgi had done ill by Olof. He lived there nine years, while the brothers worked together until at last Danes felt happier in their homes than ever since the Peace-Good. Then Helgi, restless, busked for a long-faring to lands unknown. He may have sailed west to England, or east and north to Norway and Finland and Bjarmiland, or east and south down the rivers of Russia, now raiding, now trading, ever tasting fresh winds beneath new heavens; and three years blew by ere his ships came home again.

Hardly was he gone when Grendel shambled forth. Through those three years the hall Hart lay waste, and sorrow dwelt on the brow of Hroar.

He waited for Helgi's return, since he knew of none else who might cope with the monster. Yet he could not tell if Helgi's bones bleached upon strange earth. Thus he welcomed an offer of help from the son of Jarl Ægthjof whom formerly he had saved: his kinsman Bjovulf of Götaland, the man that in England they call Beowulf.

The tale is well-known, how Bjovulf gripped Grendel and tore the arm from him, how Grendel's mother came in vengeance, how Bjovulf followed her beneath the water and slew her likewise, to win a name which will be

undying as long as the world shall stand. Enough, here,
that he had but lately gone home, when Helgi came—and
found all Denmark ringing with what that outland hero
had done, hardly an ear left open for his own deeds.

He was not so unmanly that he begrudged Bjovulf a
well-earned fame. Nonetheless he harked back wistfully
to years when he too was young. He was no gaffer—little
more than thirty winters had whitened the world since
first he yelled his way into it—but a freshness was gone
from his eyes. If naught else, folk took for granted that
Helgi Halfdansson would do things like sailing further
than men had done before. Ah, otherwise it was when he,
a boy, overthrew a king and avenged himself upon a
queen!

Maybe that was the reason why, next summer, he
planned a cruise which would take him by Als. He said
he wanted to scout out Saxon realms. He could do little
in northern Jutland before he knew how stood the south.
No doubt this was true. However . . . did he remember
crowing over honor regained . . . or, even, brown eyes
and bravely clenched fists?

He knew nothing about Yrsa. None did, save Olof
her mother, the midwife, and two grannies who had since
died. The crofter pair who were rearing her had well-
nigh forgotten that the girl was not born to them.

They dwelt on the north shore of the island, which
gives on Aabenraa Fjord. Southward reached heath,
speckled with stands of low, gnarled oak and evergreen,
till this turned into willow marsh and afterward a greenwood impassable save for a few trails. Northward were
broad yellow dunes, then water, a glimpse of mainland
on the left and otherwise waves, clouds, gulls. Often rain,
mist, snow, or endless winter nights closed in. Here was a
lean and windy land, where a few families dwelt well
apart because each needed many acres to wrest a living
from and none had much to lure robbers.

Here grew up Yrsa, daughter of Helgi the king and Olof
the queen.

She knew she was a fosterling. Besides being told so,

she looked altogether unlike the parents or their children. However, this was common. A man might drown or a woman cough out her lungs, leaving a brood behind. A child was a pair of hands, therefore always wanted. Yrsa gave scant thought to a mother whom she believed had died in thralldom, a father unknown. Nor did she think whether her lot was happy or unhappy. Later she remembered these years as better than they maybe were.

True, she knew toil, hoe and hatchet, quern and kettle, loom and broom, the untold and untellable tasks of a girl who was meant for a croftwife. But life was not wholly aching back or bleeding fingers. It could be caring for a baby, or gathering nuts and berries amidst a giggling gang, or singing and daydreaming while she grazed the geese.

Garb was harsh gray wadmal, patched and tattered. Children went barefoot in summer, at best had birchbark shoes in winter. But they grew hardy and seldom minded the weather. Food was rough and sometimes scant. But gruel, black bread, a bit of goat cheese, hoarded leeks kept one going until the seasons came for fresh-caught fish, oysters, cormorants' eggs, the harvest of woods and moors. The dwelling was a single murky room, if Yrsa did not count the part wherein goat, geese, and pig were penned. Yet those beasts breathed forth warmth as well as smells, and she knew closeness to her dozen foster-siblings, and when in the dark she heard Father and Mother thresh about, she could hope to welcome a small newcomer next year.

She knew terror. Gales whirled from the north while Father was out in the fishing boat he shared with his neighbors. Did he never come home—or did he come home a strandwasher, a staring bloated eel-eaten thing such as drifted ashore now and again—it could mean not only sorrow but hungering to death, or going into thralldom for lack of any other help. Ran grinned on the sea bottom; nicors lurked in the fen-pools; the Elmwife brewed fog; drows rode the ridgepole at night, thatch acrackle beneath their drumming heels; the least thing done wrong might bring deadly-bad luck. Or, when a ship drew close as if to make landing, or strangers came afoot, it was into the underbrush and hide, for the poorest of girls still owns what a robber will want!

Yet she also knew friendship and merrymaking, both at home and among the neighbors. Neighbors could backbite, dreadful squabbles could hatch, but in the end everybody stood together against the world. There were the four great holy times: Blessing, Midsummer, Harvest, Yule, times to be awed and afterward rejoice. Someday she would be grown, and for a year or two steal off in the light nights with youth and youth, until one of them married her and she as housewife would offer milk to the elves and beer to her guests in the sight of all. Meanwhile the children watched ships pass by, miles off, ships that clearly would never land here (oh, but if they only would!)—striding oars or boldly striped sail, a far, far spark of sunlight off metal; who knew, maybe a king was aboard, maybe a god?

Winter brought cold and darkness and tightened belts . . . likewise lessened work, ice to crunch underfoot and ice to slide across, snowballs and snowmen, time for the beloved old stories. Spring brought toil and spilling rains, likewise white hawthorns and a sky full of birds returning from none knew where. Summer was green, everywhere green, dizziness of smells, honeybees abuzz, sunlight in blinding hot torrents—save when a thunderstorm came, but that was wonderful: *flash!* flew Thor's hammer, and *crack!* it smote trolls, until the wheels of his goat-car rumbled away, down and down the reaches of heaven. Fall blazed, gave fruits with both hands, bellies got filled to bursting, heather bloomed purple, long-lived full moons drenched night in brightness which glistened on hoarfrost and on the dew over spiderwebs, and made a rocking roadway across the waters from here to world-edge; and high overhead sounded the wild goose wander-song. . . .

Yrsa did not understand why her foster-siblings paid no heed to such things. Well, they were dear, but they were different.

V

"I'd like to see for myself how this land has fared," said Helgi, "but somehow don't think I'd be very welcome under my own name." None could talk him out of his wish to tramp alone about Als. His ship let him off in a cove he remembered and would call there daily, beginning a week hence.

He looked for no trouble. Who would attack as big a fellow as him, especially when he went in rags? Besides, his staff was the shaft of a spear whose head and pins he carried next his skin, along with a dagger. He waved a cheery farewell and strode off under the trees.

The news dashed him a bit, that Olof was not at her lodge. Her overseer gave him a sour stare, but a hireling filled a bowl and let him sleep in a haymow, in swap for his songs and tales. He gave out that he was a homeless Himmerlander in search of work. "Here we've no need for you," his host told him. "If you go further, though, to the north coast, you'll find a clutch of poor folk who do some fishing. I daresay they'd be glad of stout arms on a pair of oars."

Helgi shrugged and followed the rede, mainly to spy out those beaches. Now that he had Fyn, he needed close knowledge about this side of the Little Belt.

And thus he topped a high dune, and from afar saw a girl who walked along the strand. Last night had been stormy. She was out after driftwood, amber, or whatever else might have come ashore.

He knew that if she saw him coming she would dash toward a hut, unseen behind dwarf pines, whose smoke smudged the sky. It would be pleasant to chat alone if she was not too ugly. Anyhow, when he had shown by laying no hand on her that he meant well, her kinsmen should open up to him. Else they might fear he was an outlaw, or a thrall-catcher looking them over.

Helgi crouched back down behind the dune while his eyes scouted a path. He could zigzag from thicket to bush to boulder, he could use his hunter's tricks to sneak through the ling, until he was almost upon her.

And so he did. But when he peered from behind a scrub oak, the heart soared in him.

This was a windy day. Sunlight speared through hurrying clouds, sheened on the waters, then was gone again as shadow swept across the world. Waves boomed inward, burst white over skerries, tumbled back and rushed in afresh, gray, green, and steel-blue. To one side, misty as a dream, lifted mainland hills. The wind whistled up whitecaps, roared in boughs and soughed in heather. Gulls rode upon it, mewing. It was cold and tasted of salt, it thrust and slid. It tossed the hair of the maiden who picked her barefoot way over the sand between the sprawled brown strands of kelp.

She was not tall; standing straight, which she did, she would reach halfway up his breast. A drab gown strained across small breasts, slim waist and limbs, suppleness overlaid by an endearing coltishness. Beneath soot and suntan, her skin was fair; freckles dusted a tilted nose. That face was broad and high in the cheekbones, tapering to a strong little chin, mouth wide and soft, lips parted a bit to show good teeth, eyes huge, wide-set, long-lashed under arching brows, the gray-blue of her seas. She had woven herself a garland of yellow dandelion flowers. The locks beneath flowed to her hips. When the fleeting sunshine touched them, they shone as if burnished.

Helgi trod forth. "Why, you're lovely!" he cried.

She sprang back with a stifled shriek, dropped the wood she had gathered, and ran. He loped alongside her. "Don't be afraid," he said. "I'd never harm you. I want to be your friend."

Grimly, she ran. He put on speed, got ahead of her, barred the way. She snatched a stick, spat like a wildcat and jabbed at him. He liked that grit. Spreading his arms, he gusted forth laughter. "You win," he said. "I yield me. Do whatever you will."

She lowered the stick. Her breathing slowed. He could overwhelm her—but he merely stood and smiled. What a big and handsome man he was, too! That frame did not belong in those foul, flapping tatters. His face went with the body, craggy-nosed, eyes heaven-blue, flaxen mane to the shoulders and beard closely cropped. Scars lay white among the golden hairs on his arms.

"What's your name, lady," he asked with an outlander lilt, "and of what folk do you hail?"

She pointed to the smoke. "I'm yonder crofter's daughter," she whispered through wind and surf. "Well, no, really, I . . . my mother was a thrall. I hight Yrsa."

He stepped to her. She stood as if under a spell, hearing her heart knock. He took both her hands in his, which were hard and warm. Gazing for a long time, he said thoughtfully: "You do not have the eyes of a thrall."

They sat down, backs to the blast, and talked. She had never imagined a stranger would care about the day-to-day life which was hers. "Who are you?" she kept asking. He would put her off: "Tell me more of yourself, Yrsa."

"There's something hidden about you," he said. "How old are you?"

"Why, I . . . I never counted," she answered, astonished.

"Think." He took her fingers. "This year; last year—" After a good deal of finger-play, she was flushed and half dizzy, and guessed maybe she had thirteen or fourteen winters.

"I was that age when—Well, no matter," he said. "We both come of fast-growing stock."

They shared cheese and hardtack from his wallet. Later, when he laid an arm about her waist, she did not shrink, but sighed and leaned her head on his breast.

A gull wheeled low, milk-white in a shaft of sunlight.

"I'm head over heels with you," said Helgi. "I am."

"Oh, now," breathed Yrsa.

He must grin. "You being a crofter's daughter," he said, "it's fitting that a poor beggar should get you."

She jumped from him in horror. ' What? No, no, no!"

He rose to loom above her. "Yes, oh, yes." Taking a careful, unbreakable hold: "Come away with me, Yrsa. You must. A Norn stood here today."

She started to weep and plead. He stood a while, in noise and chill and hasty shadows, before he said: "I could bear you off against your will. But your tears would hurt me too much. That's a word few women have ever had from me. I ask you, then, if you'll freely be mine."

She looked at him, and recalled the neighborhood louts she knew; and suddenly the headlong blood overran her. Crying and laughing, she came to him.

They sought shelter together. She knew a spring where trees gave murmurous lee and summer had mellowed the grass into hay.

Helgi abode in the woods, not wanting anybody to pry and leer. She sought him daily, smuggling along food which neither of them truly tasted. They in the hut marked that something had come over her, but she slipped free of their watchfulness. Not that that was very much; nobody hereabouts would take to wife a girl whose belly did not show she would give him children.

At the right time, Helgi went away. He told her not to be frightened if a ship came. When that happened and everyone else fled, she stayed. The richly clad man who leaped ashore told her he was the Dane-King. "I wouldn't have cared if you were only a gangrel," she gasped, and fainted.

Afterward she found her foster-folk and coaxed them back. Helgi gifted them lavishly before he sailed off with Yrsa.

He could not leave his fleet, which he had told to stand by at Fyn. Men would scorn him, did he give up his yearly faring and moon lovesick ashore. So he turned Yrsa over to his brother Hroar and then put out to sea. For him and her alike, the next months were weary.

Said Queen Valthjona to her husband: "I think she'll be more than just another of Helgi's doxies."

"Maybe." Hroar tugged his beard and scowled. "Ill is this. A thrall-born crofter-brat!"

"No, now, she's a sweet girl," Valthjona said. "Besides, for the good name of the Skjoldungs, I'll have to take her in hand."

There was much that a lady must know: everything about the running of a big household; arts such as weaving and brewing; good dress, good manners, good speech; the lore and rites of the high gods and the ancestors; who her man's friends were, who his unfriends, and how to deal with each. Yrsa could not learn it all in a day.

"Yet she's willing," said Valthjona to Hroar, "and had I begun that lowly, I'd have mastered what I must slower than she does."

Aside from missing Helgi, Yrsa was a gladsome soul, every day singing while she flitted about her tasks. She kept many beasts, dogs and horses and birds, and made much of them. She did not like to go hunting. On the other hand, in a boat she was as deft and gleeful as any boy. Young herself, she frolicked amongst the youngsters at Hart. Humbly reared, she was friendlier toward hirelings and thralls—even listening to their long-drawn tales of woe and trying to help—than Hroar or Valthjona, though these were reckoned kindly.

"And yet," said the queen to the king, "she knows their work so well, having done it herself, they don't twice try cheating or slacking on her. Not that she has them whipped. She asks in the mildest tone if they'd rather serve someone else. Of course they wouldn't."

"Hm, yes, I've come to like her myself," Hroar said.

"She's of good stock," Valthjona said. "Her mother may or may not have been a thrall as was told her. But if so, I swear she was a highborn woman taken captive. And her father, why, he may have been a king."

When Helgi came home and saw Yrsa in linen and furs and gold, the keys of his household at her belt, graciously greeting him, he stood as if hammer-smitten. Toward dawn of that night, he said that being his bedmate was not good enough for her. He would make her his queen.

And thus he did. Their wedding feast was talked of for years.

Hroar took that chance to befriend his new-caught islander chieftains. He invited them, and by gifts and fair

words he bound them to the Skjoldungs. "Yrsa's brought
us this, at least," he remarked to Valthjona.

"Do you hold it against her that she stands in the way
of Helgi making a more useful marriage?" she asked.
"Why, he can take as many wives as he pleases."

"None other do please him," said Hroar. "He doesn't
even keep lemans any more." He smiled at Valthjona.
"Ah, well, I'm like that myself."

Yrsa kept on learning how to be a lady, until folk said
that young though she was, Leidhra had seldom had so
fine a queen. They marked, too, that Helgi grew more
and more mild. He began to spend his summers in Denmark, doing Hroar's kind of work. If less patient than his
brother, he was equally just. Men became happy to give
their lawsuits into his hands. They thought he talked
things over with Yrsa and that she softened his stern-
ness.

Young she was, however. For two years she got no
child. In the third year she had a boy.

That was a long and hard birth, upon Yule Eve to
boot. Helgi sat in his hall, drinking, hearkening to a skald,
talking to his men. What he said made scant sense; and
ever he turned his head doorward, as if to strain through
the storm outside to hear cries of pain in the lady-bower.

At last the midwife came. In a huge hush, save for the
roaring of fires and gale, she walked, bearing a bundle
which she laid on the earth before the high seat. Helgi
sat still. Sweat gleamed on his brow and cheeks, reeked
from his clothes.

"I bring you your son, King Helgi," said the midwife.

"And Yrsa?" croaked from him.

"I hope she does well, my lord."

"Give me our son." The hands shook which Helgi
lifted, to take the baby and put him on his knee.

Next day, being sure Yrsa would live, he slaughtered
a herd of horses and oxen in the holy shaw, and called
men to a feast only less mighty than his wedding. Himself
he poured water upon the boy and named him Hrolf.
Warriors who had fared beside him from end to end of

the known world, clanged blade on shield and hailed their atheling.

Yrsa was slow to get back her full health. She never bore another child. Nonetheless she and Helgi stayed happy together. They rejoiced in their Hrolf. He was small but handsome, merry, quick on his feet and quick of wit.

Those were quiet years for Denmark. Still, the brothers held a close eye on Götaland and Svithjodh, where much was happening.

The Göta-King Hugleik—maybe in search of fame to match Helgi's—took a war-fleet past Jutland and Saxland, to Frankish country. There he harried about; but the Franks trapped him and his, and he fell in battle. Among the few Götar to win free was Bjovulf, who swam in his byrnie out to their ships. Sad was his homecoming. For this doughtiness, the Götar would make him their lord. He refused, and himself raised Hugleik's son Hærdredh before the Thing. However, as the strongest headman after Ægthjof died, Bjovulf must needs steer the land in all but name.

At that time, the Swede-King in Svithjodh was Egil. Like other Ynglings, he was a spendthrift offerer to the gods, and a wizard besides. Maybe a spell of his went wrong; anyhow, once a bull which he was about to give broke loose, gored its way past the thralls already hanged in honor of Odin, and escaped to the wilderness. Long did it roam, wreaking harm upon folk. King Egil led huntsmen after it. He rode from them in those leafy reaches, and suddenly came upon the beast. He cast his spear. The bull shook loose the barb, thundered forward, laid open the king's horse and tossed him to earth. Egil drew sword. The bull got in first. A horn stabbed him to the heart. Then the king's men arrived and did away with the brute. Afterward they bore Egil away and buried him at Uppsala.

He had had a brother named Ottar. Now strife over the lordship broke out between Egil's son Aali, and Ottar's sons Asmund and Adhils. It raged in Svithjodh for years. Asmund fell, and a beaten Adhils fled into Götaland. The Götar, under King Hærdredh, backed him. But when their host entered Svithjodh, Aali was again victorious and Hærdredh himself met death.

The Götar took Bjovulf for their new king, as they had wanted to do all along. He called on his kinsman and friend Hroar, who sent warriors. In another fight, on frozen Lake Vänern, Aali died. Adhils rode to Uppsala and was hailed King of the Swedes.

Hroar and Bjovulf thus had hopes of a lord in Svithjodh who would be thankful to them. Furthermore, this was no warlike man. Rather, Adhils went deeper into spellcraft than any Yngling before him. Having gained what he wanted, he left the world in peace as far as he was concerned.

Even so, when the Skjoldung brothers helped him they made a mistake. They did not know this right away. Other sorrows came upon them first.

Seven years had passed since the day that Helgi found Yrsa on the strand, when Queen Olof came for her revenge.

VI

The crofter dared do no otherwise than seek out Olof and tell her how a seafarer who said he was the Dane-King had borne off the girl she gave him. She sat unmoving until, very faintly, she quirked a smile. From then on she was always eager to hear news from Denmark. It did not come readily, because she never let on that anything had changed and folk still feared speaking to her of Helgi Halfdansson. But in this way and that, she learned how he and one Yrsa, whose parentage was unknown, were happily wedded.

"You shall get grief and shame, Helgi, where today you have honor and gladness," she vowed, alone with her ghosts.

Time passed, though, for she could not fare off at once like a man. Moreover, she found joy in thinking about what anguish lay in her bestowal. Foremost was her need to make sure he would not strike back. To that end she wove a web of alliances, both with other Saxons and with Jutes to the north. After what had happened in the islands, these lords knew they must stand together if they wanted to stay free. But Olof worked and waited until she was certain their greed and quarrelsomeness could not be used to pry them apart.

At last she made known that she would fare to Denmark in quest of understanding with the Skjoldungs. Folk liked this. It would much help trade if the dread of war could be lifted. She had only three ships. Therefore none thought it odd that she chose a month when she knew Hroar and Helgi would be away from home, making their round of the shire-Things. She could establish herself with their queens, sound those women out, win their friendship and thus a good word to their husbands.

The Saxon craft came down Roskilde Fjord and moored at the docks before the town. A number of merchantmen were already on hand. It bustled around warehouses and the gaily decked booths which traders had set up—men, wives, horses, dogs, cattle, swine, children atumble among the livestock, here maybe a whore, yonder maybe an outlander from as far off as the Frankish realms, a broiling racket and a swirl of colors. High rose the stockade behind, at each corner a watchtower where gleamed the helmets and byrnies of warriors on guard, and the heads of outlaws moldered on stakes. Above that wall could be seen the sod roofs of many houses, green and flower-flecked now in summer. Smoke drifted savory toward the gulls which shrieked in a snowstorm of wings.

On either side the land rolled back from sun-glittery water, cleared save for woodlots, plowed and planted, rich and peaceful. High on a hill, ringed by a holy oaken-shaw, a shingle-built temple lifted roof upon roof. Nearby, mighty amidst its outbuildings, the hall called Hart raised antlers which flamed with gold.

"They've done right well, yon brethren," said her skipper to Olof.

She stood on the foredeck, fists clenched at her sides: a small woman, her gown sea-stained, gray streaks in her

hair and lines graven deep in a face where the broad
bones stood stark, nonetheless stiff of back and haughty
of look. "Maybe they won't forever after," she said, and
beckoned the marshal of her household troops. To him
she gave a most exact message. He and several of his
men strode to Hart, in mail they had carefully polished,
spears aloft, cloaks of red and blue blowing off their
shoulders.

While Helgi was gone, Yrsa's custom was to bring her
son Hrolf and stay with Valthjona. Those women liked
each other. Besides, Hroar's dwelling was better than
anything in Leidhra. Olof had learned this.

Her men asked to see Yrsa alone. She received them
in a bower where she sat spinning with her maidens. The
girls made big eyes when the shaggy Saxons trod into
their room.

"Welcome," smiled Yrsa. "Talk has buzzed, how three
more ships have docked this day. Whence come you and
what would you?"

"I hight Gudhmund, lady." The marshal's way was as
rough as his form of the Northern tongue. Folk had not
the manners at Olof's little offside court which they did
here. "I bring you greeting from my queen." And he told
who she was.

"Why, how wonderful!" Yrsa clapped her hands,
though she reddened as deeply as any of her maidens.
While the tale of her husband's doings long ago in Als
was not common talk any more, she had heard it. "Olof
would at last be our friend? Of course, of course! Let her
come at once." She turned to a girl. "Thorhild, go find
the cooks—"

"Hold, lady," said Gudhmund. "My queen told me to
tell you, she would on no account be a guest here."

Yrsa frowned. "What?"

"She has a word for you, lady, if you will come to
her."

Yrsa's scowl deepened. Queen Valthjona might have
warned her to refuse so insulting an invitation, had
Valthjona been there. But Yrsa felt she had better learn
what this was all about. She took time to dress well: in a

white gown embroidered with green vines and leaves, linen headdress, golden chain around her neck and golden coils on her arms, shoes of kid buckled with silver, a scarlet cloak trimmed with ermine. She summoned guardsmen to ride along. Almost, she let the Saxons walk, then at the last moment thought they should not have to be humbled just because their queen was bitchy, and ordered horses saddled for them.

In color and clatter, between gaudy shields and under bright spears, Yrsa rode forth to her doom.

At the dock she dismounted, left her men ranked, and herself sprang lithely onto the foredeck of the ship. For a while she and Olof clashed eyes. The crowd ashore, goggling at the sight, grew still. Only the gulls cried, a breeze whittered, wavelets clucked on strakes, tackle creaked.

"Welcome to Denmark," said Yrsa slowly. "Why would you not be our guest?"

Still Olof stared at her. In seven years, the barefoot strand-lass had become a woman. Not tall either, Yrsa likewise walked straight and supple; bronze hair, gray eyes, gently molded face were good to see; small dimples made by laughter edged her lips. Even today she could not really glower.

"I have no honor wherewith to repay King Helgi," said Olof in a flat voice.

Yrsa bridled. "Little honor did you show me when I dwelt in your land." Yet eagerness leaped in her. She leaned forward, reached as if to take the older woman by the hands, and said not altogether steadily: "I wonder . . . can you tell me about my kindred? I've thought it may not be such as I heard—"

Then Olof smiled. "Why, yes, my dear. It's not impossible I could tell you something about that. In fact, I made this journey hither mostly because I wanted to make the truth known to you." She drew a deep, tasting breath. "Tell me, are you happy in your marriage?"

Bewildered, flushing, Yrsa nonetheless answered with gladness. "Yes, I must say I am, I who have such a brave and famous king to husband."

Shuddering for joy, Olof spoke forth, that men might hear not merely down in the hull but on the wharf: "You've less reason to be content than you think. He is your father, and you are my daughter."

One scream did Yrsa let out.

Thereafter she shouted that this was a filthy lie and Helgi would burn everything on Als to cleanse his honor. Olof pressed in, unrelenting. She had had years to make ready her words. She had brought along as a witness the midwife who drew Yrsa from her and heard how that name was given; she had even brought the skull of the dog.

Guardsmen saw their Dane-Queen sink to the deck, riven by weeping, while the Saxon woman stood above her and grinned. They hefted their weapons and shuffled forward. "No, hold, hold," mumbled their captain. "I fear . . . this is nothing . . . we can kill. O all bright elves, help us this day!"

But naught flew over Yrsa save sea-mews.

At length she rose and gasped, "I think my mother is the worst and most heartless who, who, who ever lived. This thing is unheard of. It will—will never be forgotten."

"You can thank Helgi for that," said Olof.

And, astounding those who stood there under the sun, she stepped forward, took her daughter in her arms, drew the tangle-tressed head onto her bosom, and said: "Come home with me, Yrsa. Come home in honor and respect, and I'll make everything as good for you as I can."

Yrsa drew free. She waited until she had gathered strength, then answered evenly: "I know not what the outcome of that may be. But here I can stay no longer, when I know how impossibly I am placed."

Turning, she left the ship, mounted her horse, and rode back at an easy gait. She was a Skjoldung.

The tale does not say what passed between her and Queen Valthjona, or her and Hrolf Helgisson.

Nor does it say just what Olof did. No doubt she held further talks with her daughter, and a tongue made cunning by years of kingcraft urged over and over that Yrsa come back to Als. In truth, if she forsook her husband, where else might she find shelter? A woman alone is booty. At the same time, belike Olof lingered no great while. Word would have gotten to Helgi, and he would be killing horses on his way home. The Saxons must soon have rowed off. Their best plan would have been to lie to beyond the strait which links Roskilde Fjord and Isefjord, so that they could readily flee out into the Kattegat.

The tale says little more than that Helgi and Yrsa met. This would have been under four eyes, not even small Hrolf on hand to be frightened by his father's wrath and grief. She would have sent maidens, carls, and guards out of the bower-building where he and she slept, and where once she had sat singing at her distaff while she waited his return to the news that she bore his child.

Their room was on the upper floor. Doors gave on a gallery where a man could stand, overlooking hall and courtyard and the life which swarmed there, his glance faring onward to town and bay, sweep of deep-green meadows where cattle grazed, tall rustling trees, grainfields white for harvest, roofs asmoke from nothing worse than hearthfires, on and on to a ridge and a dolmen. Clouds loomed like snowpeaks, a hawk soared, a lark sang. Sunbeams streamed in onto sand-scrubbed planks, glowed darkly in wainscoting and carven furniture, stroked the skin of a bear he had tracked down and spear-slain only to give her a warm blanket, called cedar smell forth from the chest where she kept some clothes of fine foreign make that he had likewise offered her.

Helgi bulked helpless above his love and stammered, "Foul and heartless she is, your mother. But let everything be between us as it was before."

"No, no, that can't be," she begged of him, and drew back when he would lay arms around her. "You—I—No. Helgi," she well-nigh wailed, "what luck can it bring to a land, that the king lies with his own child?"

Then he was the one who sank. Blighted fields, murrain on the stock, sickness sweeping through a starveling folk, Denmark the haunt of naught but ravens and wolves, cutthroats and madmen, until an outland ax hewed down the tree of the Skjoldungs—surely that dread left him felled and speechless.

"Yrsa," he got out at last; but she was gone.

She may have dared kiss her son farewell. She may have had a man row her in a boat, forth across the bay, through night and rain, till she found the ships of her mother.

VII

Yrsa spent three years on Als. Her mother treated her righteously if coolly. She was much alone, and in company talked little. Her least unhappy days were when she went sailing in a boat she owned, as she and Helgi had been wont to do. Even then, nobody ever heard her sing.

Though Olof's standing made Yrsa the best of queenly matches, no kings came wooing. That was mostly because they were unsure whether Helgi would fetch her back, or whether he would take it ill did she wed another.

But he never stirred. He had raved to Hroar, after his brother joined him, about leading a fleet and a host to seek his wife. "You speak nonsense, and well you know it," snapped Hroar. "We're not ready to fight half Jutland, which warfare against Als would bring on. And what could you gain? A girl, your own daughter, who'd have to be kept caged lest she flit from you—and surely the gods turning their backs on us, when you wittingly did such a thing. No!"

Crushed, Helgi spent a long while abed, staring at emptiness. Afterward he was moody, harsh, and nearly always drunk. When he took women he could do nothing with them—the whisper went that Frigg herself had smitten him—and at last he stopped trying. He built a shack in the wilds and often stayed there, quite alone, for weeks on end.

Hroar and Valthjona reared Hrolf. Whatever bane lay in his parentage did not seem to have touched him. He was a sunny-tempered lad who won the hearts of the motherliest serving woman and the starkest guardsman.

Good at those boy's skills which grow into a man's, he was likewise given to thinking, asking questions, wondering aloud if the answers he got held the whole truth: even as his uncle had been at that age.

In the third summer a fleet came to Als under the white shield. Never before had Olof guested so big and splendid a troop. At its head was Adhils the Swede-King. He had fared hither straight from his burg of Uppsala.

Olof received him with utmost respect. In his guest quarters she put the best of everything she owned. Yrsa was merely polite, and soon went back to the separate house where she dwelt. That evening Olof and Adhils drank together in the high seat.

"I have heard about your daughter," he told her, "and I see the tales were true about how fair she is and how strong the kindred she stems from. Lady, I ask for her hand."

Olof regarded him closely. Adhils was a young man, tall and broad though already running somewhat to fat. His hair and beard were long, amber-hued, and greasy; he kept running his freckled fingers through those whiskers. A sword-sharp nose looked out of place between his wide red cheeks. While he walked in gold and the finest linens, these were not as clean as they might have been; a sour smell hung around him.

Withal, he was no butt for laughter. His voice rolled heavy as North Sea surf. The little ice-pale eyes sunken beneath his brows were unwavering. He was known to be deep into wizardry. His folk felt the weight of his greed and grimness, but he steered them with a cunning beyond his years. Svithjodh was the biggest kingdom in the North, reaching from the hills of the Götaland marches to the endless wet wildernesses in Finland. Scores of under-kings and tribal headmen paid scot to Adhils. Thus he had at least as much wealth and as many warriors at his beck as did the Skjoldungs.

"You know well how it is with her," said Olof slowly. "However, if she herself wishes this, I will say naught against it."

"I should hope not, my lady," said Adhils unsmiling. And while the night was warm and fires burned high, Olof shivered a bit.

Still, she thought, granted him for an ally, she needed no longer fear Helgi or anyone else.

Next day Adhils sought Yrsa. She sat outdoors, on a bench under a willow tree in a herb garden behind her dwelling. A pair of girls helped her sew a gown. She kept only a small household, and not a single thrall. Quietly though she lived, she did not lack for hirelings, because they knew they would be kindly treated.

Today she was clad as usual in a plain dress and no ornaments. Sunlight spattered through shade to waken ruddy hues in her braids. The air lay hot and moveless, full of the smells of herbs for cooking or healing—sharp leek, chervil, wormwood, wintergreen; milk-souring sorrel; bitter rue; sweet thyme; shy cress. A pair of swallows darted woad-blue on a mosquito hunt. When gravel in the path scrunched beneath Adhils's feet, Yrsa looked up. "Good morning, my lord," she said dully.

"We missed you at the feast yestereven," he rumbled.

"I am not one for merrymaking."

"I had hoped to make you a gift. Here." Adhils held forth a necklace. The servant girls squealed. Those links and plates of burnished gold, those blinking jewels, could buy a longship.

"I thank you, my lord," said Yrsa, troubled. "You are too kind. But—"

"I will hear no buts." Adhils dropped the thing into her lap and flapped a hand at the maidens. They scampered off, to gossip out of earshot with the squad of Swedish warriors who had followed their king. He lowered himself beside her.

"Your mother is a rich queen," he said. "You should not have to lead as lonely a life as you do."

"It's my own choice," said Yrsa.

"You were happier once."

She whitened. "That's my business."

Adhils turned his head to spear her on his glacier eyes. "No, you're wrong. What a lord or lady does is the business of the whole folk. Not so much because they want to pry. Their lives hang on us."

She tried to draw away from him without seeming either rude or frightened. "I have left that," she whispered.

"You cannot leave your blood," said his slow, hammering voice.

"What do you seek, King Adhils?"

"You for my wife, Queen Yrsa."

She tautened. "No."

Adhils's smile barely touched his lips. "I am not such a bad match."

She leaped to her feet and flared: "Here there's nothing good for me to choose. Well do I know how hated you are!"

"I am feared, Yrsa," he said, shakingly unshaken.

She handed him back the necklace. "Go. I beg you, go." Wildly, she waved at the storks' nest on her rooftop. "Those birds are supposed to bring luck and children. I've gotten none. You don't want a barren queen."

"You have slept alone here," he reminded her.

"And I always will!"

He raised his hulking frame to block her off from the leaves. "You may well have gone barren since you bore that child you never should have," he said bluntly. "No matter. I've begotten others. Between your mother and her Saxon friends as allies, and you as my wife, the Skjoldungs ought to behave themselves toward me." He pressed the necklace into her clasp. "Moreover," he said, "you'll be a brighter ornament to my house than this." He did not speak merrily, as Helgi would have done; rather it was like something he had put together and learned beforehand.

"I would not cause trouble, I do not want to insult so . . . so great a king," said Yrsa. Sweat stood forth upon her; and did tears mingle? "Yet go. *Go.*"

He turned and walked calmly off. When he was out of sight, Yrsa cast the necklace down, huddled on the bench and struggled for air.

Olof learned what had happened and came to see her

in her home. That was after sunset. Dusk brimmed the room. Yrsa called for no fire to light a lamp. The two women saw each other as shadows where they sat. A window stood open to coolness. Now it was bats which darted about, and somewhere an owl hooted.

"You're a fool, Yrsa," snapped Olof. "An utter, rattle-headed fool. There's none like King Adhils."

"There is—there was a better one for me," mourned the daughter.

"Yah, an unshorn tosspot who dens all by himself!" Olof jeered. "You've heard what Helgi has become."

"You lost no chance to gloat over it."

"You lay by your own father—the same horn which gored me bloody, Yrsa. That you've not been smitten dead or blind . . . that now the mightiest lord of the lot comes wooing you, yes, gives you a gift which could be the Brisingamen itself, that you let fall in the dust—"

Yrsa tossed her head. "To get the Brisingamen, Freyja spread her legs for four foul dwarfs."

"You need only go, hallowed and in honor, to a great king." Olof was still for a time, until: "My hankering was never toward men; no, my loathing was. You're other-wise. I heard from afar how your hand in his and your gaze upon him told the whole world how glad you were with Helgi. In these years here, I've marked how you'll smile at naught I can see, or hug to you a blooming dewy apple tree by moonlight, or—don't gainsay me!—let your look stray across a handsome youth. Yrsa, you need a man."

"Not that man."

"That very one. I was saying—in spite of your coupling aforetime, like that bitch I named you after; in spite of your treating him today in such wise that he could right-fully bring war—Adhils is patient. This has to be more than luck. A Norn stands nigh, and your doom is to be-come the queen in Svithjodh."

Hoo-hoo went the owl. Yrsa cowered as if it were her that it hunted.

"Much worse could that doom be," Olof pursued. "Much worse will it be, if you let your folly grow into madness. I have no heirs, Yrsa. The Alsmen will not take you to rule them when I'm dead, nor could you if they did. What would you rather be, the prey of some viking, the willy-nilly leman of some grubby little chieftain, or the lady of high Uppsala? What's worthy of a Skjoldung?"

"No," Yrsa beseeched, "no, no, no."

"If you are his queen," Olof said, "Adhils will have a claim on this kingdom too. He can set a jarl over it when I'm gone, a strong man who'll keep it safe. Otherwise— well, think of your foster-siblings on the north coast. Think of brothers lying dead, ravens picking out their eyes; think of sisters ravaged and dragged off to turn a stranger's quern. Then they will say her mother did well to name Yrsa for a dog!"

Olof rose and walked out. Yrsa wept.

Next day she was steady of mien. When Adhils came, she gave him careful greeting. He offered her more gifts, ornaments and costly stuffs. She did not say aloud that she would be wearing those things anyhow, did she become his wife.

After a pair of weeks between him and her mother, Yrsa bowed her weary head and said, "Yes."

While the Swedes sailed off, bearing the bride away, Olof stood on the strand looking after them. As the last hull dropped below world-edge, she laughed and cried: "That's another for you, Helgi!"

She lived only a few years further. A growth killed her.

VIII

When King Helgi got the news, he grew even heavier of mood and withdrew altogether to his shack.

This building he had made himself, hewing logs as if they were foemen, in the thinly peopled north of Zealand. At need he would walk several miles to the nearest farmstead and pay for food and beer. The wagoner who brought it never lingered, and nobody came calling. They said his was a haunted ground. At its back stretched a wilderness of low, storm-twisted trees and brush. Before it, heath, broken here and there by thickets, rolled off toward a fen where mists were ever swirling and dripping. In sight of the house lifted a gaunt ridge, into which the Old Folk had once sunk a stone-lined chamber.

Scant game was around, a few deer, mostly hares and squirrels and other scuttering frightened things; yet wolves often howled. The fen drew waterfowl whose wings and clamor could fill the sky; but men hunted nowhere near those deep, green-scummed pools. Birds of prey and carrion lived off the flocks, eagle, kestrel, osprey, goshawk, merlin, kite, crow, raven, chough, and more and more. Helgi took fledglings and tried to tame them. He failed, mainly because he was always drunk. But he did like lying on his back in the springy ling, watching how they soared and wheeled.

When winter drew over him, he could watch no longer.

That Yule Eve got bad weather. In Roskilde, in Leidhra, in homes everywhere through Denmark, humans drew close, stoked fires, raised good cheer like a wall between themselves and the beings which prowled this night. Helgi bolted flatbread and stockfish, swilled down many hornsful of beer, and lurched to his bed of straw and bearskins. He did leave a stone lamp burning.

After a while he woke and frowned into gloom. The chamber was bitterly chill; night seemed to breathe out of the clay floor. Wind hooted. Where it found an unchinked crack between logs, it fluttered fingers across his nakedness. A different sound, a weak whimpering and scratching at the door . . . why had it roused him?

Some stray beast? His head felt eerily clear, as if he had drunk no common beer but instead had tasted the mead they say Odin brews for his midnight guests. He thought it would not be kingly to leave a living creature outside when he could save it.

Rising, he took the lamp, groped his way over hoar-frosted hardness, through bobbing huge shadows, to unlatch and open the door. Snow hissed on the wind. A nearly shapeless heap of gray rags huddled shuddering on the threshold. He stooped, urged the poor thing inside, closed the door again and lifted the lamp for a better look.

It was a girl. She was scrawny as death. Lank black hair

fell around an ill-shaped skull wherein clattered what teeth had not rotted away. Her feet were bare and swollen from frostbite. She squatted on the floor, hugged herself with blue hands at the end of broomstick arms, and moaned. He heard: "You have done well, King."

Helgi made a face. However—he set the lamp back down on the ground, took the two or three strides needful to cross the room, bent over and began to pluck straw and a pelt from his bed. "Put this around yourself and you won't freeze," he said.

"No, let me get in by you," whined the beggar girl. "Let me lie against you. Else I'll die. I'm so cold, so cold."

Helgi scowled. But having taken her as his guest, he could do naught else than say: "That's much against my wish. Still, if you must, then lie here at my feet in your clothes. That can't harm me." He hoped her fleas and lice had already perished.

Like an ungainly spider, she crawled where he bade her and pulled a skin over herself. Helgi got back in the straw and stretched out his legs. The forlorn wench could at least take warmth from his soles, he thought.

What was this? They did not touch filthy tatters or rickety bones. No, a silkiness glowed; the tingle of it went through the whole of him.

He sat up and hauled back the fell. There lay a woman in a sheening sark. Never had he seen any this beautiful. The straw hardly crackled as she rose to her knees and smiled at him. Full breasts and hips thrust against her garment, shone through it; their sweetness overwhelmed all winter chill and stench, he was suddenly drowned in summer. Raven's-wing locks flowed past a face pale and strange, too cleanly carven to be wholly human. Her eyes were the unblinking gold of a hawk's.

"But—but you—" Fear jabbed him. He scrambled backward and made the sign of the Hammer. She smiled, and fright whirled out of head and heart. Dim though the lamplight was, it gleamed off her skin, driving murk from everywhere indoors. Far and faint seemed the yowling wind. Shaky-armed, he reached for her.

She nearly sang: "Now I must go from here. You have

saved me from sore need, for a spell was laid on me by my stepmother. I have sought many kings. You alone, Helgi Halfdansson, had the courage to do what would set me free."

"It took no courage." As he touched her, his manhood arose.

She saw, and lifted a hand. "No," she said softly, "you must not lie with me. I will stay here no longer."

He gripped her and answered in upward-tumbling blitheness: "Well, you won't get leave to fare off that soon. We'll not part thus."

She took him by the shoulders. The feel of her went through him to his marrow. "You have done me good, Helgi. I'd not be the means of bringing woe on your house."

"You bring greater joy than I can tell you," he babbled. 'I'll wed you as early as may be. Tonight—'

Sorrow dimmed those falcon eyes. "As you will, lord." Then they flamed, and she cast off her sark and came to him.

Long, long afterward, morning stole wolf-gray across a white and silent world. He had loved her more often and burningly than he had known lay in the might of any man. Stirring half out of sleep, in the dimness he saw her stand above him. She was clad. Where had her green gown and cloak come from, or the red wreath of rowan about her head? She bent down, laid a finger across his lips, and told him most quietly:

"So you have had your will, King. Know, we got a child together. When you took me in, I wished you well; and I do not yet wish you ill. Do as I say, and it may be we can still halt the bad luck you have sown in my womb. Our child must be born undersea; for mine is the blood of Ran. Be down by your boathouses, this time next winter, and look for her." Pain crossed her mouth. "If you fail, the Skjoldungs will suffer."

King Helgi thought that then she fared away. When he came fully awake, she was gone.

He went out into the snowfields, and saw her in every blue shadow and in every glimmer off ice; after the short day ended and the stars blinked forth, she whispered around him. She was not Yrsa, though, a heart wrenched out to leave a bleeding hollowness. Elven, she was like a wind of springtime, soon gone, never really remembered, bequeathing newly unfolded blossoms.

He found that he had back both his manhood and his will to be a man. Singing, he rode home to Leidhra.

Hroar had done what he could in the years of his brother's despair. Nevertheless much had gone agley. A king was a great landholder, a great owner of trade goods and merchant ships. Helgi's stewards and skippers dared do little without orders which were seldom forthcoming. He took matters in hand and shortly set them aright. Likewise did he with the kingdom, and his brother and his sister-in-law, and his son Hrolf.

Busy as he was—among womankind as well—he forgot what his elf-love had asked of him. Indeed, she seemed so strange to everything else he knew, he sometimes wondered if she had been a dream and no more. Then who had sent the dream and what did it mean? These were daunting thoughts. He pushed them aside, he plunged back into the world of men.

On the third Yule Eve, he was again alone in that house near the barrow.

He supposed it was happenstance. A man, lately outlawed for murder, had been skulking about those parts and wreaking harm. When Helgi passed through, the yeomen asked his help. "Scant use to hunt him with a flock of beaters," laughed the king. "Well, maybe I and my hounds can track him by ourselves." They did. Helgi slew the fellow and took his head to show. By then, twilight was on him, and he recalled his hut. Undwelt in for three years, it was a cheerless enough place to keep this night. However, its walls gave some lee.

About midnight, the baying of his dogs roused Helgi. He took his sword and went to the door. The sky had become very clear and quiet. Stars frosted a vast blackness; the Bridge glowed silver-cold; snow shone beneath, save where the mound with the tomb reared.

Three men and a woman sat horses which shimmered

wan and changeable as waterfalls, long-maned, long-tailed, hoofs making the frozen snow not creak but ring—elven horses. The men were clad in byrnies that chimed, in shirts and trews and cloaks where wavered faint rainbows, in boots whose golden chasings flickered like fire. Their heads were too beautiful to be human. The woman—Helgi knew the woman.

She leaned down. In awe, he dropped his weapon to take the sealskin bundle she laid in his arms. Sadness freighted her tone: "King, your kinsmen must pay because you cared naught about what I wished. Yet well shall it be for you yourself, that you loosed me from my wretchedness. Here is our daughter. I have named her Skuld."

Swifter than flesh, those horses fled off across the world.

Helgi never saw the elf-woman again. He stood holding a child asleep, who hight Skuld: That Which Shall Be.

IX

Then grief came back upon him. He kept from his former wildness and drunkenness, dwelt in Leidhra and steered things well. But he spoke hardly more than he must, never laughed, and went for many long rides alone or sat staring hour after hour into the fire.

Hroar learned of this, and toward spring bid him to Hart for Blessing. That was a mild and early year. Hawthorns were white across the land, roads dry and heaven full of songbirds, when the kings rode forth from the temple just behind Frey's wagon. Bright was the gold of the shrine thereon which hid the god's image; stately was the lady chosen to attend him for the month; garlanded were the oxen which drew them, and garlanded the Roskilde girls who danced forth to meet them. Song lilted through the lusty mirth of swains; snow-water gurgled in every ditch; trees lifted branches across which a goddess had strewn the first frail green, into a heaven of slanting sunbeams and towering clouds; cattle stood rust-red in the mists that steamed off paddocks; a breeze blew cool and damp, swollen by the smells of growth.

Coalsack nights and huddling indoors were ended. Day had come again. New life was on its way; one could all but hear how the soil stirred. Let joy rise with the rising sap. Let man rise too, and plow his woman over and over, so that Frey and the land-elves would not fail to make fruitful our mother the earth! After the god's wagon had gone from Roskilde to carry him around the shire, there was a feast. As ever, folk left early, hand in hand, not only young ones but the gravest of householders and wives.

Helgi sat cheerless. What words he had were mostly for his son Hrolf, asking how the boy did, what he planned. At eleven, Hrolf was slim and on the short side. He moved like a deer, though, and rich garb sat well on him. His hair was a deeper shade of yellow, with reddish tints, than was his father's. His eyes were big and gray under dark brows—Yrsa's eyes—and much of her lay in his clear-skinned face, along with the jutting Skjoldung chin. He answered readily. Otherwise he was himself apt to stay quiet, watching what the rest did and thinking his own thoughts.

That night Helgi slept alone.

Hroar sought him out in the morning. "Come, let's go for a ride," said the older brother. Helgi nodded. Grooms saddled horses for them and they trotted briskly off. Their guards saw they meant to talk, and fell well behind.

The bay sparkled, woods breathed and burgeoned, wind whooped. High overhead went a flight of storks. At length Hroar said: "I'd not tell you what to do, Helgi. Still, some will call it a bad sign that you, a king, were so glum at the offering and the feast, and later gave none of your seed to a woman."

Helgi sighed. "Let them."

"You told me how the elf warned of trouble to come. Well, trouble always comes, of one kind or another, and she said she at least bears good will toward you. As for that girl-child—"

Helgi turned to him and said hoarsely: "I'll tell you what the matter is. Seeing her a second time, finding she was real after all, and ever since then seeing our daughter, who cries too seldom and whose eyes are too sharp for a baby . . . I remember Yrsa."

"What? I thought you'd put her out of your mind."

"Never. Oh, I found I could live without her. But . . . I know not . . . the Other Folk do eldritch things to our hearts . . . maybe I hark back to Yrsa because I'm afraid to dwell on her who sought me—and meanwhile Hrolf, the son Yrsa and I got together, who has her eyes—"

Helgi slumped. "She goes about in Uppsala, not gladly from what I hear," he mumbled. "I sit in the home that was ours and grow old."

Hroar peered at his brother. Bones stood forth in Helgi's face, his skin was deeply furrowed, grayness had begun to dull his locks. Hroar ran a hand across his own grizzled beard and said, "We all grow old."

"Need we rot before we are dead?" rasped Helgi.

"We've mighty works ahead of us yet." Hroar tried to smile. "Anyhow, I said to cheer you, you've won the fondness of a most powerful being—"

He broke off, because suddenly his waymate jerked straight upright in the saddle. The hair stirred on Helgi's arms; he stared before him and hissed like a lynx.

"What is it?" asked Hroar in unease.

Helgi lifted a fist. Iron rang through his tone: "By the Hammer! You're right! Why should I mope out my days?"

Hroar began, "Good, I'm glad to hear—" His brother's shout cut through:

"I'll go to Uppsala and fetch her back!"

"What?" Hroar cried. "No!"

It rushed from Helgi: "Yes. Hear me. I've brooded on this, till in a flash you made me see—" He gripped Hroar's forearm with force that left fingermarks. "I, I *do* have the goodwill of one who stands high among the Others, is of the very blood of Ran. I fathered her child, that I'm rearing myself. Would she let harm come on her own daughter? Why need I further fear any curse? Why need you, or the Dane-lands? Need we ever have? Would Hrolf be as fair and promising as he is, were there a doom in his begetting? No, our grief was from none but that she-wolf

Olof, who's dead now, may she never walk again." He lifted his hands to the sky and yelled. "We're free!"

"No man is free of his weird," said Hroar. Helgi heard him not, but instead struck spurs to horse and was off in a breakneck gallop.

There followed a whirlwind of making ready. Feverishly mirthful, Helgi overbore every naysayer. His household troopers were so glad to see fresh heart in him that they would have followed him anywhere. Those who had been to Uppsala aforetime told such tales of it that young men swarmed off the steadings to help crew the ships, as soon as the planting was done.

"We'll fare in peace," Helgi made known. "If Adhils will grant my wish, I can offer him good terms on outstanding questions such as the amber trade. If not . . . Adhils is unwise."

In vain did Hroar protest, "Bjovulf and I worked hard and spent men to get an Yngling who would not be our foe. Do you want to spill this on the ground, for the sake of your own lust?"

"What threat is that sluggard?" Helgi scoffed. "We could plunder up and down his coasts, and he'd never stir from his bloody altar stones." He tightened. "I'd count myself no fit lord, did I leave my Yrsa with one who gives her woe."

A single time he was taken aback. He and his boy Hrolf had gone hawking. Their bird struck down a crane. Helgi said into the sunlight: "Thus will I bring your mother to you."

Hrolf answered gravely: "Dead like yonder prey?"

"What do you mean?"

"They tell me she left us against your will. It may be against hers to come back."

Helgi stood still in the blowing air for some while before he said, tight-lipped, "Well, I'll have given her the chance."

Speaking alone with her husband, Queen Valthjona uttered the same doubt: "If I know Yrsa, Helgi will have had this trip for nothing."

"I hope the upshot is no worse than that," fretted Hroar. "Yrsa will do what she can for his safety and honor."

"But Adhils—I never liked Adhils, useful though it seemed he could be to us. And what I've since heard of him does not leave me unworried."

Valthjona cast him a troubled smile. "You'll never swerve Helgi," she warned. "So don't drive a wedge between the two of you. Stay quiet, wish him well, and give him as glad a sendoff as you are able."

<h1 style="text-align:center">X</h1>

Adhils seldom left Uppsala. But as wide a realm as Svithjodh, holding many different tribes, under-kings, and lesser headmen, was bound to suffer uproar from time to time. If they did not seek to withhold his scot or break away altogether, they were likely to fall out with each other. To quell this, he kept a large household troop. Foremost were twelve berserkers.

That kind of men were so called because they often fought without mail, that is, in their bare sarks. They were huge and strong but ugly to behold, unkempt, unwashed, surly and bullying. In battle a madness came upon them; they howled, foamed at the mouth, grew swollen and purple in the face, gnawed the rims of their shields, and rushed forward like angry aurochs. Then their strength was such that no ordinary man could stand before them. It was said that iron would not bite on them, either. Truth was, the wounds they got, save for the deepest, hardly bled and closed up almost at once. After the rage was past, they were weak and shivery. By that time, however, most who had tried to fight them would be dead or fled.

Goodfolk loathed berserkers . . . and feared them. The dread they awoke went along with their might to help them plow through a battle line. While Adhils was not the first king who used this kind of men, it was reckoned against him. He cared little about that.

He did care when his twelve, and most of his other warriors, were away, and a scout galloped in to gasp that a score of ships had come up the channel from the Baltic Sea to Lake Mälar, which even then they were crossing. Soon after, a boy brought a message from that fleet. It had lain to at the river mouth; upstream, escape might be barred. Its lord had gotten hold of the boy and given him a piece of silver to seek the royal hall and say: "Helgi the Dane-King comes in peace, to visit his ally and talk over what matters may lie between them."

Queen Yrsa was on hand. Adhils turned to her. "Well," he asked, half grinning, "how would you like me to receive him?"

She had stood wholly still, save that red and white flew across her brow and cheeks, down her throat and into her bosom. Now she must gulp, and her tone was less than steady: "You must settle that for yourself. But you know from aforetime . . . the man is not found . . . to whom I owe more than to him."

Adhils combed his whiskers, padded about, muttered to himself, before he said, "Well, then, we'll have him here as our guest. I'll send a man who can, hm, hm, make known without offending him—um-m—best he not bring his whole strength along."

Yrsa wheeled and walked quickly off.

Adhils did give that word. Thereafter he sought another trusty man in secret. "Hasten to where the berserkers and their following are," he bade. "Tell them to leave what they're at and come back as fast as may be. Near Uppsala, let them hide in the woods and let none but me know they are here. I'll tell them what to do next."

When Helgi got the hint in the Swede-King's invitation, he chuckled to his chief skipper: "Rightly do they call Adhils a stingy fellow! I wonder if those who stay to watch the ships won't eat better than we will who go to him."

The seaman scowled. "If treachery's afoot—"

Helgi snorted. "*I* don't think him worth being careful about. Remember, we made sure his crack fighters are afar. He'll hardly risk his own dear hide against us." He swung away, quivering in eagerness. "Come, let's be off!"

He and his captains mounted horses they had brought. A hundred men tramped after them. They were a brave sight, there along the gliding, gleaming Fyris River, between the rich farmsteads of the lowlands on its far side and the high, greenwooded west bank. Helgi rode haughty, in gray ringmail, gilt helmet, scarlet cloak. Above him, borne by an also mounted youth, floated his banner, the black raven of his forebear Odin on a blood-red field. Behind the riders, a ripple ran over sunlit spearheads.

That night, though, housed by a wealthy yeoman, he slept little. He woke his band before dawn and made them keep a hard pace. At eventide they reached Uppsala.

Its stockade loomed above them, swart against a sallow heaven, as they climbed from the river road. The king's guardsmen came forth to meet them in flash and jingle of metal, lowing of lur horns; through sundown shadows, shields shone like moons. Within the gates men found a big, sprawling town, abustle with folk who dwelt in well-timbered houses that were mostly two floors high. Yet those walls cast the ways between into gloom at this hour, making burghers, women, children into blurs which buzzed and slipped from sight. There seemed to be uncommonly many swine about—the chosen beasts of Frey, who was the first Yngling. They grunted, rooted in muck, shoved coarse-bristled flanks hard against legs.

On a height outside the burg lifted the mightiest temple in the North. It was made in the wonted way of a building raised to the gods, roof piled upon roof as if the whole were about to fly skywards. But these gables and monster-headed beam-ends stood clear against the shaw which lowered behind, being neither tarred nor painted but sheathed in gold. Inside were the images, wooden but tall and richly bedecked, of the twelve high gods—Odin with the Spear, Thor with the Hammer, Frey on his boar brandishing the huge sign of his maleness, Baldr whom Hel has taken to rule beside her over the dead, Tyr whose right hand the Fenris Wolf bit off, Ægir of the Sea whose wife Ran casts nets out for ships, Heimdal bearing the Gjallar Horn which he shall blow at the Weird of the World, and others of whom there go fewer tales. At holy times, most of the shire could crowd within. Then the foremost men slaughtered horses, caught the blood in bowls, sprinkled it off willow twigs onto the folk; in giant kettles seethed the meat, of which all partook. Otherwise women tended the temple, cleaned it, washed the gods in water from a holy spring.

But in the shaw both men and beasts were hanged up, speared, and left for the ravens. Thither Adhils was wont to go by himself, to make offerings and wizardries.

"A wonderful sight," said Helgi's flagbearer.

The Dane-King scowled. "We've more to do with men than gods, I hope," he answered.

Adhils's headquarters stood in the middle of Uppsala, a widespread square of buildings inside a stockade of its own. They were handsome, and at their middle a broad, flagged courtyard rang beneath hoofs and boots. Yet Helgi's frown deepened when he saw the hall. "Gloomy is that for Yrsa to dwell in," they heard him mutter.

Servants milled about through the dusk. A groom took his bridle. He swung down and strode toward the door which gaped for him like a cave mouth. Then he stopped dead, and it was for him as if nothing else was save that white-gowned one who came to meet him.

"Welcome, King Helgi," she said, and, faltering the least bit, "my kinsman."

"Oh, Yrsa—" He caught her hands in his. In the blue twilight he hardly saw her face; but sky-glow lingered in her eyes. Above her the evenstar blinked forth.

The chief guardsman said, "My lord awaits you." Yrsa said, "Aye, come," and led the way. Helgi followed, shoulders held stiff.

Adhils sat wrapped in furs upon his high seat. Gold shone around his brow, across his breast, wrists, and fingers, though somehow the longfires and rushlights left him in darkness. Maybe this was because much smoke drifted about, gray and stinging. "Be greeted, King Helgi my friend," he purred beneath the crackle of wood. "Glad I am that you have sought to me."

Unwilling, Helgi took the pudgy hand. Adhils talked on, in words which never quite said that the Skjoldung had come to acknowledge him his overlord. Yrsa broke in: "Let our guests be seated, let us drink in each other's honor before we dine."

She brought Helgi to the place across from his host's.

Throughout the evening she took him his ale and mead. At such times he let their fingers touch, caught her gaze and smiled a strangely shaky smile for so famous a warrior. In between, in chosen words, he and Adhils swapped news of their kingdoms. Their men mingled more cheerily. A skald chanted lays. Among them was one in praise of Helgi, for which the Dane-King gave him a whole armring. His look across the floor, to Yrsa where she sat by her husband, said: You told him to make those staves, did you not?

A week went by. Adhils housed and fed his guests well, showed them around, had huntsmen take them forth on chases, spoke about trade and fisheries and such-like business—never about that for which he must know Helgi had really come. Nor did the Dane-King raise the question. He bit back his feelings and abided his chances to see Yrsa alone.

They came more than once. The first was a couple of days after he arrived. He had been out chasing wisent and rode into the courtyard near nightfall, still wet and mud-splashed, men at his back, bow slung at saddle. Dismounting, he took the weapon to unstring it. "My lord Adhils is away," said the groom. Helgi glanced upward. On the gallery of an offside sleeping-house stood Yrsa. So high aloft, she was still in sunlight, which shone tawny on her gown and struck fire-glints from deep within her hair. The sky behind her was an endless blue.

The bowstring rang.

She hailed him. "Welcome, kinsman!" Her tone drifted down clear and cool among the darting swifts. "Come have a stoup and a talk till King Adhils returns."

"Thank you, my lady," he called, and tried not to hasten through that door and up that ladder.

A serving-girl offered them mead. Reading the queen's look, she closed the door behind her. They stood on the gallery in full view of everyone; none could backbite them, but neither could anyone hear what they said. The royal garth reached below them, and the smoky shadowy town, and the grainfields beyond where the River Fyris ran until it lost itself in southward woods. There went a faint grumble of wheels, hoofs, feet, voices; a smith was beating iron somewhere, it sounded like bells; now and again a dog barked. But mostly quietness dwelt around Helgi and Yrsa. The breeze chilled him in his wet garments.

She raised her goblet of outland glass. "To your health," she said. He clashed his on hers and took a long, warming draught. They lowered them and stood a while before either could find words.

"It's good to see you," he said at last. "After seven years."

She had become altogether a woman. Slender above the thin bones, she moved more slowly—almost heavily—then erstwhile. Shadows lay under her cheekbones and around the big grey eyes. Lines had begun to show in her skin. Paler than of yore, it seemed to drink the level sunbeams. Their shiningness washed down over her breast until it picked out how her fingers strained on the goblet stem.

"They have marked you, those years," she said tonelessly. "You've grown gaunt. You're turning gray."

"I've missed you, my darling." Helgi stopped. "Likewise has your son," he added. "It would gladden you to see what a fine boy he is."

"Your son—ours—" She twisted her head away. "No. That's forever behind me."

"Must it be? I didn't come here about herrings or—you surely understand. I want to bring you home."

"No. I beg you, by everything we ever had, no, . . . Father."

Helgi's mouth writhed. He stared beyond her, to the temple on its hill and the darkling trees. "How is your life here?" he asked.

She did not answer, save in quickened breath.

"How does he treat you?" Helgi nearly shouted.

She cast a look at the courtyard, where household folk moved, and to the door behind which her maidens sat, eyes and ears, eyes and ears, tongues, tongues, tongues. "Hush," she begged. "You'd not have me speak ill of him I plighted my faith to."

"You gave me yours first," said Helgi.

She dropped her glass. It shattered. Mead pooled about her feet and dripped down between the gallery rails. Her hands wrestled. "We knew not what we did!"

"Did you know with Adhils?" he attacked.

She straightened. "Yes."

"And—?"

"It's been about as I awaited."

"He shows you your rightful honor, does he not?" She heard how much he hoped she would say no.

"Yes," she told him. "You've seen for yourself. I go about as first lady of a strong land. He . . . has not even other women." She stopped to wet lips and clear throat. "In truth, he doesn't often seek me. Which suits me well enough."

"How lonely you are," he said like a man with a spear in him.

"No, no, no. Things aren't that bad. I have my girls— you've seen them, they look on me as a kind of mother. I hear their woes and give them my redes and, and try to see they marry well. . . . I have my duties, in the household, in the temple, in everything that becomes a queen. I can go sailing on the lake when I'm here. We have guests—"

"Many? I never heard Adhils called hospitable."

She flushed. He knew she was ashamed of her husband's niggardliness, and forbore to say he knew it. "Men who come to take service here," she said hastily. "Jarls. Chieftains. Skalds, merchants, outlanders. They bring news of a world beyond this. And I—I'm taken up in cookery." Her smile was forlorn. "You'd not believe how skillful I've grown about herbs. Also healing herbs, every kind of leechcraft, why, I, I, I'm on my way to becoming a wise-woman."

He peered back at the temple. "Or a witch?" he growled.

"No!" Horror rode her voice. He thought of dead bodies rocking in the wind below yonder branches, and of Adhils on his witching stool, hunched by a kettle where nameless things boiled. "No, I've naught to do with that!" She turned on him, clenched her fists and said shakenly: "I

won't do anything unbeseeming a Skjoldung. Not even
. . . return to you . . . oh, my dearest."

They could not speak much longer. She must go oversee the readying of the hall for her husband and the
evening. Helgi was curt at that meal and drank hugely.

He and Yrsa spoke a few more times alone. The end
was always the same. Oftener he talked to Adhils, of
course, and did his best to sound out the Yngling. The
latter stayed polite. "Yes, yes," he said, taking Helgi's
arm as if he did not notice how the Dane winced, "I am
glad you came, kinsman, glad we can reach understanding.
Strife should never happen between kinsmen, as you and
I well know, eh? And I think we two are bound closer
than most—my wife, your daughter—that unluckiness of
yours and hers which I may make bold to believe I've
set aright, by giving her honorable marriage and by offering to the gods and, hm, hm, elsewhere."

More than one of his own men warned Helgi: "Something's wrong here, lord. I'm not friends with any of the
Swedish captains, no. But I've drunk and gone fishing or
hunting or played games with a few who're at their call
—yes, ha, played games with a girl or two—and something's afoot. They've told me how their chiefs go warily
about and mutter in corners. Mark them, lord, you who
nightly sit amongst them, and see if their manner don't
strike you the same."

He, his heart full of Yrsa, would give back: "Oh, belike
that trouble northward, which has most of the household
warriors away from here. They'd take it unkindly if I
pried."

After a week, the secret came to Adhils that his troopers
had swiftly fared back at his behest and lay in the woods
for his orders. He made an excuse and hurried off. To the
head berserker, a hairy, warty, slouching hulk named
Ketil, he told what had happened and bade him and his
band lie in ambush, to fall upon King Helgi while the
Danes were returning to their ships. "I'll send a number
from the burg to help you," he promised. "They'll attack
at the rear and put our foes in a pinch. For those *are*
our foes. I'll set everything at stake to see Helgi does not

escape. Well have I marked, he bears such love for my queen that I'll never be safe while he's alive."

Meanwhile Helgi and Yrsa had a last talk which could not be overheard. "Since you won't come away," he said, "I'll take my leave."

"Live gladly," she whispered, "my darling."

"You bear up well," he said. "I can do no less. But I wish—" He smote hands together and left her. She gazed after him, long beyond the time when he was gone from her sight.

To Adhils Helgi said he would be starting home. Queen Yrsa told her lord, not loudly, yet to be heard by everyone in the hall: "I think, because our guest sought us himself to bind our houses in friendship, it behooves us to send him off with gifts that will show how much this means to us."

"Why, indeed, indeed," said Adhils at once.

"He does not even blench," mumbled a drunken man of his. "What's got into the fat miser?" Everyone else was too happy at so good an ending to pay any heed. Even Helgi brightened somewhat. None could now say he had fared for naught.

And in the morning, in sight of the many who were gathered, Adhils ordered forth a wagon drawn by six white Southland horses. "This and these I give you, kinsman," he smiled, "and a bit more besides." Cheers arose as carls brought the things out of his storehouses: heavy golden rings and brooches, silver caskets full of coins from Romaborg, shimmering axes and swords, cunningly carved ivory of walrus and narwhal, jewel-crusted goblets, garments of costly weave and dye, amber, furs, oddly wrought goods from none knew where, until the axles groaned.

Helgi reddened and had trouble finding the right words for his thanks. He could not tell whether this smirking smooth-talking young man did mock him or seek to buy him off. Then his glance fell on Yrsa, and he saw such yearning that he thought it must all be because of her.

The king and the queen of the Swedes took horse to follow him part of the way. Adhils chatted glibly; Helgi and Yrsa were still. After a while the Yngling reined in.

"Well, kinsman," he said, "I fear we must bid you good-bye, looking forward to when next we are together."

"Come be our guests," said Helgi hoarsely. "Both of you."

"We can send word about that," said Adhils. "Meanwhile, fare speedily, King Helgi, to the place where you are bound."

He turned his steed. Helgi took Yrsa's hands. "Live well," he whispered in haste. "Always I'll love you. Someday—"

"Someday," she gave him back, wheeled her beast and trotted off after her lord and his men.

Helgi rode on at the head of his own troop. The river murmured and blinked in sunlight. Tree shadows dappled it. A kingfisher darted, blue as the hovering dragonflies. Hoofs plopped, leather squeaked, metal clinked. The air was thick and hot; men sweated and swatted at bugs. Westward above the leaves was piling a violet wall of clouds, and thunder rolled across miles.

Suddenly clangor awoke. Scrambling from the brush to take stance across the ruts came a host of armed men. Among them were a dozen giants, most byrnieless, who snarled and slavered and chewed their shield-rims.

Helgi reared his horse. "What in Loki's name?" he cried.

His chief skipper said: "I think King Adhils does not mean for you to keep what he gave."

"No—no, Yrsa—" Helgi half turned, as if to retreat for the first time in his life.

At his rear, around a bend in the road, came more men. They must have taken a side-way out of Uppsala—even this far off and past the noseguards on their helmets, Helgi knew some—and lurked till he had gone by them.

Helgi got down to earth, unslung his shield from the horse's crupper and took it by the handgrip. Tall he loomed among his men; only his banner, flapping in a heavily rising breeze, overtopped him. "Well, we're between the stone and the hammer," he said. "But they may find us tougher metal than they reckoned on."

River and steep, overgrown bank gave no room for the swine-array, a wedge-shaped line of mailed men with archers and slingers behind. Crowded together, death hailing from fore and aft, the Danes raised war-shout and charged ahead as best they could. In their van ran King Helgi. His sword hissed out of its sheath, blazed and screamed.

It sped against the first of the Swedes, himself big in a bright chain-coat. His shield took the blow, but he must lurch. Helgi pressed in, yelling. His blade leaped, up, down, around, dinning on helm and shield-rim, ever driving the man backward, in among his fellows. The Swede thought he saw a chance to chop at Helgi's thigh. He tried, and his sword-arm spurted blood. He swayed and sank under trampling feet.

An ax boomed on Helgi's own shield. That weapon, wielded two-handed, by its weight can smash through most men's guard. Helgi sprang in. Sheer strength warded off those blows. He got his blade beneath the axhaft and cut a leg from under his foeman.

A spear-thrust took him in the calf. He hardly marked it. "Forward, forward!" He knew how to fling a cry from the depths of his lungs, so it soared above every shout, grunt, thud, rattle, and death-moan. "Hew past them! Win free!" For he saw, above the swaying helmets and twisted faces, that if his folk could break through those who confronted them, there would be none at their backs. Turning, they could hold the road against onslaught while they withdrew, and most of them might yet win to their ships.

That could be a long running battle. He moved against a berserker. Hemmed in, he could not get up speed. The monster swung an ax aloft and brought it down in a doomsday crash. Helgi's shield splintered. His left arm nearly did. He staggered back. He would have attacked the berserker afresh, but too many roiled in the way.

Men of his fought stubbornly at his side. One by one, outnumbered, they were slain. Spears pierced him where he was not helmed or byrnied; his blood and sweat squelched in his shoes; the blows upon his metal might go through, but made bruises down to the bone. Still he fought. His blade raved and reaped.

A berserker won to his standard bearer. That youth had no hope. Brains spattered, he toppled, and the flag went into the dust. Thereafter the Danes had nothing to tell them where they should stand. The Golden Boar waved on high. The Swedes pressed in.

Clouds drew blue-black over heaven, wind arose cold, the light turned a weird brass-yellow.

Helgi, cut off from the last of his men, backed up, fighting one-handed with a sword whose edge was dinted and blunted. The dead and the hurt marked his path. Still the foe came after him. He waded out into the river, which his blood reddened. Ketil, foremost berserker, met him there, howling, yowling, hurling blow after blow like the hailstones that now began to fall, yet never seeming to feel any that the king landed upon him.

Men heard Helgi croak, "Garm breaks loose. He has swallowed the moon—" He fell, and the river bore seaward what little was left of his blood.

Together with him died all who had gone ashore. The rest got word from scouts and fled back to Denmark. Yrsa wept. Here ends the tale of King Helgi.

IV

THE TALE OF SVIPDAG

I

Yrsa wept.

She had not known what Adhils had ordered until the thing was done. Upon him she wished every kind of ill, that his ship not sail though the wind be fair, that his horse not run though he would flee his killers, that his sword never bite till it sang about his own head—"not that you are one for ship or horse or sword, you womanish spell-cooker, you crow feeding on corpses!"

Adhils waited out her wrath in that watchful calm which frightened men. When she was only crying, he said easily: "I could not behave otherwise. Well you know Helgi would at last—and not very far from today, either —have sought to overthrow and kill me, and bear you off to a life of shame that you yourself had run from."

Yrsa swallowed her tears, met his gaze so the clang could almost be heard, and told him: "It is not seemly for you to preen yourself over having betrayed that man to whom I owed the most and whom I loved the most, and for this sake I will never be true to you when you have to deal with King Helgi's men. And I will see about having your berserkers that slew him done away with, as soon as I can find lads bold enough to do it for me and their own renown."

"You rant, Yrsa, and it's empty, and well you know that," Adhils said. "Supposing I let you go, where would you seek to? Bring no threats against me or my berserkers, for this you will have no gain of. But I will make good with rich gifts the slaying of your father, with treasure and the best of lands, if you like."

The queen departed, to return in a while and stonily accept his offer. Some wondered why she did not, instead, try to reach King Hroar in Denmark. Their fellows thought belike she had a threefold reason. She, daughter and bride of King Helgi, would not flee like an outlaw and come like a beggar. Nor would she forego the washing and laying out of him, the closing of his eyes, the binding of hellshoes onto his feet, with her own hands, and seeing that he and his followers got a burial worthy of them and that honors would ever after be paid at the howe. Nor would she give up hope of revenge; already it was plain that Hroar would not take any.

None saw the queen glad thereafter. The unfriendliness in the hall was worse than before. After trying once, Adhils no longer shared a bed with her. As often as she saw a chance to do so, she went straight against his will. Doubtless he kept her only because of her kindred, her Swedish following, and her dowry.

Meanwhile the ships had brought the news to Denmark. Hrolf Helgisson was not alone in crying for war. "That lies beyond our might," said his uncle; "but do not think I lack grief for my brother." And he went away, hood drawn over his head, to mourn alone.

Later a craft from Svithjodh made landfall. The chieftain aboard spoke for Adhils. Though Helgi had fallen on his own deeds, said the message, in that he schemed against the lord in Uppsala, yet the latter was willing to make a settlement which would keep peace between the two kingdoms.

Hroar took weregild for Helgi and gave oath to bear no spear on account of the slaying.

Adhils had looked for this. Else he might never have dared strike. Through his spies and, maybe, his sorceries, he knew well how things stood for the Skjoldung house just then. The truth was, Hroar had such troubles that he could not afford strife with Svithjodh.

His brother-in-law Sævil, Jarl of Scania, had lately died. Sævil's son Hrok was a surly and greedy young man who felt he was owed much because of the help his father had given Hroar and Helgi. When refused the great ring which

Fenja and Menja had ground forth, he raged off. In part
for the sake of Hrok's mother, Hroar's sister Signy, and
in part for fear of uproar, the king did not want to cast
him out of his seat. But Scania was no longer held in a
way that Hroar could fully trust.

Furthermore, an undertaking of his had gone awry and
he knew there would be war elsewhere.

His uncle Frodhi, whom he had helped burn, had had
a son Ingjald by his first wife, Borghild of Saxland. He
had sent the child off to be reared by the grandfather,
a strong king who lived where the Elbe meets the sea.
Now Ingjald was getting along in life; but he was a powerful chieftain and likely to become king after his present
kinsman on the high seat. And he was lately widowed.
Hroar thought such an ally would make safe his flank
to the southwest; it would not matter any more that a
Swedish jarl sat on the island of Als and had the ear of
the king in Slesvik. Hroar would gain a firm peace which
would leave him free to build up his realm.

He hoped to marry his daughter Freyvar to her cousin
Ingjald.

Messengers went back and forth, and at first everything
looked promising. But it happened that Starkadh was at
the Saxon burg.

About him goes a long saga. He was of Jötun descent,
they say, and born with six hands. Thor ripped off four of
them, yet always hated him for his kindred. When Odin,
who fostered him, said he should have three men's life-
spans, Thor said he must do a nithing deed in each of
them. Odin gave him the best of weapons; Thor ordered
that never would he own any land. Odin said he would
always have money; Thor said he would never have
enough. Odin gave him victory in every fray, Thor that
he should always be wounded. Odin made him the foremost of skalds; Thor made him forget his staves once he
had spoken them. Huge, harsh, and unhappy, Starkadh
walks like a storm through that hundred-year, and ever
his coming means trouble.

At the wedding feast of Ingjald and Freyvar he stood
forth, upbraided the groom for thus linking with the get

of the man who murdered his father, and roared forth verses which brought blood to seething. Danes and Saxons alike remembered what they had suffered from each other. It came to blows and deaths. Ingjald thrust Freyvar from him and sent her home bearing word that he himself, for his honor, would bring a brand to set Hart afire.

Thus Hroar could not have the warriors of Svithjodh on his back.

That Yule Eve, Hrolf the son of Helgi passed his twelfth year and could be reckoned a man. When the boar was passed around for the making of vows, he laid hand upon it and swore: "Never will I flee from fire or iron!"

Men shouted he was indeed his father's son. Still, some thought he did more than favor his uncle: that in his quietness and dreaminess he might become one of the sluggard Skjoldungs. After all, his had been a strange birth, and he had a sister who was more eldritch than that.

The doubters changed their minds in the following summer. When the Saxons came across the Little Belt, the Danes met them on the shores of Fyn and a battle took place which brought wolves and ravens from wide around. Hrolf lacked his full growth, which would never be great, and of course he needed the help of older men. Nonetheless he went forward so doughtily and, for his age, so skillfully that he won the goodwill of every warrior.

In clang and clash, shout and shriek, maiming and manslaughter, the Danes rolled back the Saxons and crushed them utterly. There fell Ingjald, the son of Frodhi.

There too fell Hrodhmund, eldest son of Hroar.

In sorrow the Dane-King went home. From then on, his only care was to have peace. This may well have been because his younger son Hrörik, though a year ahead of Hrolf, had made a poor showing.

And the next few years made plain that it was in Hrörik, not Hrolf, that the bad blood ran. Hrörik was lazy, cowardly, and greedy. About him clustered a gang of bully boys and toadies, and he soon learned how to flatter this headman, bribe that one, and threaten yonder.

His swiftly aging father turned more and more to the nephew Hrolf.

Queen Valthjona died.

A cookfire broke loose and Hart burned down.

Hrörik and his father were on a ship to Scania, where the king would lead the rites of Harvest, reminding the folk there of himself, overawing and—he hoped—befriending Hrok Sævilsson. The journey over the Sound is short, and those aboard were clad in their best. Upon Hroar's arm gleamed the serpent ring.

"You should give me that," said Hrörik. He was quite drunk.

"I had it from my brother," said Hroar, "and I will bear it till I die."

"Well, let me see it, anyhow," his son urged him. "It's supposed to be the top treasure we have, now your hall is gone, but never have I gotten a real look at it."

Hroar took the ring off and handed it over. Hrörik turned it between his fingers. The eyes of the snake which girdles the world glittered red. "Well," said the youth, "best might be that neither of us has it." And he cast the ring overboard.

The coxswain's chant broke and the oars sprattled wildly. A moan went down the length of the hull. This was the worst of signs.

Hroar drew a fold of his cloak over his gray head. He died that winter.

Hrörik had readied himself, though he hardly needed to. Hrolf would not stand against the son of the man who had been like a father to him. Therefore the Danes hailed Hrörik their king.

Almost at once, those lands which Helgi had laid under him began to fall away. More than olden pride brought that about. The headmen had no faith in an overlord known for his sloth and miserliness. When he made only the feeblest of tries to get them back, they felt they had weighed him rightly. "Not being fools," they said, "henceforward we look to ourselves."

The heaviest loss came when the jarl at Odense—Odin's Lake—said he would be king as his father had been.

Here was a town as big as Roskilde and far older, the holiest stead in Denmark. Soon the island of Fyn had everywhere forsworn Leidhra.

Robbers fared forth, vikings harried the coats, Jute and Saxon and Wend raided with ease and laid plans for all-out war.

Then the Zealand chieftains got together and rose up. Hrolf told them he would not fight his kinsman. They told him that they would, whatever he said, and afterward take him for their lord.

Raging, Hrörik sent men to the house where Hrolf lived. Barely did the atheling escape alive. Thereafter he had no way out of unsheathing his sword against the son of his uncle and aunt, whom he had loved.

Hrörik fell in battle. Warriors and yeomen swarmed about the Thingstone to roar that Hrolf, son of Helgi, was now their king. In sorrow he clasped the oath-rings and took over the lordship of a land breaking asunder.

Meanwhile Adhils in Svithjodh had waxed rich and mighty, till men reckoned it a high honor to serve him.

II

West of the lowlands which Uppsala overlooks, the mountains of Svithjodh rise high, steep, and thickly wooded: a land of eagle and bear, rushing streams and deep dales. There dwelt a yeoman named Svip. His garth stood far from others, yet was of goodly size and housed many folk, for he was well-to-do. In youth he had been a bold warrior and fared widely about. He was wiser than he looked—a burly, squinting, grizzled man with a broken nose—and made his own judgments of everything. Though no wizard, he was thought by some to have the farsight, and sure it was that he often got warning dreams.

He had three sons, Hvitserk, Beigadh, and Svipdag. All were strong, able, and handsome. In spite of being the youngest, Svipdag overtopped his brothers in both height and might.

When he was eighteen winters old, he sought out his father one day and said forth what he had long been brooding on: "This is a dreary life, sitting up here among the fells and never even visiting others or seeing them here with us. We should go join King Adhils and his warriors, if he'll take us in."

Svip the yeoman frowned and answered, "I don't think that would be wise. I know King Adhils of old. His words can be foul as well as fair, however great his promises. And his men are bold enough, but an ill-behaved crew." He sighed in his foreknowledge and added, "However, King Adhils is both strong and famous."

Svipdag raised a fist. "Something must be risked to win something, and none may know before it's happened how his luck will twist around. This I do know, that here I will sit no longer, whatever may lie before me."

The yeoman gazed upon his son a while. Tall, wide-shouldered, raw-boned, the yellow beard already thick on his ruddy craggy face, Svipdag stood with mane held aloft to shine beneath the sun, against green pines and blue heaven. Hay harvest was just past and the steading full of that sweet smell of peace. "Well-a-day," said Svip, "I have myself been young."

Hvitserk and Beigadh decided to follow their parents' wish and stay home at least a while longer. For the outfaring one, Svip brought forth goodly gifts: a horse big enough that the rider's feet would not dangle to the ground, the full gear of a fighting man, and a long ax, darkly gleaming and sharp. He offered many such redes as: "Never thrust yourself on others, and never brag; that wins naught save a bad name. But if anyone presses on you, then guard yourself, for the way of a skilled man is to speak softly, but in danger to go strongly forward." He had no fears for Svipdag in a fray. Himself their teacher, the brothers had spent hour upon battering hour, almost every day of their lives, training in the use of weapons.

So Svipdag hugged his kindred, his best friends among the garth-folk, and whatever girl he had lately been lying with, and rode off. For a while his song floated back to them. At last it was gone in the noise of a waterfall.

Not seeming especially safe to attack, he met no trouble.

His cheerfulness brightened houses where he stayed overnight. Asking his way, he learned that King Adhils and Queen Yrsa were not in Uppsala, but at a place they owned on the shore of Lake Mälar. She spent much time there, each summer, and he was making his royal rounds.

Svipdag arrived on an eventide. Woods and grainfields rolled broadly down to a vast sheet of water, the glow of level sunbeams across it broken by the upthrusts of islands. The air was cool, damp, very still save for shouts and clatters from the dwelling, sounds which echoed about before they lost themselves in the sky. Svipdag reined in at a gate of bars set in a stockade around hall and outbuildings. It was latched on the inside, and nobody warded it. Men swarmed about the courtyard beyond, either playing or watching a swift game of handball. Svipdag called to be let in. The few who heard merely glanced his way and went on with their sport.

He reared back his horse. Hoofs smote, the latch cracked over, the gate groaned wide and Svipdag clattered into the yard.

King Adhils sat outside the hall, splendidly clad, in a gilded chair. His twelve berserkers stood or squatted around, shaggy, filthy, surly, as foul to see as to sniff. They growled and glared through the hush which had fallen on the crowd. Adhils's words dropped slow: "That man goes heedlessly ahead. The like has never been dared before. He must think well of himself."

Svipdag halted, dismounted, and beamed. "Greeting, King Adhils, my lord," he said, "for surely so finely arrayed a man must be you. I hight Svipdag, son of Svip Arnulfsson, who dwells off in the land of the Westmen but was known to you aforetime."

"You come here more rashly than your father might have counselled," said Adhils.

"No, lord. I asked to be let in, and wasn't. Such loutishness among your men dishonors you, and I hoped you'd call it well done of me to give them a lesson in manners."

.. "What?" rumbled Ketil, foremost of the berserkers. "Why, I'll step on you like the cockroach you are——"

He lumbered forward. Svipdag, always smiling, touched

the ax at his saddlebow. "Hold!" ordered Adhils. "We'll talk first. I remember Svip. He fought stalwartly for me against Aali, that day on the ice. What does his son want from us?"

"I would much like to enter your service, lord," Svipdag said.

Adhils bade him be seated. He found a log by the chair and watched the ball game after it had started anew, while he and the king talked in friendly wise. The berserkers liked this ill, glowered and muttered. When the call to eat was heard and the king led the way inside amidst these dozen guards, Ketil told him: "We're going to challenge that wolf-head and cut him down before he makes more trouble."

Adhils picked his nose. "I don't think he'll be easy to handle," he answered softly. "Still, hm, hm, yes, I would like to find out if he's as stout a fellow as he seems."

Ketil grinned over his whole warty face. While men were moving to their seats he left the king, pushed his way to the youth, grabbed him by the cloak below the throat, and snorted, "Well, do you think you're as good a warrior as us berserkers, brashly as you bear yourself?"

Svipdag flushed in the fluttering torchlight. He struck the bulky man's hand aside and spoke for the hall to hear: "Aye, I'm as good as any of you."

A bellow lifted from the twelve. They moved to close in on Svipdag. Nobody bore arms indoors, and he had left helmet and byrnie in the foreroom. Belike a dozen could pluck one apart. Men got out of their way, trying not to make that look like a scramble for safety.

"Hold! Hold, I tell you!" cried Adhils from his high seat. "Be at ease. I'll have no fighting in here, nor any time this night."

The berserkers bayed. Ketil spat at Svipdag's feet. "Dare you fight us tomorrow?" he roared. "Then you'd have to use something besides big words and overbearingness, and we'd find out how much stuff is in you."

Svipdag flung back, "I'll take you one a time. Thus we'll see who's better."

Adhils nodded. He liked the idea of a testing, for in the

course of peaceful years it had become hard to know how useful any fighter really was.

A clear voice said: "That man shall be welcome here."

Svipdag looked through shadows and fire-flicker to her who had spoken. She sat by the king, no closer than she must: a woman not tall but proud of bearing, simply clad and marked by sorrow, yet her gray eyes alight and her hair a red-brown shiningness. She must be Queen Yrsa.

Ketil hunched his shoulders and grated at her, "We've long known you wish us in hell. But we're not such weaklings we'll fall before mere words and ill will."

She turned to her husband and said, "You'll get no good if you see this through, you who feel a need of using scum like these."

Blue with rage, Ketil howled, "I blow at you and your stiffness! We're not afraid to meet him!"

Adhils signed the women to bring drink in haste. The evening passed peacefully if not quietly. The berserkers sulked; the rest of the household were cheerier. Yrsa's look kept straying to Svipdag, where he sat near an end of the hall, talking, drinking, feasting, the blithest man beneath that roof.

In the morning the holmgang took place.

This is a usage among the heathen, when men wish to fight out a challenge. They go onto a holm, a small island, where few or none can watch them and maybe get to brawling. Four willow wands mark off a field, and he who is driven beyond them is deemed to have lost. Otherwise the blows go by turns. The business can be until first blood, or yielding, or death.

Today there were more watchers than common. Adhils had had himself rowed out together with the twelve and sat among them, on a stump, peering across the staked-off meadow. Under the trees on its far side, iron gleamed around a slight figure in a blue cloak. Yrsa had come too, and a score of those warriors who attended her and felt bound to her more than to the king.

Svipdag stood tall in kirtle and trews. Save for his helmet, he had left off mail, because he would not be reckoned unfair toward his foes in this proof of his met-tle. Nor had he a shield, his ax being a two-handed weapon. Yrsa bit her lip when she saw this; her head drooped.

Ketil glimpsed that, and leered at her before he trod forth into the long grass. He began swaying, working himself up into the rage of his kind. Slaver ran down his beard. His cheeks puffed and purpled. He gnawed his shield-rim, waved his sword, and made beast noises.

Svipdag yawned. "I'd not have said you could have the first blow," he called, "did I know how weary a while you'd take to lift up that mare's heart of yours."

Ketil shrieked and charged. His sword whirled on high and whistled down. Svipdag's ax met it midway, in a clang and a shower of sparks. Then the heavy head flew back, and forward again, to crash on shield and send the berserker staggering.

Yrsa clasped fists to breasts and breathed swiftly.

Ketil recovered. He hewed and hewed—no more thought of taking turns—and mighty were those blows. Ever Svipdag halted them, and ever he battered the shield of his foeman. His ax was gripped by hands, driven by wrists and shoulders, which had logged trees and rolled rocks across mountains. The thunder sent flocks of birds crying aloft.

Of a sudden the ax smote full on Ketil's helmet. Half stunned, the guardsman let drop his shield. Svipdag's edge went into his ribs with a meaty *thwack*. Ketil yammered and sank to one knee. His neck was bent. Svipdag sheared it through. Ketil sprawled and gaped at himself.

"Svipdag, Svipdag, oh, Svipdag!" Yrsa laughed and wept.

"By my balls," hooted another berserker, "I'll cut yours from you for that, before you die!" And he sped out after revenge.

Svipdag, though sweat-soaked and panting, flashed a grin and strode to meet him. Reckless, this man was easier game. Svipdag got back breath while playing him as, on his father's homestead, he used to play bulls for fun. At the right time, he laid his enemy's belly open. Blood foamed forth.

Maddened, a third berserker sprang from the king. He

gained speed as he charged across the meadow, his own ax swinging overhead. Svipdag sidestepped and thrust out a long shank. The monster tripped. Svipdag's weapon came down across his backbone.

Aghast, Adhils yelled to his men to stay where they were. A fourth did not heed. Svipdag spun on his heel barely in time to meet that attack from behind. The berserker leaped, trying to overrun him and knock him to earth. Svipdag's ax flew so that blood made a tail behind it. He went down under the other man's shield, indeed; but he had smashed a kneecap. He freed himself in a heave, rolled clear, grabbed the ax and sprang to his feet. The madman felt no pain, belike did not know he was crippled. Yet he could not rise, and in his raving he made a poor one-legged defense. Svipdag was quickly past his guard. Again the ax bit. Four dead men lay in the daisies, the flies already thick around. Yrsa cheered and cheered.

Svipdag, red-splashed, bearing flesh wounds, clothes sodden and hair lank with sweat, heaved after air. Wild in rage, King Adhils rose to shout, "Great harm have you done me, and now you'll pay for it! Men—all of you together—slay him!"

"Never while we live!" Yrsa cried, and ran forward. Her guards dashed past her to form a shield-burg around Svipdag as she bade.

The eight berserkers who were left circled around, growled, mewed, spat oaths and taunts, made as if to rush. The queen's men stood firm, spears and swords aloft. Behind them, their archers strung bows and twanged these, a deep sound as if angry wasps were on the way. It was no use trying to overcome that many.

Yrsa went to her husband, where he shuddered and croaked, stood before him and said, "Call off your dogs. My men are going to defend Svipdag till you give him peace."

"Oh, you're happy today, aren't you, Yrsa-bitch?" Adhils answered. He made as if to strike her. She clenched fists, gave him look for look, and said:

"This fight was none of his asking. He came in good

faith to offer us his service. They set on him, those trolls. Well, see what he's shown them to be worth! Glad should you be to get that blubber out of your battle-line. Make peace, I say! You'll win more honor with this one man than with all the berserkers who ever befouled the earth."

"What care you for my honor, Yrsa?"

"Little enough, in truth; yet more than you, it seems."

Thereupon Yrsa spoke soothingly. The years had given her a ready tongue for showing where wisdom lay. In the end she did make peace between Adhils and Svipdag. When the newcomer returned to the mainland and the household learned what had happened, they swarmed about him and avowed that never before had such a wight come to be their brother in arms.

Nonetheless the queen found a chance to whisper to him, "Be wary. Those eight will not long abide by the oath they gave you."

He nodded. Yestereven, down at his end of the hall, he had heard in full about the slaying of King Helgi nine years before. He thought in youthful hotness that that had been the worst of nithing deeds; and today, this woman who suffered most from it had saved his life.

"Yes, I think I've done them less scathe thus far than I ought to, lady," he told her.

Her eyes widened in fright. "What do you mean? No, Svipdag! Beware! Never be alone!" Then other folk drew nigh and there could be no more frankness between them.

At the queen's urging, Adhils gave Svipdag the seat of honor opposite him that evening, and courtesy and praise as long as men drank together. The berserkers were not on hand. Adhils had already talked to them, out of everybody else's earshot. He said later that he had been calming them. Svipdag had marked how they slouched off seeming grimly pleased. The yeoman's son had acted as if he awaited nothing untoward, and as if he spent the afternoon whetting his ax merely because any good workman would do so. When the king said he should not sleep on a bench tonight, rather in a guesthouse across the courtyard, Svipdag had thanked him . . . then quietly, under cover of dusk, borne mail and weapon in a bundle of underpadding, not to that house, but to a corner of the hall's foreroom.

Much drink went down. It was late when Adhils bade him goodnight. Outside lay drizzly gloom. The forechamber was like a well of pitch. Svipdag was glad of that. He could don helm and ring-byrnie by feel, unseen and thus not warning anybody.

On firm legs—he had drunk far less than he pretended —he crossed the yard. Near the guesthouse, that happened which he awaited. The eight berserkers came from shadow and fell upon him.

He laughed, got back to wall, and let them come. In the murk it was hard to see. He, alone, was free to strike anywhere, and he was iron-clad.

He had killed one when the racket of what should have been a quick and silent murder brought men stumbling out of the hall. They hastily stopped the fight, and raged at the shame that this had brought on them.

Adhils could do naught else than say likewise, and tell the berserkers they lied in claiming that he had egged them on. He outlawed them on the spot. They left under scorn and jeers, storming off into the rainy night, vowing to come back and harry the whole of Svithjodh.

"I give that threat no worth," said Adhils, indoors again. "You've shown how there's nothing to those loons."

"I'm not so sure, lord," answered Svipdag. Now that he dared, he drained a mighty stoup of mead.

"Well, you must become what they were supposed to be, and give me no less guarding than the twelve of them did," said the king with his narrow smile. His glance flicked across Yrsa, whose eyes shone upon Svipdag like suns. "The more so," he added slowly, "since the queen wants you to take their place."

"Will you?" she breathed. "May a good Norn give that you will!"

Svipdag was still for a bit. He no longer really cared to serve this Adhils. However, having today won a high name, he might hope for even more of the honor, as well as the wealth, which he had come for. And Yrsa beseeched. . . .

"Yes," said Svipdag. "I do thank you, my lady."

III

Hrolf Helgisson had but sixteen winters when the chieftains made him king of a shattered Denmark. Though they meant well in the guidance they gave him, none was a Regin or a Sævil. He must grope his way forward into the craft of masterdom. No matter how apt, he was bound to make blunders. He was too mild with his guardsmen, who thus became a wild and overbearing lot; and many folk misliked it when he followed the way of Adhils and, one by one, took a dozen berserkers into his service.

Patiently he explained to those who spoke against this: "I am more like my uncle Hroar than my father Helgi. I would rather build than burn. However, Hroar could not have been what he was nor done what he did, without his brother for sword and shield. I am alone, these are hard times, and before we can hope for peace, we must put down violence. To that end, I use what means come to hand."

He had inherited great treasures and gave them out freely. No king's men were better housed, feasted, clothed, armed, and ring-bedecked than his. Rough they were, but they loved him. Had he wanted, he could have led them in storming Asgard. (Some said it in just those words, because Hrolf, like his forebears, was no very eager worshipper of the gods.) He found plenty for them to do. And all the while he was learning.

In four years, he scoured robbers out of the Zealand woods and vikings from the coasts. Hrok Jarl made an uprising in Scania; Hrolf fared across the water and won a battle wherein Hrok fell; for the sake of Signy the mother, Hrolf gave his foe a lavish burial, but he also made sure of getting a man in that part whom he could trust. He regained Mön, Langeland, and some lesser islands. Once more safe, Roskilde flourished. Likewise did the little fishing port on the Sound, drawing traders until they began to call it Cheaping-Haven. In between his war-farings, Hrolf went about among the shire-Things, or sat in his hall in Leidhra, heard men out, gave judgments, and strove to make them agree to better laws.

"I would see you get back what you had under Frodhi the Peace-Good and Hroar the Wise," he told them, "in a kingdom so big and strongly timbered that it will not crumble again around you."

Meanwhile his half-sister Skuld was growing.

After Ingjald the Saxon sent Freyvar Hroarsdottir home, she was wedded to Ulf Asgeirsson, a mighty headman in the north of Zealand. Hrolf raised him from sheriff to jarl and gave Skuld into his keeping. Ulf steered his district well, so that the busy king had scant reason to see him. But at the end of those four years, he sent to Leidhra and invited his overlord to come visit after the Harvest offerings. The messenger added in Hrolf's ear: "He says it's a heavy matter; he did not tell me why."

Hrolf looked hard at him. "Can you yourself guess?" he asked. The man grew unhappy. Hrolf smiled, albeit with small mirth. "Well, I'll not squeeze you," he said. "I'll merely come."

He made a brave sight when he rode into Ulf's garth. Hrolf did not tower as his father had done; he was no taller than most, and of spare build. Still, he moved like a wildcat, winning fights with much bigger men by sheer speed and skill. Amidst wings of reddish-yellow hair, his face was high in the cheekbones, wide between the large gray eyes under their darkly arching brows, the nose straight and a little tilted, mouth full in the lips and quick to bend upward. But under a soft, close-cropped amber beard jutted the Skjoldung chin. His voice was light, usually rather slow and seldom loud.

He was also akin to the wildcat in cleanliness. If a bathhouse was anywhere near, he went into its steam, scrubbed and doused himself, daily. Men laughed that King Hrolf was hospitable to all the world aside from fleas. He liked good clothes. Today he wore a white linen shirt, red kirtle stitched with gold thread, belt of tooled leather with a broad silver buckle, blue breeks with white

cross-gaiters, sealskin shoes, gilt spurs, saffron-dyed cloak
trimmed with marten and held by a garnet-studded brooch,
gold around head and arms and fingers and scabbard.

He had only a score of guardsmen along. North Zealand
being a poor and sparsely settled land, he did not want to
lay a burden on its chief. However, these young man were
in iron that shone and jingled, and in colorful cloaks.
As they neared their goal, they each winded a horn and
broke into a gallop. It was a storm, noisy and full of
rainbows, that gusted into the garth.

Ulf and Freyvar made them welcome. Nonetheless,
plainly they were a troubled pair. Hrolf said he would like
to see the grounds during the afternoon, and his host and
hostess grabbed at the chance.

They went afoot from the hall, a few men following
out of hearing. This was a chilly fall day. Wind boomed
across stubblefields and the gray heath beyond them.
Clouds hastened through an ice-pale sky where a flight
of storks was outward bound, high and high above.
Closer down, some ravens flapped black and grukking.
Off on one side lifted a wood, leaves ablaze in red, russet,
brass, bronze, ripped loose and whirled away by the blast.
Afar northward, a steel glimmer bespoke the sea.

"What did you want to talk about?" asked Hrolf.

"Your sister Skuld," said Freyvar. She was a slender
woman; her husband was short and stocky. "She makes us
fear for our own children, what she may lead them into."

"I'm wary of what she may bring on the whole land,"
said Ulf. He waved around. "Here is a stern earth at best,
full of secret places and uncanny beings. There are fens
from which many a man or child or beast has never come
back. There are barrows where heatless fires and walking
shapes are seen after dark. Often have I myself heard hoofbeats and hound-howlings go through the night air. Wise
folk give such things a wide berth. I fear Skuld does not."

"She was always a strange child," sighed Freyvar. "She
hardly ever wept, even when little, or showed love or
seemed to want it. Mostly she went about by herself. She
was willful, given to screaming rages, scorning woman's
work, most fain to climb trees, swim—oh, she swims like

an otter—range the wilds, later on hunt and fish and, yes, for a task, sharpen knives—"

"I've heard somewhat about that, of course," said Hrolf. 'Well, if her soul seems too much a man's, think who her father was."

"I think more who her mother was," growled Ulf. "Boyish girls I've seen before. Mostly they change after their breasts have budded. Skuld—she's quieted, though she's no less stubborn and sharp-tongued. The servants dread her, so spitefully does she treat them. What frets me most is how she's taken to what looks like spellcraft. Not just a rune cut on a fingernail for luck; no, I've heard her mutter and seen her make passes in ways unknown to me, who've dealt with many different kinds of folk. She's been glimpsed off on the heath, squatted before a dolmen, on her hands the blood of a bird she'd torn apart. She runs into yonder woods, heedless alike of wolves, outlaws, and trolls. Then she's gone long at a time, and won't say where she was or what she did. But when her cloak slipped aside, we've seen that she carried a shoulderblade with signs carved on it. I don't know where she got such a thing."

Hrolf winced. "I don't care for this myself," he said. "She could be only playing, however, maybe teasing you. How old is she now—twelve? Let me see if I can't win her trust and sound her out."

That evening he asked Skuld to sit and drink beside him in the high seat which Ulf had turned over to the king. She came readily.

By bright firelight, in a room warm and full of the smells of woodsmoke, roast meat, rushes on the floor, where flames crackled and talk and laughter rang, Skuld did not seem like any being of darkness. She was very beautiful. The slimness of her age was on her, but not its awkwardness; she flowed rather than walked. The unbound locks of a maiden tumbled straight and black over a simple white gown, down to her waist. That was blackness which shone, as shines a starlit lake. Her face was narrow and thinly chiseled, skin swan-white, lips startlingly red. But mostly one saw the eyes, large and long-lashed, a changeable green which could shift from almost blue to almost golden, like sea-waves. Her voice was husky, though in anger it grew shrill and saw-edged.

Tonight she smiled and raised a goblet to clink upon her brother's horn. "Skaal," she said, "Welcome. I've seen too little of you."

"We must do something about that," Hrolf answered.

"When?" She was at once aquiver. "Here I sit in this wretched frog-pond, yawning and moldering, while you —Take me back with you!"

"In time, in time," said Hrolf. "You have yet to learn what beseems a wife."

"A wife!" she fleered. "To cook, brew, wash, sweep, oversee, and wait on a pack of drunken oafs—to be swived whenever it pleases that one of them who calls me his, and each year set my life at stake, in blood and anguish, to farrow—No!"

"You'll have a high standing, Skuld. But you must be worthy of it, and that means doing its work. Do you think I'd not liefer be off chasing deer than sit and listen to the dreary squabbles of dullards and search for a judgment that'll quiet them down? Do you think a war or a robber-hunt has no long treks through rain, no camps in the mud, no hunger or thirst or vermin or runny guts? Do you—"

"Have done! You dwell in great halls, you make merry with friends and lemans, you fare across lands and seas, you meet new men and hear new tales, skalds chant your praises, you play draughts across whole kingdoms with men for pieces, and when you're dead they'll remember you, you won't rot forgotten. . . . Do *you* think your father's daughter, born undersea to an elven woman, will not seek for the same?"

"Well . . . well, we must weigh the matter—" In unease, Hrolf recalled what ill things had been foretold of this girl. "Tell me, have you any memory of your first years?"

She calmed, her moods being always quick to shift; she stared before her and murmured: "I am not sure.

What does anybody remember? Sometimes it seems to me there was . . . a huge green coolness, where shapes flitted and the tides pulsed like music. . . . Songs, plucked strings and shivering silver pipes, or was it only sea-birds, or a dream? My dreams are not the same as those of other folk."

"They say you skip off by yourself. That's not safe, you know."

"For me it is."

"Where do you go?"

Skuld laughed, a sweet sound. "No, brother mine, here comes my time. Tell me about the world outside, Leidhra, Roskilde, everything splendid. Oh, do!"

Wanting to gain her friendship, he obeyed. She listened bewitchingly, head cocked, gaze bright upon him, questions clever and eager. He thought maybe their father had misunderstood and no doom was in her after all.

But the moon was full tonight, and Ulf had told how Skuld fared abroad now and again after sunset. Before the company went to sleep, Hrolf drew a couple of his best men aside and ordered: "Find yourselves a hiding place where you can watch the yard. Stay awake by turns. If you see my sister go forth, come at once and awaken me."

"Waken the king, lord?" asked one of them doubtfully. "You could be having a dream—"

"Which could be meaningful for the land," Hrolf broke him off. "I know. Well, what my sister is about is maybe graver than that. So while we're here, I set that law aside. You *will* call me—by stealth, that nobody else may know."

For the same reason he refused Ulf's offer of a thrall woman and entered the shut-bed alone. He left his clothes on. His thought was rewarded when, in thick gloom, the panel slid back and a hand shook him by the shoulder.

He followed the man outdoors, where he buckled on his sword. "She went off yonder," said the warrior, pointing toward the wildwood.

"Well done," said the king. "Wait here for me."

"You're not going alone, my lord!"

"Yes, I am, and I've no time to jaw about it." Hrolf hastened from the garth.

The moon was high and small, yet so bright that most stars were drowned. The air lay moveless, cracklingly cold. Rime covered the stubble and the heather beyond. He could barely make out the shape, in a blowing pale gown, which flitted ahead of him. She did not look behind her. He reckoned that if she did, he could stay unseen through this tricky light.

When she had gone into the woods, it grew harder to follow. Brush clawed, dry leaves rustled, twigs snapped. The moon-glow did naught but dapple blackness. Skuld fared more swiftly and softly than Hrolf had awaited.

Of a sudden he stumbled out onto a meadow. He stopped short and drew a whetted breath.

Trees lowered hoary-headed around the sere grass, whose frost glimmered beneath the moon. In the middle of it stood a high bauta stone, a lichenous slab raised long ago by a folk unknown to a god unknown. The howl of a wolf came, distance-dwindled to little save a shiver, as if the chill gnawing inward through his flesh had begun to speak.

Before the stone stood a woman. Tall and full-formed, in sheening dress and cloak, she was ringed around by awe. Hair more nightful than the sky streamed past a face which recalled his sister's. Mainly he saw her eyes. Even in the wan moonshine, they shone hawk-golden. Her upward-turned hands bore a naked sword.

"Wayfarer, halt," she sang more than said, "and wander no further, ere in the end you must."

"Am I in a dream and all unawakened?" he asked. His voice seemed as far off as the wolf's, and he as far from himself. "Did my man do my bidding?"

"Sleep you or wake you, say what you hunt here, Hrolf son of Helgi King."

"My sister I follow."

"Seek her no longer. Search would find sorrow only. Grief soon enough is given to men; never foreknow your weird. Go home again, King, take hold of the rudder, strengthfully steering forward. Mightily raise what men will remember."

"Who is this hailing Hrolf?"

"Ask me not that, for only the death-doomed need to bear names for crying."

"How are you here, and why do you warn me, lady of loveliness? Have you below your heart ever borne her, the girl who brings grief on me?"

"A word may not change when once it is uttered. Not even Norns can that. Hear me, though, son of Helgi my darling: weal do I wish for you. Let the girl go, and live out your lifespan. Deep may you drink of sunlight, live every day in love and in gladness, dreading no dark to come; at last may you stand and laugh at the Norns, so winning the war you lost.

"See what I bear, this sword that hight Skofnung. Dearly from dwarves I got it. Wield the blade well, and wide may its fame go, high as of Hrolf himself. Strike down the illdoer, stand for the folk, O Hrolf, son of him I loved."

He knelt to take it from her; and she was gone; and he went back.

With Gram, which Sigurdh bore against Fafnir, and with Tyrfing the accursed, and with Lövi of which more later, Skofnung was one of the magical swords, that never rusted and always bit. Goodly it was to see, long and broad, shimmering now brown and now blue. The haft was of a black, hard, unknown wood, gold-entwined, and on the pommel was a many-faced stone, clear white but splintering light into fiery hues. Runes were graven in the crossguard which none could read.

Hrolf tried no more to find out what Skuld did in the wildwood.

IV

Svipdag must attend King Adhils on his rounds and later at Uppsala. But when Queen Yrsa returned to the head burg, the young man was often at her side. The king was displeased. He could do nothing much about it, though, for nothing untoward happened. When those two were together, it was always in sight of others. If they were not always in hearing, such of their talk as got heard was harmless. Svipdag spoke mostly of what had gone on and what was told around his father's lonely steading, she of the wider world she knew, adding many wise redes for him.

As their friendship waxed, he came more and more to tell her his hopes and dreams, while she more and more remembered aloud for him her days with King Helgi. They did their best not to let this be overheard. Still, it could not altogether be hidden from Adhils how the wind blew.

He kept his own counsel and stayed smooth toward Svipdag. Indeed he had gain from this new guardsman. Svipdag was the strongest and ablest in the whole troop, ever the winner at most sports and games. Nonetheless, being fair-minded, polite, willing to listen when others spoke, withal merry, he kept their liking.

Thus the year passed, and spring came again, when Svipdag and Yrsa walked under blossoms, and summer's great greenness.

Then the king got war-word. The berserkers he had cast out were come home to Svithjodh. In the Baltic islands and along the shores of Finland and Wendland, they had found ships, they had gathered crews of ruffians, and now they were on Lake Mälar, looting, killing, and burning everywhere around.

Adhils blinked at Svipdag. "This is somewhat because of you, my friend," he said in his mildest tone. "Let you, therefore, go against them. You shall have as many men as you need."

The youth flushed. "I'm hardly ready to lead a host—" he began.

"And stand in its van to be killed!" said Yrsa hotly.

"No, no, here's your chance to prove yourself," smiled Adhils. "You shall be the leader."

Svipdag thought a while before he answered, "Then I want from you my own following of twelve men, whom I pick myself."

Adhils made a wry mouth. He could not well say other than: "That you shall have."

"Any of mine," offered Yrsa. Svipdag grew a deeper red as he thanked her.

He chose his dozen carefully, both from among those who favored the queen and those who unquestioningly upheld the king. All were strong warriors and glad to take him as their head below Adhils. With them he swore brotherhood, in the temple on the bracelet of three thick gold rings after it was dipped in the blood of a bullock, calling to witness Frey of the earth, Njörd of the sea, and Thor of the heavens. Thereafter he and his captains led forth a host. The king stayed home.

Well had Svipdag hearkened to older men during the past year. When he set up his swine-array and standards, he knew many tricks of war, such as laying down caltrops in the long grass.

The vikings charged. The fighting grew stiff. They were driven back, and those who got in among the caltrops fared ill. One berserker died, and a heap of rovers. The rest fled to their ships and hurried off.

Svipdag bore this news to Uppsala. The king thanked him much. Queen Yrsa said before the packed hall: "In truth, better men are housed here when one man like Svipdag sits among us, than when your berserkers did."

Sourly, the king agreed. He gave a feast and gifts to the warriors. It was as nothing to what the queen gave a week later.

The year wore away. Svipdag became marshal of the guard, which brought him a herd of duties. He was likewise often out hunting, fishing, boating, swimming, visiting as well as being visited. In his house, besides servants, he kept a lively wench or two. Yet he found ever more excuses to see Yrsa. Her husband glowered.

Meanwhile the berserkers who were left brooded on their hatred. They gathered a larger gang than before, and early next summer sailed back to Svithjodh. It seemed to them they had made a mistake earlier in landing near Uppsala, where the king's crack fighters were on hand.

This time they left their ships well north, on the Gulf of Bothnia, and trekked overland to the mountains, thence southward till they reached the country of the Westmen. From there they meant to strike swiftly at Uppsala. Along the way they plundered, slew, tortured, raped, laid waste, and drew into their band every kind of outlaw and evildoer.

Word reached Adhils. Again he bade Svipdag go against them. This time he would have fewer folk than erstwhile —a third fewer than the wolf pack—for the berserkers had also chosen their season craftily. Able-bodied men were scattered far and wide getting in the crops.

"I'll take a different way with the household troops," said Adhils, "more roundabout, that the foe be unaware. We can arrive at the same time as you, who'll be kept to the pace of older yeomen and untrained lads among those we can summon. Meet the foe head-on. When he has thought for none save you, I'll fall on him from behind."

Svipdag scowled. "Lord, it won't be easy, keeping track not just of the vikings but of each other."

"We'll use scouts and runners," said Adhils loftily, and would hear no more.

Yrsa found a chance to walk with Svipdag, down by the gleaming river, none but an old deaf tirewoman to watch them. "I fear for you," she said in woe. "I feel in my marrow, Adhils thinks it'll do no harm if you lose and bite the hillside. Then those madmen can be talked into supposing their honor is avenged. They can be bought off cheaply, or even—" a crawling went over her—"taken back among us."

He looked down at the bent head and answered low, "All men must dree their weirds. Yet what you fear shall not happen while blood remains in me, my lady."

She cast him a look he had seen before, in the eyes of a netted swan.

Awkward though their hastily gathered levy was, Svipdag and his captains arrived sooner than the berserkers had awaited. In a dale of steep red walls and rushing waters, under greenwood and across flowery meadows, a hard fight began.

The berserkers had whipped their unruly followers into a team. Back and back they drove the raw, outnumbered Swedes. Never a sign was there of the king or his trained household troops.

Now it is to be told of Svip the yeoman, that he awakened from sleep, sighed deeply and said to Hvitserk and Beigadh: "Sore is the need of Svipdag, your brother, for he's in battle not far hence and has great odds against him. He's lost an eye and gotten many wounds besides. Three berserkers has he felled; three are left."

Swiftly they armed themselves and what men they could get, and hastened to where their father had told them. When they reached the dale, strife was still going on in the light night. By then, the vikings had twice as many as Svipdag. Mightily had he fought, but he reeled from his hurts and his men lay slain in windrows. And still the king had not come to help him.

Yet the foe were also worn down. It is no slight thing to wield iron hour after hour; and they too had suffered wounds and losses aplenty. The fray had broken into knots of men who lurched about, battering with weapons blunted into clubs, or crept away and struggled for breath. Upon this burst a band small but fresh, well-led, bearing newly whetted steel, and wild for revenge.

The brothers went straight to where the berserkers were, and the swapping of blows ended in the deaths of the latter. It needed only a few more killings for fear to sweep through the outlaw gang. Svipdag's men rallied and joined a charge on them. They broke. Those who asked for their lives gave themselves over to the brothers. A huge booty fell likewise to these.

Because they wanted to go home, and anyhow no garth hereabouts could feed them all, the Swedes returned straight to Uppsala. Svipdag went along on a litter, in the care of his brothers. He had swooned and they were unsure whether he would live.

Reaching the burg and royal hall, they found Adhils already there. He thanked them aloud for this work of manhood, lamenting that he had lost touch with the levy and been unable to find it in time. But erelong word

leaked out that the king had been near the spot and forbidden his troop to go further.

Svipdag bore grievous hurts. Worst were two gashes on
his arms and one in his head, which must be sewn up.
And his left eye was gone. Sickness came into his flesh.
Long he lay in a coalbed of fever, muttering or raving or
heavily adrowse. Queen Yrsa tended him. She paid no
heed to pus and stink, she washed and soothed him as if
he had been her own child or her own man, and when
he began to mend, she brought him milk and broth and
spent as many hours at his bedside as he could stay
awake.

Healing at last, gaunt and slow-moving, he went between his brothers to stand before Adhils, at eventide in
the hall. "How good to see you back," said the king, not
as if he meant it. "What would you of me?"

"Leave to go," said Svipdag. He kept his gaze from
Yrsa, who gasped and brought a hand to her lips. "I'll
seek a lord who shows me more honor than you. Ill have
you paid me for warding this land and for the victories I
must win on your behalf."

"Well, I have said it was only bad luck which kept me
from joining you. Stay, you three brothers, and I will do
well by you. None shall stand higher."

Svipdag held himself from telling the king he lied; and
as for Adhils, he did not really urge them to abide. His
eyes kept shifting aglitter toward Yrsa. She sat dumb.
Soon Adhils asked whither they meant to fare.

"We've not decided that yet," Svipdag admitted. "I do
want to learn the ways of other folk and other kings,
and not grow old here in Svithjodh."

"Well," said Adhils happily, "to show I've no hard
feelings, I promise you safe conduct should you ever
come visit us."

Svipdag looked at Yrsa. "I will," he said.

In the morning the brothers busked themselves to go.
When they were ready, Svipdag sought the queen in her
bower. The room where she and her maidens were stood
open to sight of trees, whose rustling blew in on a green-
smelling wind, and to a heaven where clouds wandered

white. She stared long at him, his face scarred and aged, bones jutting under sallow skin, a black patch where an eye had been. Silence grew.

"I would . . . thank you . . . my lady," he said at length, very softly, "for the honor you have shown me."

"Little enough," she answered, herself scarcely to be heard beneath the wind outside. "Now Helgi sleeps well. And I, I need no more see his murderers daily about me." The distaff fell from her hands. She reached out. "Oh, why must you go?"

"This is no longer good for either of us," wrenched from him. "I've freed you of something, maybe, but— I've marked how I'm become a drawn sword between you and the king."

"There was never much else between us," said Yrsa as if her girls were not around her.

"I would only make your sorrows worse, my lady," said Svipdag. "In the end, through me you could even come into danger of your life."

She nodded. Bleakness fell upon her. "More likely, I would bring about your downfall. You're right, here is no longer a place for you. Go, then, and luck and gladness ride at your side." Her shield broke. "Will I ever see you again?"

"If that is my weird, as truly it is my will, I swear so."

They spoke only a few words more ere Svipdag left the room. She heard hoofbeats dwindle hollowly away.

V

The brothers went to their parents, where Svipdag spent the next several months getting back his strength and learning how to land his blows one-eyed. He was less blithe than formerly.

Yet he was young, and the world reached before him. Eagerness waxed as his health did. Hvitserk and Beigadh were no less fain to be off. They asked Svip where they might best betake themselves.

"Well, the highest honor, the biggest chance for gold and renown, is with King Hrolf in Denmark and his warriors," the yeoman told them. "I've heard said for sooth that thither are flocking the best fighters in the Northlands."

"Where do you think they will seat me?" Svipdag wanted to know.

His father shrugged and said, "That may in some wise depend on you. But I hear of King Hrolf that his like is not to be found. Never does he spare gold and other dear things for whoever will take them of him. He's skimpy of size, I hear, but great in his thinking and knowledge, a handsome man, haughty toward those who're not mild, but easygoing and friendly toward small folk and any who don't set themselves athwart him. A poor man has no more trouble meeting him and getting a fair word than does a wealthy one. At the same time, he's making his neighbor kings into underlings. Some freely give him their oath, for under him are peace and just laws. Aye, his name will be unforgotten while the world stands."

Svipdag nodded. He had heard the same at Uppsala. "After what you've told," he said, while his brothers added quick yesses, "I think we should seek King Hrolf, if he'll take us in."

"You must see to that yourselves," answered the yeoman. Sadly: "Me, liefest would I that you stayed home with us."

They would not hear of this, as he had foreknown. Erelong they bade their father and mother goodbye. Afterward she smote her hands together and said: "She who's hatched eagles and can't fly. . . . Well, we have our daughters and grandchildren."

Of the faring south is naught to tell. At the Sound the brothers bought ship-passage for themselves and their horses, and from Cheaping-Haven rode across Zealand to Leidhra.

Roskilde had drawn off most of those who once lived there. Hrolf, like Helgi before him, thought it best to keep his brawling guardsmen away from the town. Moreover, Leidhra was the olden seat of the Dane-Kings, founded by Dan himself, hallowed by memories of Skjold the Sheaf-Child. And it was no mere stronghold. The stockade ringed big houses as well as the royal hall, lesser dwellings, sheds, bathhouses, barns, stables, mews, kennels, workshops which made clangorous the daylit air. Even so, many who had to do with the king's household spilled forth in homes strewn across that land of farms and woodlots which rolled richly green from Leidhra to world-edge.

North, south, east, west, four well-kept highroads ran to the gates of the burg. Traffic went thick upon them, wheels, hoofs, feet. Outside the walls were always booths or tents which traders raised, for a few days of dickering before going on elsewhere: a swirl of bright garb, a hubbub of talk and laughter, maybe a roar when two men put on a fight between their stallions. Hearthsmoke made the air bittersweet, above a ripeness of roasting and hay and pitch and dung and sweat and pine planks under a summer sun. Here trundled an oxcart, there clattered a warrior, yonder a smith banged hammer on forge, a carpenter's saw went *ret-ret,* naked children tumbled amidst yapping dogs in the dust between buildings, a woman drew water from a well which tapped the nearby stream, a maiden fluttered her lashes at the three tall newcomers.

"This is less in size than Uppsala," said Hvitserk.

"Well, yes, seeing as how most of the trade is elsewhere," said Beigadh. "Here's a town for chieftains."

"I was about to finish, it seems greater in heart."

"And surely in its hall," said Svipdag, pointing. For last year, the seventh of his reign, Hrolf had built a new one, as grand in every way as had been his uncle's. Only did he leave off gilt antlers, lest they bring the same bad luck; but cunning carvings swarmed over every gable and beam-end.

"After that gloomy cave where Adhils squats . . . how bright in here!" said Svipdag as they entered.

The king was on hand, playing a board game against an older man. When the brothers greeted him, he leaned back on the bench, smiled, and asked their names. They told him, and added that Svipdag had been a while with King Adhils.

Hrolf's brow darkened. He spoke calmly enough:

"Then why did you come here? Between Adhils and me is no close friendship."

"I know that, lord," said Svipdag. "Nonetheless I would much like to become your man if it can be done, and my brothers too, though you can see they're little used to this kind of thing."

"Wait." King Hrolf sat straight. "Svipdag . . . why, yes, I've heard of you, if you're the one—how you three slew Adhils's berserkers and did other mighty deeds."

"We are those, lord," said Svipdag; and less boldly: "Your mother Queen Yrsa was a friend to me."

Hrolf brightened. He bade them sit down and shouted for drink. They talked long and long. That evening the king had them stand by his high seat, and after the guardsmen had come in, he uttered forth who they were. "I had not thought I would make any who have served King Adhils into comrades of mine," he said. "But since they've sought me I'll take them in and believe it'll pay us well, for I see that these are doughty fellows."

"Where shall we sit?" asked Svipdag a bit stiffly.

Hrolf pointed rightward, where a stretch of bench stood empty before one saw the first of the row of warriors. "By that man who hight Starulf; but leave room for twelve."

It was a fairly honorable seat. After all, the brothers had yet to prove themselves here. When he sat down, Svipdag asked why a dozen places should stand unused. Starulf told him that those belonged to the king's berserkers, who were away at war. Svipdag frowned.

Hrolf was unwed, because thus far he saw no house to which he felt sure he wanted to tie himself that firmly. However, by two daughters of yeomen he had girls of his own, Drifa and Skur. They were quite young, though old enough to serve in the hall, both pretty, both taken with the brothers from Svithjodh, and showed these goodwill.

Likewise did the other guardsmen as friendships ripened. Next year, they said, the king would take the field himself, not just have a few shipsful out. Then he would be ready to win back Fyn, second of the Danish islands. Many a chance would there be for a warrior to gain renown. Meanwhile were ease, merriment, traveling about among the Thingsteads, hunting, feasting, sports, a hearty life under an unstinting lord. Svipdag, Hvitserk, and Beigadh agreed they had come well to harbor.

So time passed through the summer and to the fall, when the berserkers came home.

Svipdag bristled to see those hairy hulks tread in, armed as if for battle, so much like those that had troubled Yrsa. He had been warned of their custom. They went from man to man, and their leader asked each who sat whether he deemed himself as good as them. Not even the king was free of this. To keep the peace with those beast-men, who were of high use in war, he was wont to answer something like: "It's hard to say, for surely you're fearless, you who have won such honor in weaponstrife and bloodspilling among many folk both north and south." The rest of the troop did likewise, hitting on different words which would not sound like outright cringing. Still, it was easy to hear both fear and shame in their voices.

A bearded giant loomed over the eye-patched Swede and hawked the question. Svipdag sprang up. His sword hissed forth. (Hrolf let his men bear arms in the hall, saying he would not dishonor them by mistrust.) "In no way am I less than every one of you!" he shouted.

Shock brought stillness along the snapping, fluttering fires. The berserkers gaped, until their leader shook himself and challenged: "Hew at my helmet!"

Svipdag did. Metal rang. His edge would not bite, either on the helmet or on the mail which this band wore in spite of their name. The berserker bawled and drew blade. They squared off to fight. Hvitserk and Beigadh snatched their own weapons out.

King Hrolf came on the run. He sprang between them, nearly getting cut down. "You must not do this!" he cried. "We've foemen enough without squandering each other's blood. Hereafter, Agnar, Svipdag, you'll be reckoned alike, and both good friends of mine."

The men snarled and glared. But their king stood in

their way and spoke words both stern and mild. Too many brawls had there been in this troop, he said. He would have no more of it. Strong they all were, and he would hate to lose any of them. Nonetheless, whoever picked a fight with a brother in arms, be it these three from Svithjodh who had slain the twelve of Adhils—at that the berserkers grew thoughtful, insofar as they were able—or somebody longer here and highly honored: that man would be sent away forever, outlawed in Denmark. Let them make peace!

In the end, Hrolf had his will. Thereafter the one-eyed newcomer was looked upon in awe.

VI

When springtime came around again, the Dane-King gathered a host and fared off to Langeland. Thence they overran Turö and afterward the whole southern half of Fyn. They had victory wherever they came. All the kings whom Hrolf overwhelmed, he made to swear him troth and pay him scot. His following swelled as the weeks went by, for men swarmed to join him, who was known to be more fair-minded and openhanded than other lords. He could pick and choose whom he would take into his household troops.

One failure did he have. Svipdag reminded him of those treasures King Helgi his father had gotten from King Adhils. The latter had sat on them ever since Helgi fell. "But they are rightfully yours," Svipdag said. "It's not to your honor that you don't claim them. Besides, the way you break rings, you have need of as many as you can clap hands on."

Hrolf chuckled, but soon did send men to his mother Queen Yrsa and asked her for the hoard.

She answered that her duty was to see to this if she could, but it lay not in her unaided might. "King Adhils is too greedy; nor does he willingly do anything that might gladden me. Tell my son that if he himself comes here to fetch the goods, I'll help him with redes and however else I can." The messengers thought she whispered, "And I will see again, Hrolf;" however, they were not sure.

They bore the word back to him where he was camped. Having so much else to do, he decided he must put off that quest.

He was then in the midst of weighty dealings. The old king at Odense, who had broken loose from Leidhra, was dead. Hjörvardh his son had taken the place, but was rather a weakling. Though he could raise more men near home than Hrolf could ferry across the Belt, he offered to talk peace. Hrolf received him well and they bargained back and forth. The Danes were ready to quit warfare for this year, anyway. By the time they got a firm grip on what they had already won, raising up trusty jarls and sheriffs, harvest season would be nigh.

Hrolf would not let go his demand that Hjörvardh become his underling, though the latter stalled and spoke of alliance instead. Was not Hrolf's sister Skuld of marriageable age? In the end, they parted in seeming friendly wise, and Hrolf invited Hjörvardh to come visit him next year.

This the Odense king did, with a following who made a grand show. Hrolf guested him in all honor. Skuld was there at Leidhra. She was now seventeen.

When Hjörvardh first saw her, he gaped. Blood rose in his cheeks. He was a ruddy young man, snub-nosed, his brown hair getting thin while his belly was thickening. On the whole, he looked good, for he kept beard and nails well trimmed and wore none but the finest clothes. "I, I had heard you were fair to behold, my lady," he stammered. "I did not understand . . . you are more than fair."

"Swart, then?" Skuld smiled teasingly and ran fingers down her midnight tresses. It showed forth the better how clear and white her skin was, how storm-green her eyes. The last childishness was gone from that narrow face. The body, in a rich gown, was slender but wholly a woman's, save that she moved in a soundless, rippling way that disquieted some.

Other men might have wooed her erenow, had it not

been for the uneasiness which hung about her. She had learned to be smooth-tongued, to seem to yield while really getting whatever she wanted. But she stayed harsh toward humble folk, given to shrieking fits, grasping for gold and chary of giving it out. Everybody knew she wrought witchcraft; nobody knew how deeply she was into it and what she did when she went off alone.

Folk were astonished that she, who had hitherto scoffed at talk of wedding, was suddenly sweet to a man whom she knew had hopes of winning her, "I could wish myself fair for you, King Hjörvardh," she murmured, and took him by the hand.

"I would, would, would wish you no otherwise . . . than what you are," he said.

"Come, let us sit and drink together," she offered. Each evening thereafter those two were side by side, so eagerly holding speech that they hardly heeded anyone else.

Svipdag drawled to his brothers: "From what I know of her, she's after becoming a queen. And not the wife of a scot-king, either. I daresay she'll stiffen Hjörvardh against giving oath to Hrolf—"

"How will she stiffen him?" asked Hvitserk, and guffawed.

"If Hjörvardh doesn't knuckle under, it'll be war," said Beigadh, "for along of him goes the whole half of Fyn that's left. Hrolf's bent on regaining everything his forebears had."

"And if these kings part unfriends," Hvitserk wondered, "how shall Skuld be wedded?" For, her father being dead, her brother ruled over who should get her and on what terms. Among the heathen, a woman may choose second and later husbands for herself, if widowed or divorced; and as for first marriage, her kinsmen seldom gainsay her wishes. Wherefore Svipdag answered:

"I'd not put it beyond her to run off with Hjörvardh. But somehow I don't look for that. Our Hrolf's a deep one, and he's working on some plan."

What that was, broke upon the world several days

later. The two kings had gone hunting at the head of a big troop. Merrily blew the horns and belled the hounds, down the long leafy halls of the greenwood; deer bounded away, their rusty coats flecked by gold spots of sunlight, till they fell before twanging bows; a wild boar turned and charged, earth shuddering as he met the spear; when the band stopped to rest in a glade, everyone was happy and at ease.

Hrolf, standing, unbuckled his sword belt. "Will you hold this?" he asked Hjörvardh. The Fyndweller nodded and took the hilt. Somehow the sheath withdrew, and Skofnung gleamed bare in his grasp. Hrolf smiled. "That's all right," he said while lowering his trews. "It handles well, no?"

"Wonderful!" Hjörvardh cried, and brandished it before returning it to the scabbard Hrolf had reached him.

Having let his water, the Dane-King took back his weapon, fastened it on, and said loud and clear: "This we both know, that whosoever holds the sword of a man while that man takes the belt off his breeches, he shall be the underling ever afterward. And now you shall be my under-king, and do my bidding like others."

A shocked hush fell. Hjörvardh sputtered that this was meaningless: that, yes, in plighting troth one did take the sword of the chief in hand, but not like this, and he'd sworn nothing, and— Softly, sometimes even smiling and clapping him on the shoulder, Hrolf spoke of his wish to stay friends, to spare both lands a costly war, to make them one. As scot-king, he said, Hjörvardh should have more renown and wealth, within a realm waxing rich and mighty, than ever before, the more so because Skuld was his sister. . . .

Haggling went on for days, often in sharp words, and men kept their arms by them. But the end of it was that Hjörvardh owned himself Hrolf's man, and wedded Skuld in a feast of overflowing splendor.

"I think our lord played no prank, that day in the glade," Svipdag told his brothers. "He must already have made plain to Hjörvardh that he could overwhelm him.

Yet it'd have meant heavy losses for us. This way, Hjörvardh can save his pride by saying he was tricked; and, to be sure, he gets the woman he wants."

"He seems to bear a grudge, even so," Hvitserk said.

"I think Skuld bears more of one," said Beighadh.

Svipdag nodded. "Aye. He'd be no danger by himself, that sluggard. Given her, though—we've not seen the tail of this beast."

Skuld and her husband went to his hall in Odense, paid scot to her brother, sent warriors at his behest, steered their land after his laws. Rather, she did, for she soon ruled Hjörvardh in every way. A hard life she led him, too, and she was barren as well. Yet he never dared lie beside anyone else, nor forbid her to bring in Finnish wizards and fare off whenever and wherever she chose.

A fisherman whispered how once he had been blown from his home waters, till at last he and his sons got their boat ashore on the lonely strand along Hindsholm. He left them to keep it while he went off looking for fresh water, theirs being gone after stormful days. At dusk, spying someone on a high bluff over the sea, black across flying iron clouds, he hefted his ax and went to see if it might be a helpful soul. From behind a gnarly brake he saw Queen Skuld—yes, surely her, he had seen her before when he sought Odin's Lake to offer for luck—standing at the edge of that headland. Wildly streamed her gown and unbound locks. She had raised a pole whereon was a horse's skull, the worst kind of ill-wishing, and pointed the empty eyes east toward Zealand. That way too did she shake her fist and yell forth curses, while she wept for sheer wrath.

V

THE TALE OF BJARKI

I

West of the Westmen in Svithjodh, the mountains of the Keel rise ever higher and steeper, until a wayfarer reaches the Uplands of Norway. Here formerly the king was named Hring. Only one of his sons lived, called Björn. While this was a promising lad, folk did not want to risk the Thor-descended royal house perishing with him. So when the queen died, they as well as the king thought that was great scathe. Everyone urged him to marry again. Though he was getting somewhat old, at length he agreed. He sent men southward to find him a worthy wife. At their head was a captain of guards who hight Ivar the Lean.

They rode down the dales to the Oslofjord, where they took three ships and steered for Jutland. Hardly were they in the Skagerrak when a frightful storm arose. Bailing, rowing, seeking naught but to claw off that lee shore, they rounded the end of Norway. Still the gale raged. The crews could only run before it, north along the coast. Each time they thought the weather had slackened and turned their bows, they got first heavy headwinds, then more gales out of the watery vastness beyond Ireland.

Two ships went down. The horny skin wore off the hands of Ivar's men; raw palms and fingers, arms from which the strength had drained, could no longer wield oars. He must raise sail and keep it poled well out, to stay clear of reefs and cliffs where he heard surf bawl through the sleety wind.

After days and nights he won in among islands, to a fjord which stabbed far into ice-helmeted mountains, and

145

beached his craft. It leaked at every seam; he dared no longer trust the tackle; broaching waves had reaved or ruined most of the foodstuffs aboard; the season was well along and foul winds kept on yowling through murky skies. He saw no help for it but to lay over that winter, hunt and salt down meat, make leather and bast rope for repairs. "Maybe we can trade with the Finns, if we can find any," he said. "We're surely in their lands." He cackled laughter. "Maybe a wizard will sell us fair winds, tied up in a sack."

His crew huddled shuddering in their cloaks. Mists blew around them, the steeps gloomed overhead, they were cold and wet and wretchedly hungry.

Once camp was made, Ivar took half a dozen men and struck inland to scout around. They climbed stony heights till they came to a pinewood where soft brown duff whispered underfoot and between the trunks they spied the gleam off a glacier. Toward dusk they found a log house, small but stoutly made. Reindeer stood in a paddock. A hound came to meet them, coal-swart and glowing-eyed, looking as huge as Garm who will devour the moon. It neither barked nor growled, but they felt something eldritch here and knocked most carefully on the door.

A serving-maid let them in. Two more women sat at the hearthstone. One was well clad and not ill to see, for all the years upon her. Ivar's band had eyes only for her companion. Like the others, she was plainly Finnish: short, richly curved of body, with high cheekbones, golden hair, slanty blue eyes; never had they heard of a face more lovely. She smiled and bade them welcome in the Norse tongue as if three women alone had nothing to fear from armed men. Ivar thought this was indeed so. Along the walls he saw runic wands and bones, flint knives, bags of odd-smelling dusts, an overly big cauldron, things that bespoke witchcraft.

Yet he and his were kindly received, given food and drink and good redes about where to hunt for what they needed. Ivar told of their errand and farings, then asked the women why they lived this lonely, as fine and fair as they were.

The oldest said into the flickering dark: "Everything has its reason, fellows. The ground for our being here is that a mighty king wooed my daughter, but she would not have him. He threatened to come and take her by force. Her father is long away at war. I thought best to hide her here."

"Who is her father?" Ivar asked.

"She is the daughter of the Finn-King by me, a leman."

"May I know your names?" For Finns often mislike giving these to strangers, lest a foe use them in spells.

"I hight Ingebjörg, and Hvit my daughter."

Ivar had his doubts, those names being Norse. However, men of that kind were already in his day making trips to Finland, trading, raiding, squeezing scot of hides and furs out of those tribes; and northward-pushing settlements were slowly driving the wanderers back. There were half-breeds, and enough other folk, who knew both tongues.

The maid here did not, but Ingebjörg was good at Norse and Hvit better still, the few times that she did more than faintly smile. Ivar slept well that night on the rushes of the floor.

In the months which followed, he was often a guest at the house, bringing gifts of meat and, at last, gold. Talking much with Ingebjörg and as much as might be with Hvit, he satisfied himself that the latter was in truth the child of a strong headman if not of one whom an Uplander would call a real king. And surely she was fair; he could lie awake lusting for her. She was not learned in what becomes a queen, but she seemed quick-minded. Anyway, the Uplands were no Danish or Swedish or Göta kingdom. Theirs were a folk who would not have understood lofty manners. It might be well to have a Finnish tie, Ivar thought. Home lay far south; still, northbound traders sailed out of Oslofjord taking Uplander men along—

He did not like everything about her. Surely she was witchy. Where did she and her mother go at Yuletide? How could they fare about over the snows? True, they had skis, like all Striding Finns. Ivar wondered, though, and could not find out, why no tracks showed anywhere around. Might they have gone well inland, to those three tall rocks that overlook a river to which the Finns make offering? The rocks stand just at that place where, northward, the sun may be seen all day at midsummer and never at midwinter. Norse travelers swore that the wizards did not welcome and bless the sun, but cursed it and drove it away.

This might not be true. And Hvit was very fair; and Ivar was weary and homesick, carrying no wish to sail forth again this year.

Early in spring, when his ship was about ready, he asked her if she would like to come along and marry King Hring.

She dropped her gaze to her lap. After a long while she whispered, "Let my mother decide."

Ingebjörg frowned before she said, "As the old saw goes, one must make the best out of the bad. I think it wrong that her father not be asked first. Your kind has never dealt well with ours. . . . However, I'll dare this, to make safe her morrow."

Ivar thought something was amiss here, the more so when the mother stayed behind. They should either have said an outright no or given him a gladder yes. But the leaves were budding, and he yearned to be off, and Hvit was very fair.

So she sailed. They had the best of passages to Oslofjord. Thence they rode to the hall of Hring and made known the woman to him. "Do you want her?" asked Ivar. "Or shall we take her back the same way?"

The king was a big man, grown gaunt and grizzled, and had himself spent a sorrowful winter. He soon fell hard in love with Hvit and married her, against the wish of some of his councillors. No matter that she was not rich, he said. She was beautiful.

But he—he was getting old. The new queen soon marked this.

II

Not far off dwelt a yeoman called Gunnar. In his youth he had long lain out in warfare, to win much renown and booty. Now, settled down with a wife, he had but one living child, Bera, a girl. As a bairn of her own age, the atheling Björn found his way over the few miles of woods, steeps, and icy fords, and became her friend. For years they played small games together and were mightily glad of each other. Later they roamed through greenwood and pinewood, scrambled panting and laughing above timberline to meadows blossom-starred between snow-peaks, lay outdoors in light summer nights which were like a lingering dream of day or stood in ringing winter chill and watched the northlights flare across half heaven.

Then once when they were undressing to steam themselves in a bathhouse, Bera suddenly reddened, and her hands fluttered across her body. Björn turned his eyes away, more flushed and awkward than she. After that they were still closer knit. Their parents smiled and nodded and began talking quietly about a betrothal some years hence.

Meanwhile the children turned into youth and maiden, both tall and handsome, he fair-haired and good at every feat of strength and skill, she brown-haired and sweet though stubborn about whatever really mattered to her. Meanwhile, also, Björn's father took his second wife.

There was much warring to be done against wild men and neighbor kings. Thus Hring often spent many weeks away from home. Then Queen Hvit would steer the land. She was not liked, being vain, cold, and overbearing toward everyone save Björn. Luckily, most Uplanders dwelt in far-strewn steadings and little thorps, so they need not look to her for much.

A time came when King Hring was making ready for such a faring. Björn was wild to go. It would be his first taste of battle. The queen, alone with her husband, said his son ought to stay behind and help her. He soon agreed. She had made this mighty man into a fish hooked on her line. Björn raved when he heard; but toward him Hring could still be stern. In the end, the atheling watched the host fare off without him.

Struggling not to weep, he sought the bed in the loft-room that was his. He had lain a while, staring and brooding, when the door opened, shut again and latched. Queen Hvit had entered. Her garb was a wanton's and her locks floated loose. She came to him, stroked his fore-head, and crooned, "Poor Björn. Poor dear Björn. Don't sorrow like this. Your grief is a grief to me."

"Well, why did you work to hold me here?" he croaked.

She smiled and fluttered her lashes. "I've seen you wrestle, race, practice weapon-use, meet boar and elk. You've no need to doubt your manhood in war. In king-craft, though, and in . . . other things . . . you've a world to learn. Here's your chance, out of your father's shadow. Now be glad, let me gladden you, my own pet bear." For "Björn" means "bear."

He sat up. "Go away!" he shouted. "Get out!"

She left, unangered. In the next few days she sought him over and over. At last she whispered to him to come to her in her bower before sunrise, secretly, for she had something great to tell. Unwilling, he did.

No women of hers were in that twilit room. She cast herself upon him, moaning of her love, striving to drag him to her bed. "Behold me, my bear, me, young and alive, bound to a dry stick like Hring! Oh, come and I'll show you the wholeness of life, I'll bring you alive!"

Too shocked to move, he stood dumb for a bit. Then rage burst forth. His palm cracked on her cheek, sent her staggering back. "You foul slut," he yelled, "haven't I told you to keep away from me?"

She breathed hard before she spoke in a voice like an adder's: "That was foolish of you. I am not used to being struck and driven off. You think it's better, Björn, to throw your arms around a yeoman's daughter than have love and goodwill from me. Well, as you will. For your hard heart and . . . and your cloddishness . . . take your reward!"

Snatching a wolfskin glove, she smote him across the face with it. "Like a bear have you treated me, Björn; no more than a bear are you, nor ever shall be. No, you shall become a bear in truth, a grim and raging bear that lives off no other food than your father's kine. You shall kill more of those than was ever heard of erenow; and never shall you be free of this shape-changing; and the knowing of it shall be the worst of all for you."

He shrieked, that strong-thewed youth, whirled and fled. Already as he crossed the yard, he shambled. Hvit's cat-shrill laughter followed him into the dawn.

What she did next is not known. Nor did anyone know where Björn had gone, what had become of him. Some feared he might have been taken by a huge gray bear which began harrying the king's herds. Cattle it slew as a weasel slays in a henyard, yet it was spied only from afar by frightened men. Hunters went to search. Their numbers were few in wartime. Wilier than was right, the bear lay in wait, attacked from behind, slew and maimed and sent the rest of them in flight. They saw nothing could be done till the king and his warriors returned.

Bera wept for her sweetheart.

Summer waned. One day late in it she was out to gather berries. On her way back, in a cold wind beneath a hastening dull sky, she stopped in mid-path, dropped her basket and wailed. For out of the brush trod that great iron-hued beast.

Wildly she looked around for help, a tree to climb, anything. But the bear only stood where he was, some yards off. She heard him make a sound more like purring than growling. Step by slow step, waiting between steps as if afraid, he neared. It came upon her that here was a wonder. She braced herself and stood fast. The bear reached her. She held forth a shivering hand. He licked it. She looked into his eyes and thought, in a wave of dizziness, that she knew the eyes of Björn the king's son.

The bear turned and trotted off. She groped after. High

they went on the mountainside, to where scrub oak grew gnarly amidst wan grasses and the eye swooped over a blue-shadowed dale to snowpeaks that seemed afloat in heaven. This eventide she saw just a chill, whistling dusk, a cave near a spring, a shape at its mouth. The bear reared . . . was it really a bear?

She ran to the arms of Björn.

After a while he said he must get on some clothes. Laughing, sobbing, hiccoughing, she clutched him and said she would keep him warm. When he went into the cave, she followed. On its sandy floor glowed a banked bed of coals. He started to feed it wood. She chattered that that was her task. As the flames bloomed, she saw a heap of hay and hides for sleeping, and drew very near to him.

"You must go," he stammered. "This is not seemly. You can't stay. I'm a man only at night. Each dawn I turn into a beast."

"So much . . . the more . . . is it right for me to abide here . . . O my darling," she cried softly.

For weeks she dwelt there. When he arrived near sundown, she cleansed his dripping jaws, cooked the torn-off ribs or haunch he had borne home, and waited for him to become Björn again. In the mornings she brushed the harshness that was his coat, kissed the terrible head, and waved farewell as long as she could see him lumber down the slope. The rest of the time she was alone with sun, clouds, rain, wind, hawks. She would sleep, gather sticks and nuts against winter, try to make the cave houselike, now and then weep a little but oftener sing.

Afterward she told no more than that of her life on the heights. It may well be that the bear did not always go ravening among men. Did she ride gleeful on his back, like the lassie she had been not many summers ago? Did he raid the bees to bring her honeycomb as overflowing as his love, and did she weave wreaths to hang around his neck?

Did he take her along when he sought out the elven folk? For surely, in light of what happened later, he knew them. Half outside the world of men, he was half into the Half-World. The spell must also have touched Bera, in however ghostly a way. Did she giggle at the antics of a niss, or flee when a nicor gruesomely broke the surface of a moonlit lake? Did she sit at the feet of a dwarf, old and twisty and tough as her oak trees, to hear his riddles and remembrances? Did she run in fear from the earthquake stride of a troll? Did she hear the Asgard's Ride of the dead halloo through the night sky, did she see the one-eyed spearman on an eight-legged horse who led them in their hunt?

Did she meet the elves? Tall and grave they are, though sometimes a wicked mirth ripples through them; they come from their hidden high-roofed halls, or from the gods whom they may serve, to dance by moonlight in rings of bauta stones raised ages ago; awful and beautiful are they, and weirdly do they work on the world. One woman among them spoke long to Björn of what had been and would be, far off in a land called Denmark. Afterward he needed from Bera what cheer she could give.

She held him close against the hateful dawn.

In fall King Hring came back from his warfare and men told him what had gone on, or what they thought had. When he learned that his son was lost, belike killed and eaten by that beast which was ruining his herds more than anyone else's, he covered his eyes. Long he sat before he went off by himself. Later the queen urged him most strongly to gather enough men and hounds to track that monster down and get rid of it. He stared sideways at her and said there was no haste about that.

To everyone he acted as if the bear did not matter much. Still Hvit kept after him, as did his friend Gunnar whose only child was likewise missing, and the kinfolk of those who had lost dear ones to the beast, and all who dreaded it. At last Hvit taunted him: "Is your manhood small where it comes to keeping the land safe *also*? Then I must betake myself elsewhere, for bad harvests will come from such a king till he's hanged on high to the gods."

Hring groaned aloud and turned from her. Next morning he sent word out for hunters to meet from far around.

Some nights later, the bed rustled beneath Björn as he woke from sleep, turned and drew Bera to him. She lay by the knocking of his heart, smelling the hay and skins and his own beloved warmth. In darkness and wind she heard him say:

"My dream has come. Tomorrow will be the day of my bane. They are bound hither to get me killed."

She cried out. He stopped her with a kiss and went on in that heavy whisper: "Well, I myself have little gladness any more, save when we two are together, and now that must end.

"Hush. I give you the ring under my left arm. Tomorrow when I'm dead, go to the king and ask him to give you what's below the left shoulder of the beast. He will. Belike the queen will guess what you've been about and offer you bearflesh to eat. You must not—"

"I could not!"

"You are with child, you know. You will have three boys; and that food would harm them sorely, for the queen is the foulest of witches.

"No, go home to your father and mother, and there birth our children. You will come to love one of them the most, though hard will they all be to cope with. When you can do that no longer, then take them back to this cave. Here you will find a chest with three locks. The runes on it will tell you what each of them should have. There will be three weapons as well, driven into the mountain, and each lad shall get the one which I, foresighted, have willed to him."

He tried to kiss away her tears. "Bestow good names on our sons—Frodhi the first, Thori the second, Bjarki the third—for long will they be remembered." She clung to him and thought she heard a fading faintness: "Yet the sign of the beast will be upon each of them. Even he who seems unmarked will at the end—" He broke off and comforted her as best he might.

At sunrise the bear shape came over him. He went outside and she followed, into dim daylight. Peering toward a noise which lifted, she saw a hundred men headed up the mountainside. Before them bayed and leaped whole packs of hounds.

The bear licked her hand, once, and charged.

Hounds and hunters went at him. That was a long and hard fight. He slew nigh every dog—ripped it open, broke its back, snapped it in bloody twain—and hurt no few men. Yet spears and arrows sank into him until he was no longer gray but red. The warriors ringed him in. He rushed about. Everywhere were shields and whetted metal. He began to stumble on the shafts and guts that hung from his belly. No way was left to slip free. He turned toward the king, struck that man who stood next by and ripped him asunder.

But then the bear was so worn and empty that he cast himself on the earth. His breath rattled with blood. Spears plunged, axes rose and fell, the men swarmed over him and slew him.

While they stood back, cheering and boasting, Bera came to King Hring. Her mouth was firm and her gait was steady. He knew her and said, "Why, Bera, my dear, where ever have you been—?"

"That's no matter, lord," she answered. "For old times' sake, will you let me have what's under the shoulder of your prey?"

He looked at her a while before he nodded his whitening head and spoke loud enough to be sure men heard: "Of course. You must be starved, after wandering lost this long. There can't be anything here, save such as I might as well let you have."

Like a carven figure, Bera watched them flay and butcher the carcass, until she could go to the formless thing and reach underneath. None saw her draw forth a golden ring and tuck it between her breasts.

Whooping, the band fared back to the king's garth. It would have seemed strange if a girl newly returned from wilderness did not come along, and did not go into the hall for merrymaking like everyone else.

Queen Hvit went about, very blithe, bidding them welcome and ordering the bear's flesh cooked for a feast. When she saw Bera, hunched unhappily in a corner, she halted. Her fingers crooked. She wheeled and left in a whirl of skirts. Well before anybody might have awaited it—men had just begun their real drinking—she carried in a trencher of spit-roasted meat.

Straight to Bera she went and said for none to mistake: "How good to know you're alive! Poor darling, you mustn't go hungry one wink longer. Here, eat."

The girl shrank back on the bench. "No," she begged.

Hvit drew herself straight. Frightening did she look, in a ghost-white gown which glimmered amidst shadows like her eyes and her teeth. "Why, this is unheard of," she said, "that you spurn food which the queen herself does you the honor to bring. Take it at once, or you'll get what is worse!"

She drew her knife, stabbed a chunk of meat, and thrust it at Bera's lips. Worn out, numbed by grief, terrified for her unborn children, the girl knew not what to do. Men were beginning to stare. If they knew the truth, what might *they* do? She clenched shut her eyes and hands. The gobbet pushed hot at her mouth. Its smell of scorched blood roared in her head. She swallowed it whole.

The queen laughed, "Well, that wasn't too bad, was it, little Bera?"—and pushed another bite at her.

It got onto her tongue. Bera won back a wavelet's worth of strength. She spat it out, leaped to her feet, and shrieked, "No, no more, not though you torture or kill me!"

Again Hvit laughed. "Could be that that morsel does something anyway." She lifted a third.

Bera sprang past her and fled out of the hall. The queen herself could ill afford to start folk wondering. "Well, well, how thin-skinned for a yeoman's wench," she said. "I was only trying to brighten her mood."

Bera went home to her father and mother; and heavy was the burden she bore. To them alone did she tell what had happened.

III

Hvit did not seek to do the girl further harm. Either she dared not, or she felt she had enough to gloat over. For at her lying in, Bera brought forth first a horribly misshapen child. Above he was human, but from the navel down he was an elk. When Gunnar the yeoman would have taken the being out to squall on a hillside till it died or a wolf found it, she said through her sweat and pain, "No. That's Björn's son. He wanted him named . . . Frodhi."

Now she birthed another boy whose feet were the feet of a dog, though in all else he was goodly to see; him she called Thori.

Yet a third boy had she. In him was no flaw. This was Bjarki, whom she came to love the most.

Of the years which followed is little to say. At first folk must have shunned that house of bad luck. However, Gunnar was wealthy and well-liked; he had built a halidom to Thor, where he often made offerings; his crops and kine throve. He and his could not be under the wrath of the gods or the land-wights. And after all, freaks were not unknown, though usually they were set out. Erelong life was going on as before, save that there was no more close friendship between Gunnar and King Hring. The queen's ever more evil temper had caused most men to steer as clear of that hall as might be.

Gunnar and his wife thought it wise to keep still about who the father was of their grandchildren. Bera told the world they were the by-blow of a wanderer she had met while lost in the high country. That sort of thing was common enough. Being comely and sturdy and sure to bring a big dowry, she had suitors, but took none.

The boys grew like grass. Elk-Frodhi on his long hairy legs, hoofs click-clicking, swayed back and forth and must needs go slow when he walked. Leaned over to run, he outpaced everyone save his loping, padding brother Thori Hound's-Foot. As he got his growth, nobody could withstand him when he wrestled or smote with wooden practice weapons.

Huge and ugly he was, uncouth and surly. He got along well only with his brothers. These were the best-looking of lads, hardly to be told apart aside from their feet. The older of them was oftener snarly than the younger. Bjarki was of a sunny heart.

Nonetheless, since he always fared in company with the other two, their ways worked on him. The bigger they grew, the louder and more unruly they became. When playing with neighborhood boys they were heartless and willful; many a one had a hard time at their hands.

Worst was Elk-Frodhi. At the age of twelve, he was broad and heavy as any full-grown man, and would have been as tall did his legs not make him slouch. He began to seek the king's garth and challenge the royal guardsmen to bouts. Several he threw around so badly that they were crippled. When the rage came upon him, he would slash out a sharp hoof or bring down a fist like a hammer. Some men died.

This cost Gunnar stiff weregilds and led to hard words between grandfather and grandson.

At last Frodhi hulked and clicked his way to Bera and said he wanted to leave. "I wish naught to do with folk hereabouts," he growled. "They're weaklings, who get hurt if you come near them."

She sighed, and knew in guilt that it was from a kind of happiness. "That would be best," she said. "First come and get what your father left you."

They went together, up onto the mountain. She had not been there since Björn was flayed. Nodding sunlit grasses, blowing flowers, soughing trees, a hawk aloft amid clouds which seemed to have broken off the snows yonder, a thrush which trilled and hare which bolted, none of these remembered him. When she and her son entered the cave, they found a triple-locked chest of bronze, lovely to see though its moldings told no human story. She had spent time learning how to read runes. Now those upon the box spoke to her. When she touched the locks, they sprang open. Inside lay bright suits of mail, fine clothes, gold rings and jewelry. The runes said Elk-Frodhi should have little of this.

"I'll take my own, then," he sneered, and tried to snatch out a helmet. His fingers slipped off. He could grasp nothing which was not his. "Well, I'll win my own, and Hel take *you!*" he bellowed. Did a few tears start forth?

Squinting toward shadows at the back of the cave, he saw steel glimmer and went for a close look. Driven into the granite which made a rear wall for the softer stone around, were three weapons: a longsword, mighty and fair; a great war ax; and a curve-bladed shortsword. "Ha!" he cried, and grabbed the hilt of the first. Though he heaved till the sweat ran out, he could not rock it, nor afterward the ax.

Said Elk-Frodhi: "Maybe he who put these here wanted they should be dealt out the same as the other goods." He took the shortsword by the haft, and at once it slid free.

A while he stared at it before he said, "Unjust has he been who divided these treasures." In howling ire he chopped the blade two-handed against the mountain. He did not break it; no, it rang as it hewed into the granite.

A while more he stared. At last he said, "What matter if I fare about with this uncanny thing? Surely it can bite."

He turned, snatched up what else had been left him, and galloped away. He did not bid his mother farewell, nor did she ever see him again.

Word came after months. Elk-Frodhi had gone into the Keel, a wild part through which one road went. There he had built himself a hut and now lived as a robber. It took more than a few men to stand him off. Were the band small, he bore off their goods, and if they fought, he left dead and wounded behind him.

King Hring heard of this, and thought he could see what witchcraft lay beneath. However, he said merely that he did not think it was his work to keep safe a traders' road to Götaland.

When their brother was gone, Thori Hound's-Foot and Bjarki grew better behaved. Yet they were restless too, and after three years the former asked leave to go.

His mother took him to the cave and those things which were willed him. His was a bigger share. He too tried to draw the beautiful longsword, and failed. The ax came free in his hand, and a stout weapon it was. He busked himself, said goodbye to his mother and grandparents, and rode off eastward.

All the brothers were keen hunters. When Thori saw traces too faint for most eyes, leading off the Götaland road, he followed them. Atop a rocky bluff, in a murk of firs, he found a sod-roofed log house. He took the lone chair inside and pulled his hat low.

Toward evening was a huge clatter of hoofs, the earthen floor shivered beneath weight, and there stood Elk-Frodhi, seven feet tall and more than broad to match. He glared at the dimly seen newcomer, drew his sax, and chanted:

"Grinning the shortsword
goes from the sheath;
well he remembers
the work of Hild."

Hild is a Valkyrie and her work is war and manslaying. Frodhi chopped his blade down into a bench, frothed and snorted.

Quoth Thori:
"I can likewise
let my ax
sing for you
the selfsame stave."

And he hid his face no more. Frodhi was overjoyed in his gruff way to see him, having long lived wholly friendless. He bade him stay, and offered him half the hoard of loot.

Thori said he would not take this. He abode there a few days, then said he would be off again.

Elk-Frodhi sighed: "I'm no woman to keep you here, am I, nor more than part of a man. As you will, brother. Hear my rede, though . . . for I get some news from those

I waylay but spare the lives of. Go on to Götaland. On the shores of Lake Vener dwell the West Götar, who pay scot to the High King Bjovulf. Their own under-king has died and they've called a meeting at midsummer to choose a new one. This is how they do it. They set a chair in the middle of their Thingstead, such as two ordinary men could hardly fill; and he who can sit at ease by himself, leaving no proper room for another, shall be king. I think already you're that size."

"An odd custom," said Thori.

Frodhi laughed. "It makes as much sense to me as whatever else men do. Either they get a giant who leads them to victory, or they get one too fat to start a war."

"Well, they do say Bjovulf is a good overlord. I thank you for doing this well by me."

"I wish . . . I could do more—be off, if you must!" Frodhi turned his coarse head aside.

So Thori fared to the West Götar, where a jarl received him well. Folk admired his height and looks. When the Thing was held, its lawman deemed he fitted the seat best, and the yeomen roared the name of king upon him.

Many are the tales about King Thori Hound's-Foot. He grew rich in friends, among them the jarl, whose daughter he married, and his overlord. When Bjovulf later fell in strife against a dragon, trouble broke forth among the Götar. Thori stood fast by that Vigleik whom the old king had wanted to follow him, and in most battles had the victory.

Meanwhile Bjarki stayed home. Three more years passed by.

His mother was happy with him. He had grown altogether good-hearted, however bold in the hunt or in breakneck sport. Did he no longer wrestle, race, or otherwise playfully contend with his fellows, it was because none had a chance and everybody knew it. For he towered a head over the highest among them. So broad and thick was he that, from a ways off, he did not seem to be this tall; yet he ran down horses and deer while hardly breathing deep, and was supple as a withe. In face as well

as size, he was from the same mold as his brother Thori:
handsome in a heavy-browed, blunt-nosed, freckled way,
his hair as red and his eyes as blue as living fire. But he
did not lope like a dog, he strode like a man.

Merry at first, he began in time to brood. Bera watched
him in growing trouble. She was not astonished when, at
last, he bade her walk with him alone in the greenwood.
There he asked her who his father was. He had gnawed
his way through her tale and would no longer be fobbed
off.

In a mingling of dread and joy, she told him about
Björn and herself, and how his stepmother had undone
her lover.

Bjarki smote fist in palm; birds fled from branches.
"We've much to reward that she-troll for!" he cried.

"Beware her," his mother begged. And she told how she
had been made to eat of the bear's flesh, "and that's
seen on your brothers, Thori and Elk-Frodhi."

Bjarki said through his teeth: "I should think Frodhi
has greater grounds to avenge our father and himself,
than to win goods by robbing and slaying harmless men.
And strange how Thori could fare away without giving
that hag a keepsake."

"They did not know," Bera whispered.

"Well, then," and Bjarki grinned like a wolf, "best that
I pay her off on behalf of us all."

She warned him about Hvit's witchcraft. He promised
to take care, and spent some while making ready.

Grandfather Gunnar had become time-enfeebled.
Bjarki and his mother went by themselves through the
woods to the hall of King Hring. They found the garth
ill-tended, paint peeling from walls, weeds rank in the
yard, few folk around save slovenly guardsmen and servants. There was no bar to getting speech with the king
in an offside room. He too was greatly aged. In him,
unlike the yeoman, was no haughtiness left, and his
hands always trembled.

Bera stood forth, her son sheer behind her, and told
him what had happened. For proof she had the ring
taken from beneath the slain bear.

The king turned it around in his chalky fingers, peered at it with his dim, watering eyes, and, "Yes, yes," he quavered, "yes, I know this well, I gave it myself to my Björn cub, and . . . and . . . oh, I had my thoughts, I was not blind, not then, but I kept still because . . . because I care so much for her."

Bjarki's deep young voice rang under the rafters: "Let her now begone, or I will have revenge."

Shivering, though the day was summery bright, Hring pleaded. He would make it up with goods, he promised, gold, every kind of wealth, heaped as high as might be wished, if only Bjarki would let this matter rest in its grave. He would give his grandson a shire to steer, yes, the name of jarl at once, and the whole Uplands to be king over when he, Hring, was gone, which would be soon. Hvit had given him no children. But oh, let her live—

"No wish have I for that," said Bjarki, "before all, no wish to call that fiend my queen—and you, you're too snared by her to rule either your kingdom or your wits aright. Never shall my father's murderess do well in the Uplands!"

Hring cowered, seemed to crumble. He might have called his guardsmen. Did he know that Bjarki, who had overcome each one of them in games, would hew a road through any shield-burg they raised? Or did he fear they would stand aside from the queen they hated? Ruthless in his youth, Bjarki walked across the yard and tore open the door of the lady-bower.

Hvit's women shrieked and scattered. She crouched spitting before him. He had a glimpse of a haggard face, of a soul more starved than any flesh could be; then he had clapped a sealskin bag over her head and drawn the string of it chokingly tight.

Blinded, she could work no spells on him. She clawed, and he heard her voice muffled from within: "Ha, I know you, I know you, and I say the hour will come when another witch brings your bane—"

He cuffed her. The hooded head snapped to one side and she fell. "This for my father!" he shouted, hauling her back up. Blow after blow: "This for my mother! This for Elk-Frodhi! This for Thori Hound's-Foot!" When she was dead, he tied her by the ankles and dragged her around for everyone to see. Afterward, lest she walk again, he cut off her head and burned her.

In this wise died Hvit the Finn-King's daughter, far from her homeland in miles and years. Most in the royal household said her doom was not too harsh.

Later Bera showed Bjarki the cave. He took the rest of the treasures, which were the largest part; and for him the longsword came easily out of the stone.

The runes on its blade said it hight Lövi and was among the best of weapons, for it was not forged by hand of man. It must never be laid under one's head nor rested on the hilt; nor need it be honed more than thrice in an owner's lifetime. Whenever drawn, it would give a death, and no second blow would have to be landed. Following his mother's word—she remembered the elves —Bjarki made for it a sheath of birchbark.

Old King Hring did not long outlive his wife. When he sickened and died, men hailed Bjarki in his stead.

He ruled for three years, and did well at healing the harm that had come under the witch-queen. Yet he was restless as his brothers had been. The Uplands were no home for a young man like him. Here were tall mountains and good hunting, and very little else. Men grew stale on their wide-scattered homesteads. At best, they might fare abroad as traders or vikings. Why not seek something this country could never give?

First he saw to his mother's welfare. Valsleif Jarl was a widower, a man of standing whom Bera had come to like. Bjarki got them married, and himself helped lead groom to bride. Thereafter he called a Thing, told the folk he was leaving, and led them in choosing a new king.

Then at last he was free to ride off.

He had a horse of size to bear him, and no other company. Most gold and silver he left behind, though with weapons and clothes he was well outfitted.

Off he rode, and suddenly after this long time he could let his glee break loose. Far up in heaven, the larks heard him singing.

Of his trek naught is told until one day, like Thori before him, he came to the lair of Elk-Frodhi. He took his horse to the stall end of the house and settled down. He knew some of the things he saw in the piled hoard— they were akin to those he had taken from the elven chest—and felt he had a right here to whatever he might need.

Toward sundown Frodhi came home and glowered at the newcomer who sat in his chair, hat pulled down to mask face in shadow. Even to him, a guest was a guest, thus holy. He brought his own horse to the stall, and found it could not get along with the other.

Turning, he said: "Well, this a froward and worthless fellow, who dares sit himself down without leave."

Bjarki kept his hat low and did not answer.

Seeking to frighten him away, Frodhi drew shortsword from sheath so it screamed. Twice he did this; but Bjarki paid no heed.

The robber drew blade a third time and rushed in. Huge though Bjarki was, Elk-Frodhi overtopped and out-weighed him. Still the guest sat calmly. Frodhi growled and slavered. "Would you like to wrestle?" he got out. His thought was that he could break the man's neck in that game and so become free to cast him out.

Bjarki laughed, sprang to his feet and seized Frodhi around the rough-haired waist. Mighty was that fight, wrenchings and tramplings till the walls shuddered.

Then the hat fell off. Frodhi knew his brother, let go, and rasped: "Welcome, kinsman! Why didn't you tell me? Too long have we fought."

"Oh, no need to end it yet," said Bjarki, albeit he breathed hard and sweat sucked his clothes to his skin.

Elk-Frodhi grew grave. "Scant luck would you have had, kinsman, if we really strove," he rumbled. "I can only be glad that I saw in time. . . . Come." He hugged his brother; the woodland smell of him filled Bjarki's nostrils. "Let's drink and eat and, oh, you must tell me every-thing!"

Bjarki stayed for some days, talking when they did not go hunting. Frodhi asked him to abide here and own half the wealth. Bjarki said no; he did not like killing folk in order to win his goods.

Frodhi sighed in the firelit gloom: "I've given ruth to many when they were small and weak."

"I'm happy to hear that," Bjarki answered. "Best would be if you let everyone go by in peace, whether or not you think you can win aught by slaying them."

"I have gotten a doom that is heavy in all ways," said Elk-Frodhi.

After a while he added: "As for you, well, I know somewhat of the world, alone though I am here. Wayfarers and—and others—tell me things. If you want riches and renown, seek out King Hrolf in Denmark. The best warriors fare to him, for he's the most bold, wise, openhanded and splendid of kings in the Northlands."

More did he have to say, until Bjarki agreed.

Next morning Frodhi followed his brother a ways along the road, doing his clumsy best to talk. At last they must speak their goodbyes. Bjarki dismounted to clasp hands on the same footing. Frodhi shoved hard at him, and he stumbled backward. A smile stole across the robber's ugly lips. "You don't seem as strong as you ought to be, kinsman," he said.

Drawing his knife, he gashed his own elk-thigh. "Drink of this blood," he said, pointing to what welled forth. Like one in a dream, Bjarki knelt and obeyed. "Rise," ordered Frodhi. When Bjarki did, he shoved him again. This time the man younger by an hour stayed in his tracks.

"I think you got good from that drink, kinsman," said Frodhi. "Now you should stand above most, as I heartily wish for you."

He chopped his foot into the bank beside him, through ferns and soil, down into rock till the hoof was lost therein. Withdrawing it, he said: "Daily will I come to this spoor and look. If you die of sickness, there'll be mold in it, and water if you drown at sea. But if you die by weapons, there'll be blood, and then will I come to avenge you . . . dearest to me of all men."

And Elk-Frodhi fled away up the wilderness road.

Bjarki shook himself free of sorrow and rode on. Naught worth telling happened before he crossed the ranges to Lake Vener. King Thori Hound's-Foot was away, whether on war or hunt is not said. Folk wondered to see him come riding back by himself—for, shod and mounted, he looked just like Bjarki.

Unsure what was going on, the latter thought best to play along till he could learn. He let them bring him to the royal hall, serve him in the high seat, and at night lead him to bed by the queen.

When they were alone, Bjarki said to her, "I'll not lie under the same blanket." She was taken aback until he told her how matters stood. Thereafter she too thought it wisest to pretend; a witch or a Norn might be in this.

Things went so for a time. While they did not become lovers, Bjarki and the queen became friends.

When Thori did get home and found his brother, that was a meeting of embraces. Having heard the full tale, the king said there was no other man in the world whom he would have trusted to rest beside his wife. He wanted him to stay on and to share in everything.

Bjarki said that was not his wish. Thori offered him men instead, to follow him wherever he might go. This likewise Bjarki refused. "I'm bound for King Hrolf in Denmark," said he, "to learn if it's true what they tell me, that more can be won as a man of his than as a king anywhere else."

"That may be," said Thori; dryly: "Though I'll stay where I am." And earnestly: "Remember, those birds which wing highest are most likely to be struck down by the hawk."

"Better that than to be a mole," said Bjarki.

Thori started to answer, but curbed himself. At leave-taking he rode a ways with his brother. They parted in friendly wise, though keeping thoughts of their own.

Now once more is little to tell save that Bjarki got to the Sound, bought passage across, and at last had not far to go before he would reach Leidhra.

IV

The year had run on to fall, each day more short and chilly than the last. Toward the end of Bjarki's trek, rain fell from dawn till dusk and gave no sign of stopping to sleep. He had pushed on hard in his eagerness, and at nightfall found himself on a lonely stretch of heathland, soaked through. His horse was badly wearied under him. It slipped and plopped about in fetlock-deep mud. Still the downpour brawled, icy through an ever deeper blackness. At last he lost the road.

A bit later, his beast stumbled against what seemed like a mound. Bjarki got off, groped forward, and made out that this was a house, one of the poor little sort built from turf and peat over a pit dug into the earth. The smokehole was covered, but light glowed dull red through cracks around a door. Bjarki knocked.

A man half opened it. Grizzled and ragged, he carried a bill. The Norseman wondered what in the gloomy hole behind him might draw robbers. Even the wife was not much to look at, seen by a clay lamp over which she huddled for some warmth.

"Good evening," said Bjarki. "May I shelter here for the night?"

The crofter, who had gulped at the great size of him, now felt safe and said, "Aye, I'd not send you on in this foul weather and murk, outlander though I can hear you are." He helped unharness and tether the horse. It must wait outside, no room being within where his one cow was stabled. Bjarki got a shabby coat to wrap around himself after his drenched garments were off, a dish of roots and hardtack, a place to lay himself on the rushes in that smelly gloom. Everybody was soon asleep.

In the morning the wife, Gydha, gave Bjarki the same food for breakfast since they had no other. Meanwhile Eilif, the man, asked for news. In his turn Bjarki asked about King Hrolf and his warriors, and if it was far to reach them.

"No," said Eilif, "only a short way. Are you bound thither?"

"Yes," answered Bjarki, "that's my thought, to see if he'll take me into his household."

"It'd be fitting for you, aye, aye," nodded the crofter, "seeing how big and strong you are." He sounded oddly sad; and all at once, Gydha broke into tears.

"Why, what are you crying about, goodwife?" asked Bjarki.

She sobbed: "I and my man . . . had an only son . . . we called him Hott. Here was a lean enough living for him . . . and this past year none, after we lost our flock . . . Eilif and I can barely last on what's left. . . . Hott went to the king's burg to see if he could get work—and they made him a scullion but—" She must stop to master her grief. "The king's men make game of him. He has to help serve, and . . . when they sit and eat, as soon as they've gnawed the meat off a bone, they throw it at him . . . and if it hits him he's hurt, knows not if he'll live or die, though where else could he go?" She leaned forward in the dimness of the hut and said more steadily, "This reward do I ask for taking you in, that you cast small bones at him rather than big ones, if they've not already knocked him to hell."

"Gladly will I do as you wish," said Bjarki, "but I think it's unmanly to throw offal at anyone or deal badly with children and weaklings."

"Then you do well," said the woman, catching his hands in her own worn fingers, "for these look mighty to me, and my Hott could never stand before your blows."

Bjarki bade the old couple farewell and rode on according to the way they had told him. The rain was past, the sky dazzling, sunlight asparkle on puddles in the brown earth and on wet boughs where a few leaves still flamed. Starlings flocked, robins hopped in fields, curlews whistled merrily through a cool damp breeze. Bjarki paid scant heed. A scowl was on his brow. He had not looked to find king's men who behaved like trolls.

Heath and marsh gave way to richer country, where

steadings stood plentiful and cattle drowsed rust-red behind fences. Here many folk went to and fro. Bjarki
stopped to talk with some. Maidens smiled at the red-
haired giant, but he was not in a mood for them today.
The questions he asked in his thick Upland burr had to
do with King Hrolf and the royal household.

Aye, said the yeomen, this was a good king, a wise
and righteous king, withal strong to fend off rovers from
abroad or ride down outlaws and hang them. . . . Well,
yes, his troopers were an unruly lot; he really ought to
curb them, but no doubt he had too much else on his
mind. . . . He'd been away this summer. Year before last,
he'd brought King Hjörvardh of Fyn under him and
(ha!) his sister under Hjörvardh. With his rear thus made
safe, all the islands in his grip, he was going after the
Jutish realms. Once he had those likewise, an honest man
could till his fields and never dread outside onslaught.
Of course, first the king must spy out the Jutland shores.
So he'd only taken a few shiploads of warriors along this
season. The rest had stayed home in Leidhra and, aye, in
their idleness gotten above themselves. . . . The king
should be home any day, now when the fall storms were
come. Maybe he already was. A yeoman wouldn't know
about that. Yeomen had their work to do, butchering
time and so forth. Let the great folk see to their own,
hey?

Bjarki rode on along the stream. In the afternoon,
Leidhra lifted before him.

At this time of year, when little traveling was done, the
stronghold lay quiet within its stockade, gates open and
unwatched. Women, children, thralls, craftsmen were
much about, but few warriors. Bjarki supposed most of
those were off hunting or whatever. He rode through
muddy ways to the richly carved wooden cliffsides of the
royal hall. Flagstones in the courtyard rang beneath his
horse's hoofs. He dismounted at the stables. "Put mine in
beside the king's best," he told a groom, "give him oats
and water, curry him well, and stow my gear in a clean
corner till I send for it." The man gaped after him.

In costly clothes, a knife and the sword Lövi at his waist, but wearing neither helmet nor mail, Bjarki strolled into the main chamber of the hall. However dim and smoky when he had trod straight in from beneath the sky, it was sunnier and airier than he had thought such a place could be. Bright shields, broad horns, fair skins, sconced rushlights, birch wainscoting lined the walls. The figures on panels and on the roof-pillars were of beasts, vines, and heroes; he saw no gods among them. The posts of the high seat bore Skjold and Gefion. A few workers moved over the juniper boughs on the floor, which lent their freshness to the air, and a few hounds lay about. Otherwise the reach of the room seemed empty. The Norseman sat down on a bench, near the door, and waited for whatever might happen.

Soon he heard a rattling in a farther corner. His eyes used to the inside, he could make out a heap of bones over there. A hand was just coming above the top. Bjarki rose and strode close. The hand, he saw, was nastily black. He wrinkled his nose at the stench of rotting shreds of meat. "Who's in here?" he called.

A youth's voice, thin and frightened, said, "I . . . I . . . I'm named Hott, wellborn lord."

"What are you doing?"

"I am m-m-making me a shield-burg, lord—"

"Woeful is your shield-burg." Bjarki reached in, got hold of an arm, and in a clatter hauled forth the one who had crouched behind the pile.

A skinny shape writhed, helpless in the big man's grasp. The voice yammered: "Now you'll slay me! Don't do that—not when I'd fixed it this well! You've pulled down my shield-burg—"

Bjarki peered. Hott was about fifteen, he guessed, tall but wretchedly thin. His locks were so tangled and greasy that one had trouble seeing they were yellow; his face seemed to be all sharp nose and huge eyes; he shook in his kirtle. "I was laying it high around me to keep off the bones you'll throw," he sobbed. "It was almost f-f-finished."

"You'll need it no longer," said Bjarki.

Hott shriveled. "Do you mean . . . to slay me . . . right away, lord?"

"Don't whimper that loud," said Bjarki. He must give a cuff or two before the starveling quieted down. Then he picked up the form, gone limp from dread, and bore him outside. It was not far to the nearest stockade gates. A short ways beyond, he had seen how the stream widened to make a pool. Few paid him any heed.

Bjarki hauled the filthy tatters off the boy, pitched him into the pool, knelt and hand-scrubbed him till no boiled lobster could have been more clean or red. Rising, he jerked a thumb at the kirtle and said, "You wash that wipe-rag yourself."

Hott obeyed, and trotted dripping after him when he returned to the hall. Bjarki took the same place on a bench as before. He pulled the lad down beside him. Hott could speak no two words. He shuddered in every limb and joint, though he saw through the haze of fear that the stranger wanted to help him.

Dusk fell. The king's warriors began to drift in. They spied the newcomer and hailed him well, for this household was proud of its hospitality. One asked Bjarki what he was here for. "I thought of joining your troop, if the king will have me," said the Norseman.

"Well, you're in luck," said the guard, "for he's come home this very evening. He's tired and dines in his own tower along of a few best friends. Tomorrow you can see him, and surely he'll take on as stout a fellow as you." He leered at the cowering Hott. "Kick that sniveler aside, though," he warned. "Over-bold are you to set him . . . it . . . among men."

Bjarki glowered. The guard looked up and down his bulk, decided not to press the matter, and swaggered off. Hott started to go. Bjarki clamped onto his wrist. "Stay," said the Norseman.

"B-b-but they'll kill me—for sure—when they get drunk . . . if I dare sit here," blubbered the stripling. "I've g-g-got to work and—let me go build up my shield-burg again!"

"Stay," said Bjarki. He kept hold of the wrist. Hott might as well have tried to drag away a mountain.

The longfires were stoked, the trestle tables brought in, food heaped on trenchers and horns filled with drink. Bjarki and Hott sat alone. None of the men would have that butt of scorn for benchmate. The more they drank, the more they glared at him, as did the kitchen servants he was supposed to help.

At last the warriors began casting small bones his way. Bjarki acted as if he did not see. Hott was too frightened to take either meat or mead. Bjarki, who could now let go of him because he dared not move out into the open, ate and boused for two.

Loud grew the uproar of voices above the fire-crackle; dogs barked and growled in the smokiness. Suddenly light flickered red on a huge thighbone which flew through the air. That was a thing which could kill.

Bjarki hooked it in midflight, inches from the skull of shrieking Hott. Rising, he took aim at him who had thrown it, and cast it back. Straight to the head it went. There was a *crack,* and the guard toppled dead.

Horror yelled through the hall. Men snatched weapons and boiled toward Bjarki. He thrust Hott behind him. His sword Lövi he did not draw, but he rested hand on hilt, knocked over the first few attackers with his fist, and thundered that he wanted to see the king.

Word came to Hrolf in his tower room. That was a broad chamber, paneled in different woods, giving on a gallery which overlooked the courtyard, more simply furnished than might have been awaited from so rich a lord. He had eaten, and sat quietly drinking and talking with Svipdag, Hvitserk, Beigadh, a few others who had been along on this summer's faring.

A pair of troopers thudded up the ladder and panted their news: that a bear-sized warrior had come into the hall and killed one of their number. Should they cut him down out of hand?

Hrolf stroked his short coppery-gold beard. "Was the man slain without cause?" he asked.

"Yes ... yes, so to speak," said the talebearer.

In the same mild tone, King Hrolf wanted to know just what had happened. The whole truth came forth.

Then he sat straight on the bench, winter came into his eyes, and they remembered that this slight, soft-spoken man was the son of Helgi the Bold. "By no means will you get leave to slay him," he said; they flinched at each word. "Here you've given yourself back to that foul habit of casting bones at harmless folk. It's to my dishonor, and the worst of shames. Often have I scolded you, but you would not heed. By Mimir's hewn-off head, the time is overpast that you got a lesson. Bring the man before me!"

Amidst bristling steel, Bjarki entered. He seemed quite unruffled. "Greeting, my lord," he said proudly.

Hrolf looked at him for a while. "What is your name?" he asked.

"Your guardsmen call me Hott-fence," laughed the Norseman, "but I hight Bjarki, son of Björn who was son of the Upland king."

"What do you think you should give me for my follower whom you killed?"

"Nothing, lord. He fell on his own deed."

"M-m-m, *I* must deal with his kinfolk. . . . Well, will you become my man and take his place?"

"I'd not turn that down, lord. Not in itself. However, Hott and I must not be parted because of it, and we must both be seated closer to you than the other fellow was. Else we'll fare off."

The king frowned. "I see no gain to be gotten from Hott," he said. After looking anew into the face above him: "Still, he can always have food here."

Bjarki took oath at once on the sword Skofnung. No one thought to demean this by asking Hott to do the same. The Norseman went back to the hall, beckoned the youth to him, and looked for a place to sit. He did not choose the best; nor did he take the worst. Nearer to the high seat than was intended for him, he pitched three men sprawling off the bench, and put himself and Hott there. When angry words arose, he shrugged and said, "I've seen how good the manners are hereabouts." King

Hrolf likewise told the men they could not gripe if they too were bullied.

Thus Bjarki and Hott abode for some weeks in the hall. None dared do anything against them, and slowly the boy put on weight and began to stop flinching. But none would be their friends either.

V

As it drew toward Yule, folk grew fearful. Bjarki asked Hott what this came from.

Hott shivered: "The beast."

"Stop clapping your teeth and talk like a man," Bjarki said.

The tale stumbled forth. "For two winters, a great and horrible beast has come hither, this time of year, a winged and flying thing. Widely it harries, killing among herds and flocks; nobody can build byres for all they may own. That was what wrecked my parents' livelihood and sent me here."

"This hall is not as well manned as I thought, if a beast can freely work harm on the kingdom and the holdings of the king."

"The men have tried to kill it. Their weapons didn't bite, and some of the best of them never came home. It's no beast, really, we think. It's a troll." Hott glanced around and brought his lips to Bjarki's ear. "I've overheard Svipdag and his brothers wonder if it's not a sending of the witch-queen Skuld. They say she broods bitterly over being wed to a mere scot-king, there by Odin's Lake where thralls are drowned to honor the One-Eyed."

Afraid to speak further, he scurried away to work. He had become the Norseman's groom, scrubber, fetch-and-carry knave. Between tasks he got bruising training in the use of weapons, which he hated and tried vainly to beg off.

At Yule Eve the offerings were ill-attended, since none dared be out from under a roof after dark. The feast in the royal hall was glum. King Hrolf stood forth and said: "Hear me! My will is that everyone keep still and calm tonight. I forbid my men to go against that fiend. Let it do with the kine whatever luck may choose; but I do not want to lose any more of you."

"Aye, lord, aye, aye," said the relieved voices. Bjarki sat quiet, unheeded.

The fires guttered low. The king and the leman he then had went to his tower. The guardsmen stretched out on the benches, wrapped in blankets. They had been drinking hard to quell their fears, and soon the gloom was loud with snores.

Bjarki arose. He prodded Hott, who slept on the floor below him. "Follow me," he whispered.

He had marked where in the foreroom his battle gear was, and fetched this in the dark. Outside, the night stretched cold and silent, clear and starry, a crooked moon casting wanness over hoarfrost and the smoke of breath. Bjarki laid his mail and underpadding on the flagstones. "Help me into this," he bade.

Hott smothered a wail. "Master, you don't mean to—"

"I do mean to tie your backbone in a knot if you wake anybody. Stop that whining and give me a hand!"

By the time Bjarki was armored, Hott was too frightened to walk. "You, you, you'll lead me into danger of my life," he moaned.

"Oh, belike it'll go better than that," Bjarki said. "Move along." The youth could not. Bjarki picked him up, slung him over a shoulder, and strode from the garth. Getting a horse would have made too much noise.

They heard racket enough shortly after they had gone out a gate of the burg. Cows bawled in terror, from one of the king's own meadows a mile thence. Bjarki broke into a hammering trot over the frozen ground, along the darkly sheening stream. Near the meadow, this broadened somewhat into a bog, where dead reeds poked stiffly out of ice.

Above the pen, a shadow blotted out stars. Through the cattle-clamor beat a leathery rustle and a rushing as of mighty winds. "The beast, the beast!" Hott shrieked. "It's coming to swallow me! O-o-o-oh—"

"Belay that yammer, you cur," Bjarki snapped. He

peeled the clutching fingers loose from his ring-mail and pitched his burden into the bog. Hott crashed through the ice and huddled down to hide under the water and mud beneath.

The Norseman unslung his shield and went to meet the monster.

It saw him, swung on high and readied itself to stoop: a featherless thing of huge sickling wings, cruel claws and beak, tail like a lashing rudder, scaly crest above snaky eyes. Bjarki planted his feet and laid hand on sword hilt.

His weapon would not leave the sheath.

"Witchcraft!" he groaned. The monster hissed athwart the bleak-bright Bridge. Wings thrust air, and down it came.

"Elven sword—" Bjarki hauled on Lövi till the sheath creaked. Then it broke loose to flash under the stars.

The troll-being was almost upon him. A rank smell overwhelmed his lungs. He held his shield firm and struck from behind it. The heavy body smote, a thud and clang, a boom of air and a whistle out of grinning sharp-toothed jaws. Bjarki stumbled back. Any other man would have been flattened, broken-boned. His blade had already bitten. In it went between wing and leg, through hide and flesh and ribs to the heart.

The monster swerved and crashed. A while it threshed around. The earth quivered under the blows of its wings. When most of its cold blood had run out onto the rime, it lay dead.

Bjarki gusted a breath and went after Hott.

He must pluck the fear-blinded, shaking, whimpering wretch out of the bog, carry him over to where the beast lay still twitching, and set him down. Pointing to the wound, from which blood welled black, he said: "Drink of that."

"No, oh, no, I beg you," Hott blubbered.

"Drink, I said! Have I not told you what my brother Elk-Frodhi did for me? Whoever called this thing forth, out of whatever hell, wanted strength in it."

Hott crawled and sobbed. Bjarki clouted him and

promised worse if he did not obey. The boy shut his eyes and put his mouth to that cup which the sword had made. However much he gagged, Bjarki made him swallow two long draughts. Thereupon the Norseman cut the heart out of the beast, handed it over, and said, "Take a bite off this."

Hott did. He had stopped shaking. When he had chewed the meat, he bounded up. "Why—" He looked around in wonder. "Why, the world is beautiful."

"You feel better, eh?" said Bjarki as he settled the elven blade back in its birchbark sheath.

"I feel . . . as if I'd wakened from death."

Bjarki felt Hott's arms. "I knew there were good thews in you, since I got you rightly fed," he grunted. "What you needed was to tauten them." He unbuckled his sword belt. "Let's try you out."

Long they wrestled before Bjarki got Hott to one knee, longer than he would have taken even for Svipdag. Raising the other, he panted gladly: "You've a bit of strength now. I don't think you need fear the guardsmen of King Hrolf any more."

Hott lifted hands to heaven and cried in young heat, "From this night, I'll never fear them—or you either, or anyone or anything!"

"That's well, Hott, my friend," said Bjarki. "I think I've paid off a debt of mine." He grinned. He was no oldster himself. "Help me set up this carcass so they'll think it's alive."

Laughing like drunkards, they did. Thereafter they stole back to the hall, lay down, and acted as if nothing had happened.

In the morning the king asked whether aught had been marked of the fiend, whether it had shown itself during the night. He got the answer that livestock around the burg seemed unharmed. "Look further," he ordered.

The watchmen did. Erelong they came pounding back, to gasp that they had seen the beast and it was bound hither.

Men clattered to arms. The king bade them be brave and each do his best to get the life out of this thing. He took the lead in the dash to meet it. When they spied the great brown shape, propped on stiffened wings in the wintry dawn, they drew together in a shield-ring, and a hush fell over them.

After a while the king said slowly, "I don't think it's even moving. Who'll take a reward to go and see what it's about?"

Bjarki spoke aloud: "It'd indeed be something for a bold man to carry that out before witnesses." He clapped the back of the youth who had followed him. "Hott, my fellow!" he said. "Here's where you can wash off that slander they've put on you, that you've neither strength nor courage. Go slay yonder pest! You can see that none of the others are minded to."

Stares went to the fair-locked head which suddenly was borne so high. "Yes," said Hott, "I will."

The king lifted his brows. "I see not where you've gotten this boldness from, Hott," he said. "You must have changed in a very short while."

"I have no weapon of my own," was the answer. Pointing to one of the two swords which King Hrolf wore: "Give me that Goldhilt of yours, and I'll fell the beast or get my bane."

Hrolf looked at him for a time before he said, "It's not seemly that this sword be borne by any save a brave and trustworthy lad."

"You'll soon see that I am like that."

"Who knows if there's not been even more of a change in you than we thought we saw? It's as if you were altogether a different being. . . . Well, take the sword, then, and if you can do this deed, I'll find you worthy to own it afterward."

Few had followed these words. They were too aware of the hideousness before them. But all saw Hott bare the steel and run toward it. In a single blow, he knocked it flat.

"Look, lord," cried Bjarki, "what a mighty work he's done!"

Stunned at first, the men broke into cheers, brandished their weapons, clanged blade on shield, rushed to hug

Hott and lift him on their shoulders. Hrolf stayed behind, as did Bjarki. The king said low: "Yes, he has become something else from what he was. Nevertheless, Hott alone has not slain the beast. Rather, you did."

The Norseman shrugged. "Could be that's so."

Hrolf nodded. "This I saw at once when you came here: that few could be like unto you. Yet I think your best work is that you've made a man out of this hitherto luckless Hott."

The troop were nearing. Hrolf raised his voice: "Now I want him no longer to be called by a thrallish name like Hott. Let him be named for the sword Goldhilt he has earned." Turning to the flushed young warrior, he said, "Henceforth you shall be Hjalti."

That means "Hilt," and the hilt he became of the king's household, as Bjarki was the blade and Svipdag the shield.

VI

From that day onward, Bjarki and his friend had the goodwill, or the outright worship of the guards. At first the lad was not seen much in the hall. After bringing goods to help his parents, he made up for lost time by mowing a swathe through all the women to be had for many miles around. Bjarki stayed graver. He won the close fellowship of the king, who made great gifts to him, and of eye-patched Svipdag. Together those three held long talks about how to widen and strengthen the kingdom and what might be done for its welfare.

Bjarki also began to see a good deal of Hrolf's oldest daughter Drifa, who was becoming a handsome lady. And, being more among the warriors then was possible for the king—who must go to Things, hear out the troubles and quarrels of folk, give judgments, play host to visitors, watch over his own broad landholdings, and on and on—Bjarki strove to make the troop mend its ways.

Svipdag told him: "I think our twelve berserkers are the root of the ill behavior here. They browbeat most of the men, who then have to take it out on somebody weaker. I wish we could get rid of them, and I'm sure King Hrolf wishes likewise, useful though they can be in a fight. But they are his sworn followers and have given him no real cause to dismiss them."

"Where are they now?" the Norseman asked.

"They've been at the head of a band which harried about in Saxon lands. See you, the king doesn't want to bring those under him. They've too many ties further south. But they have been bothering us—egged on by the Swedish jarl of Als is my guess. And we can't well haul the Jutes into Denmark, as we hope to, till it's been pounded into the Saxons that they'd better leave us alone. Our raiders decided to winter there. They'll be back in spring."

Later Bjarki asked Hjalti what to await from these berserkers. The younger man told of the way they had on arrival of bracing everyone in the hall and asking if he reckoned himself as doughty as them. "They've learned to make this only a token as far as the king goes, or those three brothers from Svithjodh; but the rest must needs humble themselves."

Said Bjarki: "Small is the number of bold men here with King Hrolf, if they bear words of scorn from the berserkers."

Time flowed on. The evening came when, as the household was settling down to its meal, the door flew open and in came the twelve huge men, gray with iron, shining to look on like icefields.

Bjarki whispered to Hjalti, "Do you dare match yourself against any of them?"

"Any or all."

The dozen lumbered to the high seat and questioned King Hrolf in their wonted words. He answered in such wise as he found prideful while keeping the uneasy peace. Next they went along the benches. One by one, in hate-filled voices, the warriors called themselves the weaker.

Agnar, their headman, had seen Bjarki and thought this was not a little boy who had come. Nonetheless he hulked over the Norseman and growled, "Well, Redbeard, do you think you're as good as me?"

Bjarki smiled. "No," he purred, "I do not. I deem myself better than you, you filthy son of a mare."

He leaped to his feet, grabbed the berserker's belt, swung him on high and dashed him to the floor so that the crash resounded. Hjalti did likewise to the next.

Men shouted. The berserkers howled. Bjarki stood holding Agnar down under his foot, a knife in his hand. Hjalti had drawn the sword Goldhilt, and from behind it grinned at the half score who milled and mouthed before him.

Hrolf sprang out of the high seat and sped thither. "Hold off!" he cried to Bjarki. "Keep the peace!"

"Lord," said the Norseman, "this knave is going to lose his life unless he owns himself the lesser man."

The king gazed upon the pair who lay stunned beneath the two friends. "That's easily done," he said, not quite able to stay wholly earnest.

Agnar mumbled something and Bjarki let him get up, as Hjalti did for the other. Everybody took his seat, the berserkers theirs with heavy hearts.

Hrolf stood forth and talked sternly to his troopers. Tonight, he told them, they had seen how none was so bold, strong, or big that his like could not be found. "I forbid you to awaken more strife in my hall. No matter who breaks my ban, it shall cost him his life. Against my foes you can be as angry and raging as you wish, and so win honor and fame. Before as goodly a flock of warriors as you are, I need not keep still. I say to you, make yourselves worthy of yourselves!"

All praised the words of the king and swore friendship.

It was but skin deep on the part of the berserkers. They kept their hatred for Bjarki and Hjalti, losing no chance to backbite these and giving them never a word which was not surly. However, they dared not make real trouble. After they stopped pestering and humbling the rest of the men, the latter soon lost their own overweening ways toward others. In a while, not only hirelings but the very thralls said that King Hrolf's garth was a happy place to be.

The warriors were much away from it, however, for in those days he was bringing the Jutes under him. Great were the deeds done on strands, hills, and heaths, in woods and dales; and wily, too, were the schemings which Hrolf set forth. The tale of his warfaring would get overly long, for it is only a tale of victories.

At home he dwelt in splendor. This is how he seated his men: On his right was Bjarki, acknowledged the foremost among them and therefore the marshal. They had come to call him Bodhvar-Bjarki, Battle-Bjarki, which fitted so well that today he is often spoken of as Bodhvar, as if that were the name his father bestowed on him. But Bjarki is right, and more than one lay calling men forth to fight is known as a Bjarkamaal. However terrible in war, he was a cheerful and openhanded soul, always spared the lives of foemen who yielded, never took a woman against her will, and loved to make small children laugh.

On his right in turn sat Hjalti the High-Minded. The king had given him that nickname. For every day he was among the guardsmen who had been so tough on him, and took no revenge even though he had now waxed far stronger than any of them, and though Hrolf would surely have found it forgiveable if he had handed out a few remembrances.

Beyond him sat several who were reckoned among the best: Hromund the Hard, the king's namesake Hrolf the Swift-Coming, Haaklang, Hard-Hrefill, Haaki the Bold, Hvatt the High-Born, and Starulf.

On the king's left were those who stood below none save Bjarki and Hjalti—Svipdag, Beigadh, and Hvitserk. To the left of these were the berserkers under Agnar. They were moody benchmates, but their strength earned them this honor. Anyhow, the brothers from Svithjodh were not very outgoing. Svipdag especially was apt to brood when in his cups, as if recalling someone from years agone.

Elsewhere, on both sides, the hall was full of picked fighting men, to the number of three long hundreds. A boisterous crew they were, a merry and breakneck lot; the burg roared with them, the whole surrounding countryside did.

There were still more household workers, and usually guests. As the fame of King Hrolf heightened, and the Danish waters and highways were cleared of robbers, ships lay to at Roskilde, Cheaping-Haven, and other ports, with goods that might come from Finland or the Icy Sea, from Ireland or Russia or the deep heart of Saxland, or further yet. To trade, the Danes had fish and amber out of the waves, meat and butter and cheese and honey off their fat farms. But they themselves were laying ever more keels and turning ever more prows outward.

It was costly to live as King Hrolf did, the more so because he was the most lavish of gift-givers. However, the wealth that came in as the range of his peace broadened was enough and to spare. Besides getting payments from his under-kings, he was himself the owner of lush acres and widely faring seacraft. He did not need to lay heavy scot on fisheries, farms, and trade; nor, when his warfaring dwindled for lack of foes, did he miss the booty he used to win.

Harder was to hold his men at rest. Mostly he found ways. Each owned something, be it land or ships, that he must often see to. Each had a leman nearby to keep him snug, and many now slept in their own houses near the hall. The king got them to practice all kinds of games and crafts; and this they came to do ably and proudly.

Whatever they undertook, Bjarki was always the best at it. He became the dearest to the king, who in the course of time gave him twelve great farmsteads scattered around Denmark—and, at last, his daughter Drifa to wife. They were a happy pair, the redbeard and the stately fair-braided young woman; folk said they looked like Thor and Sif.

Hrolf himself stayed unwedded. Bjovulf being dead and Götaland in upheaval, there was no real match for him anywhere in the Northlands—save maybe in Svithjodh, where King Adhils would hardly let him make an alliance. "Besides," he said once to Bjarki, "I've had too much to do for a woman to be more to me than a bedmate." The marshal thought he heard wistfulness.

None of this came about overnight. It took five years

from the time when Bjarki first rode through Leidhra gate; and hard was the swordplay. Toward the end, things went faster. The Jutish kinglets and headmen saw no hope of holding out. Moreover, they and those they led came to understand that whoever owned Hrolf Helgisson their overlord, got things which far outweighed what he asked of them.

They got peace. No longer might a neighbor chieftain take it into his head to come killing, burning, looting, raping, enslaving; and did outlanders seem like a threat, the High King in Leidhra could whistle up more warriors, more skilled and deadly, than anybody cared to meet. At first the crows gorged on hanged outlaws, the gulls on vikings washed ashore. Later these birds went hungry. The farmer and fisherman harvested free from dread; the merchant who had a venture in mind, the settler who wanted to clear new land, dared plan it.

The High King was just. The poorest old granny might speak to him as he rode around in the Denmark he had made, and be sure of a patient ear. The haughtiest underking, jarl, or sheriff must answer for every wrongdoing. Yet Hrolf was no harsher than he must be. In judging a quarrel, he tried as far as he was able to bring men together. "If you give a little as well as gain a little," he would say, "it does not make you the less. Rather, it means that after you are dead, folk will be glad to remember your name and offer at your howe."

Trade spread like friendly wildfire. Any islander, Scanian, or Jute could fare to the markets and dicker for what the skippers were bringing in. This was more than goods; it was arts, crafts, skills hitherto unknown, it was news and sagas and staves and songs from abroad, to lift the soul out of the narrow paddocks of home.

Thus when Hrolf Helgisson had been thirty-five years upon the earth, he steered a kingdom second only to Svithjodh in size, and far more rich, happy, and outward-looking. Mighty as a summer sky, his peace roofed it in; and to none did he give grounds for weeping, save those few who were left that hated, and one afar in Uppsala who loved him.

VI

THE TALE OF YRSA

I

In the last year that Hrolf spent building his kingdom, things went like carpentry. Some men grumbled at getting no fights. Bjarki was not among them; he had no need to show off his manhood or win booty. Nonetheless he grew more and more thoughtful, and this went on after he had come home.

Huge was the feast that Yule Eve in Leidhra. The hall was loud not only with warriors but with many guests: scot-kings, jarls, sheriffs, and yeomen from widely across the realm, as well as outlanders wintering in Roskilde. Crofters, beggars, and gangrels fared better than they would have done as heads of most chiefly households. It was a sorrow to Hrolf that his brother-in-law Hjörvardh and sister Skuld had stayed away. In everything else he was glad and prideful.

The skalds chanted their old lays about his forebears, their new ones about him, and he had no lack of rings to break for their reward, nor of goodly weapons and costly garments to bestow on other friends. The long-fires leaped and rumbled, the rushlights burned clear, to fill the air with warmth, sweet smell of juniper boughs, sheen off gold, silver, copper, and polished iron. The graven figures on pillars and panels seemed to stir, as if reaching out of their shadows to join the mirth. Talk, laughter, clash of horns and cups together, rolled under the roof like surf. The benches were crammed with lords and ladies, a rainbow of colors, a star-glitter of jewelry. To and fro scurried the servants, dodging hounds which lolled about chewing bones and thumping tails. The trestle tables had been cleared away. Ox, boar, deer, sheep, swan, grouse, partridge, whale, seal, tunny, flounder, cod, oyster, lobster, bread, butter, cheese, sausage, leeks, apples, honey, nuts, these and much else were now well-filled bellies and lingering savors. The real drinking was under weigh: beer and ale of different brews, swart or fair; mead, thick and sweet or light and lively; wine, from Danish berries or Southland grapes. Already some heads were finding it as noisy inside the ears as outside them. Yet no word had been spoken save in fellowship.

Beaming, King Hrolf looked to right and left and said, "Much strength has here met in one hall." He leaned toward Bjarki, who sat unwontedly quiet, his wife Drifa at his side. (Beyond her, Hjalti and a maid on his lap were having a gleeful tussle.) "Tell me, my friend, do you know of any king like me, who rules over men like these?"

"No," said the Norseman, "I do not. Your work will never be forgotten." Then, slowly: "I do think one thing is left which breaks down your royal honor."

Taken aback in his happy mood, Hrolf asked what that could be.

Bjarki gave him look for look and answered weightily: "What demeans you, lord, is that you do not fetch your inheritance from your father out of Uppsala, the hoard which King Adhils unrightfully keeps."

Svipdag, to left of the high seat, leaned past Hrolf's leman. The single eye suddenly burned in his gaunt, scarred face.

Hrolf could not gainsay that it shamed him to be thus treated, and therefore threatened him. What he spoke aloud was: "It would be hard to get hold of it. For Adhils is no honorable man. Rather is he skilled in witchcraft, evil, sly, ill thought of, and the worst there is to have to do with."

"Even so," Bjarki said, "the most seemly for you, lord, would be to demand your due, and sometime seek out King Adhils and find how he answers."

Hrolf sat still a while before he said, "A great goal is this you have named; for I have my father to avenge."

He glanced at Svipdag. "Adhils is the greediest and cranki-
est of kings, so let's have a care."

Bjarki chuckled, or did he growl? "I would not scorn
someday to learn what kind of fellow he is."

Svipdag breathed: "I promised when I left there, I'd
visit them again. Lord, the queen would help us."

"We'll talk further of this," Hrolf said. For the rest of
the evening he had to work at being merry.

Drifa whispered to Bjarki: "You will go. I know you
will."

"I believe it," he nodded, more content than hitherto.

She gripped his arm. "Always you go, you men. My
mother, you remember . . . my father saw her married
off to a yeoman, and she bore her husband a son who
fell in holmgang . . . she said to me, it seemed like yesterday she laid him in his crib, and now she was laying
him in his grave." Her gold-bedecked head lifted. "Go
you must, Bjarki, because you want to. But oh, come
back! I have not had you very long."

Busy though the king was, during the next few weeks
he spent a good deal of time speaking in secret with
knowledgeable men, drawing plans and making ready.
"If we're slow," he warned, "Adhils is sure to get wind of
our intention and thus time to build something nasty.
Traveling while winter is on the ground and few wayfarers about, we may be able to keep ahead of any word
of us."

"Why not go by sea?" asked Bjarki.

King Hrolf frowned. "That was no lucky road for my
father."

"Too risky this time of year, along that coast of uncounted islands and skerries," warned Svipdag. "Any sudden storm could dash us ashore; and I'm not sure but
what King Adhils could raise one."

Hence Hrolf's only rowing was across the Sound to
Scania. He gave out that he wanted to ride around and
see how that part of his land was doing. To make this
look true, as well as to go speedily and to leave plenty
of strength in his newly-made realm, he took no great

troop along. There were his twelve chief warriors, the twelve berserkers, and a hundred guardsmen.

They went on the best of horses, leading ample remounts and packbeasts. The garb they wore was thick against cold, of the finest furs and gaily dyed stuffs. Hrolf and the dozen captains each bore a hawk on his shoulder, so well trained that hood and jesses could be left off, to make a still better show. The king's was named Highbreeks, a gyrfalcon, big and mettlesome, his eyes like those golden shields that are said to light the halls of the war-gods. Alongside loped Gram, a giant red hound which had pulled down wolf, elk, boar, and man.

Where Scania faded into Götaland, the Danes struck north. This East Göta country was rugged, thickly wooded and thinly peopled. They would often have to sleep out, rolled in bags upon chopped-off boughs. To make the more haste, they would not hunt, but live off what dry food they had along. They thought nothing of that, and of their faring is nothing to tell until one dusk when they came upon the lonely garth of a yeoman.

II

This was a surprise. They had seen no spoor of the plow thereabouts. Meager snow decked a clearing walled by evergreens and roofed by a low overcast. The house ought to have been easier to make out. It seemed to stand in deep shadow, itself another darkness which looked neither small nor great. The air hung chill, blotting up hoofbeats, voices, clink of metal, squeak of leather, sighs of weary beasts. Breath smoked dim.

Clearer to see was the man who stood outside, save for his face. A broad-brimmed hat cast that in murk. Beneath flowed a long gray beard. He was very tall, wrapped in a blue cloak, and carried a spear.

The king reined in. "Greeting, fellow," he said. "Fear not if we camp on your land. We mean no harm."

Deep tones answered: "You need not sleep in the weather. Spend the night under my roof."

"It would ill become me to do what my men can't."

"I meant all of you."

Hrolf blinked in astonishment. "You're a bold one! Can you really afford that? We're not few, and it's not for a smallholder to take us in."

The yeoman laughed in a way that recalled wolves baying. "Yes, lord. But I've now and then seen just as many men coming to where I was. You shall lack for drink this evening, or for whatever else you may need."

The king felt it would be unfitting to say other than: "We'll put our faith in that."

"You are welcome in truth," said the yeoman. "Follow me."

He led them behind the house. There they found a well-timbered building of a size to hold their beasts. Apart from hay and water troughs, it stood empty. The old one said it was too dark within for any who did not know his way around, and he would himself stall the horses and see to them. This went oddly fast.

"Who are you, yeoman?" asked the king.

"Some call me Hrani," he answered.

Hrolf wondered at that, for the name is not common. His uncle Hroar had used it when hiding from King Frodhi. Even more did he wonder when he trod into the house he could so poorly see. The room beyond the door was as long and brightly lit as a hall, though as forsaken as the stable had been. Runes were cut in the walls.

"There's something uncanny here," Bjarki muttered to Hjalti.

The younger man shrugged. "Better than outdoors."

Hrani bade them sit down. Had the trestle tables already been set up, trenchers of hot swineflesh, cups full of mead? Did Hrani himself, never taking off his hat, serve them as swiftly as he had done the horses? Strangest in their minds afterward was the dreamlike way in which they took this guesting. At the time, most of the men soon grew drunk and cheerful, swore they had hardly ever come upon a finer place, and shoved their wonder aside.

Hrani sat by Hrolf. They and a few who gathered around spoke together. The king named himself and his errand. The yeoman nodded and gave counsel about the best way from here to Uppsala. Svipdag asked how he knew this, forasmuch as smallholders seldom go far from where they were born. "Though I am aged," Hrani said, "I wander widely."

"How can you live in this house by yourself?" asked Bjarki.

"I am not by myself tonight, am I?" answered Hrani with his wolf-laugh. "I have guests oftener than you think, as well as strong sons who don't happen to be here. Now as for your road—" He went on to tell them things they had never known about this land and those who dwelt in it. From there he led the talk to happenings aforetime. Never had they heard tales better told; and many were the wise saws and ringing staves which he threw in. It seemed to them this was indeed a deep fellow.

But they had ridden throughout a hard day. Soon weariness overcame them, helped by the noble mead they had drunk. Hrani bade them stretch out on benches and floor. He did not stay in the room. The fires died down.

The king and his men awoke sometime in the middle of the night. Only banked coals were left in the trench, barely enough red light to fumble by. It was so cold that the teeth chopped in their jaws. They sprang up, undid the bundles they had brought in from the packhorses, and put on more clothes and whatever they could get hold of—save for Hrolf and his chief warriors, who made do with what they already wore. Everyone froze until dawn came, and Hrani bringing wood to throw on the embers.

Then asked the yeoman: "How have you slept?"

"Well," grunted Bjarki.

The yeoman turned an eye on the king, bleaker than the winter dark had been. He said dryly, "I know your guardsmen felt it was rather cool here last night; and it was. They must not suppose they can withstand what King Adhils in Uppsala will lay on them, if they took this so ill." Sternly: "If you would save your life, send home half your following; for it will not be by numbers of men that you win over King Adhils."

"You are no common man who tells me this," said Hrolf low. "I will go by your rede."

After they had broken their fast, he found mild words which turned back the fifty warriors who had shivered most. Later no one could quite remember how the speech went or why none felt this a slur. When the rest were ready to go, they thanked the yeoman and bade him live well.

Onward they rode, over hills where the pinewoods reared and dales where the snow had drifted thick. As the cloudiness left their minds, they talked about who, or what, had been their host, and why. At last Bjarki said gruffly, "Well, more than men and beasts can flit through a wilderness, as I have good cause to know. They need not be unfriendly . . . . Although," he added after a bit, and cast a glance toward the king's helmet before him, "keeping them friendly can be a tricky thing."

At eventide they came again upon a clearing where stood a garth and a tall old man who wore a broad-brimmed hat and a blue cloak. His house was likewise hard to make out in the shadowiness around. A mumble went among them, a prickling through them. King Hrolf drew rein and clapped hand to the sword Skofnung.

"Greeting, lord," laughed the yeoman. "Why do you come so often?"

The king answered steadfastly: "We know not what kind of sleight is being used on us. You're an eldritch one."

"I will not receive you ill this time either," said the yeoman.

The king looked back down the lines of his men. "Best we stay, since we are asked," he told them. "Night comes on apace."

Once inside, nobody wondered much, and the hospitality was good. Erelong they laid themselves to sleep.

They were awakened by such a thirst that the tongues could hardly move in their heads. A mead barrel stood at one end of the room. Everyone went there and drank deep, save the king and his twelve captains.

In the morning, Hrani the yeoman said: "Again, lord, hearken to me. I think there's scant hardihood in those fellows who had to drink during the night. Worse trouble must they withstand when they reach King Adhils."

Nothing could be done right away, for a blizzard had sprung up. Blind whiteness shrieked around the house. Strongly were those walls timbered, not to groan beneath that wind. The men sat and listened to Hrani spin such wonderful tales that the day seemed very short—"as if somehow we'd ridden out of time," Svipdag mumbled to his brothers.

About sundown the storm ended. Less snow had fallen than one would have awaited; travel should be possible next day. Hrani brought in wood and stoked the fire. It blazed strangely swiftly, high and higher, red and blue awhirl over a white-hot bed, roaring as loud as the weather had done. Heat went in waves over the men where they sat. They shifted well back. King Hrolf remembered the vow he had taken when he was young, never to flee from iron or fire. He stayed where he was, and his captains beside him, though sweat rivered off them and it felt as if their eyes must soon boil.

A single light gleamed from under Hrani's hat. "Again, lord," he said, "you must make a choice out of your following. My rede is that none go on from here save you and these twelve. Then it may be that you can come home; otherwise not."

Heat-dazed, King Hrolf tried to speak firmly: "I've such a mind about you, yeoman, that I think I'd better heed your words."

The flames soon dwindled. That night the men slept well, aside from uneasy dreams.

In the morning, Hrolf sent home his remaining fifty, together with the berserkers. Again, none cried out against this order until afterward, far too late. Mounted, the king said to the yeoman: "It may be that I have much to thank you for."

"It may be you can repay me sometime," answered Hrani.

"Farewell until then," said Hrolf. His hawk fluttered

wings at sight of two ravens aloft; his hound growled at
the nearby howl of a wolf. In a while woodlands had
hidden that garth in snow and silence.

They rode on: Hrolf, King of Denmark, bound to redeem his riches because in them lay his honor and, he
hoped, revenge for his father; Bjarki, the werebear's
son; Hjalti, who had gotten his manhood from the blood
and heart of a troll; Svipdag, whose one eye peered from
years agone to days ahead; Hvitserk, Beigadh, Hromund,
Hrolf the namesake, Haaklang, Hrefill, Haaki, Hvatt,
Starulf, men whose starkness no fiend or god could daunt,
hawks upon their shoulders and looking out of their souls.
Bright were their helmets and spearheads across winter-
wan heaven, bright their mail and cloaks across darkling
green boughs and blue-shadowed whiteness; they hardly
felt the chill that made their breaths fog and their saddles
creak. Yet this was no great troop to bring against the
king of Svithjodh and the weirdness he commanded.

Entering that land, crossing open fields where farmsteads and hamlets were many, sometimes needing to be
ferried, they were seen. Though they named themselves
no longer, word about them may well have flown ahead
and Adhils have guessed the truth. Or maybe he peered
into one of his cauldrons and saw a thing in the steam or
heard a thing in the seething. One twilight he said to the
queen beside him, but for all to hear: "I learn that King
Hrolf Helgisson is on his way to us."

Yrsa gasped before she could clap a shield down over
her face.

"It is well, it is well," smiled Adhils; "for surely he shall
get such a reward for his trouble, before we part, that
the tale of it will travel far."

III

At last King Hrolf and his warriors came riding over
the Fyris Wolds. Those meadows lay streaked with dusty
old snow, otherwise brown and hard-frozen, thudding
under hoofs. Ahead was the river, and on the high west-
ern bank Uppsala town, crowned by the temple. Its roof

upon roof lifted into a bleached heaven, gold aglitter; but behind, the trees of the holy shaw were skeleton-bare. A few crows flapped and cawed through the breeze.

Hrolf lifted a horn slung from his shoulder and blew three blasts, deep and long as the challenge of a bull wisent. Striking spurs to horse, he broke into a gallop. His men came straight after, a gleam of mail and of spear-heads which moved like waves, a winging of cloaks red and blue and tawny across that winter land. When they went over the bridge, its planks thundered beneath them.

Folk clustered in watchtowers and on walkways of the stockade, to see so bold a sight. The gates stood open; nobody knew any reason to fear thirteen strangers, however well-armed. Hrolf understood that he must not for an eyeblink act as if this broad and crowded town daunted him. Up the road, through the gates, along the ruts between walls, he sped. Men, women, children, wagoners, swine, dogs, hens must scramble alike to get out of the way. Angry shouts followed him. But none dared launch a spear, especially since he was clearly aimed at the royal hall.

The gates to that garth stood likewise wide. Guardsmen filled it, spilling into the yard beyond, a moon-field of shields. None drew weapon, however; and men of the household waited in good clothes, smiles smeared over their mouths.

The Danes drew rein. Their horses reared, their hawks spread feathers across which sunlight ran, the hound Gram bayed once. Svipdag cried: "Tell King Adhils that here to guest is Hrolf Helgisson, King of the Danes!"

"Welcome, welcome," said the spokesman for the Swedes. He did not seem astounded at the news. "I am honored in greeting so famous a man and his followers." He let his gaze pass quite slowly among them. "Surely King Adhils is as sorry as I am, that you bring this few for him to give hospitality to."

"We have brought enough."

"Ah . . . Svipdag Svipsson . . . yes. You have come back, eh?"

"I said I would."

"Will you follow me, then?"

They rode among the buildings to the stables. Grooms took their bridles. As he dismounted, Bjarki said, "You fellows make sure neither the manes nor the tails of our horses be unkempt. Stall them well and have a care that they not get dirty."

The spokesman flushed at this—that here might be less than the best—and signed to a boy, who scuttled off. Thereafter he held the Danes in talk for a bit, asking about their journey. Meanwhile the boy entered the hall and told King Adhils what had happened thus far.

The lord of Svithjodh smote the arm of his high seat and grated: "Hard is it to bear, how toplofty and overweening they are! Bring back my word to the head groom and see that he does as I bid. Chop the tails off those horses, right next to the rump, and cut the manes off so the scalp comes too. Then stable them in every way as badly as you can, and let them barely stay alive."

The boy louted low and slipped away. Adhils settled into his chair. He quivered. Likewise did the weavings lately hung along the walls.

Soon the Danes were brought to the hall. None stood at its cave-mouth door to greet them as would have been fitting. Their guide smirked, "The king awaits you within," and left.

Hjalti clapped hand to sword. "They dare treat our lord like this!"

Hrolf looked across the yard. The guardsmen had withdrawn too but stood under the stockade, rank upon mailclad rank. "Don't start anything," he murmured. "Our coming was not quite the surprise we hoped for."

Svipdag tugged his drooping mustache and said: "Yes, I was afraid of this. Let me go in first. I know this house from aforetime, and I've a nasty suspicion about how they mean to receive us. Now listen—whatever happens, let none give out which of us is King Hrolf. That'd make him a target, not alone for every edge and point if things come to that, but for any witchcraft Adhils may have cooked up."

The king sighed. "I suppose I should be glad that not

even my mother has met us," he said. "Across the years, she may still have known me." He straightened. "Well, no dawdling, or they'll think we're afraid."

Svipdag rested his ax across the right shoulder—his hawk sat on the left—and trod between the grinning figures on the doorposts. After him came his brothers Hvitserk and Beigadh, then Bjarki and Hrolf, then the rest mingled together.

The foreroom was broad and dim. Svipdag passed on into the main chamber. That was like stepping into night, so gloomy was it. Barely did he see great changes everywhere. The fire-trenches gaped cold. A few rushlights flickered in brackets set far apart, to pick out weavings of heavy cloth. Otherwise the hall reached empty, altogether silent. In the freezing dark, it felt still more vast than it was, as if those rows of wavering blue flamelets dwindled on and on till they met at some edge of the world.

Svipdag strode forward, an iron glimmer. His friends stayed close behind. Whisperings went through the hush around them. All at once Svipdag tottered backward. "A pit!" he warned. "I nearly fell in."

Using their weapons as feeling-stocks, the Danes found that, while it seemed to stretch across the room, the trap was not too broad for men such as they to overleap. They did, and went on.

Next it was as if spiderwebs dropped around them. They were tangled in sticky nets, unseen and cable-strong. Something giggled. "Strike out," said Svipdag. As cold iron hewed, the strands fell away.

A thing walked toward them. It had the shape of a dead giant-woman—they saw the grave-mould and the lightless eyes—whose skin moved upon her bones and whose hands reached out to strangle. Svipdag's laughter jarred. "He finds less and less to offer us, the good Adhils," he said, and chopped at her. His ax met emptiness; she was gone.

When they covered some yards more, another shape hove in sight. High on his seat spread the gross form of the Swede-King. They could hardly see him, away off in dimness amidst monstrous shadows. Svipdag raised an arm to signal a halt. It looked as if further pitfalls lay ahead.

The eyes of Adhils, hidden from them in the blur of his face, could better stab through the murk he had made than could theirs. He called in mockery: "Well, at last you've returned, eh, Svipdag, my friend? Hm, hm, what errand has the warrior? Is it not as it seems to me, that bowed is your neck, one eye not there, wrinkled your brow, hands bearing scars, and Beigadh your brother limps on both legs?"

Svipdag stiffened. He knew he appeared older than he was; and Beigadh had taken wounds in Hrolf's service such that he no longer walked as easily as most. Therefore Svipdag's answer was harsh as well as loud. "In accord with what you promised me, King Adhils, I crave safety for these twelve men who here are gathered together."

"That they shall have. Now come into the hall briskly and in manly wise, calmer-hearted than you have shown yourselves hitherto."

"Don't let him goad you into rashness," Hrolf whispered.

"Keep ready to form a shield-burg," Bjarki added, "for I think those weavings on the walls bulge forward, as if armed men were behind."

The Danes thus went ahead with care, and found another trench they must spring over. Then they were near the high seat. Runic signs rippled on the cloths, as a fighter in mail stormed forth from behind each one.

"Make a ring!" roared Bjarki. There was no need; everybody knew what to do. Shield by shield, they stood against thrice their number.

Hrolf cast his spear. A Swede stumbled when it took him in the neck. More shafts flew, till the attackers closed. Through the air hissed the swords Skofnung, Lövi, Goldhilt, and their kin. High lifted the ax of Svipdag, whirling overhead till he struck across the shoulder of Hromund who shielded him. Metal boomed. The shield of that Swede dropped off a numb arm. The ax slewed about and its butt stove in his temple.

A tall man came at Bjarki. The Norseman brought his shield forward, to hook its rim behind that of his foe. He shoved to make an opening in the defense. Through this his edge smote; and a head rolled over the floor.

Hjalti's blade rang and sparked upon another. In blow after blow he beat it aside, got the brief chance he wanted, sliced inward and crippled a wrist. As that man howled and lurched back, Hjalti slew him. Meanwhile King Hrolf crouched, shield on high, and chopped the leg from beneath an attacker. The rest of his men struck and stabbed. Their hawks had flown to the rafters, but the hound Gram slashed with fangs, himself too swiftly dancing about to be wounded.

In din and shouting, the Danes cast back the Swedes. As these reeled in disorder, the thirteen made a wedge and charged them. Weapons played like flames. Dead and maimed lay strewn around, the darkness echoed to cries of pain. On Hrolf and his captains stood hardly a mark. "Kill them!" bawled Bjarki. "Cut them down like any other dogs!"

King Adhils sprang to his feet and screamed from the dais, "What is this uproar? Stop! Stop, I say!"

Slowly the fight ended, until there was silence but for the groans of the wounded, the heavy breathing of the hale. Eyes and iron gleamed amidst shadows. Adhils yelled at his guards: "You must be the worst of nithings, that you set on such outstanding men—our guests! Go! Clear the hall! Bring in servants and . . . and light—go, you wolf-heads! I'll deal with you later."

The warriors stared. However, they caught his meaning, and would not make their failure worse by gainsaying him. They stole out, helping those of their hurt fellows who could move.

"Forgive me!" Adhils said to the Danes. "I have foes, and feared treachery . . . . When you came in armed, as is not the wont here . . . then some of my followers grew over-zealous, me unwitting . . . . But I see now that you must in truth be King Hrolf, my kinsman, and his famous champions, as you told the gatekeeper. Sit down, be at ease, and let us have it good together."

"Little luck have you gotten, King Adhils," growled Svipdag, "and honorless are you in this matter."

They peered at the Svithjodh lord. Adhils had grown bald and fat. The beard which spilled down his richly robed paunch was more gray than yellow. Only his blade of a nose remained lean, and the little squinting, blinking eyes.

Thralls and hirelings hastened in to bear out the dead and disabled, clean up the blood, strew fresh rushes, bring lamps and build fires. With them came new guardsmen, and more must be crowding outside. It would not do to rush at the dais and try to kill Adhils. Besides, that would besmirch the name of King Hrolf, after he had been greeted in friendly words, however empty he knew those words to be.

"Sit, sit," urged his host. "Come give me your hand, my kinsman of Denmark."

"The time is not ripe for you to know which of us he is," Svipdag said.

Hjalti fleered. "Aye," he added, "it would be to your . . . dishonor . . . King Adhils, should more of your men grow . . . over-zealous."

"You mistake me, you mistake me," puffed the fat man. He dared not press the matter and thus remind everyone in the hall of his humbling. He could only sink back into his chair and gibe, "As you will. If you are, hm, hm, not wholly so bold as to make yourself known, Hrolf, well, be it as you wish." After a bit: "For I do see that you don't fare outland in the way of wellborn folk. Why does my kinsman have no more of a troop?"

"Since you don't forbear to sit in treachery against King Hrolf and his men," said Svipdag, "it makes small difference whether he rides hither with few or many."

Adhils let that pass, and had a bench brought to the foot of the dais where his guests might sit. Though the hall grew swiftly more bright and loud, hereabouts was a ring of bristling wariness. Ever did Adhils's gaze flicker across those below him. Which of them, that looked back as fiercely as the hawks which had settled anew on their shoulders, which was King Hrolf, the son of Helgi whom he had slain and of his own wife Yrsa who hated him?

Ten were here whom he did not know; nor could he slip out to cast a spell that might name them for him. Belike the redbeard, huge as a bear, was not Hrolf, who was said to be a slender man of ordinary height. But would that fit the neat one with the ruddy-gold locks beside him, or the fair-haired youthful-looking one beyond who bore a golden-hilted sword, or the rather short and dark but quick and deft one, or the lean one who had wielded so terrible a halberd, or—or was the whole tale wrong? In the town were seafarers who had seen the Dane-King. He could bring them up tomorrow. It would look too eager, though, it might spring the trap of more trouble, did he send after them this evening. Yet he *must* know as soon as might be, to lay his plans before Hrolf carried out whatever he meant for avenging his father —Hrolf, who had never sworn peace like his uncle Hroar . . . . Might Yrsa know her son, child though he was when she left him? Was that why she had stayed in her bower?

"Let us make up the longfires for our friends," called Adhils, "and let us show them the heartiest goodwill, as we have had in mind all along."

His councillors, captains, and stewards were joining him. "Forgive me, kinsman," he said, "if I, hm, must speak of something secret before you. I told you I have strong and underhanded foes who seek my life. And you yourself don't think it unmanly or impolite to, hm, keep secrets from me, eh?"

"We will not hide why we came," Svipdag said. "We are after the treasures that are King Hrolf's rightful inheritance from King Helgi."

"Well, well, that can be talked about." Adhils turned and whispered to his head steward, who nodded and went off, plucking the sleeve of the chief guardsman to bring him along. They crossed the planks which had now been laid over the pitfalls, and were lost to sight.

Rubbing his hands and blowing frost-clouds, the lord of Svithjodh said: "Yes. We can talk. We can sit and drink like brothers. For truly I do not hold it against

you, Hrolf, that your father plotted my undoing while
he was my guest, nor that you, hm, are leery of me. I
want to show you honor. So, if you'll not tell me who you
are, that you may be given the seat across from mine,
why, I'll step down to a footing with you. It's gotten
beastly cold in here, hasn't it? I ought not to make you
shiver beneath my roof. Come, let's sit near the fire-
trench."

Hrolf's band glanced at each other, but could scarcely
hold back when Adhils waddled past them. Soon they
were in a row on a bench hard by one of the longfires.
Opposite them sat Adhils and the captains of his household troops. It would have looked too much like planned
treachery had these broken the rule that only eating-
knives might be borne in here. Hrolf's men kept their
weapons, and nothing was said about that.

Horns were brought. Adhils drank their health and
chatted on, merrily, meaninglessly. He grew ever harder
to see or to hear. For men of his—guards, from the look
and way of them, though they wore the kirtles of hirelings—were meanwhile adding peat and dry wood to the
fire.

More and more high whirled the flames, red, blue, yellow over coals too hot for the eye to stray near. The
noise grew till it shook men's skulls. The roof overhead
was like a storm-sky of ruddy smoke. Heat billowed. The
hawks flew aloft, the hound slunk away.

Adhils smiled: "Folk have not talked too big when
they praised the courage and readiness of you, King
Hrolf's warriors. It seems as if you stand above everybody
else and that the word about you is no lie. Well, let's
strengthen the fire, for I really would like to make out
who is your king, and you'll never flee it. As for me,
though, I who've not been out in winter air today am
growing a little warm."

He signed to his men. They moved their bench well
back. The stokers ran to and fro, bringing more fuel. Out
of the soot on them, they leered at the newcomers.

Mail and underpadding made doubly cruel the heat.
Sweat gushed from the Danes, stung eyeballs which felt

as if baking, stank in the nostrils and steamed out of the cloth which it had glued to their skins. Lips cracked. The tongues behind were like those blocks of wood which the Swedes fetched as if they worked for Surt himself. "Hrani's house was nothing like this," Hjalti rasped low. 'What's he after?"

"He hopes to know King Hrolf by him not being able to stand the fire as well as the rest of us," answered Svipdag. "In truth he wishes death on our king."

"I swore I would never yield before fire or iron," came Hrolf's parched whisper, barely to be heard through the booming and crackling.

Bjarki leaned forward, moving his shield to give his lord a bit of shelter. Likewise did Hjalti on the other side. But they dared not help him enough that it would give him away.

Squinting through the berserk glare, they could just see that Adhils and his men had shifted as far back as could be. Surely the Swede-King grinned.

"His fine-sounding promises meant naught," groaned Starulf. "He aims to burn us alive."

Hjalti stared at his knees. "My breeks have started to smolder," he said. "If we stay here, we'll be done . . . well done!"

Three of the stokers ran to throw another chunk in the trench. Sparks raged upward. The stokers wheeled about after more. They laughed.

Bjarki looked across Hrolf at Svipdag. The same will leaped in them both. The Norseman shouted half a stave:

"Let the fire be fed
here in the hall!"

He and his Swedish friend sprang up. Each grabbed a stoker. They hurled those men into the flames.

"Now enjoy the heat you strove to give us," called Svipdag, "for we are baked through." Hjalti did likewise to a third. Maybe the rest escaped. It cannot have been as dreadful a death as it sounds, because no flesh could have lived for more than a heartbeat in that trench.

King Hrolf rose. He took his shield and tossed it into the pit while he cried:

"He flees no fire
who hops high over."

His men saw his thought at once and threw in their own shields. Thus they dampened the blaze at that spot till they could leap across it.

Adhils and his folk heard choked-off shrieks, saw bodies burst into smoke—and out of the flames came storming those thirteen men, shieldless but mailed and helmeted, sooty and sweat-drenched but thirstier for blood than for water, scorched in clothes and blistered on cheeks but with weapons aflash like the fire itself.

In horror, Adhils's troopers scattered before the band which had already wrought slaughter among comrades who wore byrnies and swords. Belike too, many felt there could be no luck in fighting for a lord who tried to murder his guests. "Here I am, kinsman!" yelled Hrolf, and sped toward him. Over Hrolf's helmet the sword Skofnung swung high as his own laughter.

Adhils fled. A roof-pillar bore the outsize figure of a god who leaned on his shield. That shield proved to be a door leading into hollowness. Adhils squirmed through, slammed and bolted the door behind him.

"Batter that down!" Hjalti called.

"No," said Hrolf. "He must be crawling along some tunnel. Shall we be worms like him?"

"He might have traps to catch us if we try," nodded Svipdag. "We're not done with that he-witch."

Adhils did indeed slip outside. Rising from the ground behind the lady-bower, he entered it. Yrsa sat there. Her woman shrank to see the king in sweating, dirty disarray. "Go," he told them. "I . . . want speech . . . with the queen."

"No, stay," Yrsa answered. "I want witnesses, that he may not afterward lie about what was said."

The women huddled aside. Adhils forgot them. "That son of yours . . . Hrolf the Dane . . . is here," he panted. "He set on me—holds the hall—"

Yrsa drew a breath of utter joy. "He did not drive you thence for no reason," she said shakily.

"Go to him. Make peace between us. He'll hear your pleas."

"Go I will, but not on your behalf. First you had King Helgi, my husband, slain by treachery; and those goods which belonged to your betters, you kept. Now on top of everything else, you'd kill my son. You are a man worse, more foul than any other. Oh, I will do everything I can to help King Hrolf get the gold, and you shall reap naught but ill from this, as well you have earned."

King Adhils drew himself straight. In that moment he was not altogether a greasy fat man who had been chased from his own dwelling. "It seems that here there can be no trust," he said quietly. "I shall not come before your eyes again." He turned and walked forth into the dusk which had begun to fall. Soon she heard him lead his guards out of the garth.

IV

Thereupon Queen Yrsa sought the hall. She found the Danes gusty with glee, shouting for beer and meat to those frightened servants who were left. But when they saw her enter, in white gown and blue cloak and heavy necklace of amber, a hush fell over them. She walked down the length of the room to the bench where King Hrolf sat; nobody now hid which one was he! A while those gave look for look by the light of the still high-burning fire.

Yrsa's back was yet straight, her body lissome, though her feet no longer danced over the earth as when she was the girl-bride of Helgi. The skin was clear on the broad tilt-nosed face, but many lines marked it, the bronze hair was rimed over, and in the gray eyes lay a bottomless weariness. Much of her lived in the features of her son, who, however, bore easily on unbowed shoulders the red-splashed byrnie in which he had been victorious.

Svipdag started jerkily forward. His gaunt cheeks seemed wet below the eye-patch; the scar throbbed in his brow. "My lady—" he began. She did not turn from Hrolf.

"Are you then Queen Yrsa?" asked the king. "I thought we'd see you earlier."

She stood dumb.

"Well," said Hrolf, "here in your house I got a torn shirt." He lifted his sword-arm, the sleeve of which had been ripped by a spear. "Will you mend this for me?"

"What do you mean?" she whispered.

Hrolf shook his head. "Hard is friendship to find," he sighed, "when mother will give son no food and sister will not sew for brother."

Svipdag stared from him to her in a stunned way. Yrsa clenched her fists. Biting back tears, she said: "Are you angry that I did not greet you erenow? Listen. I knew Adhils was plotting your death. Night after night he was at work on his witching stool, with his kettles and runestaves and bones. Surely, I thought, he'd reckon on ... on mother being there to cast arms around son ... sister taking the hand of brother ... surely this was woven into his spells."

"So at the last she stayed away," Svipdag said, "and the witchcraft came unraveled, and Adhils must try what else he could think of on the spot."

Hrolf surged to his feet. "Oh, forgive me," he cried, near tears himself. "I did not understand."

They held each other close, and laughed and stood back clasping fingers to see the better, and breathed raggedly, and babbled somewhat. After a while they harnessed themselves. She gave the warriors a stately welcome, bade the servants make food and guest quarters ready, and seated herself in eager talk beside him. They had most of his lifetime to overtake.

Svipdag stepped back. "How she has aged through these dozen winters," he said, deep in his throat. "Living with that troll-man—" He shook himself. "Well, of course tonight she's happiest to meet her son."

Drink flowed and merriment pealed. Not often had thirteen men taken the stronghold of a king! At last sleepiness came upon them. Yrsa sent for a youth who would see to their wants. "His name is Vögg," she told

Hrolf, "a bit of a simpleton but good-hearted and nimble."

The fellow arrived: small and skinny, crowbeak nose and not much chin beneath a shock of wheaten hair, shabbily clad, nonetheless hopping and chuckling. "Here is your new lord," the queen told him.

Vögg's pale-blue eyes frogged out. "Is *this* your king, you Danes?" burst from him in a boy's cracked voice. "Him, the great King Hrolf? Why, he's well-nigh as bony as me—a real kraki, him!"

Now a kraki is no more than a tree-trunk whose branches have been lopped to stubs to make a kind of ladder. In their aleful mirth and the glow of their deeds this day, Vögg's words struck the warriors as the funniest thing they had ever heard. Even Svipdag guffawed and joined in the yelling: "Kraki, kraki, aye, hail, King Hrolf Kraki!"

He laughed too and said to the stripling: "You've given me a name which may well stick to me. What will you give me for a naming-gift?"

"I, I . . . naught have I to g-g-give," stammered Vögg. "I'm poor."

"Then he who has should give to the other," said Hrolf. During the evening he had had several gold rings brought from his baggage, with the idea that he might want to reward somebody. He drew one off and handed it to Vögg.

The boy cackled thanks, put it on his right arm, and strutted around like a cock, holding the coil aloft to gleam in the firelight. It slid down to the elbow. His left arm he held behind his back. The king pointed. "Why do you do that?" asked he.

"Oh," said Vögg, "the arm which has naught to show must hide itself in shame."

"We must see about that," said Hrolf, mostly because he saw Yrsa was fond of this loon. He handed him another ring.

Vögg nearly fell over. When he could find speech again, he squeaked, "Thanks and praises, lord! This is a wondrous thing to have!"

The king smiled. "Vögg grows joyous over little."

The youth sprang onto a bench, lifted both hands toward the rafters, and shouted, "Lord, I swear that if ever you are overcome by men, and I alive, I will avenge you!"

"Thanks for that," said the king dryly. His men nodded, not bothering to hide their own grins. No doubt this fellow would prove faithful as far as he was able, they thought, but how could so sleazy a wretch ever do much?

In a while Yrsa led them across the courtyard to a guesthouse. Though far smaller than the hall, it was more snug and bright and without lingering creepinesses of witchcraft. The hound Gram went along; the hawks had already been carried to the mews. In the chill beneath numberless keen stars, Yrsa took her son's hands once more and said, "Goodnight, good rest, my darling. Yet have a care. Evil is everywhere around."

"Should we not watch over you, my lady?" asked Svipdag.

"I thank you, old friend, but no need. It's you he will be after."

"All gods forbid we bring you into danger."

"Goodnight." Yrsa and her women left.

Within, a fire on the hearthstone and lamps along the walls gave light and warmth, albeit smoky air. Vögg showed the men how their goods had been stowed and benches made ready for sleeping. Bjarki warned, "Here we can be at ease, aye, and the queen wishes us well. She's right, however: King Adhils will wreak as much ill for us as he can. It'd astonish me if we're let have everything go on as it does now."

Vögg shuddered and drew signs. "K-k-king Adhils . . . is a terrible maker of—of blood offerings," he told them. "His like is not to be found. Hoo, how often at night I've heard ropes creak under their loads in the shaw, or ravens deafen the wind by day! Yet he gives no more than he must to the high gods. No, his worship is to a horrible huge b-b-boar—" He hugged himself. The teeth rattled in his head. "I don't see how things can stay this smooth," he said, woebegone. "Have a care, have a care! Sly and ill-famed is he, and he'll do whatever he can to m-m-make away with . . . us . . . by any means."

"I think we need post no guard this night," said Hjalti, "for Vögg isn't about to fall asleep."

The warriors laughed drowsily and stretched themselves to rest. They had long since taken off their fighting gear. The fires burned out and only Vögg lay forlornly awake, his earlier bliss sunk deep in dread.

At midnight the band was yanked back to awareness of cold and gloom. A racket outside was ringing in the very walls, gruesome grunts and squeals. Something battered at the house till it rocked, as if it went up and down on the sea.

Vögg wailed: "Help! The boar's abroad, the boar-god of King Adhils! He's sent it to get him revenge—and *none* can stand before that troll!"

The door groaned and splintered under blows. Bjarki's weapon gleamed free. "Get your iron back on, my lord and lads," he said. "I'll try to hold the thing."

The door smashed down. Beyond lay frosted flagstones, black walls and roofpeaks, high stars. Most was blotted from sight by the shape whose hump filled the doorway. What light there was showed its shagginess and the tusks which rose from the snout like crooked swords. A rank swine-smell choked nostrils. The grunting made earthquake thunder.

"Hey-ah!" shouted Bjarki. His blade whirled down. It rebounded so he nearly lost his grip. For the first time, Lövi which had slain the flying monster would not bite.

The hound Gram snarled and lunged.

As his jaws closed, the troll-boar squealed, a noise which went through flesh like a saw. The two beasts ramped out into the yard. Bjarki followed. If his sword would not cut, it could still club. The boar whirled on him and charged. Gram's weight held it back, and Bjarki sidestepped. The boar tossed its head, flailing Gram about. The hound did not let go.

Hard was that fight while the king's men busked themselves. But of a sudden the boar's chuffing turned into a scream. Gram tumbled aside. Bloody in his jaws were an ear and the skin of a jowl. As if a single wound was enough, the troll fell over dead. The ground shook. Gram lifted his head and belled till echoes flew.

Bjarki did not join the cheers of his friends. "Best I don my own mail," he said. "And let's drag what we can across the doorway. This night is not yet at an end."

"You . . . y-y-you . . . met the thing that took so many men—" Vögg stuttered. "Oh, how can I evermore be aught than brave?"

The rest paid him no heed. They were listening to a noise from beyond the garth: horn-blasts, cries to war, rattle of iron and tramp of feet.

Into the yard poured the whole host of Adhils's guardsmen, and more from the town besides, to fill it from wall to wall. A humpbacked moon, newly rising over a dragon gable, made their mail and whetted metal glimmer, made their breaths a ragged fog through the cold, but left faces in shadow. The Swede-King must have had spies, for his folk lost no time in ringing the guesthouse.

"What do you want?" Bjarki shouted through the door.

"This, you who slew my brother," answered someone. After a few heartbeats, they heard the thatch overhead crackle. Flames burst into being. The house had been fired.

"Soon we will not lack for warmth," said Hjalti.

"An ill way is this to die, if we should burn in here," said Bjarki. "A sorry end to life for King Hrolf and his warriors. Rather would I fall to weapons on an open field."

Svipdag peered at a hedge of spears. "That doorway's too narrow," he said. "They'd stick us like pigs as we came out one or two at a time."

"Aye," answered the Norseman. "I know no better rede than that we break down a wall, and thus plow forth together, if that can be done. Then when we close, let each take his man of them, and they'll soon lose heart." He cocked his head. "Hear how shrilly they call around or try to taunt us? I know that note. This day's work, and now the slain god of Adhils, those have shaken them."

"Good is your rede," said King Hrolf. "This I think will serve us well."

They used benches for rams. No child's play was it to smash the planks. Over and over they rushed, while the roof blazed and embers showered down upon them, flames barked and smoke bit. Then in a sundering crash, the wall gave way. They grabbed up the shields they had taken from Adhils's storerooms, leaped out, and fell on the Swedes.

Swords whistled, axes banged, men cursed and yelled beneath the moon. At first the Danes went in a kind of swine-array, that slashed through their unready foes like an arrowhead. When in the thick of them, they made a ring. No, it was more a wheel, rimmed with blades, which rolled unstoppable to split and shatter any line that tried to stand fast.

Higher rose the moon, the burning, and the din. Wildly went the strife. Ever King Hrolf and his fellows thrust forward. Behind them they left a road of hurt men, dead men, men who stared unbelieving at lifeblood which pumped out onto the frost. Soon they won free of the garth and into the town. What ranks were left to fight them thinned out—for though they took bruises and flesh wounds, they knew well how to defend each other, and none else was so stout that he need not veer before their blows.

Wings flapped over heaven. King Hrolf's hawk Highbreeks swung from the burg, stooped, and settled on his master's shoulder. Mightily proud did he look. Bjarki panted: "He behaves like somebody who's won great honor." Nor did he flinch from the weapons which sought after his lord.

At length the fray ended. However many against thirteen, the Swedes could not bring their numbers to bear in the narrow lanes between houses. Moreover, as Bjarki had heard, they were badly shaken to begin with. What order they ever had was now broken up. Few of them cared to lay down his life for a king who was not even in sight. And their wiser leaders came to dread that the Danes would break into a house, snatch a brand off a hearth, and start a fire of their own which could eat all Uppsala.

One after the next, they cried for peace. The wish spread as swiftly as a snowslide. Hrolf gave quarter and asked where King Adhils was. Nobody knew.

Weapons unsheathed, blood wiped off to let the steel flash across night, Hrolf and his men tramped back to the garth. They found its folk toiling to keep the blaze from going further. "This work seems well in hand," Hrolf remarked. "But I see we must use the king's house after all."

He led the way in and called for lights, beer, and the making up of bench-beds. "Where shall we sit meanwhile?" asked Bjarki.

"On the royal dais," answered King Hrolf, "and I myself will take the high seat."

After they had been drinking a while, Hjalti the High-Minded said, "Would it not be best that someone go see to our horses and hawks, after this much unrest?"

"At once, at once," chattered Vögg, and was off.

He came back in tears to tell how shamefully the poor steeds had been used. The Danes roared their wrath and wished every kind of bad luck on Adhils. "Go see about the birds, then," ordered Hrolf, while his own High-breeks spread wings above his head.

This time Vögg blurted wonders. "In the mews . . . all the hawks of King Adhils—dead—ripped apart by beak and claws!"

Highbreeks preened himself. The men shouted. Thus they got back the joy of their victory.

V

In the morning Queen Yrsa came before King Hrolf and greeted him in solemn wise. "You were not received here, kinsman," she said, "as I wished and as was your right—" Her words stumbled a bit: "But you mustn't stay any longer, my son, in such an ill place. Surely Adhils is gathering a host to get you killed."

"Such takes time, Mother," he answered. "We'll not

run off like robbers. No, we'll get together what's ours, with your help; and meanwhile we'll rest and feast."

Her smile quivered. "I should gainsay you, but I can't. Not when this is belike the last meeting we'll ever have." Turning, she walked quickly from the hall.

"Lord," said Svipdag, harsh-toned, "the least we can do is guard her."

"She has warriors of her own," said Hrolf.

"Nonetheless we can show her honor for what she's done."

The king looked gravely into Svipdag's eye before he nodded. "Do as you see fit."

The Swede shouldered his ax and followed the queen. She had stopped in the yard, near the ash and charcoal of the guesthouse, her back turned to the world. Workers were moving about. A dozen warriors waited some strides away. They hailed Svipdag. He reckoned they had not been among his foes of yesterday. This morning was likewise bright and bleak. The sounds of footfalls, words, beasts snorting and stamping, a magpie's caw, came sharp as the sunlight.

Svipdag stopped behind Yrsa and cleared his throat. She showed him her face, now that she had reined it in. "Greeting to you," she said.

"I thought we might talk a while, my lady," he got out.

"Like old times? No, dead years can no more be reborn than dead men. But of course I'd be glad of your company. Let's walk down by the river."

The troopers came well behind. Nobody spoke as they made their way through the bustle and chatter and manyfold stares of Uppsala town. Beyond the gates, Yrsa headed south along the bank. Though the path was frozen hard, ice was breaking up on the river, gray sheets of it borne on a murmurous brown flow. Beyond stretched the Fyris Wolds, here almost empty save for a couple of farmsteads whose smoke rose straight up into the windless chill. On the right, the bluffs were overgrown with brush and topped with woods, leafless.

"My lady—" said Svipdag at length. He swallowed "My lady, we're taking you home . . . aren't we?"

She looked away from him. He could barely hear her. "No."

"But that's madness! Adhils—"

"I have no fears for what he may do to me." Now she sought his gaze and caught his arm. "Hrolf, though— Svipdag, can't *you* make him understand you must go? Adhils, if he has to, Adhils will raise every shire in Svithjodh, and the most frightful magics, for your undoing. You can't think how rich in hatred he is!"

Svipdag's knuckles whitened around his axhaft. "Should I . . . should your son leave you alone for that to spill over you?"

"I have my men." She nodded backward. "Not only those. Enough more. They may have sworn me no open oaths, but they're in my debt and acknowledge it. Here I helped a family through a famine, there I got a judgment softened, or I freed a thrall when I saw how his eyes would follow an eagle—well, you know what the highborn can do." Into her tone entered a shrewdness he had often heard from her son and brother: "Self-interest, too, among a number of chiefs and strong yeomen. They know how ruthless and greedy the king is. I am a counterweight to him. And he knows that they know that. He dares not touch me. Rather, he lives in fear that I'll be smitten by some deadly sickness which'll seem to be from his witchcraft. Then would his days be few!" Her laugh was brittle. "Did you not believe, Svipdag, the daughter and wife of King Helgi the Skjoldung could learn how to take care of herself?"

They walked on in silence until he said, "Even so, here is nothing for you any more. You would have honor in Denmark, and . . . and love everywhere around you."

Her fingers stroked across his. "I know, my dear old avenger. How well I know. But I have my work. What would become of those who've plighted me their troth over the years, did I leave them? What of the war against you that would surely begin, once I could no longer give redes and spin webs?" She pointed. "What of my Helgi? Yonder he and his men lie in their howe, some miles further on, where they fell. Without me, who would offer at that grave, who would tend it—" she shuddered—"who would keep Adhils from dishonoring it, yes, digging up his skull to make a drinking cup and his shoulderblades to mark with witch-runes?"

Svipdag gripped her elbow.

"They say," she went on after a while, "once in this land, when Domald Visbursson was king, the harvests failed. To make the gods friendly again, the Swedes offered many oxen; but next year was worse. Then they gave men; but still the hunger deepened. In the third year they slew King Domald and sprinkled the altar and idols with his blood. There followed good seasons and peace."

"I see. You are a queen, Yrsa."

"And you are my brother's sworn man, Svipdag."

They went on as far as Helgi's barrow, and stayed a while before going back.

That evening, and in the two which came after, Yrsa shared the high seat with Hrolf. If she seldom smiled, none saw grief upon her. The warriors were happy. More and more did they use the nickname Kraki for their king. Vögg blushed at that, and scampered around to tend their wants. Because his life would be in danger here, and because he yearned for it. Yrsa got her son to agree to take him along.

During the days she busied herself readying for Hrolf's trek home. Otherwise she spent most of her time at his side, listening to his tales of what had happened in the years since he was a tousle-haired boy whom she could kiss goodnight.

On the morning of his leavetaking, folk had gathered from far around. They filled Uppsala town, raising a buzz like bees, as they waited outside the garth to see the Danes go by. Within the stockade, guardsmen and household workers made a wall around the yard. The weather stayed clear and cold, though a wind bore the first damp breath of spring.

King Hrolf and his men stood at the middle, outfitted in the finest of clothes and mail, a shout of color and gleam, spearheads blinking aloft, Yrsa's gifts to replace what the fire had spoiled. For the heightening of his fame, she wanted everybody to see what else he took away. First trundled an eight-horse wagon, Vögg driving, heaped upon it treasures of gold, silver, precious stones, amber, ivory, furs, stuffs, goblets, weapons, coins and goods from abroad. A gasp arose at the sight.

Next grooms led forth twelve tall red Southland horses bearing bridle, saddle, ringmail, and one for the king which was white as snow.

Then the queen trod from among her warriors, richly clad. In both hands she bore a silver horn as long as an arm, whereon were molded gods, beasts, and heroes. She stood before her son and spoke into the *whoo* of the wind: "Behold what is yours."

In the hearing of the witnesses, that none might question it afterward, he asked her, "Have you now given me as much as I rightfully own and my father had?"

"This is far beyond what you had a claim on," she answered in pride. "Moreover, you and your men have won great honor."

She lifted the horn. "This will I give you besides. Here are the best rings of King Adhils, among them the one they call Pig of the Swedes and hold to be the foremost in the world." She took it out. Its blaze awakened murmurs and cries. This was no common coil, but a circlet broad and thick, studded with gems, upon it the figure of a boar, the steed of Frey.

"I do much thank you, my lady mother," said Hrolf. He gave the horn to Beigadh to carry. Bjarki nodded. It struck him as good that that mark of renown should ride with one who had been lamed in the king's service.

"Now ready yourselves as best you can, so that none may get at you," Yrsa told them: "for you will have many trials."

She could not help that last useless warning. Earlier she had begged Hrolf to take some of her men along. He felt she needed them more. Besides, those who left families behind would not likely fight well.

"Oh, luck fare with you," she whispered. "I'll be offering in the temple and at your father's howe—"

He looked down into the face which was half his own, laid hands on the slight shoulders, and said: "Better than anything else is your wish, my sister. Better than the hoard we've won has been the finding of your love again, my mother." His hawk spread wings above her, his hound licked her fingers.

"That you came to me, that outweighs any gift I could ever make you."

"Men seek fame that their memory may not die with them. Always will you be remembered in Denmark, Yrsa."

"Because of you and Helgi."

"No, because of yourself."

They fell silent, since their voices were breaking in earshot of the crowd. After a little, Yrsa went among the king's men, took the hand of each and bade him farewell in the same way as she did his fellows. Briefly she embraced Hrolf. Then she stood aside while he mounted. He drew his sword and kissed it, looking at her. She waved as he and his men rode out the gate.

When he was gone, she said to her chief guard: "We had better talk over ways of keeping peace within the kingdom. First, though, I have to see the head steward about some matters in this household."

The Danes rode more slowly from Uppsala than they had come in, for the treasure wagon could not move fast. Most of them made their spirited new horses rear and prance. Hjalti kept hailing girls he had met. Otherwise the dwellers were doubtless glad to be rid of these dangerous guests. Yet they uttered no sounds of ill will, where they crowded the ways and windows and walls of their burg. Grandfathers would tell grandchildren of this they had seen when they were small.

The bridge boomed beneath hoofs and creaked beneath wheels. Across the river, King Hrolf led a way straight south over the Fyris Wolds. It would not be easy to fetch home the huge weight of his winnings. He meant to use these open fields, where the road was still firm but snow lingered only in patches amidst puddles, as far as they reached.

Uppsala fell from sight; his last glimpse was of ravens

above the temple wood. Day wore on past noon. The land began to roll, the stands of timber to show more often and more thick. Here were no farmsteads; this was summer grazing for livestock, mast for swine. The wind strengthened, tossing Hrolf's cloak like flames, making him squint and his hawk lean forward with claws clasped hard into the ringmail. It smelled wet, the wind, and was not truly winter-cold. It drove long white clouds over heaven and their shadows swift across earth.

The king rode moodily, eyes turned downward. All at once a cloud blew off the sun and a glare was in the rutted way before him. The men saw too, and called out. There lay a heavy ring of gold. As the king's horse passed over, it belled.

He drew rein. "It makes such a noise," he said, "because it thinks it ill to lie thus alone." He took one from his arm, cast it down to the other, and told his warriors: "This will I leave off, to pick up gold though it lie on the road. And let none of you dare do so either; for it was thrown here to hinder our faring."

"Freely will we promise, lord," said Svipdag. "The hand of Adhils has reached here from afar."

The band had halted. Vögg on the wagon tried not to shudder. The men looked stern. In this stillness, they heard a lowing borne up the wind. Bjarki raised a palm. "Hush," he said, and afterward, "Aye, lurs. The hand of Adhils was not so far off after all."

"Ride on," ordered Hrolf. "Whip up those horses, Vögg."

The wagon could merely lumber, swaying, clattering, squealing. Erelong the Danes saw a host of men behind them. At first this was no more than a darkness on the ridges; but soon it was banners and weapon-blink, horn-hoots, hoofbeats, and wrathful shouts.

"Mounted," said Svipdag. "That's how Adhils rallied them so soon."

"Two or three hundred, I'd guess," added Hjalti. "It looks like a busy afternoon ahead."

Bjarki stroked his red beard. "Indeed they're setting

briskly after us," he rumbled. "I could wish they get something for their trouble."

"Let's not fret about them," said King Hrolf. "Belike they'll hinder themselves."

He took from Beigadh the horn which Yrsa had given him. "Ho-ha!" he cried to his white horse. Off he galloped, a mile to the right and a mile to the left. As he rode, he dipped into the horn and flung his opened fist abroad. Far and wide he sowed gold rings across the Fyris Wolds.

"Can we be less free than our lord?" asked Bjarki. "A share of this treasure is ours." He went to the wagon, scooped out a double handful of costliness, and did as the king did. Likewise did his fellows. Gold and silver flashed through the air like shooting stars until all the ways lay glowing.

The little troop then hastened onward. When the Swedish host saw the riches which gleamed before them, most sprang from horseback and raced to learn who was quickest to pluck this up. Glancing behind, Hrolf and his men saw how fighting broke out among them; and the Danes laughed aloud.

King Adhils caught up with his levy. However fat, he was a great lover of horses and a good rider; it was just that his weight slowed down any mount. His face burned a cock's-comb hue, his beard streamed in elf-locks over his byrnied paunch. "What is this?" he yelled at the disorder which roiled around him. "Do you call yourselves men? You, gleaning the least and letting the most slip from you!" He flailed about with the butt of his spear. "Listen, you dolts! Stop and hear your king! This shame'll be noised unendingly in every land of the world . . . that you, uncounted many, let a dozen get away! A dozen who slew your own kinsmen!"

Slowly he and a few hard heads brought others to their senses, who in turn beat and scolded more. At last, maybe half the host started off afresh. The rest squabbled on over their loot. Several were already dead. The feuds from this day would grind on for years.

Now the sun was low, shadows long, rooks seeking their nests in loud streamers across greenish heaven, wind shrill and chill. A few miles away reared the wall of a pinewood, and steeply rising lands beyond it, where outnumbered men could hope to lose their hunters.

"Ride, you coal-biters!" Adhils shrieked. Himself he leaned in the saddle as if to reach ahead of the beast he spurred and flogged. Hoofs thudded, metal rattled, helms and spears flared through gloom. "Ride, ride! Oh, if I had my besom here! If I'd had time to call my trolls—"

Hrolf looked ahead and behind. "We'll not win to safety as we're going," he said. "No matter the hoard. We don't need it. The gaining of it has been enough. Empty the wagon!"

Once more the Fyris Wolds flamed golden. Bjarki cut a draft horse loose for Vögg to ride bareback.

When the Swedes saw that kind of wealth scattered around, greed overwhelmed nearly all of them. They hurled themselves onto those rings and coins and jewels as if onto women. Adhils and a faithful few did not stop to upbraid them. Instead, these sped on; and they still outnumbered the Danes three or fourfold.

King Hrolf reached into the otherwise empty silver horn. A hundred yards from his stepfather, he drew forth the ring called Pig of the Swedes, and cast it on the road. It caught the light like another sun.

Adhils slammed his horse to such a halt that blood broke from its mouth and it screamed. Well might Hrolf have more right to that ring than he did; but this was the greatest halidom in Svithjodh.

His followers went by in full gallop. Hrolf's sword sprang on high. "Have at them!" he called. He and his twelve champions rushed to meet their oncoming foes.

Northmen are not wont to fight from the saddle. They have neither the skill nor the trained mounts. But to Leidhra had come the best of warriors. They not only sought to become peerless in the manly crafts known everywhere; they were always thinking of new ones and trying these out. Thus they could make their beasts crowd near a foeman's, and themselves wield weapons without losing reins or stirrups.

Swords sang. Axes crashed. Spears went home. The hawks came down to snatch at Swedish eyes; the great hound Gram worried Swedish steeds. Not one of those who stayed true to King Adhils went home alive.

He himself dared not dismount. While his horse jittered about, frightened by this movement and racket, he tried to pick up the ring on his spear. Again and again he poked; always it slipped off the point. He slugged his beast to a standstill, bent far down, and groped two-handed after the thing of gold.

Hrolf had slain a man who threatened weaponless Vögg. Looking around, he saw what went on. His warriors heard him laugh: "Now stooped like a swine is the lord of the Swedes!" Forward he hurtled on the stallion that Yrsa had given him.

Adhils had almost looped the Pig on his spear. Hrolf sped by. Up went the sword Skofnung and down, a whine like the wind's, a thud like a butcher's cleaver. Blood spurted. Adhils yammered. Hrolf had cloven his buttocks to the bone.

"Bear that shame for a while," the Dane-King shouted, "and know who he is that you've sought for so long!"

Adhils toppled from his saddle. Hrolf swept about. Leaning over in mid-gallop, a single foot in a stirrup, he caught the ring. That would let him say he had gotten back his inheritance. And he had avenged King Helgi better than if he had slain the murderer.

Those who wrangled over the strewn loot saw what had happened. In horror, some of them remounted and rode to help Adhils. By then he had swooned for loss of blood. They had no will to do more than staunch his wound and carry him off. Unfollowed, Hrolf and his men rode on their way.

Since that time, skalds have often called gold "the seed of Kraki" or "the sowing on the Fyris Wolds." If riches were left behind, honor was brought home which would never be forgotten.

VI

King Hrolf and his twelve came into the woods. Tall
and thick were those pines; level sunbeams that struck between them only deepened the gloom everywhere else.
The air was too cold for smelling of any sweetness. The
trail was free of snow and windfalls but covered with
duff, so that the horses traveled in an eerie quiet. They
were tired out and often stumbled. The riders felt the
same weariness upon themselves.

Then the way brought them to a clearing. They could
barely see a house under the trees, though little of its
shape or how big it was. A tall old man stood outside,
leaning on a spear, decked with a blue cloak and a broad-
brimmed hat.

The king halted. "Good evening, Hrani," he said.

"Good evening, Hrolf Kraki," answered the yeoman.

"How does he know that nickname?" whispered Vögg.
"And I . . . I've been on this path . . . no garth was ever
here."

"Hush," Hvitserk the Swede told him. "We've met this
being before—whoever or whatever he is."

"Be welcome under my roof," said Hrani.

"You are most kind," said the king.

"I think your faring was not unlike what I foresaw."

"That's right. You were not smoke-blinded."

The yeoman stabled their horses and brought them inside to the long, remembered room of fire and shadows.
Again they were taking things as these happened, as if in
a dream; but however guest-free the old one seemed,
they felt something nightmarish.

Hjalti muttered about that to Bjarki. The Norseman
nodded. "Aye, me too," he said in his fellow's ear. "Well,
after what we saw at the hall of Adhils, we're bound to be
wary of what comes from beyond our world."

Hrolf himself must strive to show politeness. Hrani's
hand was bony on his elbow, leading him toward a table.
Thereon lay a sword, a shield, and a byrnie. They were
black and strangely made.

"Here are weapons, lord, which I will give you," said Hrani.

Hrolf frowned. "Those are some ugly weapons, yeoman," he answered.

Hrani let go of him. Beneath the hat, an eye caught the flickering bloody fire-glow like a leap of lightning. Within the long gray beard, his mouth drew into a line. "What do you mean by that?" he snapped.

"I would not treat my host rudely——" the king began.

"But you think my gift unworthy of you?"

Hrolf stared upward into the half-hidden face, braced himself, and said: "We're newly come from a lair of witchcraft and trolls. There may well be spells working against us yet, or traps set to catch us in an ill doom. The sword Tyrfing goes about in the world, and each owner gets victory from it, but he becomes an evildoer and in the end the sword is his bane."

"Do you hold that these also are accursed things I have made?"

"I know not. Therefore I cannot take them."

Cold as a wind off the Swart Ice blew Hrani's words: "Little do you reckon me for, when you spurn my gifts. I deem you will get woe as great as is this demeaning of me."

"I meant no such thing, friend." Hrolf tried to smile.

The yeoman cut him off. "Call me no longer friend. You are not as wise in this as you believe, King Hrolf——" his glare stabbed each man to the marrow——"and none of you are as lucky as you think."

"It seems best we leave," said Hrolf slowly.

"I will not hinder you," answered Hrani.

No further word did he speak. He fetched their horses back out, saddled and bitted to go, and leaned on his spear in the murk. Grim was he to see beneath his brows. The men thought nothing was to be won by bidding him farewell. They mounted and rode hastily off, to get as far as they could before night was altogether upon them.

But they had gone barely a mile, enough for the mist to lift in their heads, when Bjarki stopped. The rest did likewise. Dim in twilight, he told them: "Too late do the

unwise come to understanding. So is it with me. I have a
feeling we did not behave very sagely when we said no to
that we ought to have said yes to. We may have bidden
victory go from us."

"I begin to believe the same," spoke King Hrolf. "That
could have been old Odin. Truly—only now do I know
what I saw—he was a man with one eye."

Svipdag's own single light glimmered. "Let's hurry
back," he said, "and find out about this."

They trotted under the spearhead pines and the first
wan stars. Save for muffled thuds of hoofs, faint creak of
leather and clink of metal, the whimper that Vögg could
not wholly quell, they went in silence. Dark though the
way was, they knew the place when they reached it. The
garth and the yeoman were gone.

King Hrolf sighed. "No use searching for him," he said,
"for he is an angry wraith."

They turned around again, and at length found a
meadow to camp in. None wanted food or drink, and it
was now too murky to gather sticks and tinder for a fire.
They slept badly or not at all.

In the morning they fared on. Nothing is told of them
until they reached Denmark.

Surely, though, they were quick to lift up their hearts
anew. They were bold men, homeward bound from
mighty deeds. As for their weird, they had never supposed
they could escape that, whatever it was and whenever it
would find them. Meanwhile, in leaf and blossom, bird-
song and the bright glance of maidens when they rode by,
spring was coming to birth.

But in Leidhra, Hrolf the king and Bjarki the marshal
talked long under four eyes. It was Bodhvar-Bjarki who
gave the rede that henceforward the Danes should hold
away from battle. Both felt they would not be attacked
while they themselves stayed at peace. However, the
Norseman said he was afraid the king would not be the
winner as hitherto, should war seek him out; for Odin is
the Father of Victories.

Hrolf answered: "His own doom sets the life of every
man, and not yonder spook."

"You would we lose last, if we might have our way," Bjarki said. "Nonetheless I have a heavy feeling that things will be happening to us."

So they ended this talk, but were most thoughtful thereafter.

Yet high stood their name. Low had they brought the murderer of King Helgi. The troll he served and the best of his men were fallen. The hoard he had withheld was lost to him, borne off the Fyris Wolds in a hundred different saddlebags. Shamed and lamed, lonelier than one who has been wrecked on a reef, at night in the hollowness of his hall King Adhils wept.

VII

THE TALE OF SKULD

I

Now for seven years there was no warfaring out of Denmark or into it.

This does not mean that everything was quiet.

Upon his homecoming, Bjarki was gladly greeted by his wife Drifa—who had a little son to show him—and by the folk, not just on the lands he owned but widely around. They knew that, as the king's right arm, he was their warder against outlaws and outlanders. Those guardsmen who had been sent back were less happy; they felt their honor had suffered. Hrolf found words to ease the pain: Eldritch powers had been at work, and their manhood was not less because the Norns had cut no runes above their cradles to say they should fare outside the bailiwick of mankind. Thereafter he gave them such gifts of gold and weapons that the whole kingdom could know how well he thought of them. Meanwhile Bjarki's bluff mirth got them to smiling again.

Twelve could not be soothed: the berserkers. Besides being mostly too dim-witted to grasp that no man is fitted for all tasks, they were restless. For them was nothing in life but fighting, guzzling, swilling, and swiving. The peaceful three soon palled, and Hrolf Kraki no longer sent them forth to battle.

Late in the summer, Agnar their headman flared up at Bjarki, one eventide in the hall at Leidhra. Hrolf stopped the quarrel and chided the berserker before the whole company. Agnar went off to brood. At last he slouched back to seek out the king. For the shame that had been put on him, he grumbled, no amends would do save that he got Hrolf's daughter Skur to wife, and the kind of dowry that befitted her.

In horror, the girl fled to her sister Drifa, who gave comfort and spoke to her husband. Bjarki trod before the king. Hrolf was sorely puzzled as to how to keep the peace on one hand, without breaking any oaths to his men, and on the other hand how to keep that clod out of his kin. "Lord," said the Norseman, "you have rightly forbidden fights when we are met in a body. But nothing was said about holmgangs, was it? I'd rather be dead than have this son of a mare for my brother-in-law; and surely he'll oblige me."

Agnar bellowed. Hrolf tried to mend the breach, mostly because he feared he would lose his marshal, but it could not be done. In the end, Agnar and Bjarki rowed to a small island and set out the wands.

The berserker got the first stroke. His sword that he called Höking crashed on Bjarki's helmet, broke the rivets and sent iron plates screaming from each other. Barely did it stop short of the wearer's skull; blood ran past the noseguard. Ere it could be withdrawn, the other blade was up, left hand gripping right wrist and one foot on a stump to give more strength.

Lövi smote home. Afterward Bodhvar-Bjarki made a stave:

"This will I say you for sooth, the wildest of stags did I strike,
starkly hitting in strife with the long lean weapon hight Lövi,
winning a wealth of fame on the day when I brought him down,
Agnar, the son of Ingjald; highly they hailed our names!
Höking aloft he lifted and hurled it onto my helmet.
Well that that blade was worn so its wailing edge could not wound me!
Bitterly would it have bitten if the steel had stayed on its road.
Swiftly then did I swing, and my sword did cleave him asunder,

hewing his hand off to right and leaving no foot on
    the left,
while in the whirling between, it ripped out the roots
    of his heart.
Truth will I tell: I never saw man more doughtily die.
He sank but he did not swoon, and up on his elbow
    raised him,
laughing let go of his life, unscathed in his scorn for
    death.
Happily fared he hence to whatever home is for
    heroes.
Boldness dwelt in that breast, and grinned at the
    gathering dark.
Sorely I think he suffered, in both his body and soul,
for that he had not felled me; yet stricken, he still
    could laugh."

And Bjarki saw to it that Agnar got an honorable
burial. This did not dampen the rage of the rest of the
berserkers. They set upon him while he was homebound.
Hjalti and Svipdag had come along as witnesses. The upshot was that two more berserkers lay dead and none of
the others lacked wounds.

For what they had tried to do, King Hrolf outlawed
them. They left bawling vows of revenge. But unlike
those who had been cast from Uppsala, they seemed to
have nowhere to go for help, so strong were the peace at
home and the awe abroad of Hrolf's Denmark. Everyone
agreed that not only the royal halls, but the whole land
was better off without them.

Skur later became the bride of Svipdag. They say she
was happy enough, dour though he was.

Next year came mighty tidings: King Adhils was dead.

He had been taking the lead in springtime offerings to
the female Powers. As he rode around their bloodstained
shrines, his horse stumbled. No longer able to keep well
the saddle, he was cast off and struck his head against a
stone. The skull burst, the brains flowed forth. The
strange gods they served were not overly kind to the
Ynglings.

The Swedes raised a mound over him and took for

their king Eystein, his son by a leman of years ago. Yet they, and he, still felt love for Queen Yrsa; and was she not both mother and sister to the great Dane-King? Thus she stayed in the councils of the land, and had many men at her beck. She would fain have visited Hrolf, but age was beginning to weaken her. He, for his part, deemed it unwise to thrust himself upon a new lord of Svithjodh, as if to be overbearing rather than friendly. So he and Yrsa kept putting off a new coming together.

One thing that had Hrolf Kraki busy a while was that he stopped making offerings of his own. "Odin has become our foe," he said. "Besides, I never did like the hanging and drowning of helpless men, and always gave only beasts. As for those, I can't see that the slaughters which Adhils held were of much use to him." At first the folk dreaded famine and worse, when their king would not even enter a temple. He had to talk down a number of their spokesmen. But one good year followed another; trade waxed and widened; the peace seemed unshakeable.

Everyone could do what he thought best. Aside from gifts at the graves of their forebears and to the little beings which haunt house and home-acre, the king and his men called no more on any Powers, but trusted in their own strength.

Of course, this was not true of his under-kings—least of all Hjörvardh at Odin's Lake, husband of his sister Skuld the Elf-Child.

In the years since their wedding, they had mostly kept to themselves. After Bjarki slew the cattle-raiding beast, Hjörvardh particularly grew anxious to show goodwill. A few seasons he went along in the Jutland wars, and he never failed to send men, as well as paying his scot of gold and goods. Otherwise he tended the lands he owned and the work of steering northern Fyn. He was somewhat of a sluggard, content to have things done for him, and might have ended his days happily as he was were it not for his queen.

In all that mattered, the balding plump man was ruled by the black-haired slender woman whose eyes were like changeable green lakes in a snowfield. Because of her, his judgments were harsh. Folk soon learned that it was as unwise for them to protest as it was for Skuld's own thralls. Those who gave trouble to her or her husband were likely to have bad luck: sickness, a murrain on their livestock, a blight on their crops, a fire, or worse. She made no secret of her witchcraft, though none ever dared spy on her when she fared alone into the woods or out on the heaths. Some whispered they had seen her riding at night, on a gaunt horse which galloped faster than any live beast, and that a troop of shadows and misshapen things came after.

Yet she and Hjörvardh must stand well with the gods, for toward these they were lavish. At the holy times they would give to each of the Twelve lives of his or her own kind—goats to Thor, swine to Frey, cats to Freyja, bulls to Heimdal, horses to Tyr, and on in that wise until it came to Odin. He got men.

They throve, keeping a big hall, a full household, stuffed coffers. If they did not show forth a splendor like Hrolf Kraki's, it was rather because Skuld was stingy than for lack of the wherewithal.

Bitterly did she hate that her husband was her brother's underling. Each year when the scot went off to Leidhra, it was as if her heart's blood were in the cargo.

Always she nagged Hjörvardh about his lowliness. This way of hers grew worse after the High King returned from Uppsala, to make war no longer and to stand aloof from the gods. "It must not go on," she said.

Hjörvardh sighed, where he lay in bed next to her. "Best will be for us as for the others, to suffer this and let things stay calm."

"Small manhood do you have," she spat through the dark, "seeing how you brook the shame that's put on you."

"It's unwise to brave King Hrolf. None dare raise a shield against him."

"*You* don't, so skimpy is the strength in you. He who risks naught, wins naught. Who can know before it's been tried, whether anyone can beat King Hrolf and his warriors? I think he's become altogether victoryless, and he

himself knows that, and this is why he stays at home.
Well, we can come to him!"

"Skuld, he's your own brother—"

"I'd not spare him on that account."

"Be glad of what we have, my dear." He groped for
her, feeling the cool smoothness of her skin, breathing the
summeriness of her hair. She thrust him away and turned
her back. Hjörvardh did not try to have her. He had
long since learned he could only do that when she wanted
it, and then it was oftenest her who bestrode him.

She did not push the matter further for a while, aside
from a growing shrewishness. Indeed, the overthrow of
King Hrolf was nothing to undertake lightly. For four
more years she busied herself in the deeper lore of
witchcraft.

"Have a care with those spells," Hjörvardh begged
her. "King Adhils was a great wizard. It did him no
good."

Skuld's laughter froze him. "Adhils? That poor
wretch? He only thought he knew something; and few
were the beings that heeded him. I have teachers—" She
broke off and said no more.

Then a Yule Eve came when she rode off alone as was
her wont. Folk glimpsed her from afar, mounted on the
ugly old nag she used at such times, her hair and a cloak
of the same blackness tossing around her shoulders. She
was armed only with a knife and a rune-carved staff; but
from men she had nothing to fear. She vanished in twilight, and those who had seen her go by hastened indoors
to their hearthfires.

Some miles from Odense, on the shore of the bay,
stood a hill. Wind-wrenched trees and brush, bare now in
winter, grew around its bottom. Whins and ling decked
the rest of it, up to the top where a dolmen squatted.
Snowfall had been scant thus far in the year; the land
lay dark, bushes snickering an answer to the whine of a
north wind. Clouds drove over heaven, rimmed in paleness by a crooked moon which flew between them. Waves
clashed on the strand, making stones rattle. The air
flowed raw. A taste of salt was on it, and the stench of a

dead seal which had washed shore. Inland, wolves gave tongue.

Skuld dismounted and went into the dolmen. There she had a kettle and firewood for the seething of spells. Something had already filled it for her; and she needed no toil with flint and tinder to kindle a blaze. Those were low flames, blue, heatless on the skin if not the water, making shadows move so monstrously on the stone walls that the murk was not lifted but came nearer.

Crouched in the low, narrow room, Skuld held her rune-staff over the brew and cried certain words.

A sound came as of sucking. She stepped forth. Any other horse than hers would have screamed and bolted at how the water bubbled down below, how something rose from it and moved ashore. Earth shivered at the weight of each slow footstep. He who climbed the hill dripped water which glowed coldly white. Chill breathed from his wet flesh, with a rankness of fish and undersea reaches. Like kelp were his hair and beard, and his eyes like lamps.

"Bold must you be to have called me," he whispered.

She looked up the hulk of him and said: "I have need of your help, kinsman."

He waited.

"I know how to raise beings from outside the world of men," she told him, "but they may well rend me unless a might like yours bids them stay their fangs."

"Why should I ward you?"

"That the High King's peace may be broken."

"What is that to me?"

"Do not ships plow your waters, more every year, and never a manslaughter aboard to feed your conger eels? Do men not fare out in yearly greater numbers, unfrightened, to club your seals, harpoon your whales, raid the nests of your cormorants and gannets, drag their nets full of your fish, and wreck the sky-clad loneliness of your outermost islands? I warn you, I who am half human, I warn you: man is the foe of the Old Life, whether he knows it or not, and in the end his works will cover the world—never again will it know freedom or wild magics—unless we bring him down, haul him before it is too late back into the brotherhood of Beast, Tree, and Waters. For your own sake, help me!"

"Would you not merely replace one king with another?"

"You know I would not. Not really. I would *use* folk."

Long and long he stared at her, there in the windy dark, until she herself grew frightened. At last he laughed, a strangely shrill gull-noise out of so vast a throat. "Done! You know how such a bargain is made fast."

"I do," said Skuld.

When she had taken off her clothes and followed him into the dolmen, she must bite her lips against the cold weight and scaliness and smell, clench her fists against the hugeness that battered her bloody. She knew this would happen often again.

But he would stand by her when she called horrors out of the earth.

Toward dawn she rode home. Clouds had wholly shrouded heaven. Her nag stumbled in the gloom. Dry snow blew over the ground. Shuddering with cold, her body one ache of weariness where it was not in pain, she nonetheless held her head aloft in a pride no hawk could have matched.

Of sudden, hoofs resounded. They did not thud, they rang, and went swifter than moonbeams. The steed which overhauled hers was the hue of milk and silver, unearthly fair. Likewise was the woman in the saddle. In robes which gleamed and shimmered as if woven of rainbows, she had the face and midnight hair which were Skuld's; but her eyes were golden, and sorrow was upon her.

"Daughter," she cried, "wait! Hear me! You know not what you are doing—"

Other hoofs—too many hoofs—roared over the sky. Hounds bayed up yonder, horns blew, iron flashed. He who rode before that troop was on a stallion which had eight legs, and wore a cloak which flapped like wings and a wide-brimmed hat which shaded his one eye. He hefted his spear as if to cast it at the woman. She wailed, wheeled her horse around, and fled weeping. Skuld sat where she was, watched the Wild Hunt rush by, and laughed.

In the morning, as she and her husband made themselves ready for the Yule offerings, she sent their servants away. Across the room she strode to grab Hjörvardh's wrist. Her nails drew blood. He looked at her: worn out, darknesses around the sunken eyes, yet a flame clad in flesh.

"Hear me!" Though her voice was low, somehow it shook him. "I've told you before how unfitting it is that you bow down to Hrolf Kraki. I tell you now, it need not go on, and it will not."

"What—what—" he stammered. "What are you thinking of?"

"I have gotten signs that promise us victory."

"My oaths I swore—"

"The night which is past heard other oaths. Hjörvardh, you are my man. You must then be man enough to take revenge for the scurvy trick my brother played on you long ago—and moreover get the lordship of Denmark." He opened his mouth. She laid a finger across those lips, smiled, and purred: "I've thought out a plan which should work. Listen.

"Strong is King Hrolf's household. However, we can raise more fighters than that, and if we take him by surprise, he'll have no chance to send a war-arrow among the yeomen. You ask how we'll get such a band of our own, without his knowing? Well, there are many who've no love for him, chieftains he's humbled, berserkers he's sent away, outlaws skulking hungry, Saxons, Swedes, Götar, Norsemen, aye, even Finns who'd be glad to see him cast down, and . . . others I know of.

"We need wealth for bribes and to pay for weapons from abroad, smuggled hither. I've hit on a way to get that—keep it, rather, keep what's rightfully ours. We'll send word to Leidhra, asking leave to withhold payment of the scot for three years, and at the end of that time to bring it all at once."

"Why?" Hjörvardh got out.

"We'll explain that we need it to buy ships and goods

which'll further outland trade. Hrolf ought to like that. And it'll help make the work, the comings and goings hereabouts, seem harmless to him."

"But—but—"

"What's the risk? At worst he'll refuse us, and then we must stay at peace. I don't think that'll be needful. If we can keep back the wealth, why, we'll feel our way forward, doing nothing till we're sure of our next step, making no move till any doubt is dead that we can overwhelm him."

Hjörvardh was unwilling, but Skuld kept after him day by day, night by night. At length he agreed, and messengers went off across the Great Belt.

They brought back word that King Hrolf was happy to let his brother-in-law put off payment for as long as was asked, and wished him well in his undertakings.

Thereafter Hjörvardh began searching out those who had grudges against his overlord, and every kind of ill-doer. Egged on by Skuld, his eagerness waxed as he saw his strength building up. For her part, she found cunning ways to keep hidden from Leidhra what was really going on. If one who was loyal to Hrolf Kraki began wondering aloud about some of the men who came to Odense, and if the story given out did not set his mind at ease, she had spells to blind and dazzle.

No longer did she pester her husband. Instead, she was so loving to him that he became like a worshipful puppy. Even then, he never got the courage to ask what she did on those nights when she rode alone from the hall.

Thus three years went by.

As for King Hrolf and his men during this time, what can be said other than that they lived in happiness, and the land which he steered did likewise? In the welfare and safety of folk, in righteous laws and judgments, in good harvests and burgeoning markets, in growth of towns and sowing of new fields, in man dwelling at peace with his neighbor, are no tales to tell—only, afterward, memories.

Surely the troopers found much to do. Besides attending the king, they had their own ships and farms to look after. No doubt Bjarki went back to the Uplands

and greeted his mother and stepfather, taking along many
fine gifts; and Svipdag fared away off to Finland in
search of furs; and Hjalti sailed to England to see what
he could see; and it may well be that they rowed up the
rivers of Russia or along the Rhine to Frankish countries.
If so, they were traders. Big and well-armed as they
were, nobody tried attacking them.

At home they had merriment, every night a feast in
the king's hall where the boards well-nigh buckled under
the meat and horns were always filled, skalds chanted,
wanderers yarned about their travels, and Hrolf Kraki the
ring-breaker stinted nothing. There would be daily weapon
drill, and the care of steel, and such-like chores; but
there would also be hunting, fishing, fowling, wrestling
matches, races afoot or on horseback or in boats, stallion
fights, games of skill like draughts or gambling with
knucklebones, long lazy talks, gadding about and chaf-
fering with yeomen, planning, daydreaming; and somewhere in or near Leidhra burg, each man had at least
one woman, and thus fell into those bonds which the
hands of small children weave.

There is nothing to tell about those seven years of
peace, save that Denmark has never forgotten them.

At the end, King Hjörvardh and Queen Skuld sent word
to their kinsman King Hrolf. They would come spend
Yule with him, bringing the scot they owed.

Said he to the messengers: "Tell them how glad I am of
that, and how welcome they shall be."

II

The week around midwinter was a time for feasts,
fires, meetings in mirth and love, a break in that season
when a day was no more than a glimmer in the night.
But never was there more honest joy than in the hall of
Hrolf Kraki.

On this Yule Eve the flames bawled, horns and cups
clashed together, laughter and song and talk surfed everywhere around till the walls boomed. In a sable-trimmed
kirtle embroidered red and blue, trews of white linen,

gold heavy on arms and neck and brow, the king in his high seat glowed before them all. At his feet panted the hound Gram, on his shoulder perched the hawk High-breeks, close to him were the sharers of his farings, beyond them the best men and ladies of the whole wide realm he had forged. He smiled, happy to see this much happiness. Yet a slight sorrow was in him and he said to Bjarki: "*Why* are Skuld and Hjörvardh not among us? Could they have been shipwrecked?"

"Hardly, lord, on that short a trip and calm as the weather's been," answered the Norseman. "Belike something came up that held them back from starting, and they're beached for the night on Zealand's west coast and will row into Roskilde harbor tomorrow."

"Unless she's come to grief from one of those businesses she's forever running and runing after," muttered Svipdag. He had never liked the king's sister or her dark crafts.

"Hoy, that's too uncheerful." Bjarki drained a silver goblet of beer, wiped the foam off his red mustache, and shouted for more.

Vögg sprinted to obey. The boy from Uppsala was become a young man. It could hardly be told; he was still short, scrawny, almost beardless upon what little chin he had, his hair tangled regardless of how hard he combed it. The troopers had given up trying to make a warrior of him. At weapon practice, weak, slow, awkward, he won merely bruises, and a few times broken bones. However, they liked him well enough—his pale eyes dwelt upon them with such endless awe—spoke kindly to him, saw to it that he was well-fed and well-clad. In return he fell over himself in his eagerness to run any errand or do any job. His proudest boast was that he had worked his way up to being cupbearer to the king and the twelve great captains.

"Thank you," said Bjarki. He peered through the roiling, juniper-smelling warm smoke and added across the din: "Why, you've sweated yourself as wet as a fresh-caught haddock. Sit down, lad, have a stoup and let the women serve for a while."

"M-m-my honor is to be at your beck," stuttered Vögg.

He turned his head birdlike back and forth along the row of them. "D-does anybody, any of my lords want more?"

"Aye, you can fill this," said Hjalti and handed him an aurochs horn twined with gold. As Vögg scuttled off, his arms and legs pumping, Hjalti laughed, "You know, I think his trouble is he needs to get laid. So do I, as far as that goes."

"Well, you've a right pretty sweetheart," said the king. "Why didn't you bring her tonight?"

"She was too scared at the thought of going home after dark on Yule Eve. And home she'd've had to go, because here's no place to bang her, guests stacked like cordwood." Unlike Bjarki and the other ranking guardsmen, Hjalti owned no full-sized house in or near Leidhra. He felt it was too much trouble, when he could be out hunting or fishing.

Vögg came back and bent the knee as he offered the full horn. Hjalti stroked his own short fair beard—he still did not have thirty winters behind him—and said, "Of course, we do have haymows and such around. Vögg, my friend, how would you like for a Yuletide gift that I told off a thrall girl to pleasure you?"

The youth's jaw dropped. A while he blushed, sputtered, shifted from one foot to the next, before it dragged from him: "I, I, I thank you, lord, b-b-but—no, if she didn't want—" He jerked a bow and fled.

Hjalti chuckled and shrugged. Bjarki turned a look more earnest onto the king. "My lord," he began, "I've spoken of this to you before, but being reminded—your only living children are female."

"And I should beget a son, best by a wedded wife?" said Hrolf Kraki.

"Yes. An heir for us or our own sons to raise on a shield, that Denmark may go on beyond your life."

"Goodly matches can be had in Svithjodh since King Adhils got rid of himself," Svipdag said.

Hrolf Kraki nodded. "You're right, all of you, and I've waited too long. There was a girl once—" Pain touched his voice. "She died. I ought to set her ghost free of me. Let's talk further about this, the next few days."

The Golden Boar was borne in. Though the king and his men no longer had much to do with any gods, they had not given up the old usage of making Yuletide vows. He himself was first. He rose, laid his right hand on the image, gripped a beaker of wine in his left, and spoke the words he did each year: "As best I can, I will strive to be Landfather . . . for everyone." His tone was low but carried from end to end of the room. Men sat hushed while he drained the cup. Then they cheered forth their love.

Soon after, Hjalti asked leave to say goodnight. He had several miles ahead of him before he could cool his lust. A groom, sleepy and shivering, brought his harnessed horse out into the courtyard. Over the crupper were slung mail and shield, and he bore a spear as well as a sword and knife. Unlikely did it seem he would need any of this in the king's peace. He mounted. Hoofs clattered on flagstones, pounded down lanes where houses loomed like cliffs, passed through the gates and left the burg behind.

He rode north at a brisk pace. The night was quiet and chill; breath smoke white from man and beast, hoarfrost formed on iron, the *clop* when a rock in the road was kicked rang far across rime-gray meadows and murkily huddled farmsteads. Overhead were many stars and a vast, shuddering sheaf of northlights, from which rays of wan red and glacier green fanned out over half the sky. The Bridge glittered, the Wains wheeled on their unending ring around the year. Once an owl went soundlessly by, and Hjalti thought of fieldmice huddled in fear of those wings . . . like men in fear of the Powers?

He lifted his head. Not him!

Thyra his leman dwelt alone in a hut, small but stout, which he had bought for the use of those women he found among thralls or poor crofters. When they grew swollen with child, or he otherwise wearied of them, his custom was to send them off with enough gold—and their freedom, if they had not had this before—that they should be able to marry fairly well. Nonetheless they sometimes wept.

He stabled the horse himself, feeling his way, and beat on the house door. "Who's that?" trembled from behind shutters.

"Who do you think?" Hjalti teased.

"I . . . I'd not looked for you—"

"Well, here I am, and badly in need of warmth!"

Having left a clay lamp lit, she could unlatch the door and lead him inside at once. His hands roved in the light of that wick and the embers of a banked hearthfire. Thyra was a big young woman, fair-haired, full-breasted, goodly to see.

She clung to him, her fingers so taut as to belie the rounded softness of everything else. "Oh, I'm glad, I'm glad," she whispered. "I was frightened. I kept having gruesome dreams, and waking, and trying to stay awake, only they came back—"

He scowled; for strangeness walks ever abroad on Yule Eve. "What dreams?"

"Eagles tearing at dead men, men who'd been horribly hacked . . . ravens above them, and darknesses beyond, lit by flashes like those lights out there tonight. . . . We had an old neighbor when I was little, he called the northlights the Dead Men's Dance. . . . Then a voice went on and on in my dreams, forever, as if it and I fell down a bottomless gash in the world, but I couldn't understand what it said—"

For a heartbeat Hjalti was daunted. Remembering his thought as he rode hither, he then smiled. "I've that which'll soon drive such things out of you, my dear."

They hastened to bed, where he made love to her thrice in a short time. Afterward they fell asleep in each other's arms.

But the dreams came upon him too: gallopings and shouts through a windy sky, wingbeats, cruel beaks and claws, a feeling of loss unspeakable and unbounded.

He struggled awake. "I will not fall back to that!" he said aloud. Thyra moaned at his side. And did he catch another noise, in the thick night where he lay?

Aye, something moved and shrilled, miles away across the loneliness. Hjalti glided from beneath the covers. Cold gnawed at his bare flesh. He fumbled across the floor to a window and threw back its shutters.

Still the land lay hoar and empty, beneath leaping spears of light and the utterly withdrawn stars. Here and there, trees stood like blackened skeletons. Quartering the world-rim, from Roskilde Fjord toward Leidhra, moved a host.

Hjalti had keen eyes; and he knew too well what the gleam of iron meant, the bulk of men by the many hundreds massed together, muffled sound of boots and hoofs, trundling of carts laden with war-gear. Yet this was no wholly human gang. Wings toiled dark and ragged overhead; monstrous shapelessnesses stalked, crawled, writhed on the flanks of the warriors.

The truth burst upon him. He shouted.

Thyra started from sleep. "What is it?" she wailed.

"Come here." The answer was raw in his throat. "Look."

He pointed. "Friends don't fare like that," he said. "Too late, I see what was keeping King Hjörvardh and Queen Skuld. They got fighters to meet on Fyn, landed on an unpeopled strand, and now—and now—it has to be them! Who else but that witch would bring such beings ... and she withheld the scot—O gods!"

They have a revenge in the North which they call cutting the blood-eagle. The man is held down on his belly, and a blade loosens ribs from backbone till they spread out like wings. It would not have drawn from Hjalti the shriek which the woman heard this night.

"Outnumbered, unwarned," he groaned. In another yell: "Light! Start the lamp, you lazy slut! I have to get ready—and find my king!"

It may be that she was hurt by the sudden nothingness which she had become in his eyes, and wanted to strike back a little, to remind him of herself. Or maybe she was only shallow, did not grasp what danger was upon King Hrolf, who had been almighty as long as her young memory reached, and she hoped to brighten her lover's mood by a jest. She is dead these hundreds of years and cannot speak. As Hjalti, in mail and helmet, led forth his horse, Thyra stood in the doorway. The lamp she bore cast a yellow flicker on a cloak she had thrown over her shoulders and the pride of her beauty beneath. She smiled and called, however shakily: "If you fall in battle, how old a man should I marry?"

Hjalti stopped as if frozen under the stars. At length he grated, "Which would you like best, two fellows of twenty years or one of eighty?"

"Oh, the two young men," she barely laughed. Maybe she was about to add something like, "Not that they could really replace the one of you, my darling." But he screamed:

"Those words will you suffer for, whore!" He sprang at her; his knife flared; he caught her by the hair and slashed off her nose.

She staggered back. Her lamp smashed on the earth and went out. Blood poured from between the fingers she lifted. "Remember me if any come to blows over you," jeered Hjalti, "though I think most'll find little to want in you hereafter."

Too stunned to weep, she said—her voice which had been sweet gone flat and strangled—"Ill have you dealt with me. I never looked for that . . . from you."

The knife clattered out of Hjalti's hand. He stood a while, seeing how dread on behalf of his lord and his brothers in arms had made a berserker of him. Stooping, he picked up the weapon, for it might be needed, and sheathed it, red though it was.

"None can think of everything," he said in his sorrow.

He might have tried to kiss her, but she shrank from him with horror. And . . . they were asleep at Leidhra. He soared to the saddle and was off.

The enemy host was moving fast and had gotten far ahead of him. Over the land he rushed. Wind roared in his ears, through lungs and blood. It was as if the north-lights filled his skull. He did keep in mind that he must go a long way around, not be seen by his foemen or, worse, that night made flesh which walked and flapped about them. He came to the stockade of Leidhra burg with some time to spare just as his horse fell dead.

He sprang clear, rolled over on the ground, picked himself up and shouted at heaven: "Then take it if you want!"

Past the drowsy watchmen he stormed, through the lanes to the slumbering hall. There he snatched a brand from a low-burning trench, whirled it till flames blossomed high, and cried his warning.

Out among the houses he sped, calling on every man who ever gave troth to Hrolf Kraki to rise and arm himself. An old Bjarkamaal puts words in his mouth:

"Warriors, waken to ward your king!
All who fain would be friends to their lord,
know that our need is now to fight.
I tell you that here, bearing hardened weapons,
Hrolf, there has come a host against you,
and they ring our dwellings around with swords.
I think that the scot of Skuld, your sister,
no gold has bought to gleam in the halls,
but strife with the Skjoldung seeks instead
Unfriendly he fared here, the false King Hjörvardh,
to lay you low, that lordship be his.
Doomed to the death we are indeed
if no revenge we take on the viper.
Athelings, rise up and honor your oaths,
all that you swore when the ale made you eager!
In foul winds as fair, keep faith with your lord,
he who withheld no hoard for himself
but gave us freely both gold and silver.
Strike with the swords he bestowed, and the spears,
in helmets and hauberks you got from his hand;
let shine the shields that he shared with you,
thus honestly earning the wealth he gave.
In manhood we now must be making our claim
on the goods we got in a time more glad.
Feasting and fondness have come to an end.
Horns we hoisted in drinking of healths;

broad were our boasts as the food-laden board;
we gleeful played games with girls on the benches,
and maidens grew merry when marking our passage
in colorful cloaks that we had from the king.
But leave now your lemans! Our lord has a need,
in the hard game of Hild, for a hewing with blades
to throw back the threat at his throat and at ours.
Frightened men are not fit to follow him;
rather we rally none but the dauntless
who ask no quarter from ax or arrow
and eye unblinking the ice-cold edges.
His champions hold the chieftain's honor;
best he goes forth when bold men follow
shoulder to shoulder and ready to shield him.
Hard shall the housecarl grip the haft,
swiftly to swing a sword at the foeman
or beak of ax that it cleave his breast.
Hang not back, though the odds be heavy.
Ill did it always become an atheling
if ever he truckled to tricksy luck."

They sprang up: Hromund the Hard, Hrolf the Swift-Coming, Svipdag and Beigadh and Hvitserk the fifth, Haaklang the sixth, Hard-Hrefill the seventh, Haaki the Bold the eighth, Hvatt the Highborn, Starulf the tenth, and in the forefront Bodhvar-Bjarki and Hjalti the High-Minded himself; and many another man, until the burg roiled with their noise and the clang of their weapons.

Meanwhile the troop of Hjörvardh and Skuld had arrived, to surround Leidhra with numbers which swarmed further than eye could reach through the gloom. Some readied rams to break down the stockade, though doubtless they would rather spare the town by fighting in the open if the defenders agreed. In the offing, houses began to flare where the torch was put to them. Overhead rustled queer flights, and from amidst the grumble and clash of the men came unhuman grunting noises. Black tents had been raised, of ugly shapes; it could be seen that within them glowed witch-fires.

"Now does King Hrolf have need of unfrightened fellows," said Bjarki. "They who'd not huddle behind his back must have boldness in their breasts."

"You speak oddly, old friend," his lord told him.

Bjarki shook himself. Standing hunched on a watch-tower, his big shaggy form seemed less a man's than a bear's. "The air reeks of spells," he muttered. "I feel—a stirring? Something my father knew ere I was born, and his ghost remembers—?" He shambled back into the hall.

There King Hrolf sat down in his high seat and let the messengers of Hjörvardh and Skuld come before him. They said, with a firmness that wavered under the grim looks upon them, that if he would save his life, he must become the kept man of his brother-in-law.

Hrolf Kraki's red-gold mane burned amidst firelit shadows. "Never shall that be," he answered. "I owe too much to those who have trusted me. Hearken, and bear back this word I give to my guards." He raised his voice. "Let us take the best drink we have," he called, "and be merry and see what kind of men are here. Let us strive for only one thing, that our fearlessness live on in memory—for hither indeed have the strongest and bravest warriors sought from everywhere about." To the messengers: "Say to Hjörvardh and Skuld that we will drink ourselves glad before we take their scot."

When this was told the queen, where she sat in her tent on her witching stool, above a blaze which made a cauldron seethe, she was quiet for a time. At last she breathed, "There is no man like King Hrolf, my brother. A shame, a shame—" Sorrow flickered out and she said, altogether bleak: "Nevertheless we will make an end."

So the king's men sat in friendship and good cheer. Bjarki, Hjalti, and Svipdag showed for their different reasons a sadness which they tried to keep from spreading. The rest talked of olden days, and bragged of what they would do, and praised their king; and he was the blithest in that whole house.

Dawn came across the winter land. Hrolf Kraki and his men took their weapons. Forth they went, out of the gates of Leidhra.

III

Clouds had arisen. Away from the stockade wall, earth rolled dun, thinly white-streaked, under a sky the hue of dull iron. The air was frosty but windless. Not much color was in the troop of King Hjörvardh. Even its banners seemed murky. That was a mixed lot he had gathered wherever he could, among them outlawed murderers and robbers, evil to see beneath the helmets he had gotten for them. Against this, King Hrolf's band wore cloaks of all bright shades; his own was as red as living flame. Birds and beasts romped over the many-toned standards of his captains, that were spaced along the swine-array on either side of his own green ash tree on a golden field.

"Forward!" he cried. The sword Skofnung flew free. His followers made deep-throated answer, lur horns dunted, war-hounds bayed. As one, the fighters from the burg moved toward their foes. Though badly outnumbered, they were not few. Along their ranks went that ripple as of wind across rye, which bespeaks a peak of training.

Arrows whistled aloft. Spears flew gaunt between them. Slingstones thudded on shields. Hrolf shifted from a walk to a trot to a run. His band came with him like a part of his flesh.

They crashed upon Hjörvardh's lines. Iron sang. A man smote at Hrolf with a halberd. The king was less tall and more slender than him. Yet the king was not halted. He took that booming blow on his shield while his blade leaped and shrilled. The man went down. Hrolf sprang over him and hewed a way deeper into the rebel ranks. On his right rang Hjalti's Goldhilt, on his left thundered Svipdag's ax. The hound Gram tore at legs, jumped at necks. Overhead the hawk Highbreeks soared on shining wings.

Stroke after stroke resounded on helm, shield, hauberk, on into meat and bone. Spears and arrows went thick above. Men sank, pierced, slashed, spurting forth blood. Over them trampled the onrushing warriors from Leidhra. Horsemen on the flanks, who sought a weak spot to guide an attack, found naught but a human storm, or their own deaths.

Hjalti the High-Minded chanted in glee: "Many a byrnie is now in tatters, many a helmet cloven and many a bold rider stabbed down from the saddle. Still our king is of good heart, as glad as when he cheerily drank ale, and mighty are the blows of his hands. Like no other king is he in the fray, for meseems he has the strength of twelve, and no few hardy wights has he already slain. So now King Hjörvardh can see that the sword Skofnung bites; now it sings high in their breasts."

Laughing, calling to his men, red-splashed but himself hardly touched, Hrolf Kraki led the way on. Slowly the rows before him broke apart, scattered to right and left where they did not fall or flee. Stern was that strife. Had the numbers of the two sides been more nearly even, it would have ended then and there.

But the Leidhra lord had not enough to overrun the enemy host. Though he clove through its middle, its flanks were unscathed. Beneath the banners and horn-hoots of their captains, these moved aside in an order not much shaken.

There was nothing Hrolf's folk could do but catch their breath while they waited for the onslaught. Svipdag roared at some who were over-eager: "Get back where you belong! They *want* us to wear ourselves out, chasing after them!

"However," he added starkly to his master, "if we can't break them soon, if we can't get to yonder tents where Queen Skuld is brewing her spells, we'll have worse to fight against than men. Those trollish things we glimpsed may be shy of daylight, but she'll do something about that if she gets time, the witch." His single eye smoldered across the angry dead and the writhing, groaning wounded, to the lines which rallied for a new battle.

Hjalti mopped sweat from his face, looked around and

said in astonishment: "Why, where's Bjarki? I thought . . .
he must have been our right-hand anchor . . . there's his
banner, his men, but I don't see him anywhere."

His mirth left the king. He turned about, and blinked
when he spotted little Vögg nearby. The Swedish youth
had scrabbled up a leather doublet, a rusty old kettle-
helm, and a butcher's cleaver. His knees knocked together.
Blood trickled from his bitten lips. "Come here!" Hrolf
hailed.

Vögg obeyed. "You should have stayed back, lad," said
the king.

"I . . . I am your man too, lord," he answered. "I
am!"

"Well, you can be a runner, then. Go find out what's
happened to Bodhvar-Bjarki. Has he been slain or captured or what? Somebody will have seen—a man of his
size, his ruddy beard."

Vögg scuttled off. Hrolf gazed after him. "I don't think
he shudders from fear," the king murmured. "There's a
heart in that thin breast."

Hjalti gnawed his mustache, stamped feet and slapped
arms, trying to keep warm during a wait which felt endless. Would the fight never start again? The first clash had
taken no small part of this shortest day in the year. He
failed to find the sun behind the grayness that hid her.

Vögg returned. "Lord," he panted, "none have seen anything of Bjarki. Not a thing since w-w-we left the hall."

"How can this be?" broke from Hjalti. "How can he
spare himself and not come near the king . . . he who we
thought was the most fearless we had?"

King Hrolf clapped him on the shoulder and said: "He
must be where he can help us best. His will could be for
nothing else. See to your own honor, go forward and
scoff not at him, for none of you can measure yourselves
against him." He added in haste, "I slander nobody,
though; you're all outstanding warriors."

Hjörvardh and his captains had been haranguing their
own men and getting them into better order than hitherto.
Now the mass of them rolled at the defenders. Hrolf
raised a new shout and led his folk ahead.

Once more spears and arrows whistled, once more came shock and clang and hoarse yells. Meeting foemen who had not had to do battle before, they of Leidhra might have been in an ill case. Yet they cut and beat their way on. Nothing could stand before them.

For ahead of their wedge, close to their king, went a great red bear. Each blow of his paw sent a dead man to earth; his jaws ripped; rising, he hauled riders from their seats or slew the very horses; and upon him, no edge would bite.

Few on either side could see this, so closely were the fighters crowded together. Hrolf's folk, who suffered not from the bear, knew for the most part only that the ranks against them were giving ground anew. Lustily they hewed, with thought for nothing else. Meanwhile terror began to spread through Hjörvardh's gang. He, mounted and some ways off to overlook the field, spied what happened. He called for his captains to sound retreat before their followers should bolt.

Hjalti himself had been little aware of the beast. He was too busy warding and smiting. Across weapon-clash, shields, helmets, faces that hated him, he could not make out what the bear really did. Dimly he supposed it was a sending of Queen Skuld's, which however could not help her while daylight lasted.

Mainly, through the hammering and howling, he brooded on Bjarki, his more than father—on the undying shame that would be Bjarki's, that he was not here this day.

When the foe melted away afresh, when he saw there would be another halt in the strife, Hjalti ran. Back to the burg he went, overleaping the dead and dying, setting foot in pools of blood where they steamed, frightening off the carrion birds which had settled at the rear. Through open gates he dashed, down empty streets, past barred doors and shuttered windows behind which women and children crouched in dread, until he reached the house of Bjarki.

Here no latch stopped him. He flung the door wide and burst into the room beyond. It was cold and winter-

dark, hardly touched by a small hearthfire. He glimpsed
Bjarki's wife, Hrolf Kraki's daughter Drifa, in the shadows
of a corner, her children close around her. On a bed lay
the man. He wore a byrnie, but his sword was sheathed
and he stared straight upward.

The woman cried out and moved to block Hjalti. He
brushed by her unheeding, grabbed one broad shoulder,
shook it and screamed:

"How long must we wait for the first of warriors? This
is unheard of, that you're not on your feet, using your
arms that're strong as a bear's! Up, Bodhvar-Bjarki my
master, up or I'll burn this house and you inside it!
The king's in danger of his life, for our sake! Would you
wreck the good name you've borne so long?"

The Norseman stirred. He turned, sat, rose to loom
over his friend. Heavily he sighed before he answered:

"You need not call me fearful, Hjalti. I have not
been afraid. Never have I fled from fire or iron; and today you'll see how I still can fight. Always has King
Hrolf called me the foremost of his men. And I've much
to repay him for, that he gave me his daughter and twelve
rich garths and every kind of treasure besides. I fared
against vikings and robbers; I warred the length and
breadth of the Denmark we built with our blood; I went
against Adhils, and Agnar I slew, and many another
man—"

His words, which he had almost crooned as if in dream,
broke off. His gaze sharpened on Hjalti, who was stabbed
by a sudden chill. Bjarki's voice quickened:

"But here we have to do with more and worse witchcraft than ever before. And you have not done the
king the service you think; for now it is not long till the
end of the fight." With a breath of kindliness: "Oh,
you've done this unwittingly, not because you did not wish
the king well. And none save you and he could have
called me forth as you did; any others I would have
slain." Sadly: "Now things must go as they must. There
is no longer any way out, and less help can I give King
Hrolf than I did before you came."

Hjalti bent his head, knotted his fists, and said through unshed tears, "Bjarki, you and he have always stood highest before me. It's so hard to know what one ought to do!"

The Norseman put coif and helmet on his head. Drifa came to him. He took her hands in his. "It hurts that I can no more look after you," he said. "Ward well the children we got together."

"With a father like theirs," she told him, "they will need little help."

He hugged them too. Shield in his grip, another slung across his back to use when the first was beaten to ruin, he followed Hjalti out.

Day had started to dim. Bjarki trod before King Hrolf and said: "Greeting, my lord. Where can I best stand?"

"Where you yourself choose."

"Then it will be near you." The sword Lövi gleamed free.

A runner came to King Hjörvardh from the black tent where Queen Skuld squatted. He peered through dusk and saw no more of the red bear; nor was it ever seen again. Heartened, he told his captains to egg on their troops.

His host moved forward slowly and raggedly. They had taken frightful losses. Far fewer of the Leidhra men were down, and fierceness had not slackened in those who were left. Yet—maybe because they were still more afraid of the witch—the rebels went back to battle.

Alone and yet not alone, Queen Skuld cast her runes and chanted her staves. The fire flowed higher; things moved in the smoke and in the steam out of her cauldron.

Forth from the ranks of King Hjörvardh ran a hideous boar. Wolf-gray, huge as a bull, he made earth shake beneath his hoofs. His tusks flashed like swords. The sound of his grunting and squealing struck fear into the stoutest souls.

At him sprang the hounds of Leidhra. Baying and yelping, they ringed him in. He hooked his snout to right and left. Slashed, broken, the war-dogs soon lay heaped around him. For a while Gram hung on his throat. At last the boar tossed him aloft, and as he came down gored him open.

Then onward the beast raged. From the bristles upon him, arrows began to fly. No shield would stop them. Before that sighing death, the guardsmen of King Hrolf fell in windrows. Gaps showed throughout their lines which could not be filled.

Svipdag whirled his ax on high. "Close in!" he bawled. "Have at that troll before it reaches the king!"

He sped forward. Over his head swooped the hawk Highbreeks. An arrow drove through the warrior's left shoulder. He did not feel it. The galloping beast was well-nigh upon him. He kept his weapon moving, ready to cleave that grisly skull. Two ravens flew at Highbreeks. The hawk met them with beak and claws. Unscathed, they pecked him to death. The sight caught Svipdag's one eye—only in a corner, but enough that he did not see how close the swine was. Tushes ripped into byrnie and belly. Flung heavenward in a cloud of blood, Svipdag's body was long in falling.

The boar hit Hrolf Kraki's array. Through and through it tore, swung about and gored.

It could not be everywhere. One wing it might crumple. The other went on. So did the middle, where flickered the swords of the king, of Bjarki, and of Hjalti.

Soon, however, the press broke everybody's lines. The fray became man against man, shield-burg against shield-burg, ramping, swirling, striking, gasping, falling across reddened winter earth where twilight and cold grew ever deeper.

More loudly than the beast roared Bodhvar-Bjarki. His sword shrieked, thundered, belled, crashed. Here a head went, a hand, a leg; there a shield or helmet gave way, and the bones behind; one foeman toppled across the next, and his arms were bloody to the shoulders. Nothing did he want but to fell as many as might be before he also went down.

Hrolf Kraki no longer laughed. He only struck. Hjalti

stayed near, trying to fend blows off his king. The rest of the Leidhra men fought no less boldly.

Yet as darkness gathered, it did not seem that their slaying made less the flock of their enemies. Bjarki knew one warrior from of old, when the kingdom was whole. This man was now Hjörvardh's and came at him. Worn out, many times wounded, the Norseman did not ward himself well. He felt a spear strike home through a rent in his byrnie, though that was a dull and far-off knowledge. His sword split a shield. For a while he and the man traded blows. Bjarki cut off an arm and a foot, and with a backhand return cleft the fellow through the breast. He fell so fast he did not even sigh.

The strife brawled on. Hrolf Kraki's warriors were steadily driven backward. Bjarki met the same man as before. The thing grinned at him; its eyes were empty; still it struck. Bjarki stood fast till the tide of battle parted them. This was not the only time he came upon such a being.

Those of Hrolf's captains who lived, sounded their horns. Those of his followers who could, joined each other before the gates of Leidhra. There, for a little while, they held their ground, hewing so heavily through murk that the host before them fell back from their throats. For a few breaths, then, they got rest.

Bjarki knew Hjalti in the gloom and croaked: "Mighty is our foe. I think the dead are swarming here and rising anew; and bootless it is to struggle against drows. Where is the man of King Hrolf who called me afraid?"

Hjalti answered: "You tell the truth, you say no scorn. Here stands he who hight Hjalti, nor is the way between us wide. I feel a need of fearless friends, for shield and byrnie and helm are shorn from off me, oath-brother. And though I'm slaying as often as always, I cannot avenge those cuts I take. Now less than ever may we spare ourselves."

Through the gates streamed the last of the Leidhra folk. Their king and a few others held the way—until the troll-boar came. Its thrust drove shields into ribs; men tumbled, men reeled aside. Bjarki stepped to meet the beast. His sword Lövi flared like a shooting star. The boar sank dead. First it had rammed a tusk through the marshal's ring-mail.

"Greatest is my grief," rattled in his mouth, "that I can't help my lord—"

Hjalti gave him an arm to lean on. He staggered nine paces before he fell. The shields around King Hrolf drew inside the stockade. Their enemies followed. Forth darted a slight shape. "I'll hold them!" screeched Vögg. A warrior barked laughter and swung an ax. It did not go through the kettle-helmet, but Vögg toppled, stunned.

Still the fight went on. The Bjarkamaal has Hjalti call out:

"Our lives have we lost, our last horn drained.
To death are we given, to doom our hopes.
We shall not see yet another sunrise—
unless among us, all manhood lacking,
one grew fearful and fled the battle
or does not die at the feet of his lord
but cravenly crawls to beg for ruth.
The burg is breached and the foe storms inward,
the din of axes is on our doors;
bitten too often, our byrnies hang ragged,
baring our breasts to the manyfold blows,
shattered our shields and hacked our shoulders.
Wildly the weapons crash and clang.
Who is so heartless that hence he would flee?
Men I see fallen upon the field,
battered and broken the bones of their jaws;
teeth lie ablink in the running blood,
like stones in a stream that laves their bodies.
Few are the folk I have left beside me,
though far from my king I will not fare.
Hard is our need, and help is not coming.
Our shields have been gnawed to nothing but handgrips,
our weapons blunted, and we made weary.
Then wrap around wrists the golden rings
we got from our lord in goodlier days
that the wealth he gave may give weight to the blow!
In weal and in woe we did well with our king,

and even in hell will uphold his honor.
Let us die in the doing of deeds for his sake;
let fright itself run afraid from our shouts;
let weapons measure the warrior's worth.
Though life is lost, one thing will outlive us:
memory sinks not beneath the mould.
Till the Weird of the World stands unforgotten,
high under heaven, the hero's name."

Dying, Bjarki lay on the frozen earth. Hjalti knelt
above him. The marshal peered skyward and mumbled,
"Here are so many gathered against us that we have no
hope of holding them off. But Odin have I not seen. I think
he must be hovering somewhere around, the son of a troll,
the foul and faithless. Could I only know where he is,
that wretch would go home with a wound to make him
howl, for what he has done to our king."

"It is not easy to bend a doom," said Hjalti, "nor to
stand against overhuman might." After a while he closed
Bjarki's eyes and got stiffly up to meet his own death.

The last warriors of King Hrolf made a ring around
him. Skuld herself had come through the night. Sheerly
mad, she cried forth monster after monster. Before that
tide of witchiness, which they did not know save as horrible shadows and stenches, snarling and fangs, the
guards and the great captains went down. Hrolf Kraki trod
out from the breaking shield-burg. Man after man he
felled. No one of them slew him; it took them all.

When she had her victory, Skuld made haste to send
her trolls back whence they came and bid her dead lie
quiet. Thereafter, by torchlight she sought her husband
and hailed him High King of Denmark. That was in a
few flat words, for she and he alike were too weary for
happiness. They sought shelter in the hall. Darkness and
stillness owned the burg Leidhra, save where Vögg woke
alone and wept.

VIII
THE TALE OF VÖGG

I

Later that night it began to snow, and this went on the whole following day and evening. It walled in the world, made earth and sky one, filled the utterly hushed air. The snow lay heavy on every roof, on trampled, bloodied ground, on heaped and strewn dead as if to hide them from the ravens.

Forth into the dim morning went the women of Leidhra. Drifa Hrolfsdottir led them. They wore cowls which hid their faces. With besoms to uncover the fallen, they sought their men and, as these were found, helped each other bring them home. King Hjörvardh gave orders that nobody was to trouble them. It may have been needless. The wildest robber, leaning on his spear as he stood guard, must have felt awe of those dumb shapes which moved in and out of the blindness tumbling everywhere around him. Too much had happened yesterday that was eerie. Too high had the cost been. Winning was ashen.

Those who saw the queen return from the tent she had sought, near the day's end, felt yet more unease. She went like a sleepwalker, green eyes staring blankly, narrow face pinched. The snow on her uncovered hair made her look old.

Within the hall, her husband drew her aside, into a corner away from the woefully trudging housefolk. "Well, what signs did you get?" he whispered. His fingers plucked at her cloak.

"Bad ones," she said, her tone empty, her gaze afar. "Over and over I cast the runes. Always they came up

direful. When I gazed in the cauldron, I got no sight or
hearing save that . . . that far off in a highland, someone
bellowed till the mountains tolled back his grief and
wrath; and he was not human. . . . I think maybe we have
been used, you and I." She shook herself. Her eyes
cleared, her head lifted. Haughtiness rang forth: "Well,
we are the king and queen of Denmark. Let the world
know that!"

Hjörvardh must needs hold a feast at eventide, wherein he thanked his warriors and bestowed gifts on them. It
was not a merry time. The hall seemed huge and hollow.
The highest-leaping fires could not drive night out of it nor
fill a silence which grunted talk failed to deck over.
Though King Hrolf's guests were unable to go home in this
weather, nearly every one of them had found lodging with
a widow of a man of his, or with common families who
likewise mourned their lord, and was not on hand. Aside
from thralls, no women sat on the benches or bore
around food and drink. Shadows stirred like the ghosts of
those who had been here aforetime, crowding in on their
huddled-together shabby killers. The fire-crackle was like
an echo of their laughter. The air was cold and stale, as if
this were the inside of a barrow.

"Hu," shivered Hjörvardh, and drank and drank. They
came before him for their wages of gold and land, the
hirelings, the outlanders, the outlaws, the Danish nithings, *his* men, and he must praise them, the whole while
remembering those others. Queen Skuld's shrill mirth
woke no answer in him.

When he had done what he must, and heard a skald
he had brought along say a few lame staves in his honor,
he was quite drunk. Suddenly he filled his lungs and
cried forth:

"Well have you wrought, my fighters, yes, yes, that you
have. But what a wonder it is to me, that not a one of
King Hrolf's many warriors saved his own life by flight
or surrender. Not a one. Am I right? See how faithfully
they loved their lord . . . they didn't even want to outlive
him. Eh? Unlucky am I—oh, I say nothing against you,
my good men, not a word, never misunderstand me—

but am I not unlucky . . . might it not take away the bane . . . if just one of those brave fellows lived, and would become true to me? I do want to be a righteous king. . . . Lives there a man of Hrolf Kraki's, and will he now come under my banner?"

Skuld frowned. Those on the benches muttered sourly.

Then: "Aye, my lord. I outlived yestereven," called a cracked voice. From the foreroom limped a thin, shock-headed youth in a leather doublet grimed and blood-clotted. Awkwardly he made his way down the length of the hall till he stood before the high seat.

Queen Skuld sharpened her look. "You, a man of my brother's?" she said. "Who are you?"

"I hight Vögg, my lord and lady. I . . . I own I am—I was not the best of them. But I did help them when they met King Adhils, and I, I was there yesterday, and am only alive because I happened to get kn-kn-knocked out."

"Will you become my man?" asked Hjörvardh.

"I've nowhere else to go, and, and you did win, my lord."

"Why, this is at least a hopeful sign!" Hjörvardh had a sword on his lap. He drew it. "Yes, a sign, wouldn't you say, Skuld, my dear? What was doesn't forever make war on what is. Ha." He nodded, much taken with his own wise saying. "Well, Vögg," he went on before his wife could speak, though she tried to cut him off, "you shall be most welcome, Vögg, and do better with me than it seems you did with my brother-in-law. Yes." He held forth the blade. "Swear me troth upon this my sword, and you shall, um, shall know at once how good I am."

The newcomer squared his narrow shoulders. "Lord, I can't do that. We did not swear earlier on the point. It was on the hilt. King Hrolf was wont to hand men his sword and let them hold it before him while they plighted faith."

"Eh? Hm? Well—"

"No!" Skuld began. But Hjörvardh had already leaned down, Vögg had already taken the steel from him.

"Now give your faith," Hjörvardh said.

"Yes, lord," said Vögg steadily. "Here it is."

He lunged. The point rammed into the king's breast. For an eyeblink Hjörvardh gaped astounded at his own blood leaping. He crumpled. His body rolled and flopped to sprawl on the ground.

Skuld shrieked. The guards howled and snatched out their own blades. Vögg went to meet them. While they slaughtered him, he laughed and called out the name of Hrolf Kraki.

II

Over the heights of the Keel, through wilderness, across plowland where folk shuddered to see him, swifter than any war-horse sped the great ungainly shape of Elk-Frodhi. No snowbank or blizzard could halt him; his shortsword slashed whatever he needed to eat and he gulped as he fared; he seldom rested, and never for long. Within a few days he had reached that hall in West Götaland where dwelt King Thori Hound's-Foot.

The warriors aimed spears and bows at this horror which galloped toward them. Frodhi stopped and roared for his brother to come out. The king did. Frodhi spoke: "Bjarki is dead—killed. Blood fills the track I left for a mark of him."

Thori stood very still before he said beneath winter heaven, "I'll need weeks, this time of year, to gather men for revenge. Meanwhile we can send after news."

Among their scouts and messengers was one to Uppsala in Svithjodh. Queen Yrsa heard of his coming, guested him, and told him what she knew about the fall of King Hrolf. "Set a day and a place," she promised, "and you shall find waiting there a host of my own men." She sat for a little, reckoning up on fingers which age had started to gnarl. At last she nodded. "Yes, my Hrolf knew somewhat fewer years than did my Helgi, though he wrought more. They are not a long-lived breed, the Skjoldungs. They seek too far."

The troop gathered at the Scanian border. As they

passed through, Danes flocked to join them. Queen Skuld
was ruling harshly and heedlessly; they wanted to be
done with her.

One thing she had not dared, to keep his folk from
burying King Hrolf. They laid him in a ship, drawn onto
a headland above the Kattegat he had warded for them.
By him was his sword Skofnung, and beside him were
his men, each likewise armed and richly clad. Treasures
were heaped about, and thereupon was raised a hill-tall
howe to stand for a landmark. The balefires burned, the
women keened, and around and around the grave rode
the chieftains, slowly clanging sword on shield, ringing
farewell to their lord of the good days and the luck of
Denmark.

From them the queen would get no help. She had none
to turn to but the ruffians who brought her to power.
They must be rewarded with things seized from others.
So the hatred of her grew. Soon, from end to end of the
land, the red cock crowed on the roofs of her jarls. Under-
kings held back their scot and their faith from her; and
as they stood on their Thingstones, the yeomen hailed
them as free lords who owed nothing to anyone.

The runes she cast, the beings she summoned, gave
Skuld foreshadowings of woe. They could not or would
not tell that which would let her make ready. Another
strangeness elsewhere was working against her spells,
blocking her off from tomorrow.

"I think," she cried once to him who rose from the
sea, "Odin wanted me for naught but to wreak his spite."

"Do you think it was mere spite?" he answered. "The
Father of Victories must cast down whoever might bring
a stop to war. He may well have made welcome King
Hrolf Kraki and his men, to feast with him till the Weird
of the World. Whether or not that is true, about the
afterlife of heroes, sure it is that their names will live."

"And mine?"

"Yes, yours too, in its way."

Skuld sought her husband's grave. She missed him
more than she would have awaited, the man she mocked
and scourged while he humbly loved her. The thralls

she told off to tend the barrow had been slothful about their work.

Early in spring, the host of King Thori and Queen Yrsa took ship over the Sound. Skuld had filled those waters with nicors and krakens. They swarmed at the fleet, saw Elk-Frodhi in the prow of the first dragon, and fled to their lairs. Likewise did the trolls and drows she had set to keep Zealand for her. His was a might more grim than theirs.

He led the attack on Leidhra. He burst through the rows of her fear-weakened guards and into the hall. He caught her in his ugly hands, clapped a sealskin bag over her head and drew the strings tight. "Not for nothing was I born," he said. His brother fought to his side, and between them they put to death Skuld the witch-queen.

During that fray, fire broke loose. The whole burg burned. "That is well," said Thori Hound's-Foot. "This ground is cleansed."

The avengers gave what was left of the kingdom to the daughters of Hrolf. Thereafter each went back to his own: Thori and his Götar to their dales, the Swedes to old Queen Yrsa, Elk-Frodhi to his loneliness.

Drifa and her sister were well-liked. However, women could not steer when things were breaking asunder, and their sons were too young. Erelong the lordship passed, in friendly wise, to a grandson of Helgi through a leman. He saved something from the wreck.

Long would the years and the hundreds of years be until Denmark was whole again. Now watchfires burned anew to warn of foes on their way. Vikings, outlaws, wild men harried dwellers throughout the North. They wrought no worse harm than did the kings, unnumbered and uncurbed: torch, sword, free folk dragged off to thralldom, the wariness of men and the weeping of women. Nothing but a tale was left of a day which had been.

Here ends the saga of Hrolf Kraki and his warriors.